Pink October

To Belinda, thanks for your support... Enjoy the book!

Gary Norman Jr.

Author: Gary Norman, Jr.

PINK OCTOBER
Copyright 2003 by Gary Norman Jr.

All rights reserved.
No part of this book may be reproduced, stored in a retrieval system, or transmitted by any means, electronic, mechanical, photocopying, recording, or otherwise, without written permission from the author. This novel is a work of fiction. Names, characters, places and incidents either are creations from the author's imagination or used fictitiously. Any resemblance to actual persons, living or dead, events or places is entirely coincidental.

ISBN: 0-9740118-0-0 (Paperback, revised edition)
ISBN: 1-4107-7788-X (e-book)
ISBN: 1-4107-7789-8 (Paperback)

For information, contact author/publisher at:
MID-AUGUST, Publishing
Phone #: (708) 612-6165
e-mail: luv2write@survivormail.com

Cover design by: Karl L. Ray of Pikture Perfekt.
Photo taken by: Karl L. Ray of Pikture Perfekt.
Contact Karl L. Ray at: www.musecube.com/Karl_Ray
Phone #: (773) 719-8863

ACKNOWLEDGEMENTS

First of all I want to thank God for blessing me with the patience needed to write this book (without him there would be no Gary Norman...Thanks☺). I want to thank my entire family, and close friends, for the love and support they've given me throughout the most trying times of my life. This list isn't as long as some of the ones I've seen, but it's not the shortest either...You might as well get comfortable because this might take a while☺.

I want to thank my mother, Julia and my Father, Gary Sr., my sister Tracey (she just knew her brother would be all right), my cousins, Dr. Rhay E. Street (I still have those letters you sent me when I was on vacation☺), and Bryan L. Street (I probably drove you crazy with all that talk about this book). I want to thank Mrs. Allison Street (married to Rhay) and Mrs. Robyn Street (married to Bryan) for being apart of my family for more than 15 years...Can you believe it's been that long?☺ I want to thank my niece and nephew, Cassie and Rhay-Rhay, for adding laughter to an already silly family (they're something else☺). I also want to thank my auntie, Margo, and my uncle, Rob, for all the love and support they've given. I want to thank my cousin Torrence Smith (I've gone to more Bulls' games in the past year than I've gone to in my entire life...Thanks☺) and my auntie Melvon caring. I want to thank Jermaine, Sonny, Cetrina and Lane-Lane (my editor...☺) Walker for showing a brother love...we've been like family for as long as I can remember, and that's a long time...☺. I also want to thank the Gilmores (Clark, Jessie, Nardy and Shawny) for being like family. Shawny, thanks for the five dollars you sent me...yes, I do remember☺. I want to thank Karen L. Smith for making my transition a lot easier...(I still remember the look on your face when you opened your door to find me standing on the other side...I still wish I had thought to bring my camera☺). I want to thank Renee` L. Harris and Dawn Dillard for being there for me when I needed you the most (you might not remember, but I do☺). I want to thank Wanda Baker for sending me that picture (I still have it...Thanks☺). I want to thank Shawn Hammock and Brian Cooper for hanging out with a brother when I got back from my vacation...☺. I want to thank Patricia A. Lynch (aka "Sandy") for always making sure that her dog was ok☺! I want to thank Maachah Watkins for being you☺! I want to thank Shaneen Jackson for putting up with my non-sense (I had too

Gary Norman

much going on at that time and I should've let you in, but I didn't and I apologize). I want to thank Sharina Nixon for putting up with my silliness...that, and listening to me talk about my book over and over again!!! I want to thank Jinaki Smith, soon to be Dr. Jinaki Smith, for being in my corner from day one...You're something else☺! I want to thank fellow authors Cheryl Dooley-Ponton, author of *"Po' Man's Poker,"* and Kim L. Dulaney, author of *"The Beautiful Ones,"* for pointing me in the right direction (I would've been absolutely lost without the both of you...I wish you both continued success...Thanks☺). I want to thank "Skate" and David Dugan for the letters they sent...Thanks!! I want to thank Joseph Gardner the 3rd (3rd Ward, New Orleans) for encouraging me to finish this book...Thanks! I also want to thank Kym Parker (aka "Sexyhuh") for being so supportive...I wish you much success with your soon to be finished book...just don't forget to send a brother an advance copy...I can't wait to read it☺! I also want to thank Serita (with her read head self) for her much needed sense of humor. I want to thank Keva, Fon, Evita, Crystal, Akilah and Angel for lending me their ears. Angel has her own candle business...and she's good! You can see for yourself by visiting her at www.waxydesires.com. I also want to thank Tameka (from Texas) and Tyesha for putting up with all that talk about my book...I know you all were tired of hearing me say "wait 'til my book comes out," but everybody was tired of hearing that☺! I want to thank Tiffany Seay for being just as silly as I am...as if that were possible...☺. I can't forget my newest editor, Tressa Hines...Thanks for lending your expert eye to this second edition...☺. I have to thank Towanda Brewer-Graham, thanks for being who you are...I can't thank you for much more because...well, you know why...☺. I want to thank Deborah Allen...thanks for being there for me when I needed you...and oh yeah, the book is doing fine--so you know what that means...☺. A special thanks goes to all the book clubs and bookstores that have helped make this book such a success...THANK YOU!☺ I hope I didn't forget anybody...If I forgot to mention your name feel free to stop me in the street and tell me about it... You do know that I'm joking, right??☺

DEDICATION

This book is dedicated to everyone effected by this horrible disease, friends and family alike...I'll see you at the next "breast cancer awareness" event...until then, stay safe and know that God loves you!

Gary Norman

Pink October.doc

Scene 1

"Damn! They could've done this on a Saturday!" Tasha cursed as she inched through traffic heading towards her near north side destination, northeast of Chicago's Magnificent Mile. She'd forgotten all about the Breast Cancer Awareness '10K run' through downtown, a race that had been previously scheduled for Sunday, but due to a sudden downpour wound up being rescheduled for this Monday morning. A rescheduling that would cause Tasha to miss her monthly "pre-class" staff meeting because of the rerouting of downtown traffic around the events' course, making the normally hideous morning commute through downtown ten times worse. Well, that was almost the truth. She would've at least made the last fifteen minutes of the meeting had it not been for her appetite for early morning, ass slappin', hair pullin', back scratchin' sex. And that was just the oral part. Kevin's skills, in that department, have noticeably increased over the last month, lifting him to 'lesbian' status. "My prayers have been answered, big time," Tasha praised the forty-five minute tongue massage he'd surprised her with last month, before she left for work. And that was a total surprise because prior to that, in the whole two years they'd been together, he had only taken that kind of initiative one other time. And that was to make up for his forgetting their one-year anniversary. But not even his 'I'll make you forget all the things I've done or forgot to do' effort could compare to this morning's rendezvous. It's like he'd ordered a few sex tapes and then put in the hours needed to improve his oral skills, which will be appreciated throughout their relationship.

Clad in a gray skirt suit and white blouse, a full-length dark leather jacket and matching briefcase completing her ensemble, Tasha smiled as she walked through the empty hallways heading for her office. Just thinking about the special attention she'd received this morning, before coming face-to-face with the morning traffic from hell, made her feel giddy, full of life and ready to conquer a days worth of challenges. Funny how a few minutes ago she was stuck in traffic, cursing and making the most obscene hand gestures she's made since college. She laughed as she thought back to this morning's commute, though some of the things she'd said, while stuck in traffic, blanketed her with embarrassment. "I'll probably never see those people again," She shrugged as if deleting the entire incident from her memory in just one simple movement of her shoulders. "They could've did this 'shit' on the weekend!" She thought back to how she

Gary Norman

had cursed the event while sitting at a red light, watching the race proceed a half block away, down a street that would've gotten her to her meeting late (at least she would've been there). "Move that piece of shit!" She couldn't believe she had yelled those words, out of her window, at a driver who had, for one reason or another, let two seconds elapse before preceding through the intersection once the light had turned green. "A whole two seconds, Tasha," Shaking her head, Tasha found herself laughing at her uncharacteristic behavior as she walked through the doors of the reception area right outside of her office, the principal's office. A clear-cut case of road rage, Tasha thought.

"Something funny happened on my way to work. Don't worry, I'm not going crazy," Tasha, responding to the confusion in Mrs. Smith's eyes, winked as she walked pass Betty Smith's (her receptionist) desk, heading towards her office, a few feet away.

"I don't think you're crazy," Mrs. Betty Smith gave a half-cocked smile before continuing. "Just a little special," Both women laughed as they often did when they were alone, and able to shed the professionalism for a few moments. When they were able to kick back and relax. "I placed the tape of this morning's meeting on your desk, though there really wasn't anything of importance discussed," Mrs. Smith spoke hurriedly, catching Tasha just as she reached for the door to her office. "And there's a package from the superintendent on your desk," She said this last part wincingly.

"Oh, thanks," Tasha replied sarcastically before stepping into her office where her first order of business was to find out what the superintendent wanted her to accomplish on this day. Even though she, along with every other qualified principal in Chicago, received a package (a manila envelope containing this morning's memo sent by the superintendent) on a daily basis, she still dreaded each correspondence because every so often it was accompanied by extra work. Work that would add on to the work she'd already have waiting on her from the day before. Everything from suggesting updated software for Tasha's constantly expanding computer department to acceptance and/or denial notification forms could be received on any given workday. Luckily, more times than not, it was something she could accomplish in less than half of her workday. Other times the extra work would consume a few days, piling her desk with work she'd sat aside until whenever the superintendent's assignment had been completed. And that would piss Tasha off, having her workload pile while she looked into whatever the superintendent wanted her to do. But how long could she stay pissed when she was actually getting paid to do something she loved. She was working with children, her dream job, and being paid handsomely to do so (an annual salary of eighty thousand made the sun shine on the worst days).

"Come in, Tracey," Tasha responded to the knock at her office door just as she tore open the envelope containing this morning's memo.

"How'd you know it was me?" Tracey, the school nurse, and one of Tasha's closest friends, chimed as she entered the office. She was smiling like the cat that ate the canary.

"Who else would it be this early?" Tasha sat on the edge of her desk, her legs dangling over the side, her skirt revealing a hint of thigh. The huge oak desk was her first major purchase after being assigned to Dr. Rhay E. Street Magnet Elementary, an assignment she'd received because of the extra support she received from a relative who happened to be a very influential member of the Chicago Board of Education. Not that she wasn't qualified, because she was. But like they say, "it's not what you know, it's who you know."

"It could've been Mr. Coleman. You know you excite him like no other woman can," Tracey teased, taking Tasha back to the night they ran into Mr. Coleman (the school's one-eyed gym teacher/badminton coach/basketball coach) at the health club. The mere sight of Tasha in a pair of rump-fitting sweatpants caused an un-concealable swelling in his workout shorts. Damn fool wore boxers instead of his usual "workout" briefs, so there was no mistaking what was going through his mind. He was definitely excited to see his principal out of her professional suit skirts and heels and into something tight on her backside. But what man wouldn't have enjoyed that view? At 5'7", with a caramel complexion, brown eyes and dark wavy hair, Tasha is a very attractive woman. She also has the round hips and butt that men, namely black men, love so much. "Thick in all the right places," is how she describes herself when laughing with friends.

"How do you know he wasn't checkin' you out? I mean, can you honestly say that you know which eye is the real one, and which eye is glass?" Tasha crossed her eyes, jokingly mimicking those not so rare occasions when Mr. Coleman would stare straight ahead and, because he couldn't totally control the movement in one eye, his eyes seemed to go every-which-a-way.

"You know it was the sight of your ass stuffed in those sweats that made that man stand at attention. If I were a few pounds lighter you could say it was me, but right now you got me beat in that department."

"And what department is that?"

"You know, the 'one look at my ass makes a man stand like a pool stick' department'," Tracey laughed.

"You are so nasty," Tasha shook her head, covering her reddening cheeks and gaped mouth with the superintendent's memo, as she pictured the swelling in his sweatpants one moment and his crossed eyes the next. "I might not know which eye is the good eye, but I do know, on that day, it was glued on my ass," Tasha thought conceitedly. She knew she looked good at one hundred forty pounds, much better than the near one seventy she weighed before deciding to join a health club almost two years ago. Not that she didn't look good at one hundred sixty pounds, because she did (depending on who you ask she looked better then). But at one forty, she was an absolute knockout. Things that were a little jiggly before are much firmer now, giving her ass a tighter look, which is exactly what she'd hoped for when she joined the health club. Luckily, the one hundred sixty-pound behind she toted around turned out to be good for something. Kevin, who started out as her personal trainer before elevating to lover status in the blink of an eye, was an ass man. You know the kind, "one of the millions of brothers who'd trust a big butt and a smile."

------------------ --buzz-- --------------------

"Yes, Mrs. Smith?" Tasha had to lean back on her desk to reach her phone's intercom feature, which sat behind her to the right next to the laptop she'd received as a Christmas gift from her mother. "Okay, send his mannish tail in here," Tasha half sighed-half laughed, as she released the intercom button. "Did you hear that?"

"Greg Clark strikes again," Tracey chimed, rising from her chair so that she could leave her friend to a more pressing matter. "And don't think I didn't notice the 'I got me some before work' look on your face, because I did. That's why your nasty ass missed the meeting."

"Good bye, Tracey," Tasha hid her reddening cheeks with the palms of her hands, her legs swinging over the side of her desk like an embarrassed school girl who was set to run and hide after her juicy secret had been exposed.

"Buzz me when you're finished with the peep freak. I want details," Tracey nodded as she walked to the door where she paused

**Pink October.doc** 11

long enough to wave little Greg Clark into Tasha's office, which was actually starting to feel more like his office rather than Tasha's, that's how often he's called in for questioning.

It's really too early for this shit, Tasha thought as she watched the short, frail, freckled face, red head child walk over to the chair in front of her desk. He had the nerve to flop down in the chair like he was starting to get tired of their impromptu meetings.

He's only eight years old and already in the sixth grade, so he gets pick on more than the normal sixth grader. "He can't help the fact that he's smart," Tasha could remember telling the last little boy accused of teasing him. Most of the teasing stopped when word got out that he was becoming creative with his revenge. They picked with him and he found new and more creative ways to get even. That's how it worked around here. "God, give me strength," She sighed under her breath as she walked over to close her door, which he'd purposely left open to aggravate her. "God, please give me strength…"

Gary Norman

Scene 2

"I can't believe...wait a minute...yes I can. That sounds like something his little mannish butt would do," Tracey laughed so hard she had to cover her mouth to keep from spitting tuna salad onto the table she and Tasha shared, their customary "end of the day" rendezvous table in the teacher's lounge.

"Tracey," Tasha smiled, good-humoredly waving her finger as if she were reprimanding a child. "There's no proof that it was Greg Clark, or that he had anything to do with it, but..."

"Girl," Tracey cut in. "You and I both know he did it. That fits his little perverted M.O."

"If you'd let me finish my sentence you'll see I feel the same as you, but that still doesn't add up to proof, right? At least that's how his mother sees it."

"She's a lawyer, and his mother. What do you expect her to say? My eight-year old son has been caught browsing pornographic websites at home. I'm surprised you haven't caught him doing the same thing here."

Tasha, sitting across from Tracey, shook her head in disbelief. Times had surely changed from the way children did things when she was a child growing up in one of the city's south suburbs. Back then she'd hear of how her little male friends would stumble onto their father's stash of porn magazines, dirty books is what the kids called them back then. Now things are totally different. With a click of a mouse a kid now has access to images his father could've only dreamed about as a child. And it seems one of her brightest students was taking full advantage of this new age technology.

Not that Tasha didn't believe the little boy when he sat in a chair in front of her desk, his feet unable to reach the floor, proclaiming his innocence. But since he's been accused of everything from leaving an artificial rose on one teacher's desk (a rose that turned out to be a pair of red lace panties) to slipping a condom into Mrs. Harper's (the school librarian) purse, she couldn't help but doubt the sincerity of his proclamation of innocence. Especially after she'd heard from another one of Greg's teachers how he had inquired about Mrs. Harper's marital status. His question came one week after the condom had been planted, and two weeks before the story leaked to the faculty. "And if he could do something like that, he could slander another student's name on the Internet," is what Tasha's insides told her about the innocent looking little boy sitting in her office. Especially if the other student was known throughout the school as a bully (not the 'physical confrontation' kind of bully that plagued so many Chicago Public Schools. He was more of a words bully, the kind of kid that teased other kids to the point of tears). "So if he was teasing Greg Clark, or any other child, he got what was coming to him, not what he deserved," is what Tasha told the oversized seventh grader seated across from her desk. He was looking just as innocent as his younger counterpart.

Nobody deserves to have his/her good name slandered all over the Internet, but there was nothing Tasha could do to Greg Clark. He said he didn't do it, and there was no proof that he had. "But somebody posted my son's name, photo and phone number on a web page frequented by old perverts," Mrs. Taylor, the victimized boy's mother, fumed during their after school meeting in Tasha's office. At that point Tasha thought about calling one of the remaining gym teachers into her office as a precautionary referee. She knew that if Mrs. Taylor, who stood five feet five inches high, yet weighed in at a stout two hundred seventy five pounds, had decided to charge she would've been in serious trouble.

"Luckily things didn't proceed in that direction," Tracey laughed. "But if you worked at a south side school, somebody would've gotten hurt," She smiled as she pressed the auto-entry button to unlock her car door, which she'd parked right next to Tasha's BMW.

"Don't I know it," Tasha replied as she sat down into her front seat. "I'll call you tonight, that's if I have enough energy. After a full day of dealing with kids, their parents and my aerobics class, I might not have enough energy to walk to my car, let alone make a phone call," Tasha exhaled as if she'd just experienced the toughest day of her principal life; her car door still ajar, her key in the ignition.

"So, when is Mr. Red Dick coming back to work?" Tracey asked about the male vice principal who'd taken a maternity leave. She still gets a kick out of that one. You know that times have changed when a man goes on maternity leave, she joked the day the school's vice principal made his announcement, months earlier.

"His name is Reddpeccer, pronounced 'Red Pecker', and he'll be back next week," Tasha corrected, trying hard to contain her own laughter. Tracey always made fun of the vice-principal's family name. And Tasha always tried to keep herself from laughing.

"And how's his wife and the new babies?"

"They're doing just fine. In fact, he e-mailed us a picture of he and his wife holding their twins. They looked like the happiest couple on earth," Tasha managed to muster enough strength for a shallow smile, the same shallow smile she'd present whenever she'd talk of new parents and their children. Every time one of her friends, or associates, would make the announcement that they were expecting a child, she'd feel like God was taunting her. "You could've had a child if you hadn't had that abortion back when you were in college, but you blew it," The chastising finger pointing down from the heavens, directly at her, would seem so real. When she'd awaken her sheets and pillowcase would be soaking wet with both sweat and tears, but mostly tears. Once her friend or associate would give birth things would get worse. It would feel as if everybody was taunting her, laughing and pointing as if they knew the secrets of her past. As if they knew about the inevitable price she paid for that secret, those damn nightmares, which got worse when she turned thirty, but have been non-existent for the last few years. But Tasha knew that behind every kind "Mr. and Mrs. so-and-so sure have beautiful children" lay the questions she knew they all were dying to ask, but were afraid to. I mean if she could, she'd spit out a child right now. She would've had a child a few years ago, if that had been at all possible. But things just haven't worked out that way.   Now she's thirty-four years old with no children and no husband, both of which she'd planned on having by her thirtieth birthday (failed relationships turned that dream into a nightmare). At this stage in her life she can barely stand the sight of a happy family. Not when that should be her pushing that stroller or breast-feeding on a bench along the lake front.

"And I hope you don't think I forgot about this morning's tardiness? Oh no, I want details. Maybe you'll tell me something I can use with my man," Tracey smiled. "And I know it was good because you were late for work. And you're never late for work," Unknowingly bringing Tasha's attention back to their conversation and away from the 'self pity' path she was headed for, she said as a matter-of-factly, her body language screaming for more than tad-bits. She wanted the complete lick by lick, stroke by stroke, low down on Tasha's "pre-work" love making session.

"You'll need to have your parents sign a consent form. You're just too young for the uncut version. And yes, it was that good," Tasha winked before starting her car then backing out of her parking space, leaving Tracey with a smile on her face and an overactive imagination.

"Wait a minute now," Tracey flagged her down before she could pull away. "Call me after your aerobics class. You might have some information me and my man can use."

Pink October.doc

"My information comes with a disclaimer. The events discussed here," Tasha mimicked those info-mercials that promote the use of workout equipment. "Were performed by professionals so to avoid serious injury, consult with a doctor before attempting any of the techniques you've just heard," She gave one last mischievous wink before pulling off, leaving Tracey without as much as a juicy tid-bit to hold her over until they talk tonight. Tracey hated when she did that.

Gary Norman

Scene 3

"Now this is how you're suppose to relax," Tasha exhaled as she and Kim (her closest friend away from work), along with three other towel wearing women from their aerobics class, savored the therapeutic heat in the health club's steam room.

"Yeah," Kim cooed. "I wish I had one of these in my house," Sitting a few feet to Tasha's left, she sighed as she massaged her cheeks with the tips of her fingers, which she rotated in a circular motion.

"Between your new adjustable shower-head and this, you'd never go to work. You wouldn't have the energy."

"I don't think I'd be able to use my shower-head in here...it's too hot. One good nutt and I'd pass out," Kim responded softly, attempting to keep the other women in the steam room from hearing, as if the entire gym didn't already think she was a freak. After dating three of the gym's personal trainers, two of which have since quit (they couldn't handle watching Kim flirt with other men), word gets around. That's especially true when you add a jilted lover with an X-rated home video in his possession to the mix. "I gotta be more careful," was all Kim said when she heard that the tape had started to circulate throughout the gym. She acted like she wanted people to know. "It's called free publicity," she joked one minute then cursed out her ex for making the tape public knowledge the next. "I can't let people think I'm happy about what he did. They'll think I'm some kind of freak," she'd confide in Tasha once they were alone. "The right man won't care about the tape...In fact, it'll probably be what draws him to me in the first place. You know every man wants a woman that can handle her business in the bedroom," is what Kim said of the upside she envisioned. Why she thought that way, Tasha would never know. In fact, she stopped trying to figure that out months ago. "Kim is a grown woman, who can take care of herself," is what she'd tell herself. Kim has a lot to offer a good man besides being double jointed and good head, which is the only reason Tasha had ever tried to make sense of her behavior in the first place.

Kim is a very successful criminal attorney with one of the largest firms in Chicago. She doesn't have any children, which makes her an even greater catch to those brothers who are looking to start a family. She owns her own condo, on Lake Shore Drive, and, what most men consider to be the icing on the cake, she's beautiful. I'm talking Ananda Lewis beautiful. She stands five foot eight inches tall and weighs an even one hundred sixty pounds, which is mostly in her

hips and ass, another plus if you ask most brothers. Her eyes, lips, complexion and facial features are strikingly similar to Ananda Lewis' features. So much so that Kim has signed many an autograph because people would make the mistake of not looking closer. "If my hips and ass weren't so damn big, I'd be a twelve on a scale of one to ten," Kim would conceitedly pose nude in front of the health club's locker room mirror. "If that bitch was all that she'd be able to get her own man, without having to go after somebody else's," Tasha would hear those kinds of unfriendly remarks from time to time. She brushed it off as 'nothing more than jealousy', something women everywhere have to put up with sometime in their lives. "I don't know why the women at the club don't like me," Kim would say before continuing. "But so what...who cares what they think...they're probably just mad because their men want me," Kim would smile.

------------------Beep--beep--beep--------------------

"Damn...my time's up," Tasha groaned before pushing the button on the side of her sports watch, shutting off its alarm.

"We're just starting to relax. What's it been, ten minutes?"

"No. It's been over thirty minutes since we sat down."

"That long? I guess you do need to get home. Hopefully you two will be able to pick up where you left off this morning."

"We'll get to that after we exchange gifts. That way, if I like what he gets me I'll give him some. If I don't, he'll have to jack himself off," Tasha nodded as she and Kim exited the steam room, entering the adjoining locker room.

"Exchange gifts? What's the occasion?"

"It's our two year anniversary," Tasha happily shared. "So much has gone on today at work, I forgot to tell you. I'm sorry."

"Girl, don't be," Kim took her bath towel and soap from her locker, placed them on the bench then continued. "Dealing with a kid like that Clark kid, you're lucky you still have your sanity."

"Don't I know it?"

"Well, I hope his gift is ten times better than the one he gave you this morning," Kim winked then walked off towards the showers.

"Oh, it will be," Tasha spoke mostly to herself, before reaching into her own locker for her soap and towel. "And he better not have forgotten, like last year," She closed and locked her locker, her mind going over different ways to punish her man if his memory has failed him two years in a row. Now that's highly unlikely, Tasha thought, grinning as she walked towards the showers.

Scene 4

"Yeah, I remembered. I just left your gift in my gym locker, but I'll make sure I put it in my bag tomorrow," The look on his face screamed 'I'm lying,' but Kevin tried to hide the fact that he'd forgotten another anniversary.

"Kevin," Tasha cooed as she and Kevin lay side by side, in her bed, preparing for a night of 'anniversary sex'. That is until it was obvious to Tasha that he had pulled a repeat performance of last year's anniversary night. Only then he was smart enough to wait until after the sex to attempt to lie about not forgetting. "I forgot...I have a headache," Tasha, wearing the red lace lingerie she'd brought earlier in the week, uttered before reaching over Kevin, purposely brushing her erect nipples against his chest, and turning off the lamp (light) that sat on the night-stand next to the bed.

"Let me make it up to you," Kevin, using his sexiest 'daddy'll make it all better' voice, spoke so close to Tasha's neck that his hot breath set her loins ablaze (he knew exactly what he was doing). "There ain't a doghouse big enough to contain a man that lays good pipe," Kevin had once bragged to a friend of his. "If you knew how to eat pussy, along with laying 'good pipe', you'd be able to get away with something close to murder," That same friend told him that years ago, before Kevin had ever indulged in taking trips south of the belly button.

Kevin smiled as his tongue brought Tasha closer to where she needed to be, her trembling hips and thighs bringing attention to her approaching orgasm.

Tasha's thighs tightened around Kevin's head like a boa constrictor would a field mouse. That, along with the blissful 'daddy you've done right by me' sounds Tasha filled the room with, signaled the arrival of her orgasm. Now it's my turn, He conceitedly thought as he worked his way up her body with an occasional tongue, here and there.

"What's wrong?" Kevin asked, confused about the sudden change of events. Tasha had placed both of her palms on the top of his head, stopping him just as his kisses reached the fullness of her breast, his stiffness rounding third base.

"I told you...I have a headache," She kissed his forehead before directing him off of her, then turning her back on him and his hardness. "Good night," she snapped, pushing his hand off of her thigh. There was no way he'd get any tonight, not from her. He'd

Gary Norman

made his bed, now he'd have to sleep in it. "And you better not mess up my sheets," Tasha replied, mocking the last time she got him all worked up then didn't give him any (the next morning she woke up to semen soiled sheets). Luckily for her, and her sheets, that particular night she was at his apartment, in his bed.

Kevin grunted something about 'shit being fucked up' before getting out of bed and heading for the master-bathroom. Moments later Tasha heard water running in the shower. That's what you get, Tasha smiled at the thought of Kevin jacking off in the shower. That's what you get.

Scene 5

"I'm glad I decided to leave my gift in my trunk," Tasha ranted the next morning over coffee and a doughnut, which she split with Tracey since she's counting her points (the method behind the Weight-Watchers dieting program). "If I hadn't left his present in the car I would've felt so stupid giving him an anniversary present when his dumb ass didn't even know it was our anniversary."

"The way you did him, I bet you he won't forget shit else," Tracey said as a matter-of-factly, with a hint of laughter. The thought of Kevin using his new found oral-talents as leverage, only to be used for those same talents, did have some humor to it. I mean, men have been doing it for years, sixty-eighting a woman then owing her one. This time a woman owes a man. Good, Tracey thought, grinning as she pictured a confused 'I just got played' look on Kevin's face when he first realized he'd be going to sleep without having had sex first. A rarity when he'd sleep over to Tasha's.

"I just can't believe he forgot another anniversary, our second anniversary. Damn, we've only had two and he forgot both of 'em," Tasha sat across from Tracey, in a half full teacher's lounge, venting her anger as low as she could. Who knows who's listening? Who cares?

"Girl, you have to train a man just like you train a dog. Whip his ass every time he messes on the carpet, eventually he'll learn to use the paper. Or he'll runaway. Either way, you win," Both women laughed at Tracey's ideology. "So keep doing what 'cha doing."

"After last night, I doubt he'd ever forget another special occasion, whether it's our anniversary or ground hog's day."

"Forgetting shit is in a man's blood. You just have to make 'em pay – thus breaking the cycle."

"Oh, no...He knows that, from now on, he'll be punished for messing on the rug. So consider that cycle broken. And if it's not broken yet, it will be after a week of no sex."

"That's it girl, train him the old fashion way. Get stingy with the kitty."

"Nurse Miller, you're needed in the office. Nurse Miller, you're needed in the office. Thank you." The voice blared over the school's brand new intercom system, thus bringing an end to this morning's pre-class girl talk session. Something that has become a common occurrence since they became good friends, two months after Tasha landed the principal position.

"Oh, damn," Tracey spat, disgusted about having to end their 'girlfriend' talk time, especially when the conversation started getting juicy. "Let me go give somebody a Band-Aid and lollipop and I'll be right back."

"No, I better be getting back to my office. When you're finished just come by," Tasha stood from the table then accompanied Tracey to the office, talking of other ways to train a dog along the way. "So what should I do? Grab him by the back of his neck and push his nose in the toilet every time he leaves the toilet seat up?"

"You'll be surprised at how quickly he'd break that habit if you do," Tracey playfully nudged Tasha as they entered the office.

"Miss Miller," Mrs. Smith met Tasha and Tracey as they entered the office, her head tilted in the direction of the only other person in the office – an eight year old, blonde girl sitting sad-faced on the bench to the right of the entryway, behind the door. "I think she has the chicken pox."

"Ah, Tracey," Tasha whispered so that Tracey would be the only one to hear, all the while her eyes glued on the little girl who sat scratching her arm even though Mrs. Smith had told her not to. "Remember when I said come by my office when you're done?"

"Yeah."

"Well, I've changed my mind. Don't," Tasha playfully nudged Tracey in the direction of the contagious child before heading for her office, straight ahead, and two doors to the right of Tracey's office.

"Mrs. Smith, if Mr. Coleman calls or stops by, tell him I'll get back with him as soon as I can. And tell Mrs. Blaine I've okayed her request for the new lab equipment she so badly needed," Tasha remarked sarcastically. Mrs. Blaine always exaggerated things.

"Yes ma'am." Mrs. Smith answered in her 'back to business' tone.

"Oh, you know what? Just bring me a copy of Mr. Coleman's request for new gym equipment. I'll look over it when I get home."

"Yes ma'am. I'll get right on it."

"Thank you," Tasha released the conference button then continued with her daily 'end of work-day' routine of signing the papers she'd set aside for later. These were mostly detention forms and parental consent forms – all of which she'll have Mrs. Smith file

Pink October.doc   23

before leaving the office, usually taking her less than five minutes to do so.

"Here you go, Tasha," Mrs. Smith, after first knocking on Tasha's half opened door and being told to come on in, walked over and placed the requested material on her desk.

"That was fast."

"It was sitting on my desk, so I didn't have to go looking around for it."

"I'm glad, because I'm so ready to go home," Tasha, still sitting at her desk, placed the material in her attaché case, handed Mrs. Smith the forms she needed to have filed, then stood from her chair and accompanied Mrs. Smith to the door. "Do you know if nurse Miller left yet?" Tasha asked as she locked her office door.

"Yes she did...and I'm glad you mentioned her because she told me to tell you to be strong and don't give in," Mrs. Smith shrugged her shoulders as she filed the forms Tasha had given to her, her last bit of work for the day.

"Oh, I won't give in," Tasha said, trying to gather strength from her own words. Strength she needed in order to help her stick to the punishment she'd imposed on Kevin, though she knew-he knew how to break her down, if he wanted to. A few kisses in the right spot and she was silly putty. "He didn't go after my weak spot last night because he knew he was wrong for forgetting our anniversary. He knows he's still on punishment, hopefully he'll act like he knows it...Hopefully," Tasha had her fingers crossed as she walked with Mrs. Smith through the empty hallway. Only time would tell.

Gary Norman

24

Scene 6

"May I help you?" The young, pale-skinned, woman behind the counter at Krispy Kreme Doughnuts asked after she finished serving her third customer in a line of six.

"Oh," Tasha replied, snapping out of her momentary daze long enough to place her order. She had been replaying, in her mind, last night's event over and over again, since leaving Kevin's side this morning. From the moment Kevin walked into the room, Tasha didn't stand a chance. Guilt of forgetting their second anniversary didn't keep Kevin from making his move, as was the case the night before. He went straight for her weak spot, using his tongue to weaken her resistance even more. And it worked. It always works, whether he uses a tongue or finger. The spot at the base of her neck, closer to her shoulder, on either side, has stun-gun effect on Tasha; the right amount of pressure and she's at the mercy of whomever's lucky enough to fumble onto it. And with Kevin being as fine as he is, last night's love making session was the best she'd ever experienced, actually she feels that way every time they have sex. No other man has ever come close to making her feel like Kevin could make her feel, his overall physical beauty heightening her pleasure. With his chocolate skin, chiseled 'personal trainer' body and those dimples, all of which adding to the fact that he stood six foot three inches tall (a major turn-on, ranking at the top of her 'Major Weak-Spot' list), none of her past lovers could compete merely because he was fine. A 'send your aging parents to an old folks home just so you can screw all over the house' fine. Tracey will just have to understand. I'm only human, Tasha thought of how she's never been able to keep those nights she and Kevin experienced better than great sex to herself. One smile from Tracey and Tasha would break like four-inch heels worn by a four hundred-pound cross dresser.

While sitting at one of the window booths, enjoying one of the dozen glazed doughnuts and a cup of coffee, a familiar face caught Tasha's eye just as it disappeared into the flower shop across the street. "Cynthia..." she uttered the name of her old college friend, her soror, putting a name with the face she'd just seen. Or could've sworn she'd seen. "Only one way to find out," She gathered her things, put on her coat, and hurriedly made her way out the door, across the street and into the flower shop.

"Cynthia," Tasha spoke with uncertainty as she approached the woman from behind, still unable to see her face. "I thought that was you," she sang after the woman turned to face the direction of the voice that had just spoken her name.

"Hey, ship! How've you been?" The pleasantly surprised woman gleefully responded before hugging the friend she hadn't seen since receiving her undergraduate degree.

"I've been okay, how about yourself? It's been what, twelve? Thirteen years?"

"And you haven't changed a bit...Girl, look at you," Cynthia remarked on how fit her friend had remained throughout the years.

"Thank you, and you haven't changed either."

"I guess we're both just blessed, because we both look like we belong in Hollywood," Cynthia smiled, holding her arms out wide, modeling her five foot five inch, one hundred thirty five pound, chocolate frame. Smaller on the top than on the bottom, just like back in college.

Tasha shook her head at her friend's silliness. "I thought you lived in Iowa?" She had received her information on Cynthia's whereabouts from another one of their line sisters. Since there were sixteen women on their line, it was only natural that their relationships with one another varied from person to person, therefore making it easy to lose contact with one another over the years. Especially when one of them, Cynthia, graduated a few weeks after going over. That put a strain on their efforts (Tasha's and Cynthia's) to build more of a sisterly bond as opposed to the good friend bond they had worked their way up to.

"I do live in Iowa...I'm here for the annual 10K run, and this year I actually finished the race, which meant a lot to me since my mother lost her battle with breast cancer last year."

"I'm sorry to hear that. How have you been?" Tasha asked consolingly as thoughts of Cynthia's college apartment flashed in her head, her mother's picture gracing the living room and Cynthia's bedroom, right next to the red elephants she so proudly had on display.

"I've been okay. Informing women, especially black women, of how important early detection can be has helped me deal with losing her," Cynthia announced before removing her reef from atop the cashier's counter-top so that the approaching customer could be served. The reef had red and white ribbons with red letters that spelled out 'Happy Birthday Momma' in cursive lettering.

With reef in hand, Cynthia went on to tell Tasha how if her mother had found the cancer earlier she would be alive today. "A simple self-breast exam would've saved her life," Cynthia's words replayed in Tasha's head the rest of the way to work, making the five minute trek seem more like a few seconds.

Tasha went on to split her day between taking care of her principal responsibilities and thinking about what her friend had said about a disease she had never given much thought.

"I hope you feel better tomorrow," Tracey's voice brought Tasha back to reality. She'd been slipping in and out of a daze since hearing about her ship's mother. "Because you've been out of it since you got here," Tracey stood in front of Tasha's desk, watching as she sluggishly gathered her things.

"I'm sorry, I'll be ready in a minute," Tasha finally stood from her desk, put on her jacket, then walked out of her office.

Scene 7

"Seven...Eight...Nine...and ten!" The light-skinned, twenty something, aerobics instructor's voice filled the room as she brought Wednesday's evening class to an end with an intense session of step aerobics. Wednesdays and Fridays are more intense for Tasha because she would participate in the aerobics class as well as the hour-long self-defense class.

"I'll catch up with you in a minute, there's something I need to get off my chest," Kim's anger was evident, if not by her tone, by the way she headed towards James, her boyfriend/playmate of the moment. James, her six-foot, dark skinned, model type boyfriend, was standing just outside of the aerobics class talking to a dark skinned woman who seemed to be more interested in him than she should be. Not that Kim was the jealous type, because she wasn't. Well, not all the time. If that woman had been fat and out of shape, Kim wouldn't have had a problem. But since the woman was fine, James should've known better. "You're going to play me like that? Flirt with some ho' right in my face," Kim snapped, stepping between the two of them, her back to the woman, her face inches from his. When she got mad the 'hood' would come out of her like the Incredible Hulk and David Banner. Tasha often wondered if that had ever happened in court, when Kim was arguing a case in front of a judge.

"Ho'! Bitch, who you calling a ho'?" The woman snapped, stepping to Kim's side so that she could look into the face of the woman who had just disrespected her.

Tasha made it to the locker room's entrance just as the commotion began. "Wild-wild hundreds," Looking back over her shoulder, using a phrase she'd heard on the radio (a phrase that described a part of the south side), Tasha smirked before pushing her way into the locker room. She still couldn't understand how Kim, a lawyer at one of the city's top minority firms, can still be so ghetto. Not that Tasha was uppity, because she wasn't. But sometimes Kim acted like she never left the neighborhood, like she never received a higher education, the way she would get all in somebody's face over nothing. Tasha shook her head.

After getting undressed in front of her locker Tasha, with her shower necessities in hand, walked over to the showers and joined three other women in the huge bathing area. She made sure to take the nozzle furthest from the other women. She'd heard one of the three women was gay and liked scouting potential mates while they applied soap to their well-exercised bodies. Though she didn't believe it wholeheartedly (she heard it from Kim, who can be extremely vindictive over the most meaningless things, causing her to spread an occasional untruth), she still paid more attention to her surroundings than she did before hearing the rumor, especially when in the shower.

------------------- -------------------------- -------------

"Sorry it took me so long, but I had to take care of some business," Kim said as she undressed at her locker, directly across from Tasha's. "She didn't want none of me. She knew what time it was when she saw these guns," Smiling, she flexed her biceps before walking off heading for the showers, whistling the theme song to 'Rocky' as she walked. Tasha could only shake her head in disbelief. How a successful attorney wound up in 'hood-rat' situations, was beyond her. Tasha thought about the saying you can take the girl out of the ghetto, but you can't take the ghetto out of the girl, then laughed as she unfastened the towel she'd wrapped around her body. After dabbing herself completely dry, Tasha took the newly opened bottle of lotion from her locker, dispensed more than enough in the middle of her palm, then sat the bottle on the bench in front of her locker.

Starting with her left arm, Tasha worked the lotion into her pours like a seasoned masseuse, paying close attention to her elbows. She did the same with her right arm. After finishing with her arms she began to work her way down her torso, starting with her breast. As she massaged the lotion into her thirty-six, C-cup, breast Cynthia's words hit her like a runaway train. "A simple self-breast exam would've saved my mother's life," She remembered those words as if they were spoken minutes ago. It felt as if the chastising voice from her dreams was trying to tell her something, only this time she was wide-awake.

"Now how am I supposed to do this?" Tasha mumbled to herself as she tried to remember how to give herself a self-breast exam.

Using her fingers to press into her breast, Tasha began to feel around for anything remotely close to feeling hard like a pea or stone. That much she remembered because she'd passed the 'how to administer a self-breast exam' poster, hanging inside of the women's locker room, over one hundred times since she joined this health club.

"Oh...my...God," She uttered in absolute horror after coming across an unfamiliar 'small mass' of tough flesh on the lower outside

Pink October.doc

part of her left breast, between her armpit and nipple. It didn't feel anything like what the poster had described, feeling more like tension in a muscle than anything else. Even though the mass wasn't hard like a pea or stone, its fleshy and fibrous texture was still enough to push Tasha into a mild panic. Especially after all she'd heard this morning about the disease's high mortality rate when not detected early.

As she stood at her locker pressing her fingers into the unfamiliar mass, Tasha tried to calm down. "It's nothing…it's not even hard like a pea, so I'm sure its nothing," She told herself over and over again. The fact that it wasn't like a pea or stone did calm her down a bit, but it wasn't enough to end her worrying completely. Whether it was associated with breast cancer or not, it being there nearly drove her crazy. "How long has it been there? Was it always there, and I just never noticed? Is this common?" Tasha, obviously disturbed by her discovery, uttered as she continued to examine both of her breasts for anything else she may have missed. Anything she'd categorize as unusual.

"Don't overreact…It's nothing," She exhaled in an attempt to regain what little composure she was able to hold on to. "Everything is fine…and after I eat something…I'll be able to…damn, what will I be able to do?" She winced as she pressed her fingers into the "area", fear causing her life to flash before her eyes. Her left leg started to tremble, beads of sweat began to form on her forehead. She pressed once again to make sure she wasn't mistaken.

"What do you want to do?" Kim, suddenly appearing with a huge beach towel wrapped around her torso and a smaller one wrapped around her head, asked. Her sudden reemergence startled Tasha.

"Nothing. I was just thinking about something that happened at work," Discontinuing her self-breast exam so that she could get dressed, Tasha hid her concerns by carrying on as if nothing had happened. As if finding an area of tightened flesh in one of her breasts didn't scare her half to death.

"Whatever that nothing is, it really has you out there."

"Why do you say that?" Tasha asked as she prepared to step into her pantyhose. She hoped it wasn't too obvious that something was bothering her. She didn't feel like explaining.

"Most women apply their lotion before they put on their pantyhose," Noticing how ashy Tasha's body was from her stomach to her feet, Kim laughed as Tasha set her panty hose aside then reached for her lotion.

------------------ ----------------------------- ---------------

After deciding at the last minute not to join Kim and Kevin at 'Eatin' Healthy', the health food restaurant down the street from the gym, Tasha went home to deal with her runaway emotions in private. Everything from fear of dying from cancer to outright denying the possibility of women in good shape even being able to get cancer. Fear brought ignorance along for a ride. "Look at me, I'm in damn good shape! There's no way," She stood naked in front of the full-length mirror in her bedroom, staring at her reflection as if saying those words out loud would help her to see that she was being ridiculous. It didn't work, and hadn't worked since she came across the suspicious mass. So she did the only other thing she could think of. She went on-line.

"Eighty percent of lumps or changes found in the breast are not cancerous," She thanked God after reading those words aloud, the light from her computer screen illuminating her dark room with a constant glow. "However, all changes should be looked at by a doctor," The next entry captured Tasha's full attention, taking away any chance of Tasha getting a good night sleep. It's been a few years since my last mammogram, so another day won't hurt, She thought as she logged off of the Internet, making a mental note to call her doctor first thing in the morning. "Before school, if that's at all possible," She laid in bed, lights out, knowing full well anxiety wasn't going to allow her to sleep. Not on this night.

Scene 8

Tasha's Thursday morning started at five am. She was startled out of her sleep by a nightmare she hadn't had in years. The same nightmare she hadn't had since she turned thirty-two, two years ago. This nightmare would always start out with her sitting directly behind her parents, at a funeral. Her mother cried hysterically, her father patting her mother's back repeatedly, lovingly. At this point in her nightmare Tasha's tears would start to dampen her face and pillow. "Who died? Who died?" She knew her lips were moving, but nothing would come out. It was as if she were mute. That's when Tasha realized she was there as a spectator, at least that's how she figured it. If she wanted answers she'd have to go up to the casket and see for herself. And she did just that, only what she saw would jerk her from her not so pleasant slumber. It was her body lying in that casket, she learned this years ago, but each time she had this nightmare it was like the very first time. She cried every time.

After calling to set up an appointment, which, to her surprise, she was able to schedule for three o'clock today, Tasha joined Tracey in the teacher's lounge where they found themselves discussing, of all things, breast cancer.

"Tasha…" Tracey interrupted Tasha's recap of what she found on the Internet about the importance of regular mammograms.

"Yes?"

"How did we end up talking about breast cancer? Of all the discussions we've had at this table, this has to be a first. One minute we're talking about Kim snapping on her man, the next thing I know we're talking about how important early detection can be."

"How important early detection is, not can be." Tasha corrected.

"Tasha, I am a nurse…I do know a little about mammograms."

"I know. I was just on my computer last night and I found some stuff on breast cancer that startled me. I mean, before yesterday I hadn't given it much thought. But last night I found out how deadly it can be if it isn't detected early. And I also found out that black women have the highest mortality rate when it comes to the disease. So last night I decided to make an appointment to have a mammogram exam," Tasha shrugged, purposely leaving out the part about the tightened flesh she found in her breast. No need to worry Tracey when it could be nothing, Tasha figured.

"Really! Good for you."

Just then the school bell rang, signaling the start of nine o'clock classes.

"Oh, it's nine o'clock already," Tasha sighed, checking her watch as she stood from the table. "I should be getting back to my office. I'm expecting a call from a book supplier. I'm hoping he'll be able to offer a better package than the one I already have."

"I'm ready whenever you are," Tracey stood from the table, she and Tasha continuing their discussion as they walked out of the teacher's lounge.

"It's just something I feel is long overdue," Tasha explained as she and Tracey walked the empty halls of the moderate size elementary school. "Just to be on the safe side. Better safe than sorry, right?" She said mostly to convince herself.

"You're talking like I'm opposed or something. I'm all for it. In fact, I had a mammogram just last year," Just as they walked pass the sixth grade, computer class, Tracey laughed as if she'd just remembered an old joke.

"What's so funny?"

"I'm sorry. I was just thinking about the little boy you had in your office the other day. You know, the sexually advanced, computer geek," Tracey stopped in front of the classroom door, laughing at the incident as if it had happened moments ago.

"Don't laugh at that. That little boy has some serious issues," Tasha jokingly mimicked a stern parent, waving her pointing finger from side to side as she talked. They both thought that was funny.

"Look...he's about to use the computer. I bet he enters a site that has nothing to do with today's lesson," Tracey peered through the glass at the little boy as he sat at his computer station.

"I doubt it."

"Five dollars says he does," Tracey proposed a friendly wager. "I bet he goes into an adult website," Tracey continued.

"If you want to give your money away like that, I'll be more than happy to take it," Tasha nudged her friend before walking over and standing at Tracey's side, where they both peered through the square glass window in the center of the door. They were both shocked at what they saw. Well, Tasha was shocked. Tracey wasn't. Tracey found it funny that an eight year old, white kid, would be logging on to a website called Blackplanet.com, probably leaving obscene notes to a woman three times his age. The site wasn't an adult site, so nobody won the bet, but Blackplanet.com wasn't on the lesson plan, which meant Greg Clark was in trouble. "That little mannish SOB," Tasha mumbled before easing the door open, then quietly walking across the room to Greg Clark's computer station. 'He really likes himself some sisters,' Tasha had to bite her lip to keep herself from laughing at what she knew Tracey would say. "What are you doing?"

"Nothing..." A startled Greg Clark answered, his eyes looking up at Tasha, his hand scrambling to shut off his computer.

"I think you need to come with me," Tasha helped him slide his chair back. The entire class couldn't help but wonder what the little genius had done now.

"Damn," The eight-year old uttered under his breath. Tasha wasn't supposed to hear, but she did.

Gary Norman

Scene 9

With anxiety about her mammogram appointment propelling her day forward, Tasha, having left work early in order to make her three o'clock appointment, found herself impatiently sitting in Dr. Karen Peterson's South Holland, Women's Health Clinic, waiting room. All of her questions will be answered today, one way or another. "There's only two ways it can go. Yes, I have breast cancer, or no I don't," She exhaled as she sat waiting on a surprisingly comfortable couch in a brightly colored waiting room.

After waiting only fifteen minutes, which seemed more like an hour and fifteen minutes, the slender, pale skinned, middle aged white woman sitting at the reception counter announced "The doctor will see you now" causing Tasha's heart to drop into the pit of her stomach.

"Thank you," Tasha's voice cracked with the same uncertainty all women feel when it's time to face the unknown waiting for them behind Dr. Peterson's door.

After adjusting her skirt then retrieving her full-length leather jacket from the arm of the couch, Tasha walked over to the door leading into Dr. Peterson's office where she paused just long enough to take a deep breath, hoping that that would calm her before opening the door. It didn't work.

"Please, come in," The doctor replied from behind her huge Oak desk. She was an older, dark haired woman that had been practicing medicine for over fifteen years at the same location. Her desk sat in the middle of the light colored room, facing the door.

Stepping into the office, Tasha hung her jacket on the coat rack in the corner, to the left, before closing the door behind her. Let's get this over with, is what she wanted to scream as Dr. Peterson went into the formalities

Scene 10

"Keep your back straight and try to concentrate on using your inner thigh muscles," His eyes moving from breast to crotch then back up to breast again, Kevin instructed as he stood over Kim, assisting her while she used gym equipment. I love this job, he thought as he stood watching her seductively open her legs as wide as she could, working out her thighs on the gym's expensive version of the 'Thigh Master'.

"Am I doing this right?" Wearing her usual gym attire, spandex, Kim cooed as she purposely continued to tease Kevin, adding to the sexual tension that had begun to rise almost immediately after they began working out. Over the last two weeks their workout sessions have become more of a strip tease, without the strip.

"Yeah…In fact, I don't think you need this machine anymore," Fighting to regain his composure, Kevin brought his eyes up from her crotch to meet her beautiful brown eyes. "So lets move on to another machine."

"Yeah, I was thinking the same thing," She said, startling Kevin by snapping her legs open, causing the weights to slam down against the unused plates. That little move produced more than enough noise to attract attention from everybody in the weight room.

After getting up from the thigh machine Kim started to walk off, but then turned to ask Kevin "if he was coming or was he just going to stand there staring at her ass?" He had fallen behind a few steps so that he could admire what he believed to be the perfect ass. He did this every time he helped Kim workout, mostly on the days Tasha wasn't scheduled to come to the gym. Perfect timing.

"If you don't mind, I'd rather stand here and admire the view," He replied, then watched Kim sashay towards the next machine she decided she'd use to torture Kevin a little more.

"Please, not that machine. Please, not that machine," He chanted under his breath as Kim approached the hamstring-strengthening machine. "Damn," He uttered after watching her not only stop at that particular machine, but lie down on her stomach, her behind slightly elevated, calling his name like a doughnut would a seventh day dieter. "Stay calm and we can make it through this," He whispered, to an already stiffening part of his body, as he arrived at her chosen machine, his crotch a few inches from one of the shapeliest asses he'd ever seen. He hated when she teased him like this, but he loved it at the same time. She's always been able to push his buttons, more so when they were an item a few years ago, before Tasha joined the club. Back then they were just sex-partners. During that time Kim was in a relationship with one of the other personal trainers so their little fling was strictly 'undercover'. And that was cool with Kevin. He preferred that kind of situation opposed to having the entire gym in his business. As far as he was concerned, nobody had to know. And they still didn't know. Kevin and Kim would flirt with each other from time to time, but nobody really knew to what extent their relationship had gone. They may have suspected, but they didn't know. He thought Tasha would suspect something after his oral talents improved within such a short period of time, even though that's not something they did often. But she didn't, thank God.

After the last few weeks Kevin finally decided to put his all into pleasing his partner during oral sex. The only problem with that was the partner he decided to please was Kim. She had been pleasing him for so long that he finally decided to take the time to learn how to please her. The facts were like this; Kim liked to please him orally, Tasha didn't do it at all. "Maybe when I'm married," Tasha would say whenever the subject came up, usually right after one of Kevin's sloppy attempts at orally pleasing her. That would always piss him off, but he never said a word. He figured he'd be patient and sooner or later she'd come around. Two years later and Tasha still hasn't made that turn. Thank God for Kim!

After ten minutes of standing at her side, torturing himself with a close-up view of Kim's ass, his play ground, the bulge in his sweatpants had reached 'no way in the world mere sweatpants can conceal this' status. He hated when she had the upper hand. And right now, she definitely had it.

"Is that a part of the workout, or is that a separate workout altogether," Kim asked as she eyed his crotch, which, because of the height of the machine, was a foot from her face.

"This equipment is too advanced for you," He said what she hoped he'd say.

"What time is your next session?"

"Why?" He asked, knowing full well what she had in mind, nonchalantly adjusting himself.

Pink October.doc 37

Scene 11

After wrapping her Burberry scarf around her neck, which matched her Burberry shoes, Tasha buttoned her jacket before walking out into the parking lot where the south suburban brisk October wind was as windy as its Windy City neighbor. Once she reached her car she sat inside its cool interior, soaking in the news she'd just received. "Thank God," She exhaled as if the weight of the world had just been lifted from her shoulders. "It was nothing...Thank God, it was nothing," She repeated as she started her car.

Once her car had warmed up, Tasha pulled out onto Chicago Rd. intending on heading straight home, but as she got closer to the Baskin&Robin's on the corner she was overcome by the need to celebrate her good news. "This calls for a banana split," She said as she headed straight for the huge, welcoming, sign.

Scene 12

"There you go...home sweet home," After placing a half-gallon of this month's 'Flavor of the Month' into her freezer, Tasha, standing at the counter, took the plastic cover from over her banana split then sampled a spoonful of mostly whipped cream before remembering to call Kevin. She hadn't talked to him since this morning. He called from his apartment, last night and this morning, to make sure that she was okay. She really didn't give a valid reason for declining dinner, which, to Kevin, meant that something was wrong. Luckily he had to drive all the way out to Joliet (his brother and sister-in-law's house) for a last minute baby sitting assignment, because he would've gotten suspicious if she had told him he couldn't come over. Last night was definitely one time she thanked God that they weren't actually living together. She would've had to tell him about what she'd found in her breast, which would've caused unnecessary worrying, especially since what she feared to be cancer turned out to be nothing. Tasha smiled as she dialed Kevin's number, using the phone above the kitchen counter.

------------------- ------------------ ------------------ ------------

"Baby, your phone's ringing...want me to get it?" Wearing Kevin's white T-shirt and nothing else, Kim shouted from Kevin's king size bed to the connecting bathroom, where Kevin was about to step into the shower. "It's Tasha," She added with a bit of sarcasm after checking his caller ID.

"Go ahead, answer it," Kevin called her bluff as he checked water's temperature with the back of his hand before stepping into the shower. He knew Tasha was the last person Kim would want to know about their affair. They were friends. If you can call the woman sleeping with her best friend's man a friend. That's how Kevin would tease Kim after they'd finish 'doing the do'. He knew how much their affair was starting to weigh on Kim's conscious. She and Tasha had become close over the years, which meant this wasn't supposed to be happening. She wasn't supposed to like her man's woman, if that makes any sense. But she did, which made her feel worse. That's why she put an end to their occasional outings so abruptly. She just couldn't continue to go out partying with Tasha, not when things were the way they were. It wasn't because a new 'man of the moment' was taking up most of her time, like she'd have Tasha to believe. Whomever she was with was just a substitute, a sit-in for Kevin.

Pink October.doc

That's when she actually had a man in her life. Times when she didn't have a man she'd lie and say that she did just so she'd have an excuse when Tasha would suggest that they go out for drinks. She couldn't handle looking Tasha in the face when she knew the truth about her man, their man.

The fact that the two women were friends didn't bother Kevin one bit. He loved to see the both of them out together, saying it turned him on. "I bet you can lick your own nuts like your four legged brothers," Kim would hiss one minute, then take him to bed the next. That's when Kevin began to notice Kim's feelings about their situation had changed. At first Kim would jokingly refer to their arrangement as a threesome that one participant wasn't aware of. Back then the sex was coming as often as Kevin wanted. Now it was when she'd gone a week or so without it. If she wasn't horny, he wasn't getting any. No matter how bad he wanted it.

"Did you get the phone?" Kevin entered the bedroom wearing the black, silk, boxers Kim had gotten him for his birthday. Kim lost her train of thought as her eyes moved from his chiseled chest to his washboard abs. Damn he's fine, she salivated, momentarily forgetting all about how he belonged to a friend of hers.

Scene 13

"Where are your keys?"

"I don't know...I probably left 'em at the gym," Balancing a large pizza box on one hand, carrying a two liter of Mountain Dew with the other, Kevin stepped into Tasha's foyer prepared for a verbal assault. This makes three sets of keys he's lost in the last six months. Each time Kevin paid to have the locks changed, Tasha had insisted. Better safe than sorry, she said the first time he showed up at her house ringing the doorbell instead of letting himself in. "This is your last set...Lose these and you won't get another," she playfully warned after the second set. But Kevin knew she was serious. At least that's how she wanted him to take it. "Anyway, what's the good news?"

"What do you mean, 'anyway, what's the good news?' You better find my keys!"

"I will."

"You better, because the last set I gave you will be the last set you ever get," Tasha stood at his side, akimbo.

"I will, I promise...now what's the good news you sounded so happy about on my machine," Kevin asked, successfully taking the focus from his lack of maturity when it comes to adult things such as keeping up with house keys.

"I went to the doctor today," Tasha captured Kevin's attention with a collection of words that have been known to scare single men to death. She retrieved two champagne glasses from the cabinet over the microwave, unintentionally scaring Kevin even more. "I know what you're thinking...I'm not pregnant," The look of relief on his face saddened her a bit, but she continued. "Yesterday I felt a lump in my breast...well, it wasn't really a lump, but anyway, I set up a doctor's appointment for a mammogram...my good news is, what I thought was something turned out to be nothing. Nothing at all," She poured Mountain Dew into each of the champagne glasses while he placed a slice of pizza on two separate plates.

"Baby that's better than plain old good news, much better...but I have one question...Why didn't you tell me? I am you're man, I should've been there with you."

"I'm sorry, but if I had told you we both would've been worrying over nothing," Tasha kissed the side of his face, adding sugar to her apology.

"Yeah, but yesterday you didn't think it was nothing."

"You're right, and I'm sorry...I didn't look at it like that."

"You don't have to apologize, just think of me the next time you find yourself needing someone to talk to," He said this while looking deep into her eyes, all sincere, like he wasn't just laid up with a friend of hers.

"I will, I promise. Now let's eat, I'm starving," Taking both plates from the counter, preparing to enjoy her pizza in front of the evening news, she successfully diverted attention away from her insensitivity, the same way he diverted attention away from his immaturity.

Scene 14

"Baby, it's after six o'clock. Time to get up," Kevin nudged Tasha's side after turning off the clock's annoying alarm.

"I was sleeping sooo good," She stretched, yawning before rolling out of bed, once again treating Kevin to his own private lingerie show.

"Damn!" He adoringly watched her half-nude body walk into the bathroom.

Once inside the bathroom, Tasha reached behind her shower curtain and turned on the hot water, letting steam fill the room while she brushed her teeth. After rinsing out her mouth she stepped into the shower where the hot water, along with the steam it created, helped her to shake off the drowsiness associated with waking up this early in the morning. With the hot water massaging her back, Tasha, for the hundredth time since receiving her mammogram results, pressed her fingers into her breast, sending a brand new wave of uncertainty up her spine each time her fingers touched what she dubbed 'The Area'.

Over the next seven days Tasha grew more and more uneasy about the lump in her breast, even though her mammogram found nothing. "But it feels like something," she'd say to the reflection in her bathroom mirror every time she'd stand in front of it pressing her fingers into 'The Area'. "On the other hand, it did turn out to be nothing," She'd gone back and forth so much Kevin stepped in with a stern, yet caring, "If you don't get a second opinion you're gonna worry yourself sick. Now do it before you drive me crazy."

Tracey gave the same advice after listening to Tasha go from trusting in the results she had received to questioning the doctor's competence. "Tracey, I just have a bad feeling," is all Tasha gave as to why she 'all of a sudden' didn't trust the results she received. Of course she left out the part about how one bad dream after another started with her finding cancer and ended with her funeral. A funeral she witnesses all the way through, even to the point of viewing her own body. She'd wake up right after seeing her own lifeless body, but at that point she'd be too scared to go back to sleep, whether it be 11pm or 3am. Sometimes she'd wake up just before viewing her body, but she knew who was in the coffin. She's known for years. She started having this particular nightmare when she turned thirty and she didn't have the family she thought she'd have at that stage in her life. By the time her thirty-first birthday had rolled around her nightmares were far and in between, eventually stopping within the

Pink October.doc 43

next twelve months. "If this is upsetting you that much, just go get yourself a second opinion, I know they have other procedures for these kinds of situations. That way you'll be sure," Tasha spent a few days pondering over Mrs. Smith's endearing words before setting up another appointment, only this time with a different doctor.

Tasha left the remainder of Monday morning's "beginning of the week" memo to be handled by vice principal Reddpeccer so that she could make it to her appointment on time. This was vice principal Reddpeccer's first day back to work so, needless to say, he wasn't a happy camper. Tracey thought it was funny. Not the work he had to do, but the fact that a man took maternity leave. She still joked about that one.

Clad in a pair of jeans, red sweatshirt and black soft-soled shoes, which she wore more for comfort than for style, Tasha, with her shoulder length hair in a ponytail, sat impatiently in Dr. Jordan's Beverly office waiting room. Luckily she hadn't forgot to bring along her CD walk-man and her favorite Sade CD. She needed Sade's smooth tunes to calm her out-of-control emotions. It didn't work. As the mellow sounds flowed through the headphones, her mind entertained every negative 'what if' scenario imaginable. Maybe hearing about Cynthia's mother and how she lost her battle with breast cancer caused her to continue worrying, even after she had received good news following her mammogram exam. "Things happen for a reason," is what she told herself, and that meant running into Cynthia was God's way of trying to tell her something. She's always known about how her own grandmother lost her battle with colon cancer, but she never thought of it as something that she needed to concern herself with. But now here she was, in another doctor's office, preparing to undergo an ultrasound and a needle biopsy.

"The doctor is ready to see you now," The young, dark skinned, receptionist announced after finally getting Tasha's attention by waving her hands in her direction, bringing Tasha back from Sade's concert.

"Thank you," Tasha nodded courteously, her heart pounding like African drums as she gathered her coat from the arm of the couch then headed for the door leading into the doctor's office. Tasha paused for a brief moment after opening the door, inhaling deeply as if a deep breath would bring her heart rate back down to normal.

"Please, come in and have a seat," Dr. Jordan, the puffy-faced, dark skinned woman, invited Tasha into her office.

Gary Norman

After her negative mammogram results had failed to put her fears to rest, Tasha decided she'd take Tracey's 'You should get your second opinion from a black doctor' advice. Not that it made a difference what color her doctor was, because it didn't, at least it didn't make a difference to Tasha. "If we don't support us, who will?" Tasha could hear Tracey's words as she sat down in one of the plush leather chairs facing Dr. Michelle Jordan's desk, her plaques and certificates decorating the wall behind her desk like graffiti on a New York subway car.

To help Tasha feel more at ease, Dr. Jordan began by properly introducing herself then filling Tasha in on her credentials (graduating at the top of her class from the University of Chicago, her many years of experience, her work in the community, etc....). From there she discussed the forthcoming ultrasound and needle biopsy, which they'd begin shortly.

Pink October.doc

Gary Norman

Scene 15

Still feeling discomfort in her left breast from the invasive needle used in the needle biopsy, Tasha, who under normal circumstances never eats in her car, sat in the driver's seat spooning Baskin&Robin's frozen yogurt into her mouth as she sat staring out over lake Michigan. In warmer weather the Oak street beach would be swarming with beach-goers and picnickers consuming every one of the few parking spaces. But on this cool, wet, October afternoon Tasha had almost the entire parking area to herself. As she sat unable to keep her mind from traveling to the same negative places it had visited before and after her mammogram exam, she sobbed as if bad news was inevitable. "Why am I crying?" She wiped her tears away with the back of her hand, knowing that any other woman would've been happy receiving negative mammogram results. But something just didn't feel right. Could the mammogram have missed something? "Naa, that's not possible," she uttered. She was unable to convince herself with those mere words. Her mammogram showed nothing unusual, which meant her biopsy would probably turn out to be nothing more than wasted time and money. "So why do I still feel like bad news is right around the corner?" She sighed before pulling out of her parking space, heading for the place most adults go when fear starts to get the best of them.

Scene 16

"I hope I'm not bothering you with my silliness," Tasha smiled as she sat at her parent's kitchen table watching her mother fill two cups with cherry Kool-Aid, a slice of lemon in each cup.

"You know you're not bothering me. I just wish there was something I could do to help you get a grip on that imagination of yours before it runs you ragged," Tanya, Tasha's short and plump mother, set a cup in front of her daughter before taking a seat next to her. Tanya was a shade or two darker than her daughter, but you could still see the family resemblance.

"You know, you're probably right."

"I know I'm right," She watched her daughter drink from her cup before continuing. "Look, you've already had a mammogram exam and it didn't find any cancer. So you'll get the same results from your biopsy, so don't worry yourself sick over nothing," She reached over and took her daughter's hand.

"Okay, momma," Tasha smiled, feeling like she did when she was little, back when a few words from her mother would make any situation seem as though it wasn't all that bad.

"Now let me fix you a plate," Tanya laid her hand on her daughter's arm before continuing. "You look so tiny. Have you been eating, or are you dieting again?" She got up from the table to start fixing Tasha a plate, whether she wanted it or not. 'You can always take it home, if you don't feel like eating it now,' was the unwritten rule at her mother's house so Tasha didn't object. Besides, her mother made the best lasagna this side of the Mississippi. Even if she'd just come from having dinner, Tasha wouldn't have been able to turn down a helping of her mother's specialty. It was that good.

"Yes, I have been eating. Thank you very much for the compliment."

"I'm not complimenting you on being skin and bones. I bet losing all that weight was Kevin's idea, wasn't it?"

"No. And I've only lost twenty-five pounds. The same twenty-five pounds I told you about the last time you asked about my weight, three months ago, so cut it out," Tasha laughed, mimicking the tone her mother had used on her when she was a little girl and in need of some straightening out. Cut it out said in the right tone of voice could stop an avalanche. At least that's how it seemed to Tasha when she was a little girl.

"Look Tasha, I don't want you to worry about this all week."

Gary Norman

"I won't momma," Tasha replied like she was actually telling the truth, but she wasn't and Tanya knew it. Tasha has always been the kind of person to worry over silly stuff, is how Tanya had referred to it back when Tasha was a little girl worrying about oversleeping and missing her favorite Saturday morning cartoon. Tasha would worry about the same thing each and every Saturday morning.

"I better be going," Tasha downed the remainder of her Kool-Aid. "Since I took the day off I'm going to go to the gym today, so tell daddy I'm sorry I missed him and I'll talk to him later."

"Okay, I'll tell him."

"And momma please don't tell him about this. At least not until I get my results," Tasha nearly pleaded as she and her mother stood in the foyer with an aluminum foil covered plate of lasagna in one hand, holding her mother's hand with the other.

"You know he's going to be upset with you if you don't tell him. I mean, you didn't even tell us about the toughness in your breast and how it prompted you to have a mammogram."

"Ma, you can say lump."

"Well, you said yourself it didn't feel like a stone or pea, but was more of tough flesh-like feeling. Like the muscle had a frog in it."

"You're right."

"I know I'm right," She smiled a motherly 'I'm here for you' smile before nudging Tasha's arm. "So like I was saying, how do you think he's going to feel about being left in the dark about something like this?"

"I know, I just don't want everybody worrying until I know for sure."

"Tasha you're our only child, we're going to worry. But I'll explain the entire situation to him and I'm sure he'll see things just as I do. Your imagination is running you ragged, as always," She smiled, hoping her daughter would see things her way, at least over the next week. But how could she? After talking with Dr. Jordan she found out that mammograms don't always detect cancerous tumors. Tasha didn't tell her mother that part. That would've scared her to death.

"Well, at least I'll be able to get a nice workout in, which will probably help take my mind off things," Tasha told herself as she, after promising to call her father later, drove off heading for the gym. At least something good would come out of this day.

Scene 17

The look on Pam's face puzzled Tasha as she stood listening to her ramble on and on about B.S. she had little or no interest in. It seemed more like she was stalling for time than actually attempting to engage in conversation. "Or maybe that's just my mind playing tricks on me," Tasha shrugged before excusing herself, leaving Pam (the woman working the information desk) so that she could surprise Kevin before he saw that she was there.

"Oh hey!" The surprised look on both Kevin and Kim's face set off that alarm called "woman's intuition." It was just something about their closeness that just didn't seem right. Something about the way he leaned over her, supposedly helping her with barbell shoulder presses. "Girl, you're really trippin," Tasha brushed those negative thoughts aside as plain old stress from all the worrying she'd been doing. "Maybe this is a blessing in disguise," She thought of how this non-sense had taken her mind off of the biopsy results she'd receive in a few days. But the more she thought about what she saw, or thought she saw, the more she began to suspect that they were having an affair, even though she knew neither of them would betray her like that. That only happens on Jerry Springer, at least that's what Tasha told herself. And what about James? Wasn't Kim still seeing James? "There's only one way to find out," After days of pondering over what her next move should be, Tasha entered the gym on a Thursday evening, a day and time she would normally stay away from the gym.

Wearing her favorite workout sweats, her gym bag hanging from her shoulder, Tasha's plan to surprise Kevin was set in motion. There was no turning back. Her intuition wouldn't allow her to do so, even though she knew her current situation was to blame for her sudden feelings of being betrayed. Whether she was wrong about what she thought she saw or not, what she was doing today would silence that alarm once and for all. Or it would provide proof of something she hadn't expected.

Spotting Pat and one of the personal trainers standing at one of the gym's vending machines, down the hall from Pat's station, Tasha waited until she saw that they were deep in conversation before attempting to walk by the both of them. She didn't need any unnecessary distractions. She'd come too far to be spotted because she'd stopped to engage in meaningless conversation with one of the gym's employees.

She made it by Pam without being noticed. Finding Kevin without him seeing her first wasn't going to be as easy. She's an active member at this gym so there was no way she'd be able to go more than a few minutes without being seen by someone both she and Kevin knew. Someone who'd probably tell Kevin that she was here before she'd have a chance to catch him in the act. That's if he was actually up to no good, which he probably wasn't. That's what Tasha told herself as she walked through the gym trying to look as normal as any woman attempting to spy on her man could look. Like a poorly skilled private investigator, Tasha nonchalantly scanned the weight training area, but Kevin was nowhere to be found. "I know he's here," She uttered, her heart rate quickening with each step as she proceeded with her search to another section of the gym. While walking from the free-weight weight training area down to the universal-weight weight room, she spotted Kevin and Kim. They were standing outside of the restroom, which were down a short hallway to Tasha's left, a short distance away from the free-weight weight room. Tasha hid behind the wall where she peered around the corner watching in total agony as Kim, after groping the swell in Kevin's gym shorts, motioned for Kevin to follow her into the women's room. "I wish I could," He said, turning down her invitation, patting her ass as he did so. "I have to attack poor defenseless women today...the regular guy is home sick with the flu. But I'll take a rain-check," He smiled that same dimpled smile that Tasha found so irresistible. And that was more than enough to make her sick. Not an actual illness kind of sick, but the kind of sick one feels when their heart has been crushed by someone who takes the trust they've been so freely given and drags it through infidelity's mud.

"Son-of-a-bitch!" After taking in more than her fragile heart could stand, Tasha walked away mumbling to herself as tears from an unbelievable pain began to swell in her eyes.

Slipping into the women's locker room unnoticed by any of her gym acquaintances, Tasha sat at her locker fuming, wiping tears of anger and pain from her face before the women entering the locker room could notice. "How could he? How could she? How long have they been playin' me for a fool? Did he ever love me? Was she really ever my friend? That bitch! How could she? How could they?" Her mind raced through the same set of questions before sweet thoughts of revenge invaded her mind like U.S. troops and Iraq. Scratch up the paint on his truck, slash his tires, smash his windshield or trash his apartment. These thoughts eased her pain a bit, bringing a brief smile to her face, but her reasonable thinking side wouldn't allow her to do

Pink October.doc

anything that would end with her having a criminal record, so she had to think of something else. Then it hit her...

Gary Norman

Scene 18

"Our usual attacker is out with the flu so tonight we have a stand-in that I'm sure you all already know and love. For those of you who haven't had to pleasure of meeting him, this is Kevin Banks, one of our personal trainers," Instructing tonight's self-defense class, Chris introduced Kevin, who was then serenaded by the room full of women with flattering catcalls that grew even louder when he took a bow. "Ladies he's the attacker, not a potential date," Chris jokingly reminded the room, shaking his head when one of the larger women shouted "says who" in response. "He can attack me anytime he wants to. That's if he's man enough to handle all this," an even larger woman added, winking at Kevin flirtatiously as the rest of the women zealously agreed.

Known as a male hoe by more than few of the women present, Kevin smiled before putting on the huge padded headgear, which also covered his shoulders and most of his chest. Today's lesson in self-defense was focused on gouging the eyes to fend off an attacker. Everybody will have an opportunity to take part in the exercise.

As the third volunteer successfully fought off the heavily padded attacker, Tasha entered the room without being seen. At the end of the simulated attack she made her move, seizing an opportunity before Chris could choose Kevin's next victim. With her tears having dried from the heat revenge emitted, Tasha briskly walked to the front of the room taking her position as the next victim. One woman snared. Obviously she was next in line.

"Hey baby," A cautious Kevin managed to say as he stood staring like he'd seen a ghost. She wasn't supposed to be here. Not on a Thursday, his paranoid mind repeated over and over.

"Hey yourself," She stared into his eyes with disgust for him and his nonchalant attitude about what he was doing behind her back. "I guess it's my turn to be attacked," Her smile hid her true feelings of hurt and betrayal, a dangerous combination in a black woman.

"I'll try to take it easy on you," Unaware of the fury raging beneath Tasha's smile, Kevin smiled underneath the protective headgear before instructing Tasha to turn her back to him so the attack could begin.

After a brief moment of stillness, Kevin, with every eye in the room glued on him and his victim, slowly approached Tasha from behind. He suddenly sprang forward, grabbing her in a full body embrace, beginning the simulated attack. In one quick motion, Tasha, grabbing his hand in a way that she would gain control, twisted out of his hold then, with Kevin bent forward, sent him tumbling to the floor with a knee to the ribs. He rolled over once then rose to his feet just like he'd trained himself to do. This particular move allowed him to create enough space between himself and one of the class' advanced participants. This allowed the attack to continue uninterrupted.

Having been educated on this particular move, Tasha stepped to his left and waited until he made the mistake of trying to kick. When he made that mistake her pain and anger erupting like a volcano as she delivered another crushing knee, only this time to his groin. A collective gasp filled the room. Every woman present could only imagine how deep his pain went as they watched him curl into a fetal position, whimpering something only he could understand.

"You won't be screwing that bitch tonight," Tasha kneeled down bedside him and whispered before standing and laying her eyes on Kim, who, with a look of absolute terror in her eyes, witnessed the entire incident before turning to run. She didn't need the "psychic friends network" to tell her that Tasha had found out about the affair. She could see it in Tasha's eyes.

"Don't run from me you back stabbing bitch," Tasha muttered mostly to herself as she started after Kim. "Now where did you go?" After reaching the hallway and finding that Kim was nowhere to be found, Tasha was set to give up her chase, that is until she noticed the people looking in the direction of the woman who had almost knocked them over when she passed. "Oh no you don't!" Tasha ran towards the automatic sliding doors hoping to catch Kim before she reached her car. What she'd do once she caught her, she did not know. She'd figured that out once she caught that bitch, were her thoughts as she gave chase.

Just as she stepped onto the soft rubber padding that opened the automatic sliding doors, she heard the loud crying sound of tires spinning.

"Crazy bitch," Kim yelled out of her window at Tasha, who was standing in front of the gym's entrance. Kim didn't mean a single word. Fear did all the talking, forcing Kim to say such a thing even though she knew she was wrong. She regretted those words before the last syllable left her mouth.

"You can run, but you can't hide," Tasha said under her breath before returning to the gym where she retrieved her bag, cleaned out her locker, and left for home. She didn't mean most of what she had said either. The knife in her back did all the talking.

Gary Norman

Scene 19

After witnessing what added up to the end of her relationship, Tasha spent Thursday night, the eve of receiving her biopsy results, broken hearted and alone. With tears in her eyes, she thought back to the good times she and Kevin shared. Times like the night he came over after a day at the gym and pulled off his sweatpants to reveal a pair of her thong panties, the same thong panties she had talked him into wearing to show how much he loved her. He passed that test with flying colors. How silly he looked in those panties, prancing about the room as if there was no test silly enough to keep him from proving his love for her. "His love didn't mean shit...It was all a lie...A sick joke...you heartless bastard!" She cried out as she lay in her bed, her tears running down her face and onto her satin pillowcase.

With receiving her biopsy results only a few hours away, Tasha wasn't able to spend Thursday night pampering herself like she'd planned to do. Instead, she spent most of the night between throwing all of Kevin's belongings (which had accumulated over the course of their two year relationship into more than half her closet) out into her backyard and calling to inform him as to where he could find his 'shit'. That eased her pain a little, watching him retrieve his things from puddles of water left behind by a late evening shower. But it wasn't enough to keep her from thinking about how she had put her all into another relationship, only to receive the most disrespectful form of infidelity in return. He could have chosen any other woman in the city to cheat with, why did it have to be someone she considered a friend?

By the time she calmed down enough to where she could think of something other than Kevin, it was too late to call her mother like she had promised so she made a mental note to call her first thing in the morning, before her appointment. Waiting until the morning to call her mother would also give her enough time to gather herself so that her mother wouldn't detect the broken heart Kevin left behind. Which is easier said than done since all parents are equipped with radar specifically for that reason. As for tonight, she needed her rest. And with today's events taking so much out of her, and with it already being past her usual bedtime, falling asleep wasn't as hard as she thought it would be, just more painful. Thank God her mammogram exam turned up negative. If it had been positive she wouldn't have been able to sleep a wink. Thank God...

Pink October.doc

Scene 20

Friday morning started like any other Friday, yet it was totally different from any other day she'd ever experienced. With thoughts of her impending results finally outweighing her much less important domestic situation, which she dwelled on most of the night, her uneasiness blossomed into full fledge fear.

"I've already had a negative mammogram, so there's no reason for me to be so uptight...I'm fine," She stood in front of the mirror on her dresser pressing her fingers into her breast, rambling on and on, searching for that something that might help ease her unfounded worrying. After finally picking out a comfortable pair of jeans and a sweatshirt, she did what she knew would help her to ease her worrying. She called her mother...

"You'll be just fine," Tanya said just as she'd done when she was a little girl worrying herself sick about the possibility of scars being left behind once her chicken pox cleared up. But this was a lot more serious than facial scars being left behind by a childhood disease. This was something that could actually turnout to be a life or death matter, though Tanya did feel like her daughter was overreacting. "Call me as soon as you get the good news, so I can say I told you so," She laughed into the receiver, hoping that Tasha would see that she was being silly.

"Okay momma, I'll call you as soon as I get the good news," Tasha returned the laughter as their phone conversation came to an end. "I love you momma," She said before hanging up. She checked her watch one last time. Only an hour to go before her appointment. Just one hour. It seemed more like ten.

Scene 21

"Have a seat, Miss Mills...I hope I didn't keep you waiting too long," From behind her desk Dr. Jordan could see the concern in Tasha's eyes as she cautiously sat in one of the empty chairs in front of her desk. Tasha had been waiting for what seemed like an eternity for these results, so her patience for small talk was less than thin. She hadn't been seated a good two minutes before she said to Dr. Jordan, "Please, just get right to it. Do I have cancer?"

As she watched Dr. Jordan open the file in front of her, her heart began to pound so loud that she could've sworn the doctor was able to hear every thump. Then, with a calmness only seasoned doctors can maintain, Dr. Jordan proceeded with the biopsy results, ending Tasha's four days of agony with twelve words she'd never forget. "The biopsy confirmed that the lump in your breast is indeed malignant," The words left Dr. Jordan's mouth in slow motion. At least that's how Tasha will remember it.

Paralyzed by the shock of what she'd just heard, Tasha felt a tightening in her chest. It became hard to breath, causing her to violently hyperventilate for the first time in her life. Dr. Jordan, having prepared herself for a variety of possible reactions, retrieved a brown paper bag from her desk before rushing to Tasha's side.

"Miss Mills, please try to calm down," Dr. Jordan tenderly instructed while assisting in placing the paper bag over her nose and mouth.

"How....am....I....supposed....to....stay....calm....when.....you ....just.....told...me....that I have....cancer?" With tears running down her face like a dam that had sprung a leak, Tasha managed to say in between huffing and puffing.

"I understand what you're going through, trust me. But please, try to calm down. There are a lot of things we need to discuss and besides, it'll be a lot more helpful if you can talk to me without having to breathe into a paper bag. So if you want, I can reschedule our talk for whenever you think you'll be well enough to talk..."

"No...I'm....okay...Please.....just...give...me....a minute."

Once Tasha had given Dr. Jordan the okay to continue (after a fifteen minute recuperating period) Dr. Jordan went on to walk Tasha through the next steps. First she educated her on the mechanics of the disease, how it's able to travel from one part of the body to the other. Then she told her how they (doctors) go about finding out where the cancer had spread, if it had spread at all. Once that's known, the patient usually undergoes chemotherapy in order to shrink

Pink October.doc   57

the tumor before surgery, unless the patient's tumor is small enough to where chemo isn't needed. Which seems likely in Tasha's case.

"Hopefully a lumpectomy, followed by radiation therapy, will be the course of action, which is probably the case here. I'm saying that based on how small your tumor is, but that's just my guess before finding out whether or not the cancer has spread. After that's determined we'll be able to choose the appropriate course of action, okay?" After realizing Tasha's breathing had returned to normal, Dr. Jordan, her elbows on her desk, her head resting in her palms, struggled with her own emotions as she watched Tasha wipe tears from her face. The fear in Tasha's eyes was unmistakable. The look of despair was as familiar to Dr. Jordan as the look a police officer sees in the eyes of a gunshot victim. A type of blank stare that is common with people unfortunate enough to be on the receiving end of this conversation, the look of absolute bewilderment. And even though she's seen this look more times than she'd care to mention, Dr. Jordan still cries at the end of each of those days she has to tell a patient they have cancer. Not a hysterical kind of cry, but the kind of cry a person cries when they hear of tragedies; Like hearing of a stray bullet killing a mother of three or a drunk driver walking away from an accident unharmed but the family of four in the mini-van perish. That's how Dr. Jordan has always been, forming personal bonds with her patients no matter how long they've been a patient of hers or the color of their skin or how much money they earn. None of that played a part in how she would become so personally involved with her patients. "Hey girl, how are you doing?" or "Hey Mr. Man, how's everything going with you?" She'd go out of her way to greet her patients, and the parents of her patients, when she'd run into them outside of the office. This was what helped her to achieve that special bond she has with each of them.

"Thank you, doctor...I'll see you tomorrow," Tasha's voice reeked of defeat as Dr. Jordan escorted her to her car. She was still visibly shaken, that was apparent by how she fumbled through her purse for more than five minutes looking for the keys she had in her hand. Obviously she wasn't in any condition to drive.

"Miss Mills, since you don't want to leave your car here, let me drive you home in your car and I'll catch a cab back?"

"No, I couldn't ask you to do that. Besides, I'm fine. Really."
"Miss Mills..."

"Please, call me Tasha," Tasha interjected.

Gary Norman

"Tasha you don't have to ask me, I'm offering. Plus, I can look at you and see that you're not fine. Look at you. You're shaking. Please allow me to drive you home, it'll make me feel a lot better knowing you made it home in one piece," Dr. Jordan's concern was evident, making it impossible Tasha to turn down her gracious offer.

After placing her car keys in the doctor's hand, Tasha got in on the passenger side then leaned her seat back as far as it would go. It was the only way she could hide her tears from the rest of the world (which began to fall as soon as she sat in the car).

Scene 22

Once Dr. Jordan's cab left, Tasha ran to her first floor bathroom, kneeled in front of the toilet, and threw up like she'd drank a half pint of gin on an empty stomach. News of a cancerous tumor being found in her breast, which could lead to her early demise, literally made her sick to her stomach. After more than forty-five minutes of uncontrollable crying, she gathered herself from the floor, stepped over to the sink, then splashed water on her face before looking into the mirror. The emotionally drained eyes looking back at her scared her to the point of more tears. "Come on girl, pull yourself together," She spoke to her reflection like she was speaking to another living being. "Get it together...everything will be just fine, you'll see...you'll be fine...trust me," She said in between sniffling and wiping her runny nose with the back of her hand. "Did the disease spread to any other part of my body? Is it in my lungs? Liver? Brain? If it has spread, how bad is it? Will I need to have my breast removed? Is it so bad that I probably won't live out the rest of the year? Month? Week? Oh my God, I don't even have children!" She cried out, the terror of her nightmares becoming a frightening reality right before her eyes. "Will I be able to have children? If so, will I live long enough to be a part of my child's life? Will I live long enough to see them off to school? Elementary school? High school? College? Will I live long enough to see my child get married? Will I live to see my grandchildren?" Tasha stood teary eyed in front of the mirror, staring at her reflection as if it would some how give her the answers to all of her questions...it didn't.

Scene 23

"Okay, honey...I'll see you in a little while...I love you, too...and don't forget the milk!" Tanya blurted out that last part just before William hung up the phone. "I said I'd get the milk, didn't I?" Tanya jokingly mimicked her husband's usual response, tone and all, before he could even get it out of his mouth. They both got a good laugh out of that before ending their conversation with William promising not to forget the milk, something he'd probably end up doing.

Standing over a hot stove, Tanya laughed to herself as she prepared dinner for her husband, Dr. William Mills ob/gyn. She did that from time to time, laughed for no reason at all. Some people would say she was crazy, but the few people that have experienced true love understand. She married the only man she'd ever loved and that was enough to make her laugh for no reason whenever she felt like it. And why shouldn't she laugh out load for no reason? The man she chose to marry delivered on his promise to love, honor and respect her, plus to also take care of her sexually, emotionally and financially. He's given her thirty-five wonderful years filled with everything from a beautiful daughter to the kind of happiness people make movies about. He's been the near perfect husband, attentive, caring, and a good cook. He's everything she'd dreamed her husband would be, so much so that she often finds herself wishing she'd saved herself for him, unlike the lie she told him in the beginning of their courtship. She sincerely wished she had not fallen for that loser, Kinney, who lived a few blocks away from her childhood home, on the south side of Chicago. But how could she not have fallen for him, with his slick hair, slick way of talking, and that bad ass '68 Camaro he got when he got back from Vietnam. But he was a mistake. A big mistake. And with time Tanya saw how much of a mistake he really was. "He wasn't the kind of man she needed, he was the kind of man she wanted," Liz, Tanya's closest friend back then, use to say. Maturity eventually taught her that what you want is not always what you need. Once Tanya realized that William was her man, she was his and his only from that day forth (Well, except for the night of her bachelorette party, but other than that time no other man has even gotten close to sampling her goodies). What happened between her and Kinney has since been buried within her mental archives like Jimmy Hoffa somewhere in the world, never to be heard from again.

---------------------------- Ding-Dong ---------------------------

Pink October.doc   61

    "I'm coming! I'm coming!" Tanya yelled as she left the kitchen, heading for the front door to confront the person who was losing their damn mind on the doorbell. That person was probably her husband, who would get so caught up in his work that he'd leave his keys at his office from time to time. "Don't tell me you left your keys at the hospital...Oh, I'm sorry. I thought it was your father," Tanya said after opening her front door expecting to find her husband on the other side, but finding her daughter standing there instead.

    Without noticing the disturbed look on her daughter's face, Tanya turned to head back to the kitchen, talking back over her shoulder as she walked. This was Tanya's first time preparing swordfish steaks and she wanted to make sure she followed the recipe to a tee, so she was a tad bit preoccupied. "I was just thinking about you...I was wondering why you hadn't called. You know I've been waiting all day to hear what your results were, even though I've already told you what your results would be...but still, I wanted to hear it from you. You know, so I can say I told you so," So confident that Tasha's biopsy would prove that she was cancer-free, coupled with tonight's dinner needing to be placed into the oven, an entire seven minutes passed before Tanya finally noticed the emotionally drained look in Tasha's eyes. She looked as if she had been crying, her arms folded across her chest to keep from fidgeting.

    "Momma," Tasha's voice cracked, the pain of having to tell her mother the news was just as excruciating as hearing the news for the first time in Dr. Jordan's office. "I have some bad news," Unable to keep her tears at bay for another second, Tasha stood in the kitchen's entranceway, her bottom lip beginning to tremble, her eyes telling her news without Tasha having to mouth a single word. The look on her face said all that Tanya needed to know. And that was too much for her to handle while standing, so, with her mouth gaped from what she knew her daughter's eyes were saying, she eased herself into a chair, silently staring at Tasha until she too had tears running down the sides of her face.

    "It can't be...it just can't be," Tanya uttered as Tasha joined her at the table. The look in Tasha's eyes confirmed what she had said.

    "Momma, the lump turned out to be malignant," She paused, silently praying for enough strength to continue. "I have breast cancer," She reached over and took her mother's hand then sat in deafening silence for more than ten minutes, allowing her mother enough time to take in the news, cry, think, and pray.

Ever since she could remember, she's been able to say the right words that would make the worst situations no longer seem as bad. But today Tanya was at a lost for words. What could she say when she sat at her daughter's side, crying just as hard as she was. How could she offer the kind of support needed when she needed that same support? How would she be able to lend a shoulder to cry on when she needed that same shoulder? Maternal instinct, that's how. No matter how dire the situation, she could rely on her maternal instincts to step in and take over when she was too weak to do what needed to be done. This is one of those times.

Quietly, she sat listening as Tasha explained everything from the mechanics of the disease to the estrogen and progesterone tests that had been done on the cancer cells taken from the tumor in her breast. She explained how, because of the estrogen and progesterone test, doctors are able to give information on the chances of the cancer recurring. In Tasha's case, the chances were good that the cancer would not return. "There's no guarantee that the tumor won't return, but my chances are good that it won't," Tasha used her thumb to wipe tears from her mother's face, leaving her own tears to drip to the kitchen table.

"I'll have the lump removed, along with a section of my lymph nodes. Some doctors take a piece of their patient's lymph nodes so that they can see if the disease is hiding there," Enlightening her mother on what was to come was interrupted by the blaring smoke alarm posted on the wall nearest the stove.

"Damn, look at this," After springing from the table and over to the stove, where she retrieved the charred remains of tonight's dinner from the broiler, Tanya could only shake her head at what she'd done to that poor swordfish.

"At least it's done," Tasha and Tanya looked from the charred dinner to one another then burst into nervous laughter, which, in a way, helped lighten the mood a bit. Just a bit.

------------------- ---------------------------- -------------

"Thank you, sir."

"You're welcome," William tipped the pizza delivery-man a twenty dollar bill. His eyes were still red from the tears he shed in the upstairs bathroom after hearing the news. He couldn't allow his already fragile wife and daughter to see him cry, not when he could tell that they had been crying before he arrived home. Who knows how long they would've cried if he had broke down in front of them. They needed his strength more than ever. At least that's what he told himself before leaving his wife and daughter in the kitchen, excusing himself so that he could use the bathroom. Once out of their site, using the bathroom was the furthest thing from his mind when he stood between the toilet and the window crying for more than fifteen minutes, making sure to flush the toilet every so often just in case they were listening.

At five foot eight inches tall, medium built, brown skinned, with his neatly trimmed hair, beard and mustache, all salt and peppered with age, Dr. Williams has always been whatever his family needed him to be. He was supportive of his wife when, after Tasha was born, she wanted to set her promising accounting career aside so that she could stay home with their first and only child. Eventually she chose full time motherhood over a nine to five, catching William completely by surprise with her sudden decision to stay at home (He truly believed that she'd eventually go back to work). He was Tasha's shoulder of support when, after practicing so hard for the state's 'high school' cheerleading competition, she had to miss the trip because she caught the chicken pox. She cried so much, that weekend, that William did the only thing he knew would cheer her up. He brought his little girl a puppy, a German Shepherd puppy. Tasha had a cat when she was seven but it was mauled to death by a stray dog that had somehow gotten into their yard. She cried for weeks, resulting in Tanya's vow to never allow another animal into their house again. She couldn't stand seeing her daughter cry like that. Tasha literally cried herself sick. William, feeling both his wife's and his daughter's pain, agreed with his wife only to change his mind years later when his little girl's pain from having to miss her cheerleading competition forced him to do what any good parent would have done. He made his child happy. The look in Tasha's eyes when she saw that puppy was enough to erase all of their pain, hers from missing the competition. His from watching her cry over it.

"William! Our baby is starving up here," Tanya yelled from the top of the stairs, snapping William out of his sorrowful trip down memory lane.

"I'll be up in a minute," He responded, wiping tears from his face before flipping the pizza box open.

------------------- --------------------------- ---------

"Thank you, daddy."

"Baby you don't have to thank me," William said as he took the empty plates and cups from the nightstand. Tasha decided to stay for the night, in her old room, in her old bed. "Your mother's going to wash these," He added, smiling as he handed the dirty dishes to Tanya, who, in turn, handed them right back to him.

"Baby we're just glad you decided to stay over in your own...I mean your old room," Tanya leaned down and kissed her daughter's forehead.

"That's right, baby," William agreed. "So expect to be treated just like the little girl that used to live in this room," Following his wife's lead, he leaned over and kissed Tasha's forehead.

"So you're saying you're going to spoil a thirty four year old woman?" Tasha managed to smile.

"Whatever it takes to make my baby girl happy."

"Okay you two," Tanya interrupted. "You need to get some rest. Now if you need anything else, we'll be right down the hall."

"Okay momma."

"Come on, William, let her get some rest," Tanya playfully nudged William from behind so that he would walk towards the door.

"Okay, okay...we'll see you in the morning, baby."

"All right...Good-night ma. Good-night dad."

"Good-night, baby," Tanya said, turning off the lights before she and William left the room.

After her parents left the room Tasha laid in bed staring at the ceiling for hours. How could she sleep? This was literally a life or death situation, only time could decipher the two. Though being back in her old room did help in keeping her fear from running rampant, as it had earlier, but its therapeutic feel couldn't ease the pain she felt as a result of having to watch both of her parents shed tears. The look in her father's eyes said it all. He was on the verge of losing it, but she knew he wouldn't. Maybe when he was alone, but not in front of her.

Her mother was a totally different case. She would have cried herself sick had it not been for the burnt dinner that, because of Tasha's quick wit, added a much-needed laugh at a pretty somber point. Her parents were completely different, yet they were still so much alike. He enjoyed the style of Jaguar and Range Rover, while she enjoyed the more practical Honda Accord and Ford Expedition. He enjoyed dining at the finest restaurants, while she preferred a pizza and a Mountain Dew to wash it down with. Not to say that she didn't like dining out, because she did, just not all the time. He

Pink October.doc   65

preferred the opera, while she'd rather rent The Nutty Professor 2, laughing until her side hurt. The love they shared for one another made up for their differences, compromise being the key to their success as a couple.

"Baby are you okay?" Having left her daughter's room some thirty minutes ago, Tanya poked her head in on her little girl. She still had not fallen asleep.

"I'm all right, considering what's happening in my life right now."

"You need me to get you anything? If you want, I can make you a peanut butter and jelly sandwich just like you like it, with extra jelly," Tanya asked from the doorway, hoping her artificial smile would mask her worried soul. It didn't.

"No, I'm okay...Just look after daddy for me. He took it pretty hard."

"I'll take care of him, that way we can take care of you," Using every bit of the strength she had, Tanya smiled supportively. "Speaking of support, where's Kevin?" Even though she could care less, she asked anyway. He was her daughter's boyfriend so she had to at least act like she liked the fact that they were a couple, even though she hated it. "Tasha is too good for him," she said to William years earlier, as the two of them lay reading in bed. That was a few hours after their initial meeting. The way she saw it, Kevin should only be viewed as a booty call or sex toy and not a serious candidate for a life partner. He wasn't as accomplished as Tasha, and to Tanya that meant a lot. "My baby deserves better," is every parent's battle cry when it comes to his or her child's significant other. Tanya took that saying to heart when she found out that her Ph.D. wielding daughter had fallen for a mere personal trainer. "I know his type," Tanya told William, that same night in bed, referring back to that time she wasted with slick ass Kinney, whom William still knew nothing about. Yes she did know his type, but it wasn't her place to object so she accepted him because her daughter loved him and she loved her daughter. Besides, why risk jeopardizing her relationship with her daughter when she knew Tasha's relationship with Kevin wouldn't last. "He'll eventually mess up," Tanya was sure of it, she just didn't know when.

Tasha sighed before telling a well-rehearsed lie about how Kevin was out of town visiting family and how she didn't want to call and tell him her news because she knew he'd shorten his trip, which is something she didn't want him to do.

"Baby, let her get some sleep!" William yelled from he and his wife's bedroom, down the hall.

"Well, let me let you go before somebody has a fit," She motioned, with a nod, towards the direction to which William's voice came. "Good-night, baby."

"Good-night, ma," Tasha said, watching as her mother blew a kiss before retreating back down the hall, leaving Tasha to toss and turn until two o'clock in the morning.

Scene 24

"...In Jesus' name, Amen," Pastor Jentry brought tonight's funeral service to an end with a heartwarming prayer before pointing out that now is the last chance to view the body.

Dr. and Mrs. William Mills, the two lone attendees, slowly rose from their seats. William supported Tanya with an inner-strength he knew could've only come from God, that, along with his sturdy shoulder. He felt sick. His stomach held knots the size of fist, but he still had enough strength to keep his wife from falling to the floor.

"Come on, baby," Tasha sat so close to her parents she could smell the alcohol on her father's breath, the alcohol he consumed just enough of to numb his pain, but not enough to hinder him in any way. She could even hear her father's whispered words as he struggled within himself to keep his own sanity.

Like all of her other nightmares, Tasha sat directly behind her parents. She was invisible to the only other people present at her funeral, her parents and the pastor. She sat so close that, at the same point in each of her nightmares, she'd even offer to help her father escort her mother to the casket, but he never takes her hand. She then follows them to the casket where she, after her parents continue on back to their seats, lays her eyes on her own well dressed body. It's at that point her own tears woke her up by dripping into her ear.

After spending the weekend at her parent's house, Tasha started the week by first going up to her school to inform them that she'll be taking some time off, though the exact number of days she couldn't say. She would be taking at least two weeks to get herself together, emotionally.

"I'll add you to my prayers," Tracey sighed, tears building in her eyes as she watched (from her window) Tasha pull out of the faculty parking lot. "Tasha is too young to have cancer," Tracey's mind replayed those words about a million times that day.

By Monday evening Tasha was able to face one of her meaningless fears, which was only meaningless because losing one of her breast to cancer couldn't compare to losing her life. Besides, the fear of having cancer in other parts of her body was more than enough to worry about. Whether or not that was the case could only be addressed after further tests (a stage one, ductal carcinoma in situ is what she had. This is a very early stage breast cancer that can possibly develop into an invasive type of cancer).

Gary Norman

With all that had occurred during the past week, Tasha still found the time to dwell on Kevin, and how their relationship came to a screeching halt. She had more than enough love and support coming from her parents, but it wasn't the same as the support she could receive from having a strong man in her corner. "The man you thought was yours," as Dr. Jordan put it, after Tasha told her the whole sordid tale during one of the three times she visited Dr. Jordan's office during the past week. She was right and deep down Tasha knew it, but the extra support he could give was still missed. It showed in Tasha's eyes as she sat across from Dr. Jordan pouring her heart out like weak coffee at a truck stop. Her relationship woes added more stress to an already stressful situation. So much more that Dr. Jordan was prompted to suggest a support group, for that much needed understanding and support. The kind of understanding and support only cancer survivors can give. But the group she would suggest couldn't be just any old support group. It had to be something a little different from the norm, something with more of a family feel. With all that she felt was needed in a support group, to help Tasha through these trying times, Dr. Jordan could only think of one group special enough to help...Mrs. Green's Kitchen...

Pink October.doc   69

Scene 25

Two days before her lumpectomy, one day before she was scheduled to go into the hospital, Tasha decided she'd "give this support group thing a chance." "It wouldn't kill me to attend a meeting," She spoke to the reflection in her bathroom mirror as if it would somehow let her know whether or not she was making the right decision. Three days after her reflection failed to give her any answers Tasha finally worked up enough nerve to attend her first meeting. And now here she was, standing on a stranger's front porch, a little after seven o'clock at night, in hopes of finding that extra support she wasn't able to get from her family and friends.

"How bad can it be?" She nervously sighed before pressing her finger into the doorbell of the huge south suburban home, which wasn't that far from her University Park home. "This is Monday? Unless I got the days mixed up," She began to second-guess her choice of days after receiving no answer. "Maybe this is the wrong house," She uttered as she turned to step down the porch steps, only to be startled by the sudden sounds of chatter that had escaped out into the quiet October night once the front door had been opened.

"Hey Tasha," The Nell Carter-size woman chimed jovially, surprising Tasha by speaking her name as if they had already been introduced. "I'm glad to see that you've finally decided to join us...Oh, I'm sorry," She said as if suddenly remembering that it was cold outside. She then stepped aside so that Tasha could enter her home. "My name is Mary, but every one here calls me Mrs. Green. That's only because I'm the oldest member of the group and they think I'm ready for a nursing home," She said jokingly as she hung Tasha's coat in the closet nearest the front door, all while looking over her shoulder as if someone were trying to eavesdrop. She wasn't being serious, and Tasha could tell.

Stepping further into Mrs. Green's house Tasha was immediately drawn to an assortment of people gathered around a huge birthday cake, which sat at the far end of a dining room table to the immediate left of the foyer. There were six women and one man. "He must be someone's husband," is what Tasha thought of the lone male attendee.

"Oh, I'm sorry...how are you?" Tasha tore her attention away from the people laughing and talking in the dining room. "I hope I'm not intru..."

"I hope you're not about to say intruding, because if that's what you're about to say, then cut it out. You're not intruding, now lets go introduce you to everybody."

"Thanks for having me," Tasha's voice was barely audible as she followed Mrs. Green into the dining room.

"Hi Tasha, I'm Carla. I'll be your unofficial tour guide for the evening," Carla, a thirty-two year old Hispanic woman, said as she stood to Tasha's left preparing to introduce everybody assembled in the dining room. Her olive skin would've been flawless had it not been for the crescent moon shaped scar above her right eye. She was of average height with a shapely figure. "Too hippie" is how she describes herself.

"Child, don't you get too close to her...that girl is crazy," The medium built, dark skinned woman who looked to be around the same age as Mrs. Green, laughed as she looked back over her left shoulder at Carla, Tasha, and an approaching Mrs. Green. Tasha's widening smile successfully hid her uneasiness from the people assembled near the birthday cake, each of them holding a slice of cake on a Styrofoam plate.

"Anyway..." Carla jokingly rolled her eyes and neck as if she were trying to bring an old dance back in style. Most of the members laughed at her expected response; the others just shook their heads. "That's Michelle," Carla continued. "She's the comedian of the group, but, as you can see, she's not funny," She stuck her tongue out at Michelle before continuing. "We were expecting you a few days ago, but better late than never," She smiled before being interrupted.

"Excuse me Miss Carla, but the rest of us would like to meet her, that's if it's okay with you," The tall, slender, light skinned woman said as she cut a slice of cake from the huge, brightly decorated birthday cake. It had the words 'Happy Birthday Erica' spelled out in pink and green letters over a white, pink and green cake.

"Oh, I'm sorry," said Carla. "The tall woman cutting the cake is Erica, the birthday girl. The woman sitting to the left of Michelle is Amanda. And to her left is Thomas, the only male member, as you can see. And last but not least, standing between Michelle and Erica, is Rhonda. That's everybody. Everybody, this is Tasha," Each one of the group members waved, or made some other kind of acknowledging gesture after Carla's introductions.

"I hope you like coconut," Erica, clad in a pair of dark colored, loose fitting jeans and a light colored blouse, walked over and handed Tasha a large slice of cake on a medium size plate. This girl must be from down south, Tasha thought as she looked over the Texas-size slice of cake Erica had put on her plate.

"Thank you…and happy birthday, Erica" Now beginning to feel more comfortable and less out of place, Tasha smiled graciously after accepting the offering from the attractive woman with an uncommonly even skin tone.

"Go on over and take a seat at the table while I get you something to drink…what would you like?" Mrs. Green interjected.

"Bottled-water will be fine, thank you," Tasha replied before taking the empty chair closest to where she was standing.

"I'll be right back," Mrs. Green walked off towards what Tasha figured to be the kitchen.

"You just missed their awful rendition of Happy Birthday. Maybe if one of them had at least a week of voice lessons it would've sounded better, because believe me, it sounded terrible," Erica shook her head as she cut another Bedrock-size slice of cake. Nobody rebutted her statement. "I guess after drinks start flowing you can't expect Star Search kind of talent to emerge. But then again it's not like any of the women in this room had that kind of talent to begin with," Erica laughed.

"Girl, with all those damn candles on that cake you're lucky we had enough oxygen in this room to hum, much less sing happy birthday," Re-entering the room, Mrs. Green responded with her own bit of humor before setting a bottle of water on a coaster to Tasha's left.

"Ha Ha Ha…You see what I have to put up with? And she's supposed to be my girl," Erica nodded in Mrs. Green's direction, laughing along with everyone else.

Laughing for the first time since being diagnosed, Tasha found herself talking about things she had only discussed with her parents and her doctor. The family type of atmosphere, combined with the fact that everyone in the room had stood where she now planted her feet, made talking about her disease a lot less painful. Especially when you're in the company of such a handsome man, Tasha thought as she sampled her cake, her eyes, every so often, finding the unwed male on the other side of the room.

Thomas Brown, the only male member of the group, is a forty-five year old professor at the University of Chicago. Tasha couldn't help but overhear those tid-bits about Thomas, especially when he and Mrs. Green weren't standing that far away from where she and Carla were standing twenty minutes ago. It's not like she noticed how

Gary Norman

attractive he is, or his bare ring finger. Well, yes she did. "Old habits are hard to break," she thought, shaking her head at the fact that she could scope out a single man while attending her first breast cancer support group function.

"He's taken...that's Mrs. Green's man," Carla had been talking with Tasha until she noticed Tasha's attention was somewhere else. But who could blame the group's neophyte? They all thought Thomas was a fine piece of a man, at least that's how Michelle describes him when Mrs. Green isn't around. She didn't want Mrs. Green to think she'd been checking out her man, because some sisters can get pretty jealous when it comes to that kind of thing. With his dark skin, neatly trimmed salt and peppered hair, beard and mustache and hazel eyes, which topped his six-foot frame like a cherry atop a sundae, Mrs. Green had reason to keep an eye on him. He is definitely what most women would consider fine. Not a Tyson 'two percent body fat with rippling muscles' fine, but more of a height and weight proportionate, well groomed, mature fine. "Some girls have all the luck, huh?" Carla gave a smirk before telling Tasha something about each of the members, something personal. This was Carla's way of helping Tasha to get to know the other members, before she actually got around to getting to know them...if that makes any sense.

"That's Rhonda," Carla started with Rhonda, who was headed to the kitchen with her cell-phone pressed to the left side of her face. Rhonda, dressed in expensive, yet casual garments, was tall (five-ten) and slim with shoulder length blond hair and blue eyes. By the way Rhonda dressed, Tasha could tell that she had expensive tastes. From her Gucci shoes and purse to her overly priced jeans (the same jeans Tasha had seen in a downtown boutique, but was unconcerned with the name because she would never pay that much for a pair of jeans), Rhonda was the All-American woman, depending on whom you asked. "She was definitely reaping all the benefits that came with marrying an old, rich man," Carla whispered. "But those benefits came with a price," She continued, shaking her head before continuing. "Rhonda's breast cancer was the result of leaking silicone implants, the same implants she received as a gift from her husband."

Ain't that something, Tasha thought as she listened to Carla tell of how another woman had bent over backwards to please a man, almost breaking her back in the process. He wanted her to have bigger breasts, so she got them. She also got a little something extra in the deal, something she didn't figure into the equation. Tasha couldn't imagine how Rhonda must feel knowing that her husband's selfishness could've killed her. "Did she really need him?" Tasha's mind began to race in an attempt to shed light on why a woman would even think about putting her life in danger for the sake of a man. Rhonda is a beautiful woman who, even at thirty-nine years old, can still have any man she wanted from a doctor to an Indian Chief. And her breasts, even though the implants have long been removed, were still more than a handful. An ample 36C, the size most women would kill for.

"That's Amanda," Carla said, pointing at the young white woman preparing to leave. Rhonda's story was more interesting than all the others, which is why after fifteen minutes Carla was finally moving on to the next member, Amanda Thompson, a twenty six-year old housewife who's only been a member for three months, even though she's been cancer-free for two years. With her girlish looks and pale complexion, short dark hair and petite frame, she's often mistaken for being a lot younger than her birth certificate reads. She still gets carded every time she tries to buy alcohol or cigarettes. It's definitely a compliment.

Even though she, along with everybody else in the group, joined the group hoping to find that extra support from people who were going through the same thing, Amanda has yet to fully open up to the group. "She seems more withdrawn than anything...always checking her watch and either leaving the meetings early or declining to join us when we decide to have a girl's night out," Carla shrugged as if to say go figure.

"For all I know she could be a serial killer," Carla whispered as she and Tasha watched Amanda leave the room then reemerge wearing her coat. "See you next week," Amanda said amongst hugs and kisses as she stayed true to her routine of leaving early.

"It's like that every week with her, you'll see..." Carla continued. "I mean, she talks like the rest of us, but not in the same way. Wait, I don't think that came out right...put it this way, she's been coming here for the last three months and all I know about her is she's married to a guy named, Mike, who works as a correctional officer down at the Cook County Jail. She's cancer-free, and she doesn't have any kids. That's really it, unless I forgot something, which I probably did. Oh yeah, her husband picks her up every so often, but he seems to be more interested in who's here than picking his wife up. You should see how his eyes scan the place when he steps through that front door. He's a trip," Carla laughed at the thought of his last visit, moving her eyes from side to side like a security camera next to an ATM machine. They both laughed when Carla mimicked his behavior.

Last but not least, the three people responsible for keeping each of the other members grounded in the soil of positive thinking. First there's Michelle Taylor, a fifty-two year old grandmother who can easily pass for a woman in her late forties. She's five foot three and one hundred sixty something pounds, most of which is in the lower half of her body. She has a caramel complexion, which doesn't do much in hiding the blue vein in her face and neck that stands out like a clown at a wedding. "She lives with her son, his wife and their new baby boy. Oh, did I mention her daughter-in-law is white? Needless to say the sista has some serious issues with that arrangement," Carla nudged Tasha's arm as if saying 'I know you know what I mean.' Tasha knew exactly what she meant. Most black mothers would rather their sons be alone and miserable than happy and with a white woman. "And she ain't even that cute," Michelle had once stated about her extremely average looking daughter in law. Whether she was right or wrong didn't matter to her son, nor did it matter to his wife.

"That's Rhonda's best friend," Carla said, pointing towards Erica, who was in the process of cutting another slice of cake while swaying her hips to the Carl Thomas CD Michelle had just placed in the CD changer. "I think she's the luckiest one here. She has a loving husband, three beautiful little girls, and a good job, how much better can it be?" Carla paused, adding emphasis with her silence.

At five ten and a half, Erica is the tallest member of the group. She wears her hair in twists that reach the base of her neck. Her chocolate complexion, big eyes and high cheekbones reminds you of a Sudanese model, only older. "Not only is she beautiful and a physical therapist, she also has a family," Tasha's jealous mind replayed those words over and over, like a scratched record. "She kind of looks like Tyra Banks, only darker...You'd have to subtract about thirty pounds and add twenty pounds of forehead to see the resemblance, but if you squint just right you can see the resemblance," Tasha thought, laughing on the inside as Carla continued.

At fifty-six years of age, Mrs. Green is the oldest member of the group. She's also one of the group's founders (she and Michelle decided they'd do this just over two years ago). Her hair is short and curly, naturally curly, her face round and pie like, sort of like Sister Souljah or Nell Carter. And at two hundred plus pounds, she can easily pass for a smaller version of Nell Carter.

"Does that candle say forty?" Tasha asked in amazement, looking from the cake to Erica, who looked closer to thirty than forty. "This woman must've found the fountain of youth," Tasha thought.

"Yup, she's now an official member of the 'Big 4-0' club," Carla replied as she and Tasha watched Erica and Rhonda lead the rest of the group in their direction.

"Okay Miss Carla, you've had her to yourself long enough," Erica smiled, everyone else agreed. "It's our turn now."

Gary Norman

Scene 26

Amanda's watch read 8:45pm when she pulled her husband's bright red '99 Camaro into the parking lot in front of their apartment building. She nervously scanned the lot for Steve's Nissan Pathfinder, but it wasn't there. Even though Steve's parking space was empty, Amanda had to be sure his SUV wasn't parked anywhere else. Mike road to work with Steve this morning so that Amanda could attend her weekly meeting. So if Steve's truck wasn't in the lot she probably made it home before her husband, just like she's supposed to. She left the meeting a good ten minutes before her usual departure time, but, because of an accident on the expressway, she feared she didn't make it home in time. "Was he home? And, if so, is he drunk? He hates to have to wait on his dinner, especially after a bad day at work," Her mind had been through the same routine so many times before, that it was second nature for her to react this way. If she thought she was late getting home she would automatically ask herself the same questions over and over.

"I can at least get dinner on before he gets home," Relieved by the fact that Steve's truck wasn't in the parking lot, which meant her husband wasn't home, Amanda exhaled before exiting her car and hurrying into her building.

With beads of sweat beginning to form on the bridge of her nose and forehead, Amanda, after sprinting up two flights of stairs to her apartment, entered her abode then headed straight to the kitchen. Luckily she remembered to take the pork chops out of the freezer before she left for the meeting. Now all she had to do was season them and place them in the broiler.

Just as she reached into the cabinet, next to the sink, her relief quickly turned to fear when the familiar smell of Jim Bean assaulted her sense of smell like Jack the Ripper and a streetwalker.

"Dinner will be ready shortly, dear," Without turning to face her husband, Amanda reached in the cabinet, but because of her fear, forgot what she was reaching for. She knew he was drunk, the stench of alcohol gave that away. She fiddled around in the cabinet until it came back to her that she needed a pan to set the pork chops in.

"You're late..." The drunken voice slurred behind her.

"There was an accident...I left early...but...but there was an accident," Her eyes began to swell with tears as she struggled to explain. She still had not turned around to face her husband.

Through the deafening silence that followed her tearful explanation, she could hear him unfastening his belt.

Pink October.doc

"And you don't even have dinner ready," His voice hardened as he pulled his belt from around his waist, snatching it through the last two loops. "Why do you always have to do shit like this? HUH?!" The sudden volume in his voice startled Amanda. She winced then started to tremble as if it were five degrees and all she had on was a pair of panties.

Turning to face him, she found herself desperately pleading her case while back-peddling around the table in an effort to keep a comfortable distance between her and her leather belt wielding husband, who was half walking, half staggering towards her.

"Baby, I'm sorry...Please don't do this. Please," She cried, pulling her arm away just as he tried to grab her.

"You know you only make it worse when you make me chase you," Mike hissed between gritted teeth before suddenly flipping the table on its side, cutting off her path to the front door, then charging forward with his belt raised above his head in a ready to strike position.

"MIKE!"

Scene 27

Entering her home through the connecting garage door, which led into the kitchen, Tasha, for the first time since her relationship with Kevin ended, actually felt comfortable in her own house. The house she and Kevin created so many wonderful memories in. Her mood was no longer as dismal as it had been prior to her attending tonight's group meeting. The moping had vanished. There was a smile on her face and laughter in her heart as she hung her coat in the closet closest to the front door, switching her hips while humming Carl Thomas' Summer Rain. Rhonda had played that song so much Tasha couldn't get it out of her head, no matter how hard she tried.

"That woman is crazy," She burst into laughter after Mrs. Green's response about the number of candles on Erica's cake popped into her head.

Just being in a room filled with so many breast cancer survivors was enough to ease her fear. They had all been through the same thing (some of them faced worse situations), and they still laughed amongst themselves as any old, dear friends would do. They lived one day at a time, same as everyone else, yet they seemed to have a better understanding of how precious life is.

"Before I forget," Tasha uttered as she picked up the kitchen phone mounted on the wall above the counter.

---------   -------------------------   ---------------------------------

"What time is it?"

"Baby it's nine twenty three, exactly three minutes after the last time you asked. What's so important that you need to know the time every few minutes?" William teasingly asked from his seat on the couch. Tanya, who was standing in front of their fifty-five inch television, retrieved one of the three DVD's he'd picked up on his way home from the hospital while her husband spooned ice cream into his mouth.

"You know I'm waiting on Tasha's call," Tanya said, returning to her seat on the couch next to her husband.

"Give her some time, baby," William responded calmly, kissing Tanya's forehead just as the phone rang. "Look, that's probably her right there."

"God I hope so, because I won't be able to enjoy the movies you brought home if I don't hear from her first," Tanya pushed herself off the couch and walked over to the phone above the counter that separated the kitchen from the entertainment room. "And don't start the movie without me," with her hand on the receiver, Tanya turned and gave William her best 'don't even think about it' look before answering the phone. She knew how impatient he could be, especially when he was ready to watch a movie he hadn't seen.

"Would I do something like that?" He returned a smile. "But since you're over there, hit the lights for me," He winked just as she picked up the phone.

---------- ------------------------ ---------------------------

"Okay, then…I'll see you tomorrow, that's if your father doesn't kill me first," Tanya smiled at her husband. He had been impatiently waiting over thirty minutes for his wife to get off the phone. "Okay…I love you, too…Bye," She hung up the phone then immediately turned her attention to her loving husband. "I'm sorry…Tasha sounded so much better than she did the other day, I just couldn't bring myself to get off the phone any sooner," She kissed his cheek as she reclaimed her seat next to him. "She said the people there were really nice and they really seemed to be more like family than just friends, oh yeah, she also said it was one of the girl's birthday so she had some cake while she sat and talked with everyone. She also said…"

"Slowdown, motor mouth," William laughed, hardly able to get those few words in between his wife's verbal onslaught. "Funny you can remember all that, but you couldn't remember me saying that I wanted to talk to our daughter before you hung up."

"I'm sorry…I got so caught up in hearing about her day, and talking about her going into the hospital tomorrow, I just forgot…Here, let me go call her back," Tanya attempted to push herself off the couch, only to be pulled back down.

"That's okay, I'll call her later. You've talked enough for me, you, the neighbors, and their kids," William nudged her side before taking the remote from the coffee table. He finally started the first film of the night, which they should've started watching over forty minutes ago.

"Better late than never," Tanya winked. William shook his head.

Gary Norman

Scene 28

"Shhh...shhh...Don't cry...Mommy would want you to be strong, okay," She could hear the tall, dark skinned, man whisper down to the teary eyed boy and girl attached to his leg as if it were a life jacket and they were in the middle of Lake Michigan. Tasha could hear his raspy voice as clear as if he had whispered those words in her ear. She could see the redness in his eyes, the tear stains in the corners of his eyes. He whispered something to his children before standing and leading them to the casket. The youngest child didn't want to go near the casket because it scared her. The oldest child wasn't scared at all. He needed to see his mother one last time. Daddy said that mommy would want him to do it. "You're a big boy," He remembered his mother's words. The words she uttered from her hospital bed, not even a week ago. She asked him to be strong for his daddy and little sister, who was only three and needed to see that her six-year-old brother was a big boy.

"It's okay, son," The man comforted his son with a pat on the shoulder. "Big boys cry too," He whispered, vindicating the tears his son fought so hard to keep from falling because big boys weren't supposed to cry. At least that's what he thought until his daddy said it was okay for him to cry, even though his daddy wasn't crying. His tears didn't come until he looked down into the casket and saw his wife in the dress he had gotten her last mother's day. The dress she had asked him to bury her in because he had told her that the kids picked it out. She loved that dress for that reason alone. "When my time comes, bury me in that dress," She said from her hospital bed. He smiled a heartbroken smile at the memory before continuing past the casket, allowing the only other person in attendance an opportunity to view the body.

Tasha stood close to the pew, giving the grieving family of three enough room to mourn in privacy. When the family moved on she made her way to the casket, her heart pounding hard enough to crack a rib.

Just as she reached the casket the little boy broke down, screaming for his mother like he was lost amongst the crowds at Great America. Tasha froze, paralyzed by the sting inflicted on her by a few simple words. "Did he say, mommy?" The boy's heart wrenching words echoed as she turned around to face the family seated in the pew behind her. As she stood there watching the dark suited man console both children with huge loving arms, tears began to run down the sides of her face, dripping from her chin and onto her

Pink October.doc   81

dress. My family, Tasha uttered, tossing and turning until she woke from her restless slumber at two o'clock in the morning.

Hours later the Tuesday morning sun sat high and bright, but offered little warmth on this unseasonably cold October day. Today Tasha was scheduled to go into the hospital, the thought of which causing her stomach to hold in its depths knots the size of fists, her palms sweating like a Texas death row inmate. If it weren't for her parents calling early this morning insisting on treating their little girl to an IHOP breakfast, she probably would've worried herself sick.

After breakfast William and Tanya drove their daughter to the hospital where they did just as any loving parents would do. They fussed over Tasha's hospital bed, making absolutely sure she was more than comfortable.

"Baby, can I get you anything?" William asked as he and Tanya stood over her bed, he on one side Tanya on the other.

"No, I'm fine...but tomorrow, after the surgery, you can bring me a banana split," Tasha flashed as wide a smile as she could muster, attempting to raise her parent's spirits by showing them that there was nothing to worry about. Tasha had a hard time believing that one herself.

Scene 29

It was after twelve o'clock when Amanda tenderly rolled out of bed, careful not to step, breath, or even blink too hard. Mike left for work twenty minutes earlier, kissing her on the forehead before leaving their bedroom, as if he didn't know his wife was pretending to be asleep. He knew she was awake. She knew that he knew. It was kind of like their unspoken 'after an ass whippin' rule. He'd act like nothing happened and so would she. In her mind she looked at this as a phase that he was going through, even though this phase is more than a few years old. "But this is all my fault," She still remembered crying herself to sleep after Mike's first attack, over five years ago. That was the day Mike found out about her affair, an affair that wouldn't have happened had he paid more attention to her. At least that's what she told him. That was the first time he physically assaulted her. His eyes were as red as chili peppers. His neck sported veins she had never seen. He was pissed, more so about who she had the affair with than the affair it self. He couldn't be mad at the fact that she cheated because they had a different kind of relationship. They were 'young and having fun', is how Amanda later thought of their college years, when partner swapping and one-night-stands were often occurrences. But the 'just having fun' line was crossed forever when she not only had an affair with a black man, but tried to hide it as if she were considering a change of venue. Amanda swore that that wasn't the case, but Mike wouldn't believe it. He never believed it.

Mike became the campus joke amongst the white students. "The white man that couldn't satisfy his white girlfriend, so she went to a black man," is what one of his so-called friends yelled out at a frat party. Needless to say, Mike, who has always been in great shape, kicked that ex-friend's ass. After that he went back to the off campus apartment he shared with Amanda and, for the first time, took his belt to her ass like he was her mother and she'd been cut from a Texas high school cheerleading team. That night he gave her what she deserved. He knew it, and so did she. To this day she still feels like she's getting what she deserves. I mean, it was her affair that forced Mike to leave school within a year of receiving his degree (a man could only take so much snickering). That meant it was her fault that he worked as a correctional officer at The Cook County Jail and not for the Chicago Police force. "You didn't have to follow his dumb ass," Keri, Amanda's neighbor form across the hall, replied after learning of how Amanda had followed Mike, leaving school a year shy of

Pink October.doc   83

completing her own mortuary science studies. "I couldn't let him leave by himself...not when it was all my fault," Amanda cried over the pint of Canadian Mist she and Keri shared at Amanda's kitchen table, almost a year ago. One year after leaving school, Amanda and Mike were married. That was eleven months, three weeks, and six days after the first sign of abuse.

"I'm coming...I'm coming," Standing over a sink filled with dirty dishes, rinsing suds from her hands, Amanda yelled to the only person known to beat rhythmic tunes on her front door.

On her way to the door, Amanda made sure to tie her green bathrobe closed. She didn't feel like hearing it from Keri, not this morning.

"Enough with the tunes already," Amanda snatched her door open, catching Keri just before her next annoying knock.

"You don't have to hide your bruises because I'm here...I've seen them before," Keri strolled past Amanda with a look of disgust as evident as the sun in the sky. The same look of disgust she had the last time she saw the bruises Mike's belt had left on her friend. "Didn't you learn anything from your mother," She stopped in the middle of the living room to turn and face her abused friend, who stood with her back pressed against the door, her left palm held up and out, wordlessly saying 'not today'.

"I shouldn't have told you about my mother," She uttered under her breath, passing by Keri as she headed back to her dirty dishes. She knew that Keri was right. She, of all people, should know better. When she was a little girl she witnessed her stepfather beat her mother, with his fist, on several occasions. "If it weren't for the tragic accident that claimed his life, he'd probably be in jail for killing me," Gretchen (Amanda's mother) later revealed during her first and last 'baby, Mike is no different from your stepfather' sermon. Amanda wouldn't give her another chance to tell her what she didn't want to hear.

"And after all that happened last night, I bet you still fucked him...didn't you?" Keri prompted almost demandingly. The pitiful look on Amanda's face answered the question without a peep from her mouth.

"Look, it wasn't like that," Standing in front of the kitchen sink, Amanda turned towards the dishes so that she could avoid eye contact. She hated when Keri would start with her about her choosing to stay with her husband. To Amanda, talking about why it was happening was just as painful as the actual abuse. Her mother would point out reasons why it shouldn't be happening, which is why she and her mother haven't spoken in quite sometime.

"What in the hell is wrong with you?" Keri spoke as calmly as she could. She hated when Amanda would try to skate around the truth, trying to make things seem not as bad as they really are. "You don't think you deserve better than what you're getting out of this bullshit marriage? Damn! Why don't you just leave his ass? Or do you like getting your ass whipped? Is that it? Huh? Stop washing those damn dishes and come talk to me!" Keri motioned for Amanda to join her at the kitchen table. Amanda turned off the water, turned and faced Keri, and just stood there at the sink like she had no idea what her next move should be. "Did you hear what I said? You deserve better...and don't give me that shit about he loves you, 'cause if he did he wouldn't be putting that belt to your ass," Keri smirked, no pun intended.

Saying nothing in response, Amanda dropped her shoulders to a droop and just stared at Keri with the most dismal look in her eyes. She was truly in pain, emotionally as well as physically. Keri could see that her friend was hurting, which is why she did all she could to get her to see that she'd be much happier without Mike. Not that she would have a chance at a relationship with Amanda if Mike were out of the picture, because she wouldn't. Amanda had made that perfectly clear without causing the slightest ripple in their friendship. "I think you're a beautiful woman, but I just don't go that way," is how Amanda shot down her advances. During that time Keri was on the off part of her relationship with Micki, a stripper at Club 'O'. Their relationship was one of those "on again, off again" relationships, but mostly off. Now Keri has a new steady partner, Sam, who's the stereotypical lesbian (a man looking, man acting, deep voiced, medium height, short hair, husky white woman), whereas Keri is the exact opposite. Keri's feminine to the core with the kind of beauty you'd find in any music video. A perfect tan, light colored eyes, juicy lips and hips, soul-sister ass, thick eyebrows and naturally long eyelashes. Keri is every woman's nightmare, black and white women alike. She has the blond hair, blues eyes and slender frame that white men and women find so attractive. She also has the full lips, hips and round ass that black men and women love so much. "Fine as hell," is how black men describe her, "Hot," is how white men describe her. Women are a little more descriptive, more aggressive. "Especially after they've had a few drinks," Keri had once said of the women patrons that visited each of the clubs she's danced at over the years. From *The Sexy Boot* (a north side club) to *Club 'O'* (on 170th and Halsted) to *Expose'* to *D`LOS* (on 152nd South Dixie Highway) then back to *Expose'*, the women were all touchy-feely after they'd have a few drinks.

"Look, you don't understand," Amanda said somberly, finally walking over and taking the chair next to Keri. "We love each other, and besides, what kind of woman would I be if I left my husband because times are a little hard for him at the moment?"

"A damn smart one," Keri looked at her friend with disbelieving eyes, not believing her own ears. Is this woman losing her damn mind? She thought as she looked into Amanda's eyes.

"No, really...don't you think people can change? Don't you think..."

"Hell no!" Keri abruptly interrupted what was to be another one of Amanda's attempts to get her to see a meaningless point. "No...Hell no...I would've left his ass a long time ago. Does that answer your question? No, I don't think he can change...other people, yes...Him, no. Anyway, I wouldn't have stuck around long enough to find out. And you're right, I don't know how it feels to be in a relationship like the one you're in," Keri said, beating Amanda to the punch before she could resort to her old 'you don't understand' line. "My old boyfriends knew better. They saw my three, crazy ass brothers," Keri continued, laughing as if she had recalled a specific episode.

"Things aren't really all that bad. We go through the same ups and downs that other couples go through."

"He whips your ass with a fuckin' belt and you're gonna sit there and say that your relationship is no different than anybody else's. He really does have you brained washed, if you believe that. And it's really sad to see you, of all people, like this. It's like you don't even realize he's holding you back, and that really is the worse part."

"Look, we've been through this before and I really don't feel like going through it again. So if you came over here to talk about me and my husband, you can leave now," Amanda said defensively.

"Okay, okay. I'll let it ride...Oh, I mean I'll leave it alone," Keri nudged Amanda's left arm as if insinuating that Amanda didn't understand slang because she was white, even though both of them are white. Since half of Keri's "sugar-daddies" are black she has the upper hand when it comes to understanding slang, at least that's how she sees it. "So, since I'm staying, do you need any help? If so, just let me know so I can cut my visit short," Keri continued, finally bringing a smile to Amanda's face. There was no way she was going to change Amanda's mind about her marital situation, and she knew it. So instead of continuously hounding her about what she needs to do, which always upsets her, Keri would find ways to lighten the mood only to try just as hard another day, hoping that one day Amanda would wake up before she wound up dead.

They finished cleaning the apartment, which wasn't that dirty to begin with, then spent the rest of the day in Amanda's apartment talking about Keri's newest sugar daddy, a black drug dealer named Keith. How she was able to keep her sugar-daddies a secret from Sam, without once getting caught, was something Amanda couldn't figure out. Keri has had a thing for black men for as long as she could remember. They were the only ones to tell her that the round ass she carried around was attractive. "Fat-ass," is what the white boys called her. "Girl, you're fine as hell," is what black boys used to say when she'd walk by, switching her "sista" ass on her way to her fifth period class. So it was no surprise when she started to find black men more attractive than her own kind. That was years ago, back when she was in high school, and she still loves to hear those kinds of compliments from black men. Her hips and round 'ethnic' butt is what attracted them to her, and she used what she had well! Sam just didn't know it.

Thirty minutes before Mike was scheduled to make it home, Keri went back to her apartment while Amanda waited for Mike to come home with his usual "after an ass whippin" box of candy and a single red rose. That was all it took to smooth things over, until the next time…

Pink October.doc

Gary Norman

Scene 30

After what seemed like the longest night of her life, Tasha woke to a cold and rainy Wednesday morning, the kind of morning one would associate with an impending tragedy. That's if this were a motion picture. Thank God it's not a movie, Tasha thought as she sat up in her hospital bed, sipping the orange juice that came with the breakfast she wasn't going to eat. Not that she wasn't hungry, or didn't need the nourishment, because she was hungry and she did need the nourishment. She just couldn't eat. Her anxiety wouldn't allow her to.

By mid-afternoon Tasha's parents had made their way to their daughter's side.

"When you're ready for visitors I'll go get you that banana split," William said before the tall and extremely thin, light skinned, nurse wheeled Tasha out of the room.

"Miss Mills, are you ready to have that pesky kidney removed?"

"KIDNEY!" Tasha, Tanya, and William, caught by surprise, blurted in unison.

"I'm just kidding." The nurse's laugh was high pitched and nasal. "I thought a little joke would lift the mood a bit," Seeing the relief on everyone's face made the nurse laugh even louder, which in turn, made Tanya, Tasha, and William laugh even louder. How that woman laughed like that was beyond them.

As the nurse wheeled Tasha down the hall, she, for some unknown reason, began to think about Kevin. Not the Kevin that had broken her heart, but the Kevin she had loved dearly. The Kevin that had once surprised her with five dozen long-stemmed red roses, just because. The Kevin that fed her chicken-soup while making those silly choo-choo sounds as he guided the spoon into her mouth. That's the Kevin she loved. Not the son-of-a bitch she left sprawled out on the floor in front of her self-defense class.

"Here we are," The nurse smiled down at Tasha as the short ride in the wheelchair came to an end right next to an uncomfortable looking gurney.

"I'm ready," Tasha exhaled so low the nurse barely heard her, sweat was beginning to bead up on her forehead, the nervous twitch in her lips becoming more pronounced.

Pink October.doc   89

Scene 31

Alone in the huge, cold, dull painted waiting room for what seemed like three hours, but in actuality was a lot closer to an hour, William and Tanya did all they could to keep their emotions in check while waiting on news of their daughter's surgery. The suspense was enough to drive a sane person crazy, William thought as he checked his watch for the tenth time in twenty minutes.

"You know what's funny?" William's laugh was a nervous one.

"What baby?" Tanya, now lying on the couch, her head resting on William's thigh, responded before licking her thumbprint then lovingly smoothing out his bushy eyebrow.

"This is the first time I've ever been in a hospital waiting room waiting on news about my own daughter."

"She's our daughter…and that's because you were delivering someone else's baby while our baby was lying in the hospital with a broken leg…I bet the doctor that delivered Tasha still wishes you had stayed in the waiting room. The way you picked on my doctor, you should've been ashamed of yourself," Tanya smiled facetiously at her husband.

"I wasn't picking with him…I just asked a few simple questions. I didn't think he'd get all bent out of shape."

"A few simple questions!" Tanya smiled up at her husband, the events of long ago replaying in her mind like it had happened yesterday. "You asked the man if he had washed his hands. Then you asked him if the room had been cleaned, and when he said yes you asked him if he was sure. You even asked the poor doctor if the lack of sex could play a part in whether or not he would be able to keep his hands steady. And if so, when was the last time he got laid," Tanya burst into a thunderous laugh as the last words left her mouth.

"It wasn't that funny," He purposely shifted the leg his wife rested on which only made her laugh even louder.

"Excuse me…Dr. Mills. Mrs. Mills," Stepping into the waiting area, Dr. Clark, the surgeon in charge of performing the lumpectomy, cleared his throat in order to get their attention. "The surgery was a success. The lump was removed along with a portion of the axillary lymph nodes," The doctor then went on to discuss the next course of action, which involved radiation therapy.

"Is it okay if we see her now?" Tanya asked.

Gary Norman

90

"If you'd like, you can go in now, but she's still going to be drowsy so don't stay too long. And try not to whoop it up like you two were doing in here. She needs her rest," Dr. Clark smiled.

"I tried to tell him to keep it down, but he just wouldn't listen," Tanya winked at the doctor as she walked out of the waiting room, heading for her daughter's room.

"That wasn't me...She was the one making all that noise...really."

"Dr. Mills, how could you blame all that noise on your beautiful wife?"

"Easy...She was the one making all that noise."

"You should be ashamed of yourself," Dr. Clark teased. He knew it was Tanya, he just had to harass his old med-school buddy.

"No, really...that was her," William continued. Dr. Clark shook his head, turned and left the room, laughing to himself at how William was still trying to convince him that it was his wife making all that noise.

"Okay, she got me," William laughed to himself as he proceeded out of the waiting room.

---------   -------------------------   -------------------------------

"Hey baby," Tanya cooed as she walked over to her daughter's bedside. "How are you feeling?"

"I'm okay...A little tired, but okay."

"Your father went to get you that banana split. He told me to tell you that he loves you," She bent down to kiss her daughter's forehead.

"Did he send that?"

"No, that kiss was from me, he'll have to give you his kiss himself."

"I'll tell him you said that."

"Tattletale."

Tasha's laugh was a tired/groggy laugh. Her mother has called her a tattletale for as long as she could remember. Daddy's little girl, is what she's always been. And she was definitely spoiled by her daddy. Whatever she wanted he'd bend over backwards to make sure she got. And in a way, Tanya encouraged this behavior. How could she not allow her husband to spoil their only child? How could she not allow daddy's little girl to fully become daddy's little girl?

"I found her," A familiar voice suddenly came from over by the door.

"Hey..." A pleasantly surprised Tasha responded after seeing that the familiar voice belonged to Carla, who, after peeping into the room and discovering that it was actually Tasha's room, had turned to alert others about her find.

"I'm sorry...if we're interrupting we can come back some other time."

"No, please come in," Tanya responded just as the door opened and two other familiar faces stepped into the room.

"Hey, girl," Both Rhonda and Erica chimed as they entered.

"Hey!" Tasha happily responded before turning to her mother. "Momma, these are some of the ladies I told you about, from the support group...That's Carla, Rhonda, and Erica...everybody, this is my mother, Mrs...."

"Tanya! You all can call me Tanya," She interrupted her daughter.

"Nice to meet you, Tanya."

"Nice to meet you, too," They exchanged warm smiles and handshakes. "Nice to meet all of you, and thanks for helping my daughter get through such a difficult time."

"You're welcome," Carla smiled. "But you really don't have to thank us, that's what we do for one another. We're just like any other family, except we don't have the same parents."

"That's so true," Standing at the foot of the bed, between Carla and Rhonda, Erica smiled at Tasha as if they've known each other for years rather than twenty-four hours. "We are more like a big family opposed to being a regular old support group."

"And that's why we're here, to check on our newest sister," Rhonda playfully tugged Tasha's blanket covered toe.

"I'm sorry, I must have the wrong room," After pushing the door open with one hand, holding a Baskin&Robin's 'banana split in the other, William was set to retreat until the sound of his wife's voice stopped him in his tracts. "William!" Tanya blurted before the door shut behind him. "These are members of Tasha's support group...ladies this is my husband, Dr. William Mills...Honey, that's Erica, Rhonda, and Carla," Tanya pointed to each member as she said their names.

"Nice to meet you," William said as he walked over to his daughter's bedside, nodding graciously as he passed. "We've heard so much about you. We've also seen the difference in our daughter since she came back from her first group meeting. We really want to thank you for that," He handed Tasha the banana split.

Gary Norman

"You're welcome," Watching as William made sure that Tasha had extra napkins nearby, Carla responded with a widening grin. Watching William fuss over his daughter reminded Carla of how her own parents had fussed over her right before her lumpectomy. "We weren't going to let our newest member face this without any of us being here to show our support."

"Now all I need is some ice cream, because watching you eat that banana split has made me want one," Erica laughed, but she was serious. The way she savored each spoonful, Tasha made that banana split look like it was the best banana split ever made.

"Me too," Both Carla and Rhonda seconded the sentiment.

The smiles and laughter were exactly what Tasha needed at this stage of her survival. This is beat-able, so I can beat it, she thought as she lay in bed looking at living proof: Erica, Rhonda, and Carla. They're survivors, as is millions of others. I'm no different, is how each member viewed their situation. Most of them have been cancer free for more than two years, so it's no wonder most of them don't even think about the disease. They've gotten used to the idea of living their lives just as they had before they were diagnosed, which allows them to live worry-free. At least that's how it seems.

Unfortunately this visit had to come to an end. Tasha needed her rest. After exchanging good-byes, her parents, Erica, Rhonda, and Carla exited the room continuing their conversation all the way to the hospital parking lot. During their conversation, Tanya learned that she and Erica had attended the same high school, only at different times. They reminisced about everything from teachers that have been there through both eras to the air conditioner that never worked, also through both eras.

"Oh my God," William sighed as he checked his watch for the third time, in the last ten minutes, while he impatiently waited for his wife to end her conversation and get in the truck. How they could stand out in the cold and talk like old friends, when the Chicago hawk wasn't being the least bit friendly, was beyond him.

Scene 32

"Damn," Mike cursed as he impatiently waited at the kitchen table for his wife to emerge from the bathroom. "Get the lead out. The movie starts in less than an hour!" He shouted before lifting a slice of pizza from the Styrofoam plate in front of him.

Just hearing his voice made Amanda cringe as she stared into the bathroom mirror, applying the finishing touch to her lips, which she painted fire engine red, Mike's favorite. On this night, he wasn't drunk. Nor was he in a bad mood. In fact, he was exactly how he should always be. The way he was when they were dating, before her brief affair. Before all the bills brought on by the cancer. Before alcohol became an excuse. This was the Mike she loved so deeply. And if she had to put up with his abusive side from time to time, in order to be with the loving and caring side of him, then that's what she was willing to do.

"Okay, I'm ready. How do I look?" Amanda asked as she stepped into the kitchen wearing her new 'out-on-the-town' lamb skin pants, which hugged her hips tighter than an emotional parent on his/her child's graduation day, a black sweater and a pair of black leather shoes. The ass whipping she received not too long ago was a distant memory. She talked as if what had happened that night had never happened. Just like she always does.

"You're beautiful," He said as he stuffed the pizza crust into his mouth. "I really mean it. You're beautiful."

"Yeah? How about the backside?" She asked flirtatiously before spinning around to show off how great her butt looked in those pants.

"I love it. Damn, I love it!"

"It looks that good?"

"It looks even better," He spoke at a near whisper, staring at his wife's ass as she smiled back at him.

"Well, if it's that good we better get going before we end up missing the movie," She grinned mischievously.

"You know, I think you're right," He managed to say after finally breaking his appreciative stare.

Mike's response was enough to smooth over what he'd done only two days earlier. That was apparent by the look on her face. The way she smiled at him as he lovingly looked over her assets. The way she teasingly brushed her ass against his crotch as he helped her with her coat. Funny thing is, just yesterday she was seriously considering leaving him, moving back to her mother's. She could even finish school and go on with her life, just as she and Keri had talked about. Well, mostly Keri, but Amanda really did consider it, just as she does every time Mike physically attacks her. But just like each of those times, she ends up forgiving him and going to bed with him. She ends up doing a lot of things she knows she shouldn't be doing, which, in Keri's eyes, makes her dumb. Dumb for not leaving. Dumb for taking his shit. 'Dumb! Dumb! Dumb!' is how Keri would stress her point after each attack.

The only thing Keri felt Amanda was being smart about was her decision to hold off on having children, even though Mike desperately wanted to start a family. It was Keri's idea for Amanda to start taking birth control pills, which Amanda has successfully kept hidden from her husband for the last six months. If Mike ever finds out there'll be hell to pay, and she knows it. But that day may never come. She may decide to have his baby. Or, she may decide to leave him. Either way, whatever happens won't be happening tonight, enabling Amanda to enjoy the movie she and Mike will attend at the Water Tower and the dinner afterwards. A nice walk through downtown will cap the evening off perfectly, like icing on a cake. Everything will be perfect, that is until the next time Mike breaks his promise and takes a belt to his wife's tail...

Pink October.doc   95

Scene 33

Friday morning Tasha opened her eyes to find her mother sitting in the 'not so' plush green chair by the door, stretching and yawning like she'd just woke from the same restful slumber Tasha had just emerged from. Beside her daughter's bed, on the night stand, was a aluminum foil wrapped plate, a pitcher of orange juice and a small carton of milk, all of which Tanya had smuggled into the hospital so that she could baby her baby. Tanya needed to do this. She needed to spoil her only child, more so for her own sanity than her daughter's comfort. It helped her to deal with the fact that her little girl had just undergone a lumpectomy. Maybe she needed to join a support group. One that helps parents of children diagnosed with cancer to better deal with their emotions, because their emotions are just as out of control as their children's.

By late afternoon, after being released from the hospital, then enjoying lunch with both of her parents, Tasha's cravings for something sweet led her and Tanya to Jewel in search of the perfect sherbet. They ended up returning to her parent's home with a host of snacks to munch on as they watched movies later that night, just like they used to do when Tasha was a little girl and William was at the hospital bringing a new life into the world. 'Mother and daughter night' is what those nights became. They didn't give those particular nights a title, but that's what it was. Those nights were special to them because that time strengthened their already steel-solid bond. A bond only a mother and daughter could understand.

Saturday morning, after enjoying the kind of breakfast her mother usually prepares on Sundays (scrambled eggs, grits, sausage, biscuits, and French toast), Tasha stood at her mother's side, an ear-piece dangling from her ear, her cell phone in her pocket, listening to her voice mail messages while helping her mother rinse dishes before placing them into the dishwasher. Tracey had called to check on her. There was a message from Mrs. Green, Carla, Erica, and Rhonda, all of them sending their best wishes and reminding her to stop by Mrs. Green's house on Monday night. Carla asked that she call and let her know when she was starting her radiation treatment. There was even a message from Kevin, which surprised her the most.

"I'm sorry about how things went down," His sorry ass voice spilled into her ear like castor oil into the mouth of a disobedient child. "I know being friends is probably out of the question, but I at least want to apologize...See you around, okay...Bye," The sorry son of a

Gary Norman

bitch didn't even ask about my health, Tasha thought. After all we've been through, he didn't even remember ...Did he ever care about me? Lies. All lies. Everything he's ever told me was a lie, Tasha tortured herself with trying to figure out how a person that supposedly loved her can act as if they never really cared at all.

"No you don't...You better not shed another tear over his sorry ass," Snapping out of her momentary daze, standing at her mother's side supposedly helping with the dishes, Tasha wordlessly chastised herself before attempting to rejoin the conversation she and her mother were having. Tasha had been paying attention the entire time, well, that's the impression she gave.

"How can you waste time and energy thinking about an asshole like that when you're in a life or death situation?" Tasha asked herself while her mother rinsed off a plate, talked about her drunk uncle, Brandon, and chewed gum all at the same time.

Tasha woke to face a Sunday that was just as physically relaxing as the previous two days at her parent's home, yet emotionally she was an absolute wreck. The closer she got to her first scheduled radiation session, the more she'd ponder over the fact that she would battle cancer for the rest of her life, the tumor may have been removed but there's always the possibility that the cancer will return, and return with a vengeance. Nobody could promise her that the cancer would not return to her breast, her liver or her brain. There was no way anyone could promise her a long and healthy life, so the tears she cried were tears mere words could not comfort. There's a real possibility that she'd die without having had her first child, and that scared her more than anything.

By Sunday night, Tasha, having lived through one of the most emotionally draining days she's had thus far, crawled into bed where she had a surprisingly tear-free night of restful sleep. Maybe it was because she had cried so much earlier that she had no more tears to cry. Maybe it was her mother's loving words, "If millions of people beat this, why shouldn't you...Isn't that what your group says?" Tanya held her daughter's hand as they both sat on Tasha's bed, both women fighting in vain to keep their tears at bay. Tasha crying because of fear and anxiety and Tanya crying for the same reason.

Whatever it was that had enabled her to achieve such an unexpected, tear-free, nights sleep also allowed Tasha the pleasure of thinking positively. 'She's right. They (members of her support group) were right. I can beat this. I can,' Her positive thinking led to her having the strangest dreams in which she was a beautiful rose nourishing a bumble bee with her nectar. That was strange.

Pink October.doc

Scene 34

Monday afternoon Tanya and Carla accompanied Tasha to her first radiation treatment session. The ride to the hospital wasn't as grueling as Tasha had expected it would be, thanks to Carla's non-stop chatter, which added humor to an otherwise earnest situation. Oh, could she talk. From the time she sat in the back-seat she lightened the mood with her un-compromised view of "their"(the group's) reality. To say that she was overflowing with life was an understatement. As far as she was concerned, they had all battled cancer, and won. Tasha was the group's newest victor.

Once they arrived at the hospital, Dr. Jordan and the radiation physicist spoke more about the method that would be used when administering the radiation. They would be using high-energy radiation Monday thru Friday, for six weeks, with each session lasting approximately fifteen minutes. Tasha would only be exposed to the radiation for one to five minutes each session.

"Whenever you're ready, there's a radiation therapist waiting on you down the hall," Dr. Jordan remarked in a suggestive, yet polite sort of way.

"Go ahead, baby," Tanya kissed her daughter's cheek before Tasha walked off, ascending down the long hallway until she disappeared behind a set of doors at the end of the hall.

Gary Norman

Scene 35

"What time did she say they'd be here?" Standing at the kitchen table wearing her favorite 'Kiss The Cook' apron, Michelle asked as she spread chocolate icing over the three layered yellow cake.

"She said they shouldn't be much longer because Tasha's radiation session has just ended...So pleease try to have a little patience," Mrs. Green, who was standing at Michelle's side, wished her friend had just a little more patience, just a little.

"You said that over twenty minutes ago," Erica taunted from her seat next to Amanda, who was standing at the kitchen table.

"So that means they should be pulling up any minute now...Right?" Mrs. Green responded to Erica's remark, then elbowed Michelle's arm just as she licked the icing off of the butter knife she used to decorate the cake.

On this day, Michelle, Erica, Amanda, and Mrs. Green all gathered at Carla's Hyde Park home preparing to surprise the group's newest member. This planned "beginning of treatment" surprise gathering was a way for group members, those who were able to attend, to help Tasha take her mind off of her fight with cancer, if only for a fleeting moment. All of the group members know what it feels like to be newly diagnosed. They've all experienced that fear at some time or another. The kind of fear only persons diagnosed with cancer can even attempt to describe. The kind of fear that would lead to stress, stress that eventually led to fatigue and loss of appetite.

"Thanks for the ride, I really appreciate it," Having been caught up in their conversation, neither of the women assembled in Carla's dining room realized that Tanya's car had pulled in front of the house. That is until Carla's 'it's obvious there's a surprise gathering in here' voice reached their ears as she crossed her own threshold with Tanya and Tasha in tow.

"No problem...It's the least I can do," Tanya replied.

"Well, can I at least get you two anything while you wait? Water? Pop? Anything?"

"No, I'm fine." Tanya and Tasha responded.

"Well, how about some cake?" That was Carla's cue to let the other's know that she was leading Tanya and Tasha into the dining room.

"Surprise!" Amanda, Erica, Mrs. Green and Michelle joyously emerged from the adjacent living room. Michelle carried the cake, which held a single 'happy face' candle as its centerpiece.

"What's all this?" An obviously surprised Tasha asked from the dining room's entranceway.

"We wanted to commemorate your first radiation session by doing something that'll take your mind off of whatever it is that may be bothering you. Now come over here and blow out this candle," Carla walked over to Tasha and, as if they were the closest of friends, led her over to the far end of the dinning room table where Michelle had sat the cake. Tanya stood at her daughter's side.

With that said, Tasha, smiling from ear to ear like the Joker, looked at each of the attendees before closing her eyes and blowing out her candle, wishing the same wish each of the group members had wished before her. "To remain cancer-free."

After the applause had died down, Michelle handed Tasha a knife and suggested that she be the one to cut the cake.

"Wait a minute," Suddenly realizing her own mother was in on setting up this surprise, Tasha turned her huge smile towards her mother. "This cake is chocolate...my favorite. How did they know that chocolate cake is my favorite, mother?"

"ESP?" Tanya jokingly shrugged her shoulders before coming clean under the pressure of her daughter's slant eyed stare. 'That look works every time,' Tasha grinned, hugging her mother forgivingly.

"While you were undergoing your treatment, Carla told me about the surprise, but they didn't know what kind of cake to make for you. So I told her and she phoned that information back here. Surprise," Tanya kissed her daughter's cheek before lovingly nudging her towards the cake.

"Here you go, ma," Tasha handed her mother the first piece of cake. "And thank you...Thank you all," Her words prompted a group hug.

"I thought you'd start to suspect something when I said that I needed a ride back to my house to find the number to my brother's towing company," Smiling as Tasha handed her a slice of cake, Carla nudged Tanya's arm in a 'you know you could've helped me come up with a better excuse' sort of way.

"Believe me, my mind was somewhere else when you said that. Besides, that story wasn't so strange."

"I did have my cell phone and the number to information as always been the same."

"When you put it like that, I guess it wasn't a very sound story."

"You can say it was stupid...I know it was," Standing at Carla's side, Erica added sarcasm causing Amanda to burst into a high pitched squeal of a laugh.

"It's not that funny," Carla rolled her eyes at Amanda, who, after taking the slice of cake Tasha had cut and handed to her, walked to the other end of the table where she continued to laugh while she ate her cake.

"I'm telling you she's crazy. Nobody believes me. When they finally see that I'm right, it'll be too late. She would've already slit their throats and ate their hearts...And when that happens, they better not come crying to me," Carla whispered into Tasha's ear, playfully dragging her hand underneath her neck for extra drama.

"The other's couldn't make it so they wanted me to apologize to you for their not being here," Walking over from the dining room's entranceway, Mrs. Green interrupted Carla's jest before taking a plate of cake from the table.

"No need to apologize. This is more than I expected...And I thank you for it, and I thank them for being concerned enough to want to be here. Besides, I'll get to see everybody next Monday, anyway."

"Don't count Rhonda out just yet, she said she's going to try and make it here today," Michelle, now seated at the table eating her cake, explained.

"She won't be appearing today, not unless she can be in two places at once," Erica corrected.

"What do you know that we don't?" Michelle responded, the grin in Erica's voice making her as curious as a cat. "Does she have to go to work?" She added, poking fun at the fact that Rhonda is a trophy wife.

"She will be working tonight," Erica grinned, her tone mischievous.

"Ooooh..." An acknowledging chorus rose from each woman in the room.

------------ ------------------------------- -------------------------

"Will that be all, Mrs. Carter?" The 'Sexy Undies Lingerie and More' saleswoman asked as she placed Rhonda's selected lace garments in one of the store's more colorful gift box and bag.

"No, that'll be all. These will do just fine. In fact, they're more than enough to do the trick," Rhonda winked a wordless 'girl you know how powerful lingerie can be' wink before taking her purchase and heading out to her car. Tonight she planned to re-ignite the fire that had once burned so brightly in her marriage that you needed a welder's mask to protect your eyes.

"Maybe a little spice is all my marriage needs," is what she told herself when she stood in front of the dressing room mirror moments ago, admiring her well kept figure in the red lace bra and panties she decided to go with as tonight's "gift wrapping." "This should keep his eyes where they need to be," Her ass looked to be in its twenties, at least that's what the mirror told her, thanks to those hours spent on the Stair-Master.

As she walked towards her car, she could hear Erica's voice as clear as if she were standing a few feet away. "Are you sure he's worth the fuss?" Erica's question hurt like salt on an open wound. "Of course he's worth it," Rhonda would respond, half smiling to conceal the pain of not being absolutely sure of her own response. She was almost sure. That, along with the fact that she still loved her husband, was all that mattered. Love can conquer all. Deep down she knew he had at least one younger woman on the side. She's always known, but, since she never actually caught him in the act, she was able to pretend it wasn't going on. But she knew. She started out as his mistress back when she was a stripper at Club Lace, and he was the "silent investor" responsible for getting the club up and running towards financial success. He would come in after a long, stress-filled day, looking to unwind with his favorite girl, Honey, a stage name Rhonda had chosen because, as she would coo so flirtatiously to her customer, 'I'm as sweet as honey, and just as sticky under the right circumstances.'

After hearing those words come from such a young, beautiful woman, Harry was hooked. He was more taken by her youth than her beauty. "That's how older men are," One of the other dancers had said about Rhonda's sugar daddy. And Harry was definitely no exception. Back then Rhonda had just turned twenty-nine, but looked twenty-five, and he was in his late fifties. That was over ten years, and one divorce ago. They married three years after their initial meeting, and have been married for seven years. Cathy was his wife when their affair started. She was ten years older than Rhonda, which really meant 'she didn't stand a chance.' Rhonda was prettier, more voluptuous, especially after receiving the breast implants Harry had talked her into getting, the same implants Cathy had refused to get because of the rumored cancer-causing effects. And, the most important part as far as Harry was concerned, she was younger. Youth is what ultimately tilted the scales in Rhonda's favor.

Gary Norman

Therefore, even though Harry has denied all accusations, Rhonda is left to assume the worse whenever Harry says he'll be late coming home because of a late meeting. How could she assume anything else, especially with her having been on the other side? She was the younger sex toy and he was the older sugar daddy, spending money like it was going out of style. Rhonda still remembers all of those lame excuses he'd give Cathy about his whereabouts and why he'd be late coming home, if he went home at all. On many occasions Rhonda would be lying in bed beside him when he'd make his "excuse" calls to Cathy. Sometimes Rhonda would orally please Harry while he'd be in the middle of conveying his fabrication, then laugh as he reached over to hang up the phone, hoping Cathy would hear. That was the ultimate slap in the face from the other woman. That's how Rhonda saw it back then, but now she found herself wearing the same shoes Cathy wore so many years ago. But she could do something about it, unlike Cathy, who was in her forties and had gained thirty pounds in the last six months of her marriage to Harry. Rhonda was still a knockout. So there was no way she would give Harry up without a fight…A catfight if needed.

Scene 36

"Thanks ma..."

"You don't have to thank me. I just hate that your father couldn't make it...He did tell me to let you know that he loves you, and he's sorry he couldn't make it."

"I love him, too."

"He knows that...now hurry up and get out," Tanya playfully nudged Tasha's elbow from the armrest. "It's after four and I wanna get dinner on before it gets too late," Tanya leaned over the armrest to kiss her daughter's cheek.

"Now that's cold...I'm your only child and this is how you treat me...That's cold."

"Girl, you know I'm playing with you."

"You better be," Tasha smiled as she stepped out of her mother's warm car and into the cold November night's air.

"I'll call you when I get home, okay?"

"Okay, ma," Carrying an aluminum foil wrapped Styrofoam plate of cake, Tasha leaned back into the car to retrieve the gift Mrs. Green had given her. A gift from the entire group; a white T-shirt with a slanted pink ribbon on the front and the words 'Mrs. Green's Kitchen' in cursive letters. "I almost forgot my shirt."

"You'd forget your head if it wasn't attached."

"I used to hate it when you'd say that," Tasha said as a matter-of-factly, still holding the car door open.

"I know, that's why I said it," Tanya smiled.

"Bye, ma."

"Bye, baby...Now go ahead and get in the house before you freeze to death. I know I didn't see a sweater underneath that coat."

"I love you too," Tasha shook her head. Tanya will treat her like a little girl until the day one of them no longer exists. Knowing that, Tasha smiled on the inside as well as the outside.

"I love you too, baby," Tanya said as she watched Tasha walk to her front door and enter her house before driving away.

Once inside, Tasha hung her coat in the closet nearest to the front door then headed into the kitchen where she placed her cake in the frig, fixed herself a cup of hot chocolate, and checked her voice mail. There was only one message. Tracey had called to check on her. That was nice of her, Tasha thought as she dialed Tracey's number, courteously returning her call. After their brief conversation, during which she revealed her intention to return to work tomorrow

Gary Norman

and Tracey talked about her boyfriend and her 'soon to be released from prison' brother. Tasha went upstairs and started her bath water, letting it run while she gathered her bath aids; washcloth, bubble bath, and her therapeutic cup of 'Dannon's' banana yogurt, and Sade's greatest hits CD.

As she sat soaking in the hot sudsy water, savoring both the yogurt and Sade, Tasha, for the first time during one of her yogurt baths, began to cry. A loud sobbing kind of cry. Tears ran down her face as she spooned the last bit of yogurt from its container and into her mouth. Then she laughed, a sudden laugh, surprising even her. She had something to cry about as well as something to be happy about. She did have cancer and it's possible that it may return, thus giving her something to cry about. But she did catch it early therefore increasing her chances of survival, giving her something to be happy about.

"I'm really going to beat this," She said, setting the empty yogurt container on the edge of the tub before emerging from her bath.

Scene 37

"Damn, I'm hot!" Rhonda cooed seductively as she stood in front of her full-length mirror donned in her newest lingerie, her favorite sheer nightgown and her red snake skin pumps with the four-inch heels and gold tips. Tonight will be perfect. Rose petals covering their king size bed. Chilled champagne and strawberries. The dinner she prepared with her own two hands, a dinner consisting of a liqueur marinated main course, a recipe she got from the maid; A maid Harry is probably fucking, is something Rhonda has always believed, but has never said a single word about it. If all goes well, Harry won't be concerned with dinner, he'll crave dessert, Rhonda's inner voice whispered.

Her excitement began to build when she heard her husband's car pull into the garage. She stood in front of the door leading from the garage into the kitchen with a bottle of champagne in one hand and a bowl of strawberries in the other hand, beaming with anticipation as the doorknob turned.

"I guess dinner won't be served in the dining room this evening," Stopping in his tracks after opening the garage door and finding his near nude wife on the other side, Harry responded in a way that gave Rhonda every indication that tonight would be very pleasurable. Those blue, diamond-shaped pills will definitely come in handy tonight…Definitely!

Scene 38

Tuesday's early morning traffic into downtown would be at its usual snail's pace, which is why Tasha would sometimes exit onto 95th and Stony Island, taking it until it merged into Lake Shore Dr.. Not that Lake Shore Dr.'s traffic moved a hell of a lot faster than the traffic on the Dan Ryan, but it would move a little smoother. And today's commute seemed less congested because Tasha was still thinking about yesterday's surprise party and not the traffic in front of her. In fact, she hasn't been able to keep the party out of her mind for more than a few minutes since leaving Carla's house. Or should I say, after Erica opened her purse and pulled out two 'wallet-size' photo-albums, both filled to capacity with pictures of her husband and three adorable little girls. A picture perfect family. The family Tasha yearned for. "That's my husband, Carl, and these are my three little angels, Kim, 9, Teri, 7 and Jessica, 2," Tasha could still hear the joy in Erica's voice as she introduced Tasha to her family via photograph. Her tall, light skinned, 40ish husband, with his neatly trimmed beard, mustache and low cut hair. He had bushy eyebrows, full lips with a broad and distinctive nose. The kind of nose usually associated with darker skin, probably earning him the 'number one teased child in school award' when he was growing up. The three children, who were as different in height as steps leading up to the front porch, all three sporting ponytails, the two year old sporting a T-shirt that had the words "Future AKA" across the front. Tasha's eyes swelled with tears as she thought of her own little ponytail wearing daughter clad in a "Future Delta" T-shirt. A little girl she didn't have, and had no idea when she would have her. Unfortunately, last night's nightmare didn't end when she opened her eyes to face a brand new day.

Pulling into the faculty parking lot for the first time in weeks, Tasha began to feel that same 'first day on the job' feeling she felt a few years earlier, when she first arrived at Dr. Rhay E. Street Magnet Elementary as the school's newly appointed principal. It was a little over two years ago when she, not too long removed from grad school, pulled into this same parking lot filled with the same excitement and anxiety every post graduate degree possessor feels when they finally start that job they've studied so hard for. Tasha couldn't be anymore blessed, landing a job as principal of such a prestigious school. "Thank you, uncle Perry," Tasha had included him in her nightly bedside prayers after learning of her appointment. She was assigned to a school with a reputation of helping its students succeed. Not that the other Chicago Public schools are designed to make students fail, that's not the case at all. It's just that this school, Tasha's school, is devoid a lot of the problems plaguing most of the inner city schools. Prospective students have to score well on placement exams, which only secures them a spot on the school's extensive waiting list, thus weeding out undesirables. The classrooms aren't overcrowded and students must maintain a certain G.P.A. to remain. This is exactly the kind of school Tasha dreamed of one day running. There was no way she was going to one of the overcrowded, gang infested, inadequately supplied inner city schools, which would have no doubt added unwanted stress to her life. Besides, she wasn't accustomed to dealing with problems associated with those schools, be it as a part of the administration, or as a part of the student body. Tasha grew up in the suburbs where she attended both elementary school and high school, away from the problems inner city kids had come so accustomed to seeing that they began to accept as being normal. Tasha did spend time in the city, sneaking off with friends to parties, shopping, dining out, etc. But that wasn't the same as actually dealing with everyday "city" life.

"Hey there principal...It's nice to have you back," Miss Dorsey, a dark skinned, young and very shapely English teacher, standing just outside of her classroom's doorway ushering students into class, happily replied as Tasha was about to pass by without speaking. It was obvious that Tasha was off in her own world. It was also understandable.

"Hey!" Stepping over to where Miss Dorsey stood, Tasha responded with the universal reply. "I'm sorry, I didn't see you standing there. My mind is somewhere else," The combination of stress, fear, and anxiety overwhelmed Tasha for a moment, causing her to literally look right pass Miss Dorsey.

After snapping out of her daydream state, Tasha was able to clearly survey her surroundings for the first time since she entered the school. And that's when she saw him, Greg Clark. Little mannish Greg Clark, standing behind Miss Dorsey looking up her skirt with a small mirror that appeared to be taped to the front tip of his left shoe, which he stuck out just far enough so that it was directly between her feet.

"That's okay, I understand," Miss Dorsey spoke tenderly, shifting her stance a bit and accidentally bumping the mannish student behind her, almost knocking him to the floor. "Oh! I'm sorry Greg, I didn't see you standing there," She lovingly messed his hair, totally unaware of the invasion of privacy taped to his shoe.

"That's okay, Miss Dorsey...I'm okay," He smiled before his eyes landed on Tasha. He was so occupied with the color of his teacher's panties that he didn't even see her approach. He didn't hear her voice until it was too late. In that instant, he knew that she knew what he'd been doing. The way her eyes went from his shoes to his eyes then back to his shoes told the whole story...He was in trouble, again!

"Escape!" His brain yelled down to his feet, only to have his getaway halted before it even started.

"Miss Dorsey, can I borrow Mr. Clark for a minute?" That was all Tasha needed to say to keep him planted right there.

"You can have him," Miss Dorsey playfully whispered just as the tardy bell sounded, signaling her retreat into her classroom.

"Now to you, mister man...give me that," Tasha held out her hand awaiting his visual aid.

"Oh...umm...you...umm...saw that," He stumbled through his words, half-laughing to conceal his fear of what was to come.

"Yes, I did. Now get in there before I decide to punish you," Tasha arched her left eyebrow just as the mirror was placed in her hand.

"Yes, ma'am," He uttered. He couldn't believe what he was hearing. He was being let off without being punished, even though he was caught in the act. He eagerly opened the classroom door and immediately entered so that she wouldn't have time to change her mind. Tasha laughed. Not at Greg Clark's brisk escape into Miss Dorsey's classroom, she laughed at the entire picture. Here was this eight year old, frail, white kid with freckles and straight, un-styled, red hair, looking under the dress of a black woman with thick hips, thighs and ghetto booty. At least that's what the construction workers across the street howl whenever she'd step out of her car and into the summer heat.

"I just hope he didn't see too much," Tasha snickered as she thought back to the time she and Tracey ran into Miss Dorsey at Secrets, a Dolton nightclub. That night, after a few too many apple martinis, Miss Dorsey began to share too much information. "I usually go without panties," Was the first shocker of that night. "I hope she wore some today, because if not that little boy may be scarred for life," Stepping into the reception area of her office, Tasha shook her head before greeting her secretary with a surprisingly chipper "hello."

------------- -------------------------- -----------------------

Pink October.doc   109

On her first day back to work since being diagnosed, Tasha found that, because of the seriousness surrounding her situation, dealing with her usual everyday duties was a lot harder than she figured it would be. She was unable to focus on anything for an extended period of time, nothing that didn't have anything to do with breast cancer. It was now five minutes before twelve and she hadn't even glanced at Mr. Simms' (the head of the biology department) detailed request for new lab equipment, a proposal he hand delivered at eight o'clock this morning. "Thank God for vice principal Reddpeccer," Tasha thought as she glanced at the paper work sitting in the middle of her desk. He would have to be the one to go over Mr. Simms' proposal, not Tasha. Not on this day, a day when her mind has been so overwhelmed with the fact that she had a cancerous tumor removed from her breast that she's already given herself five self-breast exams. And that's just since she arrived at work.

By twelve o'clock, Tasha, having added one more self-breast exam to the list, headed for the teacher's lounge for a cup of coffee and a slice of coconut cake. As she passed through the halls she thought back to Greg Clark and his peeping tom-styled technique and suddenly the morning didn't seem so bad. Her situation no longer seemed insurmountable. She smiled.

Stepping into the teacher's lounge, Tasha immediately noticed a gathering of about eight or nine teachers around one of the far tables. "What's going on?" She asked. The answer she received was totally unexpected. When the gathering parted she saw Tracey, standing in the middle, holding a coconut cake that had the words "Welcome Back!" spelled out in red letters across the face of the cake. This surprise would be the highlight of her much anticipated return to work. And she loved every minute of it.

Scene 39

"I said I'm coming, so please stop knocking on my damn door!" Amanda barked before snatching her front door open to find Keri on the other side, laughing at how easily her rhythmic knocking always agitates her neighbor. "That's not funny," Amanda snapped, leaving the door open as she walked off towards the kitchen, wordlessly granting Keri permission to enter the apartment. "You know I hate that."

"You hate that?" Keri twisted her face. "That's one of my favorite songs by Ice Cube," Closing the door behind her, she smirked sarcastically as she followed Amanda into the kitchen.

"No, I hate when you use my front door to beat the drum line to Once Upon a Time in the Projects. My front door is not your personal drum set."

"Would you rather I knock the baseline from Dumb Girl?" Keri shrugged.

"That's not funny, Keri!" Having heard both Ice Cube's hit as well as Run DMC's hit while visiting over at Keri's, Amanda's response was curt.

"All right, I'm sorry...I shouldn't have said that. I won't start today, I promise."

"You better not," Amanda's attempt at a stone face stare was ruined by a slow developing smile. "Or I'll start knocking on your door using beats from whatever song women shake their asses to," Amanda struck a blow at Keri's chosen profession. "It pays my bills, and my tuition," is how Keri used to respond. That's before she stopped pursuing her education.

"If you want I can get you a job down at the club."

"And why would I want a job down there?"

"So you can learn how to work it," While reaching into Amanda's freezer for the last grape pop-sickle, Keri seductively gyrated her hips, her back facing Amanda. "These are for eating, right? I don't want to take your last chance at some good lovin,'" Keri made the kind of lewd remark she's known for making, holding the frozen treat inches from her crotch as if she were about to demonstrate.

"Just eat the popsickle," Standing in front of the kitchen sink, Amanda's red face screamed embarrassment. She's always found it hard to hide her embarrassment when Keri decided to pitch those kinds of sexual innuendoes.

Pink October.doc 111

At a glance you could see that Amanda and Keri were the best of friends. Actually, Keri was Amanda's only friend outside of the women of Mrs. Green's kitchen. Keri was the only person Amanda had ever opened up to about the problems in her marriage. She's also the only woman Mike would allow Amanda to go out with, besides those weekly meetings at Mrs. Green's house. And that was mainly because of Keri's bi-sexuality and Mike's dream of one day convincing his wife to fulfill his threesome fantasy. But that'll never happen. Not in this lifetime, is what Amanda thought about the mere possibility of even considering turning Mike's fantasy into reality. Amanda loved men, period. 'Strickly dickly,' is how she joked the night she spurred Keri's advances. Amanda had never even thought about being with another woman sexually. Well, except for the time she and Mike watched three porno movies in a row. All three were girl/girl films that Mike had picked, claiming he just picked them at random so that he could get out of the adult section as quick as possible. Actually, he was hoping that by getting his wife to watch the girl/girl movies he'd get her to see that sex between two women was a beautiful thing…It didn't work.

"I gotta go," After peeping out of Amanda's moderate size picture window, Keri cut their conversation short abruptly.

"So you're just going to cut me off like that! You just got here…I'm talking to you!" Amanda huffed as a matter-of-factly. "Who's that?" She asked as she, after walking over to the exact window Keri had just occupied before heading for the door, peeped out of her window at what appeared to be a dark colored 600Benz. She couldn't see the driver's face because of where he chose to park, but she did see his hands on his steering wheel. He was definitely a black man, which happens to be the only men Keri has ever allowed the privilege of meeting her outside of the club. "They're willing to pay more, and the sex is good," she had once confided in Amanda.

"Now you're being nosy."

"Must be one of your sugar-daddies," Amanda's suburban, white girl, tone made them both laugh.

"And he loves his little cream filled cup cake," Keri winked before picking up the phone just above the counter, which separated the kitchen from the living room. "Baby, I'll be right down…Okay?" Keri cooed into the receiver, indirectly answering Amanda's question.

"Does Sam know about this?" Amanda teased.

"And she'll never find out about this either," Keri said before hurrying out of the apartment, down the stairs and out into the cold

November night, leaving Amanda to be beckoned back into the kitchen by the faint smell of smoke.

Pink October.doc   113

Scene 40

The verbal abuse she received for burning the meat loaf was minimal compared to what Mike was capable of inflicting. There was no physical abuse, which Amanda had prepared herself for by hiding all of his belts, just in case, so she was able to deal with the harsh words he so easily spat. She'd heard it all before so she was immune to the spirit-poisoning effect. "How stupid can you be? You didn't think my dinner was that important? Do you think money grows on trees?" were a few of the questions he asked during his ranting, all of which she had to answer in order to keep Mike from reaching the point where he feels that physical abuse is the only way she'd see that she was wrong. He usually does his questioning when he's sober, though even a sober Mike was capable of physical abuse. But if he had decided to become physical, hiding his belts would have only made things worse. Thank God things didn't go that far, she thought while sitting through Tasha's official introduction into the group, an introduction each one of the group members remembers well. Tasha's introduction opened Monday night's meeting, immediately following the customary "opening prayer." It feels more like an initiation, is how Michelle had once described the way they all, at one time or another, had to stand and give their name along with a short story as to how they arrived here at Mrs. Green's kitchen.

"We need to celebrate the inducting of our newest member," Mrs. Green cheerfully announced as she stood at the head of the huge dining room table, each member seated about its length, holding up flutes filled with champagne as if their silent toast was a nod of approval. "And I know just the place," she added with a sly grin.

Amanda knew the place as well. Since Tasha was new to group activities, she was the only one present that didn't know the place. But just like all of the other times before, Amanda couldn't go. Mike wouldn't allow it. Funny thing is Amanda joined the group so that she would have somewhere to go, not because she needed help dealing with cancer. At the time she joined the group she had been cancer-free for more than two years. She needed to get out of the house. She needed to go somewhere other than Keri's place. She needed to talk to people besides Keri's friends. She needed her own friends. "You have to join a breast cancer support group just to get away from your husband, that's a damn shame," Keri's words always seemed to hit Amanda when she least expects.

Scene 41

"You didn't have to make such a fuss over me...but I'm glad you did," Tasha winked before taking a bite out of the seafood stuffed pasta shell she retrieved from the salad greens decorated serving trey Mrs. Green held out in front of her.

"These are good, aren't they?" Carla interjected as she took another one from the trey then held a napkin underneath her mouth as she bit into it. "We all love 'em," She added. Amanda and Mrs. Green nodded confirmingly.

"These are my favorite," Amanda chimed.

"These are delicious...I hope they didn't take up a lot of your time," Tasha said, figuring Mrs. Green had to be the chef.

"No...Ronald made them earlier, but he couldn't stay because of a prior engagement."

"Ronald? Is he your son?"

"I do have a son, but he lives in Texas. Ronald is the unofficial member of the group who handles the cooking. Don't worry, you'll meet him. And I'm sure you'll like him...You're not married, right?" Mrs. Green's deep-rooted "match-making" mechanism took over.

"If you don't watch her she'll have you married with kids before you even knew what hit you," Carla playfully pulled Tasha away from a wide-eyed Mrs. Green. She led Tasha towards Erica and Rhonda, where things were a lot safer.

"Speaking of Texas," Standing at Mrs. Green's side, Thomas spoke up after first clearing his throat and rubbing his cheeks and chin as if he were troubled by what he was about to say. Everyone could see the uneasiness in his eyes, the same uneasiness that was suddenly noticeable in Mrs. Green's eyes as well.

Before anyone could verbalize their questions, Thomas blurted, "I'm moving to Texas," undoubtedly catching everyone in the room by surprise, everyone except Mrs. Green. She knew he would be moving to Texas when he told her he was considering pursuing the soon to be vacant position at T.S.U., a historically black college in Houston, Texas. "'Vice President of the Thurgood Marshall school of Law is a title I would wear well," Thomas had beamed, saying the words as if he were trying them on for size. At least that's how Mrs. Green saw it. "I guess we better make every second count because who knows how long it'll be before you have to move to Texas," Mrs. Green can still remember the words she spoke that night, two months ago, right before a night of "different" sex, which she's now grown accustomed to.

"Congratulations! Congratulations!" Everybody got their turn at wishing Thomas the best. As the night went on they went from congratulating him to talking about their initial feeling about the only male member of Mrs. Green's Kitchen Breast Cancer Support Group. "I thought you were gay," Carla said, half joking/half not. They all felt that way in the beginning.

"I'm sorry Thomas, but what were we supposed to think?" Erica could hardly get her words out, she was laughing so hard. "You were single, with manicured nails, flawless skin...like you spend thousands of dollars on skin care products. You know women are the only ones allowed to have flawless skin and manicured nails," She laughed. "The icing on the cake came when we found out that you're a huge E. Lynn Harris fan. Individually, what I've just told you doesn't mean a thing. But when they're added together they usually equal gay!" Erica emphasized the word gay, adding two finger snaps for drama. Amanda laughed so hard seafood and pasta shell came out of her nose. Mrs. Green thought that was hilarious, not Amanda's seafood shooting nostrils, but they were actually on the right track. Wrong train, but right track.

Mrs. Green smiled at Thomas, who returned an "I know what you're thinking" grin of his own. His sly grin only made Mrs. Green laugh out loud. She could still see Thomas bent over her couch, just as he was last night, taking as much of the strap-on as he could handle. "I'm not gay now, nor have I ever been," Mrs. Green still remembered the uneasiness in his voice the first time he had asked her to push a string of beads into his butt, which she snatched out just as he reached his peak. Next thing she knew she was fucking her man. Things had progressed just that fast. At first she was uncomfortable with the idea of screwing her man. 'Gay tendencies' is what she thought of his enjoying to be entered. Eventually she became more at ease with it, figuring 'he's a fine man, and I'm a fifty-six year old, single woman with needs. If I have to fuck my man in the ass from time to time to keep him happy, who, in turn keeps me happy, then all he had to do is bend over.'

-----------------------------Ding-dong-----------------------------

"I'll get it," Carla headed off to answer the door.

"So, are you ready for a girl's night out?" Erica asked as Carla left the room. Tasha smiled.

"I'm more than ready...I mean I've been on an emotional roller coaster since I found out I had cancer. Now I'm ready to have some fun," Tasha said with earnestness.

"I know how you feel, we all do. And I know this may sound crazy, but try not to think about it. You'll only make things worse by worrying. Shoot, you should be counting your blessings. You did catch it early, which almost ensures your survival," With that said, it was easy to see why Erica and Carla were so dear to the group.

"When I look at it like that, I do feel lucky... but then when I think about all the 'what ifs'..."

"That's just it, there are no what ifs as far as I'm concerned. You will beat this, I know you will," Those last words were followed by a brief, awkward, moment of silence. A child's high-pitched laughter shattered that silence.

"Who's that?" Tasha asked about the laughter coming from the foyer.

"That's probably Tara, Ronald's precious little girl," Just as Erica said that a little girl, clad in the cutest green and red plaid dress, green knee high socks, black patent-leather shoes, and green and black face paint, walked passed the kitchen's entrance-way.

"Tasha! Can you come here for a minute, please?" Carla called out from near the front door.

"Excuse me," Tasha shrugged, excusing herself before heading for the foyer.

Stepping out of the kitchen, through the living room, and into the foyer, Tasha saw Ronald Marks for the first time. A tall, dark-skinned, mature-looking Ronald Marks; just how she likes her men to look. He wore a dark colored, full length, leather coat that draped over a dark colored Italian suit. He has dimples, Tasha's insides smiled, her eyes taking inventory. She stopped less than five feet away so that she could see everything she needed to see concerning Mr. Marks.

"Hello, I'm Ronald Marks. Glad to finally meet you," He smiled invitingly as he shook her hand.

"Oh, I'm Tasha," Carla had to elbow Tasha's side to break her out of her momentary daze. Tasha's smile was just as inviting. "Tasha Mills," she continued, her insides blushing. He was absolutely handsome. Not a male underwear-model kind of handsome, but a more realistic, everyday, professional-man kind of handsome.

"I'm sorry I can't stay longer, but I have a play to attend. My little girl is making her stage debut," he smiled the kind of smile all proud parents smile. "She's a tree," he added, his eyes sparkling with glee.

"That's okay, there'll be other opportunities for us to chat," Oh my God, I'm flirting, Tasha couldn't believe what she'd just said. Not that what she said could be viewed as flirting, but she knew what she meant.

"Ronald!" Mrs. Green walked up from behind Tasha, unintentionally interrupting Tasha's awkward moment, handing Ronald a side-view camcorder with one hand while holding Ronald's seven-year old daughter's hand with the other hand. "I was going to bring it tonight," Mrs. Green walked over and kissed Ronald's cheek.

"I know...I didn't come for the camcorder. Tara wanted to make sure you didn't forget about her play. Plus somebody needed to make a pit-stop, even though I asked that somebody to do so before we got in the car," He looked down at his daughter, who hid her face behind Mrs. Green's thigh.

"That's okay. I'm glad you stopped by, that way we can all leave together," Mrs. Green said. "Surprise!" She turned and smiled at Tasha as only a true matchmaker could.

---------- ------------------------ ------------------------

From the play's opening curtain, the tiny actors and actresses stumbled through the dialogue of Little Red Riding Hood, forgetting some lines altogether, which they'd ad-lib in the most comical, yet extremely cute, way. With his trusty camcorder glued on the stage, Ronald was probably the most active of all the parents. He got up from his seat and hurried to the front of the stage every time a scene change brought his little girl back out on stage. When her scene ended he'd return to his seat. There was no mistaking the fact that he was the proudest parent in the auditorium. The fact that he loved his daughter was evident to everyone in the auditorium, especially the people he had inconvenienced with his constant comings and goings, to and from the stage. Tasha thought his behavior was the sweetest thing she'd ever seen. He was the kind of parent that would overdo things when it came to his daughter's happiness, and wouldn't care what people thought about his actions. The smile Tara displayed when she looked out into the audience and saw her dad filming her every move, even though she stood absolutely still, was enough to justify his every move. That's all that mattered to him, seeing his little girl smile.

From where she sat, three seats to his left, Mrs. Green and Carla occupying the two seats in between them, Tasha could watch the play and check Ronald out without him noticing her admiring stares. Something about him captured her full attention. It wasn't just his handsome face and dark skin, which has always been her weakness when it came to choosing a mate. It was something else. Maybe it was the way he and his daughter seemed like characters from the Cosby Show. Or maybe it was the way he paid her little attention, which will always get a woman's attention. Those men end up being more of a challenge than the ones that lose themselves in her beauty.

After the play ended, small crowds of family and friends gathered with their little actors and actresses throughout the auditorium and foyer. It was here, in the foyer, that Tasha got a really good look at his bare ring finger, not like the brief glance at Mrs. Green's house. Wordlessly, she thanked God.

"Is your wife here, or do I meet her later?" Tasha asked, attempting to conceal the fact that she had already noticed his bare ring finger. She also let him know that she was interested, without having to come right out and say it.

"My ex-wife," Ronald emphasized the prefix 'ex'. "Couldn't make it...." Sensing the curiosity behind her seemingly harmless question, Ronald, wanting to smile yet keeping his composure, looked directly into her eyes as he responded to her inquiry. "I'm a single dad," His stare only heightened the awkward silence that followed, a silence broken by the group's unofficial comedian.

"The way you're looking at her I'll say you're in the market to change that as soon as possible," Carla's blatancy embarrassed both Tasha and Ronald. Mrs. Green, Michelle, Rhonda and Erica felt embarrassed for the both of them. They will definitely laugh about this later.

"We'd better get going," Mrs. Green said, hoping to keep their embarrassment to a minimal. "I'll see you later, Ronald...And I'll see you later too, apple tree," Mrs. Green reached down and tickled Tara's side, causing her to retreat behind her daddy's leg while doing a combination of laughing and screaming.

"Thanks for coming, all of you. We really appreciate it."

"You don't have to thank us. We're more than happy to be here. Next time, I just hope Mrs. Green tells us ahead of time. That way we can dress accordingly," Erica, dressed in jeans and a blouse, as was the entire group, jokingly elbowed Mrs. Green's side.

Pink October.doc 119

"If I had told you, then it wouldn't have been a surprise," Mrs. Green returned the elbow.

"Don't worry about how you're dressed, because you all are beautiful," Ronald complimented, his smile beaming with sincerity.

"Thank you, Ronald," An always confident Rhonda took his compliment as being nothing but the truth, at least it was for her.

"Now was that compliment meant for all of us, or someone in particular?" Carla put Tasha on the spot, once again.

"That compliment was meant for all of you. Right apple tree?"

"Yup!" Tara chimed from her safe-zone away from Mrs. Green's tickle finger, behind her father's leg.

"Well, we'll see you two later...I have one more surprise up my sleeve for these ladies."

"Sounds like you're taking us to a magic show," Carla replied sarcastically, as if she didn't already know what Mrs. Green had planned for the night. At least she thought she knew.

"In a way, you can call it a magic show...things won't be what they appear to be," Mrs. Green grinned mischievously.

-------------   --------------------   -------------------

"Oh...my...God!" Mrs. Green couldn't believe her eyes. The female impersonators performing tonight at The Baton Room were absolutely beautiful. I mean 'lingerie model' beautiful, body and all. Tasha, Erica, Rhonda, Carla and Michelle all felt the same way, Erica going as far as questioning the gender of one of the performers when he passed the group's stage-side table.

"I told you that you wouldn't be able to tell they were men," Michelle, the only one in the group to have visited the Baton Room prior to tonight, laughed in Erica's ear. Erica's state of awe was exactly the kind of response Michelle had told Mrs. Green she experienced during her first visit. That's why she suggested this place for their next girl's night out. Ever since her first visit two months ago, Michelle has been more than anxious to introduce a new experience to the group's old, yet entertaining, girl's night out trek to a north side all male strip-club. And they loved it, just like she figured they would.

"We have to stay for the next show," Mrs. Green, who was definitely approaching her alcohol-intake limit, stated at the conclusion of the first show. The group agreed.

By the time the third performer stepped out from behind the curtain, something soothing by Janet Jackson filling the room through the strategically placed speakers, Mrs. Green was well pass her limit, which, when exceeded, usually ends their night of fun a lot sooner than expected.

"Shake it to the east! Shake it to the west! Shake it to the one you love the best!" A drunken Mrs. Green joyously cheered as the female impersonator swayed his hips seductively while he lip-synced to one of the year's chart topping singles from Faith Evans.

"Is she always like this?" Tasha laughed as she watched Mrs. Green tip the performer a twenty, all the while staring at his crotch, which was at her eye level due to the elevated stage.

"Mrs. Green, let him go!" Carla demanded. "You know they said the next time you did that they'd put you out," Carla bellowed over the blaring music and the even louder laughter coming from the patrons close enough to see what Mrs. Green had done.

Mrs. Green had gotten close enough to the fifth performer of the night to reach under his mini-dress and seize her proof that he was in fact a man. That was funny, at least Tasha thought so.

"Too late...Here he comes," Rhonda nonchalantly nodded in the direction of the club's bouncer headed their way.

Letting go of the performer's once tucked manhood, Mrs. Green drunkenly flopped down in her chair and tried to act like she hadn't just broke the club's no touching rule for the third time. It didn't work.

------------   --------------------   ----------------------

"I'm sorry, but I just had to make sure."

"You just had to make sure when we went to that strip-club on the north side. You just had to make sure when we went to that strip-club on 91st and Stony Island. You just had to look when..."

"Ok...Ok...I won't do it again," Mrs. Green laughed before asking Rhonda, "Why didn't you cop-a-feel?" Her slurred words caused Carla, Tasha, and Rhonda, who were riding in the back seat, to erupt into an ear piercing laughter just as Erica pulled in front of Mrs. Green's house. They couldn't stop laughing, even while unloading their drunken cargo and seeing to it that she made it into her house safely.

Girl's night out had, once again, been used to help a new member forget about her situation, if only for a moment. This also helped new members to become better acquainted with the other members of the group. A feat that was accomplished at the beginning of the night, when each one of the members stood up and formally introduced themselves to Tasha, sharing their personal stories just as Tasha was asked to do. This helped Tasha to feel more at ease when it came time for her to stand and introduce herself. After listening to their stories she couldn't do anything but feel better about her situation. She did catch her cancer a lot earlier than Mrs. Green, who is the only member of the group to have undergone a mastectomy. Most of her left breast had to be removed, leaving her no choice but to have one reconstructed in its place. "It looks just like my other one, it just doesn't have a nipple," Mrs. Green spoke candidly about her left breast.

When Mrs. Green mentioned how the entire group had, at one time or another, experienced nightmares, though most didn't last as long as Mrs. Green's, Tasha knew it wouldn't be long before her own nightmares would cease to exist. Once they realized that they had beaten the disease, whether realistically thinking or not, their nightmares stopped. "Oh," Mrs. Green said before taking her seat, allowing the next member to introduce herself. "I'm not married, I just decided against going through all of the hassle involved with getting my maiden name back," she said this, but didn't mean a single word. Fact is she'd never stopped loving her ex-husband. "Besides, I got the house and half of the three apartment buildings in the divorce. That means I'm still getting paid like I'm sleeping with him, so why not keep the name," she added. Tonight's meeting was full of surprises, Tasha thought. Too bad Amanda had to leave right after the play ended. This night would have benefited her just as it had Tasha. But, just like all the other times when the women got together for a night of letting loose, no matter how bad she wanted to go, she didn't go because Mike wouldn't have approved. She could've gone out with the girls if she really wanted to. He didn't own her. But she knew that if he were to find out she had gone somewhere other than where she said she'd be, there would be hell to pay. Thus introducing the ingredient that had kept her from forming a tighter bond with any of the group members after all this time (almost six months). She felt more like a distant cousin, rather than a sister. On the contrary, Tasha had already begun to form a sisterly bond with the group, though she was closer to Carla than anyone else.

Through Carla, Tasha was able to see things in a more positive light. It seemed as if Carla's positive way of looking at things had rubbed off on Tasha, which she more than welcomed, considering how she drowned herself in fear after finding out she had cancer. Carla's ability to get people to feel better about their situation was heaven sent directly to Tasha, at least that's how she saw it. Carla made her laugh when she didn't think she could.

During the next five weeks Tasha's bond with the group was solidified through the love and support they showered her with when the radiation treatments had physically exhausted her. She didn't have time to sulk in depression, or wallow in fear, because just when she was about to head down that negative path someone from the group was there to lift her spirits. From shopping with Rhonda and Erica to pizza and rented movies with Carla and Mrs. Green, along with the love and support she was already receiving from her parents and friends/co-workers, Tasha's mind stayed focused on the positive. Her nightmares ended after two and a half months, thanks to Mrs. Green's Kitchen.

Thanksgiving came and went, along with Amanda's birthday, Michelle's birthday and Rhonda's, Erica's, and Mrs. Green's scheduled mammogram. Each mammogram turned up negative. During this time you would've thought that Tasha and Ronald would've gotten a little closer, but they didn't. In fact, during that five week span she only saw him three times. Two of those times he was only dropping off one of his pre-prepared dishes at Mrs. Green's house, and the third time was during the farewell gathering for Thomas. During Thomas' farewell gathering, Tasha had an opportunity to talk to him, even ask him out if she wanted, but she let that opportunity slide on by. "I'm not asking that man out. That's code for 'I'm desperate as hell, please do me...you can think of it as charity'," Tasha explained her stance to Carla, who could only shake her head. "If you want something, you have to have the nuts to go after it," Cupping her hands as if she were holding tennis ball-size spheres, Carla responded to Tasha's negative way of looking at the dating game. Deep down Tasha knew she was right, but she'd become so accustomed to being pursued that she never learned how to pursue. That's where Carla was able to add assistance, not that she was used to being the pursuer, because she wasn't. She was just as attractive as Tasha, body and all. She was just a little more outspoken than Tasha. Carla had the steel-to-the-core nerve to go over to a man's house unannounced to ask him out. Tasha didn't have that kind of nerve. At least that's what she thought.

Pink October.doc   123

Scene 42

"Come on girl, it's time to take that next step. You can do it. We're right here with you!" Sitting in the passenger seat of Tasha's BMW, Carla offered encouragement as she sat in the parking lot with Tasha and Amanda preparing to enter the health club. The same health club Tasha hadn't visited since the day she kneed Kevin in the groin in front of the entire self-defense class. "He was cheating with my 'then' best friend," Tasha justified her actions five weeks ago, the night she formally introduced herself to the group.

"She's right Tasha. You can do this. Just by walking through that door you'll be starting your healing process. And with that you can finally say fuck 'em, and mean it," Amanda's choice of words startled both Carla and Tasha. Amanda's usually so passive, so quiet. Every now and then she'll get worked up over something, but most of the time she would keep her emotional side well in check. She's always been quick to form an opinion on how someone else should deal with their problem-plagued relationship, but couldn't fix the problems in her own marriage with a tube of super-glue. At least that's how Keri describes Amanda's ability to see the wrong with everybody else's relationship, but not her own.

Looking from Amanda, who was seated in the back seat, then back to Carla, Tasha took a deep breath before exiting her car and heading straight for the health club's entrance. She walked as fast as she could, fearing she'd get cold feet and not go through with this much needed, Carla and Amanda dubbed, "Cleansing Process."

"Slow down, girl," Carla and Amanda called behind Tasha, quickening their pace in order to catch up.

As they entered through the health club's sliding glass doors, the same glass doors Tasha chased Kim through almost two months ago, Tasha's heart pounded as the mere thought of actually running into either Kevin or Kim, or both, became more and more feasible with each step. "What if he's here? What if she's here? That backstabbing bitch! What should I say to her, if she's here? What should I do to her?" Tasha's mind wandered as she fearfully entered the cardio area at the far end of the gym. "It's too late to turn back now," She said to herself as she sat her gym bag down beside one of the three unoccupied treadmills in front of a two-way mirror facing the parking lot.

"I think we should stretch before we get started. It's been a while since I've seen the inside of a health club, let alone worked out in one," Carla began to stretch right next to the treadmills, warming up her muscles for what was sure to be a physically exhausting evening.

Amanda joined Carla moments later, leaving Tasha to scan the room for any sign of either Kevin or Kim. She wanted to make sure she saw them before they saw her. If there had to be a confrontation, she wanted to see it coming. Tasha was actually surprised that Kim hadn't talked Kevin into filing charges against her. Shit, with Kim being a criminal attorney, papers were probably sitting on some judge's desk at this very moment. Come to think about it, if Kim is as good an attorney as she was a friend she probably doesn't know how to file the papers correctly, Tasha laughed to herself, her eyes going over every inch of her immediate area.

"So far so good," It's been so long since Carla's last visit to a gym that after running only one mile on the treadmill she sounded as if she were hyperventilating, the way she struggled with her words in between breaths.

"Yeah, so far so good," Tasha's breathing was more controlled as she jogged alongside Carla and Amanda. She thought Carla was referring to her steady, yet shaky, pace. She wasn't. She was referring to the fact that they've been at the gym for over twenty minutes and they haven't had a Kevin and Kim sighting.

After completing her 'pre-workout' five mile jog alone, Carla stopped running after reaching a mile and a half, Amanda stopped after reaching two, Tasha suggested that they take a walk down the hall to where the self-defense classes were held. After that they could wind down the evening with a light aerobics workout. Since neither Carla nor Amanda were gym regulars, a light aerobics workout would be better for them than just jumping into an intense routine.

The self-defense class began with the instructor (Chris) first laying out the evening's exercises for the class. The self-defense technique used at this health club was a combination of boxing and karate, mostly karate, which allows class participants to receive a full body workout while learning the art of self-defense. The women and the few men in attendance were shown how to correctly stretch before the punching, kicking, and hip-tossing exercises were to begin. The pad-protected attacker is used during Thursday night exercises which, since it is Friday, gives tonight's class participants enough time to practice their exercises over the weekend in the comforts of their own homes.

After the self-defense class ended, it was off to the aerobics class, which Amanda skipped altogether. She was totally taken aback by the self-defense class. Her self worth seemed more pronounced with each kick, punch, and hip-toss. She focused on Chris' every word, and move, as he demonstrated the proper techniques. It was as if she were taking notes in honors chemistry, the way she gave her undivided attention. She phased out Tasha and Carla as if she and the instructor were the only two people in the room. "She was serious about her self-defense," Tasha later joked as they left the gym, walking out into the parking lot. All in all, Amanda thought the evening was exhilarating. Especially since Kevin and Kim were nowhere to be found, though that luck only went so far. During their next visit to the gym that inevitable face to face reunion happened, but it wasn't exactly how Tasha had fantasized. There was no screaming, no eyes being scratched out, and no foot needing to be extracted from Kim's ass. Their confrontation was a lot more civil than that, yet uncomfortable. Apologies were given and accepted, at least that's the impression Tasha gave. "I can't believe I actually cared for this asshole," She chastised herself as she listened to the sorry ass apology Kevin offered, of course while Kim was in the locker room. It was during Kim's brief time away that Kevin found the nerve to even attempt to imply that there could still be a chance for he and Tasha to work things out. "I'm not married, and I don't plan on getting married …at least not to Kim...so who knows, maybe down the line...." Tasha cut in before he could finish his ridiculous statement. Her words would've been straight to the point like a Montell Griffin jab, had she chosen to use them. "Fuck you," is what she wanted to say, but "I don't think my new man would approve," came out instead. She knew it was a lie, but he didn't. Just seeing the shock in his eyes was worth every fabricated word, but slapping his face would have made her feel a lot better. A knee to his groin would've been the icing on the cake.

Scene 43

Pulling into the parking lot designated for the residents residing in her building, Amanda continued to rehearse her lie, the same lie she's been rehearsing since Tasha dropped her off at her car back at Mrs. Green's house. She also needed to think of a lie to cover up the fact that she'd started going to the gym with Tasha and Carla. And it had better be good or else her days of going to the gym are numbered.

Even though it's barely after eight o'clock, and Mike's probably not even home yet, Amanda still made sure she had her lie straight, just in case. She did inform him about the possibility of staying late at Mrs. Green's in order to celebrate Tasha reaching the end of her radiation treatment, but she didn't tell him about the self-defense classes she planned to attend afterwards. "Why am I trippin? He'll never know, so calm down," she tapped her head against the steering wheel as if trying to force herself to believe her own lie. The part about going over to Mrs. Green's house to celebrate was a lie, why should the rest be any different? She had only gone over to Mrs. Green's house to park her car, just in case Mike talked Steve into driving by. That was Keri's idea. She felt that Amanda should lie about her whereabouts from time to time in order to be able to do the things she wants to do, most of which Mike wouldn't approve of.

Amanda didn't see Steve's Pathfinder in either its usual parking space, or anywhere else in the parking lot, but she still prepared herself for the worse as she entered her apartment, inhaling deeply, testing the air for the faintest hint of hard liquor.

"So far so good," She nervously laughed as she stepped into the kitchen. Then, recalling their last confrontation, she cautiously searched the other rooms to make sure he wasn't home. He wasn't. There will be no belts slapping across her back today.

Amanda had gotten so used to her dysfunctional relationship that if for some reason Mike suddenly decided to change his ways, she would feel more uncomfortable with that than her present state. The fact that she was living in fear, whether she admitted it to herself or not, had become second nature. Something she could overlook, or live through. Like catching a cold, you know you'll feel better in no time. That's how she's been able to overlook Mike's, occasional, abusive outbursts.

"Boo!" Catching Amanda totally by surprise as she stood over the stove preparing Sloppy Joe for tonight's dinner, Keri grabbed

Amanda by the waist, scaring her half to death with her sudden presence.

"BITCH! You dirty bitch!" Amanda cursed once her screaming had stopped. "You almost gave me a fuckin' heart attack. That's not funny, Keri. How did you get in here, anyway?"

"You left these in the door so I thought I'd bring them to you, and teach you a lesson at the same time," Keri handed Amanda her keys before retrieving a cold Mountain Dew from the frig.

"I can't believe I left my keys in the door like that. If Mike would've found them he would have had a fit."

"And you, of all people, know how bad his fits can get," Standing at the frig sipping her Dew, Keri joked in bad taste. Amanda knew she was right, so she didn't pay it any mind. Paranoia is why she left the keys in the door in the first place, a justified paranoia. She was too worried about Mike's whereabouts, and his state of mind, to pay attention to anything else.

"I came over to ask if you wanted to go shopping with me tomorrow, while Mike's at work?"

"Yeah, I'll go. I need to pick up something sexy," Amanda stirred the Manwich sauce until it covered the ground beef entirely.

"Oh really?"

"Yes, really…I like to get just as sexy as the next woman."

"Really?" Keri asked, her facial expressions advising Amanda not to make any plans without talking to Mike first. "And what do you plan on telling Mike?" She asked in a 'I gotta hear this' sort of way.

"You know Mike won't mind, as long as I'm with you."

Amanda knew that Mike loved it when she spent time with Keri. Their spending time together kept his silly fantasy alive. She also knew that he'd be home any minute now, and he hated to come home from a hard day's work to find his wife entertaining company. That was supposed to be his time to unwind with his wife alone. It didn't matter if that company was a key ingredient to the threesome fantasy he'd never see materialize, at least not with his wife.

Keri knew about his dislike for company when he got home from work so she left when she saw Steve's SUV pull into the parking lot. She'd come back after Mike had his unwind time, which consisted of a shower, dinner, and some TV.

Scene 44

Since Mike's hours were from 12pm to 8pm, Amanda was able to enjoy a long day of shopping with Keri, even though, because of her limited spousal allowance, she was only able to pick up a few of the things she had hoped to get. And most of the items she purchased were items to please her husband. From the red, form fitting dress that flattered her every curve to the red, lace, crotch-less panties and matching lace bra with the holes where her nipples would be, her day of shopping turned out to be all about Mike and what he liked. The crotch-less panties have always been his idea. He likes her to wear them when they go out, that way their spontaneity wouldn't suffer. In other words, so they can get their freak on any and everywhere they felt the urge. Like the time they had sex on a crowded dance floor, right in the middle of a New Years Eve party. No one at the party noticed because they danced just as close as everyone else did. All it took was an unzip here and a slightly raised skirt there and 'waa-laa', Happy New Year, so to speak.

"And hurry up!" Amanda pleaded, hoping to by-pass an hour-long stay in yet another store. They stayed in the last store for forty-five minutes because Keri just couldn't make up her mind.

"I will. I will. Now hold this, I'll be right back," Keri handed Amanda her purse before turning and heading for the dressing room with at least three different outfits, all of which needing to be checked by the store employee seated at the dressing room's entrance.

This is the fifth store they've entered this afternoon, and the fifth store that Keri saw something she just had to have. "Stripping must be paying well," Amanda mumbled to herself as she browsed through the price tags hanging from each of the garments on the display rack to her immediate left.

"Excuse me, I hope I'm not bothering you," Caught by surprise, Amanda turned to face the direction from which the husky voice came and quickly interjected.

"I'm sorry, but if you hadn't noticed, I'm married," Amanda wiggled her fingers in front of her so that the heavy-set, dark skinned gentleman standing in front of her could see that she did in fact wear a wedding band and an engagement ring.

"No, you got it all wrong…Amanda. Amanda Carter was your name, wasn't it?" The dark-skinned gentleman smiled the widest smile, his hands held in front of him with his palms up as if he were saying, 'remember me?' "This should make it easier on you," He continued after the perturbed look on her face said it all. She didn't recognize him. "Minus, give or take, twenty pounds," He knew he'd gained over forty pounds, but he smiled nonetheless.

"Peter! Peter Thorton!"

"In the flesh."

"God, it's been almost seven years since I've seen you last...What have you been up to? Wait, before you answer that, give me a hug," Amanda said emphatically before hugging him the way old friends do when they run across one another after going years without exchanging as much as a postcard.

They met during freshman orientation. His thick bifocals, and tore up shoes, had most of the other freshman laughing. "And he had the nerve to ask me out," Amanda thought. She replayed that awkward day in her head as she stood face to face with a changed man. Thirty days, some contacts and new shoes after that embarrassing day, he ended up dating one of Amanda's closest friends, which allowed her to get to know him. Every time Amanda would visit her friend's off-campus apartment, there he was. It was like they had no choice but to become good friends.

Peter was as dark as night, and Joy, his girlfriend, was the palest red head in America. That's how Amanda used to joke of their coupling. "We make each other look good," was Joy's typical response about their difference in hue. And they did look good together. So good that Amanda began to see inter-racial dating in a whole new light. She began to seriously consider dating a black man, even going as far as to fantasize about the black guy on her school's swim team. Then it was the black guy that sat next to her in her Chemistry lecture hall. Then it was the black guy that delivered her pizza. At that time Mike was having problems figuring out whether or not he wanted to be in a committed relationship. Amanda had caught him cheating with one of his many ex-girlfriends, and she began to yearn for the love and commitment Joy and Peter enjoyed. The next thing she knew, she and Mike were back together and she was cheating on him with a black man. Revenge is a mother...

"Well, after receiving my bachelors, I went on to grad-school where I received my masters in three years. From there, I worked for a while, saving up as much money as I could all the while hoping to find something I'd like to invest in...Then earlier this year, this place fell right into our laps."

"You mean you own this place?" Amanda asked, running her eyes over the entire room as if she were appraising the place. She didn't even hear him say our, that's how taken she was by the fact that her old friend was doing so well.

"Yes, I'm the co-owner...You do remember Joy, don't you?" As if on cue, Joy stepped up from Amanda's blind-side and into Peter's waiting arms.

"Joy Henry?"

"Close...It's Joy Thorton, now," The still very petite, and very pale, woman smiled the widest grin before sticking out her left hand to show off the expensive looking wedding ring. A wedding ring that held as its centerpiece, what looked to be a two or three-karat diamond embedded in a platinum band.

'BITCH!' Amanda's insides screamed, but her mouth yielded a more pleasant "Hey, how have you been?" He was supposed to be hers, if she hadn't chose Mike's sorry ass instead. Peter had romantically pursued Amanda during the first few weeks of school, but she had eyes for a much cooler, much whiter, Mike. Damn eyes. If those eyes could have seen the future she would have dropped Mike back then and now she'd be happily married, with a successful business, but instead she's standing across from Joy, who looked to be gloating.

Joy made the decision to not give up on her pursuit of a man who, at the time, was obviously interested in someone else. Her persistence paid off. She's now happily married to that elusive man and the co-owner of a very successful husband and wife business, which looks to be on its way to yielding a sizable profit in its initial year of existence. They were happy, successful and, the icing on the 'slap in the face' cake, expecting their first child in eight months.

Running into the both of them was all Amanda needed to re-ignite her own passions. They were living the life she was supposed to be living, and with a little persistence she will be. Now all she has to do is get Mike to feel the same way. She has to go back to school, but first she'll have to convince Mike. Damn!

Pink October.doc

Scene 45

"That's his house right there...The one with the truck in the driveway," Carla pointed Tasha in the direction of the black Range Rover parked in the driveway of Ronald's plush Pill Hill home. His beautiful dream home, which sat one house from the corner, had a three-car garage, an upper level, and a large, gate secured, backyard. It was the kind of home that screamed success.

Having just left Mrs. Green's house with an excuse to stop by Ronald's, Tasha found herself preparing to put Carla's 'snag a man' plan into action. The plan was simple. "We'll return the cookware he left at Mrs. Green's house. I'll drive so that you can say we were on our way somewhere else, but since we were headed his way we didn't mind dropping this off for Mrs. Green. Of course I'll stay in the car while you're macking him down," Carla laughed as she divulged her plan, two days ago. "I'll hunk the horn after a few minutes so that it looks like we're going to be late for our previous engagement. That way you can ask him if he'd like to have dinner with you sometime. If you ask him this while you're walking away it won't seem like you planned the whole thing," Carla had it all planned out. The plan wasn't perfect, but it was simple, just like Carla wanted it to be. Now all Tasha had to do was ring the damn doorbell...

"Push the button, scary cat!" Carla leaned into the passenger seat and called out to Tasha, smiling as if her plan had a hidden agenda. An agenda Tasha knew nothing about.

"I did, now shhh!" Tasha shushed, her pointing finger held to her lips before turning back to the door just as it opened.

"Hello, Tasha," Ronald greeted her with a smile, stepping aside as to allow Tasha enough space so that she could enter his comfortably heated home, leaving the December weather on the other side of his seasonally decorated security screen door. "Can I take your coat?"

"That's okay...I can't stay long, we're on our way..." Looking back over her shoulder to acknowledge Carla's presence in the car, Tasha watched in disbelief as Carla drove off without as much as honking her horn. "That was dirty," Tasha said under her breath before turning back to Ronald and accepting his offer to take her coat.

"I'm sorry about this...She must've...Well, I don't know what made her drive off like that. I'm sorry..."

"No need to apologize. Whatever her reason is for leaving you, I'm sure it's nothing to worry about. If I have to I'll take you home myself. Deal?"

Pink October.doc   133

"Deal," Tasha said as she watched Ronald hang her coat in the closet, to the left of the foyer. She then accompanied him down the hall to his spacious kitchen where he was in the middle of preparing dinner. In the kitchen there was a small counter-perched TV broadcasting news of the 'still too close to call' presidential election. "And the way that things are going, it'll probably take at least another week before a new president is named," The news anchor replied just before switching to breaking "local news".

"Where is Tara?" Tasha asked just as the station went to commercial.

"She's upstairs doing her homework. I'll call her down when dinner's ready."

"Now that makes me feel even worse. Why didn't you tell me you were cooking dinner when I called? I feel like I'm intruding."

"If I had a problem with you stopping by I would've said something on the phone. Now just relax and let me fix you a plate," Standing at the stove stirring the sauce he had simmering, Ronald smiled invitingly at Tasha, who was seated at his huge glass table a short distance away from where he stood.

"Hi," The sweet little voice interrupted from the doorway leading into the kitchen.

"Hey, apple tree...How have you been?" Tasha chimed. Tara smiled. She loved her new nickname, the nickname she received the night of her play.

"Fine..." She said in the most adorable, seven year old, voice. "I just finished my homework and now it's time for my daddy to check it."

"Not right now, baby. Daddy is cooking dinner. I'll check it before we eat, okay?"

"Okay."

"If you'd like, I'll check it for you," Tasha spoke up just as Tara was about to walk off, obviously not a happy camper. She held her math book close to her chest in a bear hug kind of way.

"If it's no trouble."

"It's no trouble at all."

Tara smiled widely as she walked over and took Tasha's hand after it was clear that Tasha would be checking her homework.

"Tara, what are you supposed to say?"

"Thank you," She said, satisfying her father before leading Tasha into the living room where she proceeded to bombard her with the kind of endless chatter associated with young children.

Everything from playing kickball at recess to coming in second place in her school's spelling bee, she went on and on like the Energizer bunny.

Tara has her father's dimples, but her complexion is a few shades lighter. Her mother must be a lot lighter than Ronald and her hair must've come from her daddy, at least the extremely dark shade of her hair did. The rest of her features had to come from her mother, those high cheekbones, and those big ears that stuck out on either side of her head like a pair of Satellite dishes. Yup, they had to come from her mother, Tasha thought, smiling as Tara continued with her third story in just over ten minutes.

----------------------------Ding dong----------------------------

"I can get that for you if you'd like...It's probably Carla," Tasha announced after the doorbell saved her from yet another story.

"That's okay, I'll get it...It could be my ex-wife. She's supposed to be dropping off Tara's social studies book. The book she said she accidentally left at her mother's," On his way to the door, Ronald paused momentarily. He saw straight through Tara's plan to avoid extra homework.

"Please don't be his ex-wife. Please don't be his ex-wife. Please don't be his ex-wife," Tasha, suddenly feeling out of place, wordlessly prayed over and over.

"Come on in."

"I don't get a hello?" Tasha heard a woman's voice say. "Smart ass," that woman's voice went on to say.

Trying to keep her cool, a bead of nervous sweat trickling down her back, Tasha listened to their exchange get closer and closer until Ronald and his female visitor stood in the living room's entranceway, looking down on her as she sat on the couch going over Tara's spelling homework. Tasha picked up Tara's spelling book when she heard a woman's voice at the door.

"Hi mommy!" Tara said excitedly, springing from her seat like she hadn't seen her mother in weeks.

"Hey baby. I brought your social studies book. You know, the one I told you to put in your book bag, remember?"

"Sorry mommy," Tara sounded so adorable as she hugged her mother's thigh.

"That's okay, but you do owe me five dollars for the gas I had to use to make this special trip," The proud mommy bent down to

Pink October.doc

accept five kisses as payment instead. She smiled from ear to ear, that is until her eyes met Tasha's.

Feeling an uneasiness thick enough to cut with a knife, Ronald, standing beside his ex-wife, noticing that 'who's this bitch' look in her eyes, began the introductions, which were made even more uneasy when Tamara just had to state the fact that she hadn't gone back to her maiden name. "Tamara Marks," She said, emphasizing Marks as if she were stating her claim. He was hers, is what her statement screamed. That's what Tasha heard, anyway.

"Shit!" Tasha said over and over in her mind. She knew Tamara's presence would make things more interesting. "Where in the hell is Carla?"

Scene 46

That was her plan all along, to get Tasha over to Ronald's house and leave her there so that the two of them could finally talk to one another. It was obvious that they liked each other, but for some reason they haven't been able to sit down and talk, which is where Carla's plan was supposed to help. But who knew Ronald's ex-wife would show up. And by the way Tasha described things from the passenger side of Carla's car, a very jealous ex-wife. She didn't get ugly or anything like that. She just made it perfectly clear through her actions, that, not only was she Ronald's ex-wife, but she was Tara's mother. "I, if not her father, will help Tara with her homework," her body language screamed when she sat next to Tara and took up where Tasha had left off.

"She had a right to be a little shocked at the fact that her ex-husband actually had company, seeing that he has not made time for anyone other than his daughter, and our group, since his divorce two years ago," Carla replied. "You're lucky she didn't go off," She added teasingly.

"Thank God she didn't go off," Thinking back to Carla's comment, Tasha thought as she got comfortable underneath her bed's warm comforter later that night. "I would've felt bad about kicking her ass in front of her little girl and her ex-husband," She half grinned before grabbing the remote control from the night stand and turning to one of the many late movies playing on one of the billion channels her satellite disc picks up. She hardly ever watches any of the movies, even though she pays an arm and a leg for the service. She managed to watch forty minutes of The Nutty Professor 2 before nodding off, leaving the TVs auto-timer in charge of turning off the TV

------------- ------------------------- --------------------

Sunday morning Tasha went over to her parent's house for a Sunday breakfast reminiscent of the days back when she was a little girl filling herself with momma's 'Sunday breakfast' before heading off to church. Grits, scrambled eggs, two kinds of sausages, homemade buttermilk biscuits, orange juice, and fresh fruit. Tasha has always loved Sunday breakfast with her parents, more so now than when she was younger, but, as of the last few years, for one reason or another, she hasn't been able to get by as often as she'd like. Something would always come up, especially over the last two years when Kevin was her number one priority, but not any more. Not after finding out

Pink October.doc   137

she had a cancerous tumor in her breast. Too bad it took something as serious as cancer to put the spotlight back on the importance of family.

With the cancer cloud hanging over their lives, this Sunday breakfast was just as painful as it was a symbol of love and support. Tanya was having a hard time dealing with the fact that her little girl is a cancer survivor, and Tasha knew it. She's always known when something bothered her mother, and now was no different. To Tasha, her mother's anguish was as noticeable as a second thumb, even though her mother did an excellent job of hiding her feelings. Well, she thought she did. But what could Tasha do? There isn't a parent on earth that wouldn't be overly concerned about their child's well being, especially under these circumstances. So Tasha would have to deal with her mother's feelings as best she could.

Monday morning's commute to work was as unbearable as any other Monday in history. At least it was that way to all the people that had gotten used to doing nothing over the short weekend, which is too damn short and should be extended to four days. Well anyway, the commute was excruciating, yet it wasn't bad enough that it put a damper on Tasha's entire day, not with someone as silly as Tracey adding laughter to an otherwise drab day.

"You're lucky she didn't go off," Tracey echoed Carla's sentiment from her seat across from Tasha at the teacher's lounge table. "Because I wasn't there to help get that woman off your ass," Tracey's laughter was enough to brighten the darkest of nights, and she didn't even know it.

Scene 47

Monday night's meeting carried a tone that Tasha had been introduced to three and a half weeks ago. The beginning of the night was all about sharing information. From reduced cancer risks diets to new improvements in mammography, this night was the most informative night Tasha had been apart of since joining the group. In fact, the information about the new improvements in mammography had recently become more than just an article in the October Ebony for Michelle since Patrice, a friend of hers, accompanied her daughter to her first mammogram examination. There's usually nothing unusual or unique about a mammogram, but this was a part of a research project aimed at improving the old method by making it digital (computerized). This method uses lesser doses of radiation per mammogram than its predecessor, making it less harmful than mammograms of the past.

After the important information had been shared, the group took on its usual sorority/family type of atmosphere, void Amanda's presence as usual. Erica put on Mrs. Green's Best of the Isley Brothers CD, pulled a deck of cards from her purse and in no time at all a spades marathon was underway. A marathon that wouldn't end until 9:45pm.

"The heifer wouldn't even let me put the dinner rolls in the oven," Michelle's words began to slur, signaling that her alcohol intake limit had been reached and passed. "He was my son before he married her stank-ass," She slammed an ace of spades to the table, taking her fourth book of the game. She was obviously still fuming over the fact that her daughter in law did not let her participate in preparing Thanksgiving dinner. "Not even a measly sweet potato pie," Michelle's blood boiled.

"Is she supposed to let you into her kitchen when she knows you have a problem with her being white?" Erica, Michelle's partner, spoke over the table as Rhonda, Mrs. Green's partner, cut the suit with a two of spades. Erica had a point and Michelle knew it, rather she chose to admit it or not. "How could you prefer Author's wife over Robin simply because Robin is white? Didn't Author's wife have a drug problem? Didn't he lose everything he had because of her drug problem? Didn't he have to file for bankruptcy because of his wife's addiction?" Erica shook her head. "And Robin has been a super woman to your son and grand son. Your only grand son," Erica had been questioning Michelle's character for the last two years ever since she first heard Michelle speak of her other son's wife, Pat, and how she still favored her simply because of her skin color. Pat has caused her son nothing but trouble, emotionally and financially, all the way to the bitter end. When they finally divorced Author's credit was so bad he couldn't even get a Blockbuster card, let alone an apartment. That's what being married to Pat, the black woman Michelle loved so much, has done for him.

"If I was Robin, I'd put your ass out...Or I wouldn't give your son any until he put your ass out. Either way, you'd be getting your ass out," Mrs. Green added as she pulled the winning suit to her side of the table. 'If I wouldn't have gotten sick, I wouldn't even be in this situation,' Michelle thought as Mrs. Green's words soaked in like water into a sponge. It's only been a year and a half since she'd been forced to move in with her son, and that's only because her CHF (congestive heart failure) had swollen her feet so badly that it hurt her to walk. After learning about his mother's fragile heart, there was no way Bryan was going to allow his mother to live alone. Michelle's arthritis had already earned her monthly disability checks, but CHF was the last straw. Bryan wanted his mother close by, just in case, whether Michelle approved of his wife or not. He figured she'd eventually get over whatever it was bothering her. Michelle felt the same way. Not about getting over it, but about needing to be close to family, just in case. Though she wished Author had enough room for her, at his place. He'd still have that nice three-bedroom house out in L.A. if it weren't for his ex-wife's addiction. The same ex-wife Michelle had advised her son to stand-by. Who knew that standing by someone you loved could cost so much?

"So, have you snagged Ronald yet?" Mrs. Green asked over her fan-spread cards. That question caught Tasha by surprise.

"No, not yet," Standing at Mrs. Green's left, enjoying the game from the sidelines, Tasha said as she watched Rhonda take another winning book. "Right now I really don't think I'm ready to date. I guess I'm just feeling him out...so if, and or when I decide I'm ready to date, and if he's worthy, I'll..."

"Yeah, yeah, yeah...You know you want to feel him up," Rhonda smirked. And just like that Mrs. Green's harmless inquiry went from being squeaky clean to down and dirty.

"When was the last time you had some?" Mrs. Green asked like she was a doctor trying to determine the origin of a STD, straight face and all.

"I had a Mountain Dew about thirty minutes ago," Tasha responded without a bit of embarrassment. She'd gotten use to those

Gary Norman

kinds of questions coming from any one of the group members. Though the questions were usually aimed at someone else.

"You know what I'm talking about, smart ass. When was the last time you got some dick?" Mrs. Green's choice of words reddened Tasha's cheeks.

"When was the last time I got some dick? What kind of people do you associate with when we're not around?" Tasha laughed, hoping to avoid the 'on the spot' question.

"Answer the question, Tasha," Carla added from her seat on the couch some ten feet away from the portable card table, directly across from the basement's floor model television. It was time for the sports segment of the WGN's news at nine. And since both Carla and Michelle were huge Bulls fans, they left the card game for tonight's scores and highlights.

"It's been a few months," Tasha sighed. Why did she say that? Before she knew it her sex life, or the lack there of, was the topic of conversation. It was as if they thought her vagina would close up if she didn't use it regularly. Thank God tomorrow is a workday, that way Tasha was able to dismiss herself without seeming rude.

After arriving home, Tasha went through her nightly routine of checking her messages while preparing for her bath. Surprisingly, the third message was from Ronald. He wanted to know if he could cook her a special dinner tomorrow night to thank her for dropping off his cookware, and to thank her for putting up with his ex-wife's childish behavior. "Call me and let me know if you're okay with it," his message ended. Tasha shouted a joyous Yes, like his voice mail message would actually relay her response.

Scene 48

Today had to be the worse Monday of Mike's life. Not because of the argument he had with Steve that ended with him having to drive his own car to work, with its recently busted tail light and cracked windshield, both adding up to Mike receiving two early morning tickets from the first police officer to notice the infractions. Nor was it because of the wildly thrown punch that landed just below his left eye, which required five stitches to close the gash it left behind (Damn gang fights, but when you're a correctional officer at Cook County Jail, it's part of the job). None of the day's unfortunate incidents could compare to what he'd heard about his loving wife. Then again, after what he'd heard 'loving' might not be the case.

Apparently Jake, Mike's staff sergeant, was downtown the other day, shopping for one of his many girlfriends, when he spotted Amanda talking to 'a brother' for, as he put it, "quite a while". And to make things even more disturbing, it was just the two of them. No Keri. Or at least he didn't see Keri, even though he watched from a safe distance for a few minutes, hoping to see her. Keri never appeared. Jake had hoped to run into Keri because Mike had yet to make good on his promise of hooking the two of them up. So yes, he knew exactly how Keri looked and he didn't see her or anybody that resembled her. Jake, who is black, was no different from any of the other black men that have seen Keri. He wanted her, badly. "She has to be mixed," Jake would say, speaking of her extremely ethnic hips. The same hips he'd seen sliding down a pole at *D`LOS*, in Harvey. "This club is home to the finest sista's in and around the city...So you know this white girl is fine!" Mike had heard Jake describing his next door neighbor to another one of his co-workers on occasions, usually another black guy. This infuriated Mike, having to listen to his black co-workers talk about white women in a sexual manner. Usually this wouldn't bother him, but that wasn't the case today, a day when he's had the misfortune of learning about his wife's new affair with another black man. "Is she fucking another nigger? She has to be, because if she wasn't why didn't she tell me about the old friend she ran into while she was shopping? That's who the guy was, an old friend. He had to be...but ...if he was an old friend she would've told me about their chance meeting, seeing that we know a lot of the same people, if their running into each other was innocent. Maybe they met each other there before going back to his place where they fucked each other's brains out!" As Jake talked about

Keri's hips only a few feet away, Mike's mind juggled past truths, falsehoods and assumptions like a seasoned circus clown.

By the end of the day he could hardly keep his hands from shaking, he was just that upset. He hadn't been this upset since he found out about his wife, who was then his girlfriend, and the transfer black guy who always wore his fraternity colors. To this day Mike hated crimson and cream.

"YOU BITCH!" Mike cursed, pounding the steering wheel as he sat at a red light three blocks from his apartment. Every negative scenario that had ever crossed his mind added to his fury like gas to a flame. He was going to be the butt of private jokes, spread throughout the jail, just like back in college. Even though Jake didn't seem to be insinuating anything about Amanda being unfaithful, not seriously, that's how Mike took it. He had already gone through this, dealing with her infidelity. He could add. Two plus two equaled his wife fucking another nigger. "Who knows what she let him do to her," his mind raced through an endless number of possibilities, just like years ago, stopping at the one thing she's never allowed him to do. "If she can let a nigger do it, she's gonna let me do it too," is what his damaged ego whispered into his ear, prompting him to purchase a tube of k-y jelly before going home.

By the time he had reached his apartment his anger was immeasurable. Amanda had already been tried and convicted. All that remained was the administering of the punishment, which would be something severe. His anger would make sure of that. He'd replayed the same scene, in his mind, all day. A scene in which Amanda was being satisfied by a name-less, faceless black man. A black man that satisfied his wife in ways she wouldn't even allow him to discuss, let alone try. That was enough to drive a man insane.

"How could you?" He uttered just loud enough for his wife to hear, the vein in his neck throbbing, his palms sweating.

Startled, Amanda turned to face him. She immediately noticed the stitches under his eye. "What happened?" she asked, tenderly taking his face in her hands so that she could get a closer look at his battle wounds.

"Breaking up a fight," He replied, pulling his head away from her hands. The same hands she probably used to arouse a nigger, his ego cursed so loud his ears rang.

"What's the matter?" A deafening silence blared after her question. He had swore after their last confrontation that he would never raise his belt towards her again, but the rage he felt at this moment was unlike the mere anger that had provoked previous assaults. His rage inched closer to extreme hatred. A hatred for what she'd done. For who she'd done it with. Her lying...her...SLAP---His near hatred pushed him over the edge, causing him to slam his left hand into her face, knocking her to the floor before he could think to put it back down to his side. "Get up, you unfaithful bitch!" He hissed through clinched teeth, standing over her with his fist balled so tight he could turn coal into diamond.

"Mike please! Please stop!" Amanda cried, crawling underneath the kitchen table, where its protective shelter provided a brief moment of safety.

"What's his name?!" Mike demanded before heaving the small wooden table on its side.

"Who are you talking about?" She cried, blood starting to seep from her lip, her eyes still seeing flashes of light as she scampered into the nearest corner, her heart beating so fast it felt like it would burst out of her chest. She had never seen Mike this way, his eyes darting back and forth, the vein in his neck visible.

"You know who the fuck I'm talking about!" He began to unbuckle his belt. "The guy you're fucking!"

"I'm not fucking anybody else!" She cried, her back pressed into the corner next to the refrigerator.

"You're lying!" He shouted, drawing his belt through the loops around his waist.

"Please listen to me," Amanda pleaded, rising to her feet, hoping that she would be able to get through to him before he started swinging. "You know I've been faithful to you. You know I haven't been seeing anybody else. Please, just think for a minute. When would I have time to do something like that?" She attempted to reason, tears running down her face, her heart pounding so hard that it felt like an alien was trying to escape. "We're together all the time. And when I'm not here, you know where I am, and you know who I'm with," Trembling with fear, she held her hands out in front of her body, her palms facing him, as if wordlessly pleading with him to stop.

"Who was that guy you were with on Saturday?"

"What guy? I was shopping with Keri. You said I could go, remember?"

"The guy Jake saw you talking to in one of those stores downtown," He said, raising his belt into a ready to strike position.

Amanda's facial expression said it all. Now she knew what this was about, which meant she'd be able to clear up this misunderstanding. She hoped.

Gary Norman

"He was just an old friend from college. He and his wife..." Before she could continue, Mike slammed his belt against her shoulder. By admitting that she had in fact talked to some guy, she had also admitted her guilt. If their meeting were totally innocent she would've mentioned running into him on Saturday, not today.

"Lying Bitch! Lying Bitch! Lying Bitch!" he screamed each time his belt struck her fleeing body.

"Come here!" Running behind her, grabbing her by the back of her neck, bringing her forward progress to a violent halt, he spat angrily before pulling her ear close to his mouth. "You know what happens when you're disobedient, don't you?" His voice was half crazed, his eyes red, his grip tight as a python's hold on a small mammal.

"Please listen?" her voice trembled. "I'm not lying. Please..."

"No!" He angrily interrupted. "Now get in the room and take off your clothes," He ordered, shoving her neck forward then watching her somberly walk into their bedroom. He suddenly realized he had left the k-y jelly in the car. "Damn!"

Scene 49

On this day, there will be no excuses made for her husband's abuse. Licking her wounds and going with her day wasn't an option, not on this day, the day after a physical attack like none before, this one being the absolute worse. Not only did he strike her with his bare hand, which is something he'd never done before, but he also violated her, anally. "If you can let niggers do it, you're not gonna keep me from doing it!" were Mike's exact words before he forced his k-y jelly coated penis into a place she'd never allowed anyone to penetrate.

Last night's sexual assault forced her to finally realize that her husband wasn't going to change, at least not for the better. The assault was the exclamation point at the end of a relationship that had been doomed from the start. Last night was the first time she'd actually feared for her life, the previous times felt more like a stern parent disciplining a misbehaving child, with Mike being the parent and Amanda being the child. And whether wrong or right she came to accept his brand of discipline because, just as a punished child knows his/her parents wouldn't do anything to put their life in any real danger, she knew Mike wouldn't intentionally harm her. She knew that she was to blame for his behavior, so a spanking every now and then didn't mean he didn't love her. That's how she felt until last night's beating and sexual assault, when, instead of seeing anger in his drunken eyes, she saw hatred in his extremely sober eyes. He hadn't had a single drop of alcohol, yet he assaulted her like he'd never done before. The welts left behind by Mike's thick leather belt bled. Her lip bled. Her ass bled. He was relentless. The entire ordeal was so far from the normal encounter that at one point fear had completely taken her voice away. She couldn't scream. She couldn't plead. All she could do was cry, soundlessly, as Mike humped away at her rear-end, stopping once his fluids were spent, starting once more when the rigidness returned.

"I swear I didn't cheat on you," Amanda tearfully sobbed after his second go at her rear. At that point he was through with his sexual assault and was leading her to the door by her neck, where he put her nakedness out into the hallway. She stood on the outside of her apartment door for fifteen minutes, screaming to be let back inside. At least three other tenants saw her standing naked, crying and bleeding outside of her apartment. Two of them called the police.

"No sir...there's nothing going on here," Having been allowed back into her apartment two minutes before last night's visit from the boys in blue, Amanda stood in her living room wearing a bathrobe, covering all of her bruises, all except for one. "What happened to your lip?" The taller of the two officers asked as his partner talked to Mike in the kitchen, not even twenty feet away.

"I was wrestling with my husband...you know ...playing around and..."

"Look lady," The officer interrupted. "I've seen this a million times. I know what's going on here, but I can't do shit about it unless you're willing to press charges. But I'm sure you already know that, right?" He asked sympathetically, adding something special to last night's encounter, something that made Amanda accept the truth about her marriage. She nodded. "So what's it gonna be? You're either going to continue getting your ass whipped, or you're going to stand up for yourself. It's your choice," Tired of seeing women allow their mates to continue to abuse them, he cursed, his anger obviously getting the best of him.

With that said, Amanda took a deep breath and glanced over at her husband, who looked to be getting more agitated by the minute. With tears threatening to overtake the borders of her eyelids, she made the biggest decision of her life. "I'm going to press charges," Her mouth proclaimed before her heart could intervene.

Mike exploded when the officer told him he was under-arrest and needed to put his hands behind his back. "You bitch!" Mike cursed before his struggling ended with him being slammed to the kitchen floor, all the while his eyes were glued on his wife, burning a hole through her like a torch and sheet metal. "Tell him I didn't do shit! Do you hear me!" he ranted as he was lifted off the floor and led to the front door.

"Step back, ma'am," The taller officer ordered before leading Mike through the living room. He had hoped Mike's hostility would lessen when he figured his wife was out of his reach. It didn't. As they passed Amanda, the two officers sandwiching Mike between the both of them, his hands handcuffed behind his back, Mike spit in Amanda's face. He definitely paid the price for that move. The officers slammed him to the floor, making it look like Mike's slight struggle caused them to lose their balance and fall on top of him. Hard! They then snatched him up from the floor and, after suggesting that Amanda move further back, continued on out the front door.

From her bedroom window Amanda watched the officers place Mike in the back seat of their patrol car then drive away. It was at that point that she began packing her things, crying as she packed. Packing to go where, she didn't know, but she did know that she

Pink October.doc

couldn't be there when he got back. But where could she go that Mike wouldn't think to look? Where?

"Girl, are you all right?" Keri asked as she hesitantly peeped from behind the door, into Amanda's room. She was last night's lifesaver, just as a true friend should be.

Scene 50

Standing in front of her bedroom's full-length mirror, Tasha, preparing for tonight's dinner with Ronald, turned her nose up at the seventh dress she's tried on in the last twenty minutes. This one, a red strapless number that paid homage to her every curve, needed the right shoes to complete the ensemble. The first three dresses, which were all black, weren't new enough, even though each one had been purchased no later than five months earlier and had been worn a total of two times between the three of them. The last three dresses she's worn one time or another during her relationship with that loser Kevin. Those were definitely going back into the closet, if not the morning trash.

"I guess it's the black one," Tasha gave the second dress a favorable nod. This one, a black form fitting dress with spaghetti straps, was the kind of dress Tracey had suggested she'd wear. "Something that'll make his mouth water, and his dick hard," were Tracey's exact words while she and Tasha talked over coffee and doughnuts before arriving to work. "And make sure you spray something sweet smelling down there," Tracey winked, motioning towards her own crotch. "Just in case he has room for dessert," She smiled.

Carla wasn't as subtle, suggesting freaky things like crotch-less panties and/or edible underwear.

"The more I talk to you, the more I realize you're probably the biggest freak I know."

"Not just a freak, but a Latin freak."

"What's the difference?"

"We're much hotter," Carla said, adding her usually undetectable accent for emphasis. "And don't use any of those feminine sprays. That stuff takes away from a woman's natural scent, which drives men wild."

"Oh, does it?"

"Just ask my ex-husband."

"You and your ex-husband are nasty," Tasha laughed to herself, thinking back to her earlier phone conversation with Carla while she modeled tonight's chosen dress for her mirror. That was the first time she'd heard Carla speak about her ex-husband, other than the fact that she had one.

"Now that the dress is picked out, what kind of shoes should I wear?" Tasha stood barefoot in front of her closet, wiggling her pedicured toes. But this decision wouldn't take as long to make as deciding on the dress did. After a quick twenty-five minutes, Tasha finally decided on the black boots with the three-inch heel. The boots went with her dress as well as her Coach bag.

With those major decisions out of the way, Tasha could now focus on her hair before getting into the tub. Since she didn't have time to squeeze a trip to the salon into her schedule, she decided to pin her hair up, allowing her face to be the absolute center of attention. Not only that, the style was simple.

After her bath she sat at her vanity table going over everything from lipstick to finger and toe nail polish. This was her first date with Ronald, so of course she wanted to impress. She was as giddy as a teenage girl on her prom night, spending her entire day either thinking about her plans for the evening or talking about her plans. Needless to say, concentrating during this morning's special meeting with teachers and staff wasn't easy. Her mind, for the first time since being diagnosed with cancer, was completely occupied with thoughts of having a wonderful evening with a member of the opposite sex. She felt like the pre-cancer Tasha, before self-breast exams every morning, noon, and night were a top priority. She didn't wake up thinking about whether or not the cancer would return, not this morning. Today was all about being excited. Happy. Anxious. Beginning anew. This was the first man, besides Kevin, she'd been out with in years so she planned on leaving a memorable impression.

"He won't know what hit 'em," She winked at her reflection before exiting her room, leaving her adoring mirror in darkness.

-------------   ---------------------   ---------------------------

"I'm glad you made it," Ronald spoke loud enough, from the kitchen, so that Tasha could hear every word.

"I'm glad you invited me," Sitting on the living room sofa, taking in the room's ambiance, Tasha responded with the same heightened volume. The fire dancing in the fireplace made the room cozier.

"Here you go," Wearing a dark colored blazer and slacks, with a light colored shirt, Ronald appeared from the kitchen with the glass of white wine Tasha had requested. "Dinner will be ready, shortly. I hope you're into trying new things, because I've prepared something special for tonight," He said, handing her the glass before taking a seat next to her.

"So, you're saying this is a special night?" Tasha asked flirtatiously, seducing him with her eyes as she took her first sip.

"It will be," He smiled, exposing those deep dimples.

'God, I hope so,' Tasha's body screamed, yet her mouth released a more appropriate, "And where's Tara on this special night?"

"She's at her mother's...And she should be in bed right now," He glanced at his watch, verifying that it was in fact pass Tara's bed time.

Damn, that means Tamara knows I'm here. Damn! Tasha had to take a gulp of wine on that thought.

"So that's your plan. Get the house all to yourself so you can get me drunk and take advantage of me."

"I need to get you drunk in order to take advantage of you?" Ronald returned her flirtatious serve with a confident 'I wouldn't need the alcohol' return.

"I think you need to check on dinner," Tasha said, hoping to conceal the fact that she was actually blushing.

"But I'm just getting comfortable," He jokingly protested before rising to his feet. "Then again, we have more than enough time to get better acquainted. I mean, the night is still young," He smiled before heading back into the kitchen.

"Calm down, girl," Tasha said to herself after almost licking her lips as she watched Ronald leave the room. "I'm going to take this real slow," she nodded as if she could actually convince her over-heated hormones to cool down a bit.

-------   -----------------------------   --------------------------

After a wonderfully prepared meal, consisting of grilled marlin with spicy papaya vinaigrette, Tasha and Ronald moved from the romantically set kitchen table to the living room where they shared the only dessert capable of capping off an evening as perfect as this one. A banana split. Carla told Ronald about Tasha's fondness for banana splits, information he would no doubt use to his advantage.

"So, you've been asking about me?" Tasha asked, even though the answer was obvious. Somebody had to tell him the flavors of ice cream and the kinds of toppings she preferred with her banana split, he didn't just guess.

"I did ask Carla if she knew what you'd like for dessert," was all he'd admit to even though he'd been asking about Tasha ever since he happened to run into her at Mrs. Green's house.

"And that's all you asked?" Tasha smiled before lifting a spoonful of her dessert to her mouth.

"That's all," He lied and she knew it. He wanted her just as bad as she wanted him, if not more.

It's been two years since he'd last been with a woman sexually. And he hid his frustration well. He did this by strategically dividing his time between his daughter and his job so that his need for female companionship wouldn't become unbearable. On those rare days when he was not working and Tara was at her mother's, instead of seeking out the opposite sex for a little one on one, he'd read a book or masturbate or do yard work or prepare delectable entrees for Mrs. Green and her support group. Preparing meals for Mrs. Green's support group is something he's enjoyed doing ever since the day he found out a woman in his, then, neighborhood, who was also a breast cancer survivor, was doing something to help other women to better deal with life after being diagnosed. He just had to be a part of something so meaningful and important to a woman's mental and physical health. This was his way of not only donating his time to a worthy cause, but a way for him to deal with the fact that he was both lonely and sexually frustrated. At times he felt like he would burst. "Now I know how people in prison feel," Ronald once joked with one of the chefs working under him at Lynda's, the downtown restaurant that's been his place of employment for over ten years. But all of that was about to change. Over dessert their conversation became more and more intimate, starting a sensual blaze within the both of them. The look in both of their eyes screamed for fulfillment, and they both heard it loud and clear.

As the distance between them shortened, their hearts beating as if they had run a marathon, their eyes closed in preparation for their first kiss.

"RONALD! RONALD!" A woman screamed frantically from Ronald's front porch, destroying the mood with her repeated pressing of the doorbell. "Tamara called! It's Tara!" The woman added, knowing that if Ronald were within hearing distance he'd respond A.S.A.P. A perfect moment ruined in the blink of an eye.

Gary Norman

Scene 51

"Not even a cold shower works as fast as a piece of butter scotch candy," Tasha laughed a disbelieving laugh as she drove along I-57, heading home after dropping Ronald off at University Hospital, in University Park. Tamara would have to take him home because he needed to know what happened, and how.

Tara was fine, but the experience frightened her. She was playing with Pepper, her mother's German Shepherd, when she accidentally swallowed a piece of butter scotch candy, cutting off her oxygen supply long enough to scare the hell out of her and her mother. Thank God Tamara, who was upstairs at the time, after noticing the sudden absence of Tara's laughter, decided to check on her when she did. The fear she must've felt at the moment when she saw her daughter frantically gasping for air, Tasha couldn't even imagine. It must've been the scariest moment of her life, watching her own daughter's life pass before her eyes. The happiest moment coming when she, using the Heimlich maneuver she'd learned back in college while volunteering at a local hospital as a part of her sorority's pledge period, dislodged the candy, allowing her child to take another breath.

"Where in the hell are you going in such a hurry?" After positively identifying the 600Benz that had just passed her doing about 100mph as Rhonda's, Tasha spoke as if Rhonda could actually hear.

Rhonda's mission was clear. She was going to find out if Harry was actually held up by a late meeting, or was he lying? Two board meetings in the last five days didn't sit too well with her. 'Alibi board meetings' is what she called them when she was his mistress. But now that she's his wife they're supposed to be board meetings, and nothing more, yet they still feel like those same old board meetings from years ago. And this is not just paranoia like Erica tries to describe them as being, even though she knows how Rhonda started off as Harry's "pussy on the side." Rhonda has always known about Harry's fondness for big breasted, younger women, which was fine when she was sporting those leaking breasts. Back then she was one of the "big breasted" women her husband had eyes for. But now she's, as she puts it when she's one on one with Erica, "returned to being among the average women since having her faulty silicone breast removed." Now she has to go that extra mile to keep her husband satisfied, even if it means engaging in fantasy role playing, which she hates. If their personal home video collection ever found its

Pink October.doc   153

way to the Internet, lets just say children all over the world would no longer participate in the tradition of sitting on Santa's lap.

Cathy, Harry's first wife, was too wise to put up with his shit, not when she didn't have to. A divorce meant that a sizable piece of Harry's hard-earned fortune would belong to her, and she earned every dime after putting up with his numerous affairs. After Cathy's lawyer produced those pictures of Rhonda and Harry at a supposedly secluded villa somewhere in the Florida Keys, Harry's lawyer felt it would be best that Harry settle, thus making Cathy one rich and happy woman. Now it was Rhonda's turn to go through what she'd put Cathy through. Now she was the wife losing sleep because her gut told her that her loving husband was cheating.

Her tears blurred her vision as she drove back to her Olympia Fields home expecting to walk into an empty house. The security guard at the front desk wouldn't let her enter the building, but Rhonda knew he wasn't there, and he wouldn't be home either. And she was right; he hadn't made it home and probably wouldn't be in until late. But when he did make it home you better believe he will have his lie straight, a good lie and a very expensive gift. The gift-giving thing works every time, after he's fucked up. At least that's the impression Rhonda gives. Tonight she'll cry herself to sleep, but first she'll trash the foyer, guaranteeing her a wake up call as soon as Harry gets home, no matter what time he gets in.

Tasha, on the other hand, with her hair still damp from her shower, curled up on her couch with a bowl of rainbow sherbet and the nine o'clock news. Bush won the election even though Gore had more votes. I guess your vote doesn't count when you're black and from Florida.

Disappointed in the entire election process, Tasha turned off the television then headed for bed, stopping in the kitchen to grab her cell phone. Mom called. Tracey called. And Ronald called, wanting to know if Tasha would like to join him this coming weekend for some last minute Christmas shopping.

"Yes I would, Mr. Ronald," Tasha chimed as if she were a teenager that had just been asked to the senior prom by the most popular guy in school.

As she lay in bed thinking back to the wonderful evening she spent with Ronald, she found herself twirling a lock of her hair around her pointing finger. The same way Kevin used to do when they'd lie in bed talking after a session of good 'hair pullin', ass-slappin'' sex. How they would lie there in each other's arms, talking until one of them fell asleep. And just like that, thoughts of Kevin paraded through her head, the good and bad thoughts. He used to love playing in her hair and she used to love it when he'd play in it. But that was then, now she was interested in somebody else. Somebody different. Something needed to be changed so that she'd finally be able to rid herself of Kevin. And she knew just what that something was.

Scene 52

After re-scheduling her afternoon physical therapy session for Thursday, Erica spent this Wednesday afternoon consoling her dearest friend. Rhonda was a total mess, though that was only apparent after Erica told the girls to go play in the basement while mommy talked to auntie Rhonda.

No matter how bad Rhonda feels she can't help but smile when she sees Erica's little girls, Kim, Teri and Jessica; The two oldest were out of school enjoying their Christmas break. Just hearing their squeaky voices saying, "Hi auntie," always brought a smile to her face. And she'd always have something for them. Candy, money, toys. You name it and Rhonda had it for them. It was as if the girls were hers as well as Erica's. But they weren't hers, she couldn't dream of being so lucky. She didn't even have a husband as good as Carl, so being lucky enough to have kids as bright as Erica's three bundles of joy was out of the question. Carl was a good man, while Harry was the exact opposite. And it's been that way for quite some time now, but Rhonda just refused to accept the obvious. "I was upstairs in a meeting and I told the security guard not to disturb me for any reason," Harry said with a straight face after waking Rhonda up in the middle of the night in order to confront her about the broken vase and flowers cluttering the foyer floor. The smile on his face told the real truth, whether or not Rhonda chose to listen was another story.

"If you know he's lying, and has been lying for some time now, why don't you leave him?" Erica suggested, handing Rhonda a box of Kleenex. "You're a beautiful woman, you don't have to put up with his shit. Look at Cathy. You can do the same thing," Erica offered Cathy's situation as a possible solution. Hitting Harry in his pockets sounded like a plan to Erica. But, as always, Rhonda eventually found a way to make things seem not as bad as she'd led Erica to believe. "I'm probably just overreacting about nothing," She tried to get Erica to see something she herself didn't see. "Maybe he was there. Maybe this is just a huge misunderstanding...and I'd hate to initiate divorce proceedings over a misunderstanding," Rhonda added, patting her tears away with a Kleenex.

On the inside Erica was disgusted. Rhonda looked so pitiful; crying over Harry's no good ass like he was actually worth a single tear. Rhonda knew he wasn't, and so did Erica. But what could Erica do? Rhonda was the only person who could get Rhonda to see that she'd be better off without Harry. Erica was powerless when it came to getting Rhonda to see that she deserved, and could do much better than what she had. All Erica could do was listen because her suggestions about leaving Harry would always fall on deaf ears. Rhonda's mind has always been made up when it came to her marriage. Leaving Harry was out of the question. Not when she loves the man. Erica thought of it as fear, not love. Fear of starting over, especially with her fortieth birthday was right around the corner. Fear of starting over is something that most people can relate to. Add that to the fact that she's getting older and Erica could almost understand her point.

"It's too late in life for me to even consider starting over," Rhonda wore this excuse like a badge. "When you truly love someone you don't just up and leave when things start to look a little shaky, do you?"

"When that shaking starts to feel more like an earth quake, hell yeah!" Erica responded with the kind of laugh meant to lighten the mood.

Rhonda absorbed those words like she'd actually considered leaving her husband. Erica knew different.

"It's not as bad as an earth quake," Rhonda smiled for the first time since the kids left to go play in the basement. She just needed Erica to listen, not give advice. In her eyes, her marriage was worth fixing and Erica knew that she felt that way. That's why she never pushed Rhonda too hard about leaving her husband. "When she feels like she's had enough, she'll leave," is how Erica had come to view her friend's problem-filled marriage. 'The coffee was strong, but Rhonda just couldn't bring herself to smell it,' Erica thought as she listened to Rhonda go on and on about how this was probably a misunderstanding. She wanted to scream.

Scene 53

With her ear pressed against Keri's front door, Amanda listened for Mike's afternoon departure for work. For the moment, Keri's apartment had to be the absolute safest place for Amanda to be. Mike would never think to look for her here, not right across the hall. Yesterday he asked Keri if she might know where Amanda could've gone, but he didn't expect his wife to be hiding right across the hall. That's why Amanda's been able to disappear for two days without as much as a sighting. And if this were a perfect world, he'd never see her again. She'd sever her ties by simply snapping her fingers. But this wasn't a perfect world. And separating from her husband will bring stress and an even greater financial burden into her life, both of which she could do without.

As she listened to Mike exiting the apartment, Keri's words echoed through her mind like a scream at the Grand Canyon. "Girl, fuck him…It'll hurt for a little while if you leave now…but if you stay it'll hurt a whole lot longer," Keri drove her point deep into Amanda's psyche before taking her afternoon shower. Keri was too tired to shower when she came home last night so she settled for an afternoon shower, which is actually her normal routine.

Feeling more relaxed now that she knew, for sure, that Mike had left for work, Amanda took the remote from the coffee table then turned on Keri's fifty-five inch television. Then, still in pain from the whipping and sodomy she endured a few days earlier, she lowered herself down onto the couch as easily as she could, like a new mother suffering from a severe case of hemorrhoids would. She stared emotionlessly at The Young and the Restless while the painful truth pounded in her head like native drums. Your marriage is over, now what?

"If you're really serious about leaving, then the first thing you need to do is file for divorce. And I know a really good lawyer who'll take you as a client for free…but you'll have to pay court costs," Still damp from her shower, Keri grinned that 'girl my sugar daddy takes care of me' grin.

As much as Amanda would've loved to just forget about this entire incident, she couldn't. She knew that Keri was right, and had been for quite sometime. There needed to be closure, an overdo ending to a marriage that had never truly felt like one. Amanda's excuses for Mike's behavior no longer made up for what he'd done. True, she cheated once. And even though she had no regrets, she was genuinely sorry about the pain she caused Mike. He didn't deserve it. But then again, neither did she.

Scene 54

At 6pm on Friday evening the butterflies in Tasha's stomach were in full flutter. She had made the decision a few days ago to chop off her beautiful locks, and today was the day of her scheduled hair appointment.

The salon, We Care Salon and Spa, on Michigan Ave., was packed with its usual assortment of professional women, trophy wives, girlfriend's of local drug dealers, and regular hard working nine to five women. Tasha has become familiar with a lot of the women at the salon since she first visited over a year and a half ago, after Tracey suggested the place. And their work, along with the salon's ambiance, was just as Tracey had described, "soothing".

"What's up, Tasha," Shawnda, a petite and very expensively dressed sister spoke in passing.

"Hey girl," Politely stepping aside, allowing her enough room to exit the salon, Tasha turned and exchanged a brief smile before entering the salon.

"Giving good head obviously has its rewards," Shawnda hadn't even reached her new man's waiting Range Rover and already Paris, the unwed mistress of a small time drug dealer, spoke with pure jealousy to an audience of two.

"Hey, Paris," Tasha said, smiling a 'girl you need to quit' kind of smile, shaking her head as she hung her coat on the rack designated for Ivy's clients only.

As she walked towards Ivy's area of the salon, three chairs down the aisle, on the other side of the gray partitions, she heard Paris say, "I bet he's fuckin' around."

"Probably with somebody like your no-good ass," Tasha huffed to herself as she walked up on Ivy's empty chair.

"She's in the back, on the phone as usual. She told me to tell you she'll be with you in a minute," Bee, the six month pregnant, light skinned beauty who's station is next to Ivy's, looked up from the head she was doing long enough to relay the message. "I haven't seen you in a minute. Where've you been hiding?" Bee asked, her attention back on the woman's head.

"I've been extremely busy over the last few weeks, but, believe me, I really missed you guys. Can't you tell by looking at me?" Tasha smiled, motioning to her head with both hands. There was no way she was going to tell any of them the real reason behind her hiatus. Not that she was ashamed, she just didn't want any special treatment because of her recent bout with cancer. Nor did she want to be the object of their sympathy. She could also do without the questions that were sure to follow. "When did you find out?" "What did you do when you found out?" "Did the radiation make you sick?"

"I should definitely keep this to myself," Tasha thought as she watched one of the salon's most popular, and outrageously overbooked, stylist work his magic.

It was another fifteen minutes before Ivy emerged from the back room, but when she did the shocked look on Tasha's face was as apparent as the sun in the sky. Ivy entered the room carrying a medium size chocolate cake with a single candle in the center.

"What's all this?" Bemused, Tasha asked.

"It's to celebrate your being cancer-free," Ivy smiled, bending at the waist so that Tasha could blow out the candle.

"How did....."

"This is a salon, that's how we knew," Ivy cut Tasha off before she could finish that ridiculous question. "Glad to have you back," Was all Tasha needed to hear. And that's all Ivy was going to share about how she found out.

Scene 55

Moving from Keri's apartment to Wanda's Oak Park apartment was the smartest thing Amanda had done since deciding to leave her husband. Mike's work hours allowed her to get out of their building without having to worry about a confrontation, physical or verbal. But how long can she expect to stay at Wanda's without becoming a burden? Especially when she's unable to contribute financially. "Girl, don't be silly...you can stay here as long as it takes for you to get yourself together," Wanda insisted as she rearranged her things so that Amanda could have drawer space. "You never know how long these things will drag on, so I figured drawer space would be a lot better than living out of your duffel bag," She shrugged before showing Amanda where she could store her cosmetics.

Wanda and Amanda met at Keri's apartment six months ago during an all girls night of cards and drinking. She and Amanda were teamed against Keri and Sam, and, even though they suspected that Sam and Keri had won two hands by cheating, she and Amanda still walked away with the night's winnings. The winnings usually consisted of the winners not having to chip in on whatever they chose to drink or eat that night, making the game that much more interesting.

"Where do you dance?" Wanda sprang the question in between gloating over their winnings, six months ago. "With that kind of beauty, you'd break the bank if you were a dancer," She replied after learning that Amanda wasn't a dancer.

"With or without clothes?" Amanda had jokingly responded to her compliment. And coming from Wanda, she could only take it as a compliment. Especially since it came from a woman as beautiful as Wanda, who didn't have the "in your face" Pamela Anderson Lee-kind of beauty, but more of a subtle 'Sandra Bullock' kind of beauty that screams wholesome. She has shoulder length, sandy blonde hair, which she kept permed, blue eyes, and a small pointy nose, all topping her petite, yet curvaceous, five foot three inch one hundred thirty pound frame. And to top it off, she was just as sweet as she looked wholesome. You wouldn't guess, in a million years, that she was a stripper, unlike the strippers you'd see on Jenny Jones in dire need of a make over. That's not the kind of person Wanda wanted people to see, which is why she dressed tastefully when away from the club, just like Keri. Yet her tastes were a tad-bit expensive, just like Keri. This explained why both women lived in apartments opposed to owning their own homes. If it weren't for their extravagant spending on clothes, shoes, men, partying, and men, they could have purchased homes years ago. Let Keri tell it, she's outlived that stage after her first year of dancing. "I don't spend money on men anymore. They spend it on me." She'd boast. "But that's my only vice," is how Wanda defended her decision to spoil her men. "No drugs, alcohol or gambling. I just fall in love too fast, and spoil whomever I'm with," Wanda spoke as if she were proud of being the same sucker Amanda has been for the last few years, up until now. Her hell-ride was over. Now it was time for Amanda to heal, mentally as well as physically. "Thank God for Wanda," Amanda thought.

Pink October.doc

Scene 56

When Tanya opened her front door then stepped aside so that Tasha could enter, she couldn't tell that a change in her daughter's appearance had taken place. But when Tasha stepped into the foyer and removed her thick, beret styled hat, Tanya's mouth fell to the floor in utter surprise.

"So...what do you think?"

"It looks really nice on you," Tanya answered. The look on her face said she was still in awe over her daughter's Tamron Hall/Halle Berry styled cut. "But why?" She asked the question Tasha was sure to hear over a million times.

"It's a new look to go with the new me," Tasha smiled, slowly turning around so that her mother could see her new cut from every angle.

"Your father has to see this," Tanya shook her head before taking Tasha's hand and leading her into the den where William was relaxing in front of the television. He was enjoying an episode of Soul Food, which he had Tanya record for him over a year ago, while he was at the hospital. He saw this episode over twenty times, but you couldn't tell that by the way his eyes were glued to the screen.

"Baby, guess who's here?" Tanya announced before motioning for Tasha to step from behind his comfortable recliner and into view.

The smile gracing her father's face was reminiscent of a famous painting. He loved it, just like she knew he would. He still viewed her as his little girl, so she could stand in front of him with a pink mohawk and he'd still love it.

"Thanks daddy," Tasha leaned over and kissed his cheek before taking a seat on the couch, across from the fifty-five inch television. Tanya went to the kitchen to re-heat a plate of tonight's quick and easy dinner, Sloppy Joe and French fries.

"You look so different with your hair short." "Are you going to let it grow out again?" "Has anybody else seen your new look?" "If so, what did they say?" Tanya was so taken by her daughter's new look that William jokingly asked her to "let his little girl eat before talking her ears off."

"She can listen and eat at the same time, smart ass," Tanya responded, playfully rolling her eyes then kissing her husband's forehead before taking a seat on the couch, next to her daughter.

Tasha laughed as she dipped three French fries into the ketchup her mother had placed on the edge of her plate, washing them down with an ice-cold Mountain Dew. "Leave my daddy alone," She twisted her face in the silliest way. Both Tanya and William laughed.

Later that night, while standing in her own kitchen, Tasha still found herself laughing at her mother's sarcastic remark about her being able to listen and talk at the same time. "Ma's crazy," She said to herself as she stood in front of her wide open freezer door, spooning sherbet into her mouth. After satisfying her taste for something sweet, she headed upstairs to prepare her bath and listen to her voice mail messages. There was only one message, and that message was from Ronald. "I hope you remembered our date tomorrow. Or is this your way of telling me you've changed your mind. You don't have to start screening your calls," He couldn't keep himself from laughing after saying that. Tasha's heart smiled at the sound of his laughter. "I'm just kidding…I'll be out there at seven…Well, good night," He hung up.

Yeah, she remembered. In fact she's been thinking about their date since deciding to cut her hair. And when the final snip of her stylist's scissors sent the last of her locks floating to the floor, Ronald was the first person to pop into her mind. He would see her new 'do before any other non-family member. That's only because she'll meet with him tomorrow for some last minute Christmas shopping. But, in a way, she wanted him to be the first non-family member to critique her new 'do. She wanted a "non-related" man's opinion.

After wrapping her head in her DST bandanna, and another self-breast exam (number fifteen for the day), saying her prayers, then giving herself another self-breast exam, Tasha climbed into bed, lulling herself to sleep with thoughts of her up and coming date. This time she'll do better with containing her passion, the same passion that would've gotten her into trouble if it weren't for Tara's candy accident.

"Slow and easy," Tasha reminded herself, tssk, tssk, tssking as she thought back to the previous time they were alone.

Scene 57

Prior to stepping out of her car, Tasha tilted her rear-view mirror so that she could take one last glance at herself before heading up Ronald's walkway (she took that same "last glance" at the gas station around her house, at the red light on 95th and Stony Island and again at the light on 95th and Jeffery). The hat she wore sat perfectly atop her head, as to not reveal the secret underneath.

"Come in while I grab my coat and scarf," Ronald greeted her at his front door with a quick, yet warm kiss on the cheek before stepping into the living room where he retrieved his leather jacket, gloves and scarf from the arm of his couch. "I'm ready," he said, fastening his jacket as he stepped back into the foyer.

With Tasha leading the way back out into the brisk air on this Saturday evening, Ronald made sure his front door was locked before taking notice of Tasha's sexy strut. The way she seemed to glide across the pavement reminded him of a Spike Lee film.

Once she and Ronald were in her car, Tasha let the heat circulate before she took off her hat, revealing her new 'do in one simple motion.

"So what do you think?" Tasha asked, turning her head to the left then to the right, allowing Ronald full view of the sides as well as the back. Her heart pounded. She hoped he'd like it, though she wouldn't care if he didn't. Well, yes she would.

"I think you look damn good," Ronald answered her question, nodding approvingly as he readjusted the car's automatic seat belt across his torso. Her hairdo reminded him of a recent picture he'd seen of that news anchor with the short hair, the sister. But he had enough sense to keep that to himself. Some women didn't appreciate being likened to another woman, especially when it comes to their new look. But then again, being likened to a woman as fine as the sister on TV could be considered a compliment by some. Ronald wasn't going to take that chance.

"Thank you," Tasha smiled as she pulled away from the curb. "I told my hairdresser what I wanted and crossed my fingers."

"And she did a great job...but you do know that by cutting your hair you may have lost an admirer."

"Is that so?" The uneasiness in her voice was evident. 'Was he saying that since my hair is short he no longer finds me attractive? Is that what he just said to me? Because if that's what he's saying he can kiss my...'

"Before you go off on me, I love your new look," Sensing Tasha had taken his statement the wrong way, Ronald interrupted Tasha's train of thought before she could turn a sharp witted thought into a phrase. "But Tara might not feel the same way. She really liked your long hair, now I don't know what she'll think…You do know that she thinks girls aren't supposed to cut their hair…Maybe you should wear a wig the next time you come over," They both laughed at the thought.

Tasha's new look dominated their conversation during the remainder of the ride into downtown. Ronald admired her for having the strength to go through with such an extreme change, especially going from long to short hair. He knew plenty of women with short hair who spent small fortunes on weaves, wigs, and extensions for the temporary illusion of having long hair. He didn't know many women with naturally long hair who desired the short look.

"So you're saying I'm unique?" She smiled as she handed the State St. parking lot attendant her keys.

"Absolutely," Ronald answered after playfully running his eyes over the entire length of her body, starting at her head then scrolling down to her feet.

"I think we better get to our shopping," Tasha turned and walked off in order to conceal the fact that he had made her smile.

"That's how you're gonna play a brother? Just leave me standing here cold and alone. That's why you dropped your ticket."

"Where?" Tasha stopped and scanned her immediate area while at the same time rummaging through her purse for that ticket. "I didn't drop my ticket," She said after locating the ticket in a side compartment on the inner wall of her Coach bag.

"Now it's your turn to play catch-up," He nudged her with his elbow as he passed, leaving her behind just as she had done to him moments ago.

After an unbelievably pleasant evening, during which time Tasha learned that Ronald not only donates to their group but he's also a mentor to inner city kids through the city's 'Big Brothers and Sisters' program, Tasha drove over to the downtown bookstore Mrs. Green had told her about. Karen Lewis, who, along with her late-husband, James, was a one-time member of Mrs. Green's Kitchen, owned the bookstore. Their involvement with the group was unique because neither of them had breast cancer, or any other form of cancer. James Lewis was HIV positive. A simple affair cost him his life, yet, through the grace of God, his wife and child were spared.

"Will there be anything else, ma'am?" The petite, dark skinned, saleswoman asked as she placed "My Soul to Keep," by Tananarive Due, and "Bailey's Café," by Gloria Naylor into a plastic bag baring the stores name, number and address on its side.

"No, that'll be all. Thank you," Tasha slid the young woman her credit card just as Ronald stepped up to the check out counter with his two choices.

"Will this be all, Mr. Marks?" The saleswoman asked. Ronald still stops by every now and then to check on Karen, so the saleswoman was familiar with him.

"Yes, this will be it," He handed the saleswoman his credit card, which he sat on top of the two books he'd chosen. "Po' Man's Poker," by Cheryl Dooley-Ponton, and "The Beautiful One's," by Kim L. Dulaney, both of whom live in the Chicagoland area. Ronald met both women through Kym Parker, one of his ex-wife's closest friends, who happens to be a soon to be published author from the south side of Chicago.

At the end of the night, after a late evening dinner at Dixie's Kitchen, in Hyde Park, Ronald and Tasha exchanged the books they purchased, satisfying their gift-giving obligations. Since they weren't a couple, nor were they officially dating, they had agreed to exchange inexpensive gifts. The trip to the bookstore topped the evening off perfectly.

Pink October.doc   169

Scene 58

Sweating profusely in her dark colored sweatshirt, sweatpants and her light colored Nike fitness shoes, Amanda curbed her stress with a thirty-minute workout, during which she practiced all of her self-defense techniques in the middle of Wanda's living room. Kicking. Punching. Rolling. You name it...she did it. Earlier in the day she called Mike to let him know that she had dropped the assault charges against him, but she had decided to file for a divorce. Naturally he exploded. Never mind the fact that there has always been a thick cloud of verbal and physical abuse looming over their "so called" marriage like a storm cloud following a particular character wherever they go, raining specifically on them just like in those Peanuts' cartoons. "You're letting people outside of our marriage influence your decision. You don't want to leave me. You know I love you, and I'm doing everything in my power to change. I love you more than life itself, and I need you even more. So please, give me another chance. I'll prove to you that I've changed. Things will be different...I promise things will be different," Mike pleaded, sounding more sincere than he had ever sounded after any of the other physical attacks on his wife. Maybe it was his knowing that this time Amanda meant every word. Or maybe he did decide to finally change after years of whipping his wife's ass. Whatever the reason, it was too late. And when Amanda rejected his pleas the Mike she came to know all too well was back in full force, making her decision that much easier to make. "Fuck you then, bitch!" His words struck as hard as any belt he'd ever used on her. "You'll regret it. You're nothing without me...You'll be..."Amanda abruptly hung up before hearing the rest of his statement, which was sure to be proven a lie. Her mind was made up. If it wasn't before their phone conversation, it was afterwards. She was filing that divorce, ASAP!

Once she finished practicing her kicks and punches, which looked more like an aerobics routine than self-defense techniques; Amanda headed into the bathroom where she soaked in a hot bubble bath. By the time she got out of the tub her fingers and toes looked like they had aged fifty years; she stayed in that long. Since Wanda left for the club over an hour ago, Amanda's therapeutic bath went undisturbed, allowing her enough time to weigh the few money earning options available to her. And no matter how bad things seemed right now, she was not going to become a stripper. It didn't matter how easy Wanda and Keri made it seem. "I'm not going anywhere near that club," She huffed at her reflection in the mirror above the bathroom sink. And at this particular point, she meant every word.

Scene 59

Declining his invitation to join him over a cup of coffee before her drive home was probably the smartest thing she'd ever done. There was no way she would've been able to resist his charm had he gotten her alone in his cozy home, in front of that damn fireplace. Especially considering how fast things had progressed the last time she was alone with him. Who knows how far things would've gone if they had been allowed to go through with that kiss. Tasha knew. She knew exactly how far things would've gone had they actually kissed. "It would've gone as far as breakfast," She smiled, thinking back to the conversation she had with Tracey, as she climbed underneath her sheets and comforter, preparing for what ended up being a very pleasant "dream-filled" nights sleep, with Ronald as the dream's leading man.

Sunday morning (after her routine self-breast exam) she showered, dressed then waited an hour before driving over to her parent's home for Sunday breakfast. When Tasha was a little girl Tanya would stress that after taking a bath or shower, she should wait at least an hour and thirty minutes before going out into Chicago's weather. Flu season is how Tanya described every cool breeze, whether spring, summer, fall or winter. This morning's gospel program was so good that she forgot all about her mother's long-standing rule, leaving her house thirty minutes after stepping out of the shower. Actually, she hadn't adhered to her mother's wise words since leaving for college so many years ago, though she tells her mother something totally different.

Later that morning, breakfast would become Sunday brunch because of a late night, early morning delivery William assisted. Tanya could have called last night to inform Tasha about the change in plans, but she didn't. Why waste an opportunity to do what mother's and daughter's do best, which is to talk about whatever crossed their minds, in Tanya's case that something usually involves Tasha's love life. That's just how mothers are when their only daughter reaches a certain age and is still single with no children, and Tasha hated it. She always felt uncomfortable talking to her mother about her love life, especially when she and Kevin were an item. Tanya had always said that Kevin wasn't the marrying type, at least not the type of guy Tasha should marry. Differences in their social status led Tanya to that conclusion. In her mind, it was as simple as one, two, three. Tasha has a Ph.D. and she's the principal at Dr.

Rhay E. Street Magnet Elementary (one of the most academically recognized schools in the state). She also has an annual salary close to one hundred thousand dollars. Kevin, on the other hand, is a personal trainer. That's it. That's all Tanya cared to know about her daughter's boy toy. "It's all right to have your fun, but I hope you're being careful. You don't want to end up pregnant with this man's child. Not when he's just a pit-stop on the way to a much better man," Tanya had often teased, hoping that by doing so Tasha would begin to realize that Kevin should be looked upon as a pleasure ride. People enjoy rides for only a short period of time, then they get off.

"Ma, we haven't been a couple for almost two months now," Tasha responded after her mother mentioned how she had not heard Kevin's name in quite sometime. Needless to say, Tanya was more shocked about hearing the news so late than she was about hearing the news at all. She knew it would eventually come to pass.

"What happened? Why didn't you tell me? Are you okay?" She asked in one breath, before sitting her glass of orange juice down on the coffee table as if news of their break up would upset her so much that she'd drop her glass.

Reluctantly, Tasha began to share with her mother all that had transpired between her and Kevin and that "back-stabbing" bitch, Kim. Tasha left nothing unsaid. From the gut feeling she experienced when she popped up unannounced at the health club to the time she visited the gym with Amanda and Carla and ran into both Kim and Kevin. She even told her mother about the knee she planted in Kevin's groin, which Tanya found extremely comical.

"Serves him right," Tanya laughed at the thought of Kevin in the fetal position, whimpering in pain.

"That's not funny. I could have really hurt him. Then I would've been in serious trouble, because it did happen in front of the entire self-defense class. What if I had seriously hurt him? What if he had decided to press charges?" Tasha nudged her mother's side while trying to keep her own laughter from erupting.

"Now that you mention it, he can still file those charges," Tanya got her daughter's full attention with her sudden seriousness. Tasha's laughter faded, only to return when her mother added, "I guess the balls are in his court. Literally," Tanya nudged Tasha's arm, both women laughing so hard tears began to flow.

As their conversation continued, Tasha told Tanya about Ronald, and how they've seen each other a few times outside of group meetings. Tanya found this to be promising news. "Sounds

Pink October.doc
173

like someone more your speed," she followed her statement with a motherly, 'umm uhh.'

"He's the head chef at one of Chicago's finest restaurants. He's divorced, and he has custody of his seven-year-old daughter, which shows he's responsible and he has his own home in Pill Hill, so he's also financially stable," The fact that he was established brought an even larger smile of acceptance to Tanya's face. "He's not my man or anything like that, but we do enjoy each other's company," Tasha added after noticing that 'now this sounds like it could lead to something' look on her mother's face.

"If you're anything like your mother, that will change real soon. Trust me," She winked before pushing herself off the couch so that she could go answer the wall phone over the counter, between the kitchen and the living room. William was calling to tell his wife that, due to circumstances beyond his control, he wouldn't be able to eat brunch with his family. "Go ahead and start without me, and if I'm able to make it home before you're finished eating, I will," He said before adding his usual "I love you" to the end of his message. That always put a smile on Tanya's face, the same smile she smiled over thirty years ago, when he said those words for the first time.

"I love you, too," Tanya cooed back into the phone before hanging up and motioning for Tasha to join her in the kitchen. She wanted to hear more about this Ronald character while she went on preparing Sunday brunch as if William would make it home in time.

It's been more than two months since they've shared a mother and daughter moment like the one they shared today. A mother and daughter moment absent Tanya's inadvertent display of pain and sorrow, which undoubtedly made Tasha feel uncomfortable at the very gathering meant to ease her fears. But today was different. Just last night Tanya promised William that she would keep her worrying in check so that she wouldn't dampen Tasha's mood. He had started to notice how Tasha was more concerned about her mother's mental well being than she was about her own, causing the rekindling of the negative thoughts Tasha had just recently been able to bury.

"Thanks ma…And tell daddy I said I'm sorry he couldn't make it, but, on the other hand, I'm glad we had a chance to talk like we used to," Tasha fastened her coat then hugged her mother before heading back out into the cold, yet sunny mid Sunday afternoon. After starting her car and waving bye to her mother, who was standing behind her energy conserving screen door, Tasha pulled out of her parent's driveway and headed back to her own home where she lazed around the house the rest of the day. Tomorrow she'll spring her new 'do on the group, and Wednesday she'll meet with Dr. Jordan for the first time since completing her radiation therapy. She didn't bring up her doctor's appointment while she was with her mother, saving Tanya from unnecessary worrying. But Tanya already knew about her daughter's appointment. She didn't bring it up because she didn't want Tasha to think she was starting to worry. Like mother, like daughter.

Pink October.doc

Scene 60

Since Monday night's group meeting was the last gathering before Christmas, Mrs. Green decided to surprise everyone with a pre-Christmas Christmas dinner instead of their usual "girl's night out", which everyone seemingly enjoyed the last few times they've gone out as a group. The dinner would give their holiday gathering more of a family feel rather than the "grown women gone wild" kind of feel they'd get if they had gone out. "Besides," Mrs. Green considered the upside. "We can always go out after we eat," She smiled as she took her famous marshmallow sweet-potato pies into the dining room where she placed them on the dessert table between the three layered chocolate cake and a pound cake. But it was her dining room table which overflowed with such holiday delectables like chittlins (Chitterlings for those not familiar with the ethnic pronunciation), ham, dressing and cranberry sauce-with the ceremonial turkey holding center stage, that would capture everyone's attention.

One by one, group members arrived and, once inside the dining room, were rendered speechless by Mrs. Green's holiday surprise. "What have you done?" Michelle muttered, hardly believing her eyes as she stood gawking at the beautifully set dining room table, covered with more than one main course and just as many side dishes. "You could've let me help...You know my 'fat-ass' daughter-in-law won't let me bake a biscuit," Michelle remarked playfully on the outside, seriously on the inside. Rhonda and Carla had the same reaction as they stood over a table covered with enough food to feed a group three times the size of theirs. "You could've at least let us make a pie, or something," Rhonda playfully fussed as she hugged her good friend.

"If I had allowed you all to help this wouldn't have been a surprise, now would it?" Mrs. Green smiled, breaking their embrace so that she could answer the door. Tasha had arrived with a surprise of her own. A Surprise she's been dying to reveal since the last snip of her stylist's scissors. This was the moment she had rehearsed a thousand times over the weekend. She had even contemplated toting her camera along so that she could immortalize the looks on their faces at the exact moment she'd unveiled her new do.

"What's all this?" Tasha stood smiling in the dining room's entranceway, momentarily forgetting about her own surprise which still laid hidden underneath her winter hat.

"It's a "pre-Christmas" Christmas dinner slash surprise that Mrs. Green cooked up without giving anyone of us as much as a hint as to what that mad scientist mind of hers was moving her body to do," Looking up from rearranging silverware, Michelle happily added her two cents.

Mrs. Green's surprise was more of a lifesaver to Michelle than just a pre-Christmas dinner. To Michelle, it would amount to the best holiday dinner she's eaten since moving in with her son, grandson, and the 'white woman.' During her first few weeks at her son's house a few years ago, she sat through numerous season-less dinners to know that holiday meals would be no different, though they could be, if Robin would welcome her into her kitchen. But how was Robin supposed to welcome her mother-in-law when her mother-in-law hadn't truly welcomed her into her family. Michelle accepted her only because her son loved her and she gave birth to her only grandbaby, but she didn't welcome her into the family like her parents welcomed Bryan. Michelle knew it. Bryan knew it. Robin knew it. "When she welcomes me into your family, I'll welcome her into my kitchen," Robin had declared after Michelle's first week at their home, during one of her late night discussions with her husband. Michelle's behavior made it blatantly obvious to Robin that she liked her other son's 'drug-addicted' wife more than she did her. Not because Pat was a better wife, but because she was black. A blind man could see that. This amounted to Robin's unofficial, "the only time Michelle would be allowed in my kitchen is during tax time" rule. That's when Robin would spend most of her time on filing the family's return. "And things will remain this way until Michelle truly welcomes me," Robin said it, and meant it. Those feelings haven't changed.

"You forgot to take off your hat," Sampling a small piece of ham at the far end of the dining room table, Carla pointed to Tasha's head, unknowingly reminding her that her hat still concealed her surprise.

"Oh, I forgot," Tasha slyly grinned before removing her hat. "Surprise," she announced as she modeled her cut, slowly turning a full circle.

"What have you done?" Appearing from the kitchen just as the hat came off, Rhonda was the first to respond. Tasha had gone from having the longest hair in the group, to having the shortest and Rhonda couldn't understand why she'd do something like that. For as long as she could remember she has loved having long hair. And for a long time, assumed that every other woman in the U.S. felt the same. Especially black women, with the amount of money they spent on additives. But Rhonda made sure to keep her opinion about black women, and weave, to herself. She still winced at how back when she was dancing at Shay's, a predominantly black club on the city's north side, she had infuriated one of the black dancers, who had short hair, by asking if she ever considered getting a "phony pony," is what the black girls called it. Rhonda didn't mean anything by it, since most of the black dancers she knew were proud of their fake hair. Obviously that particular dancer didn't feel the same. By the way her neck swayed and fingers snapped, as she verbally tore into Rhonda, you would've thought Rhonda had used the 'N' word instead of asking about fake hair.

"I'm sorry…I guess I'm just surprised at how short you cut your hair. Shoot, if it wasn't for the Chemo I would've never cut my hair… But it really does looks nice," Rhonda blurted before Tasha could respond, hoping that her first comment wouldn't be taken out of context.

"Thanks Rhonda… And don't worry, you're not the only person I've shocked half to death with my new short look. Every time I look in the mirror I have to do a double-take to make sure that's my reflection staring back at me," Tasha laughed as Mrs. Green stepped up from behind.

"It does look nice. Maybe now people will stop thinking we're sisters," Mrs. Green smiled, nudging Tasha's side before continuing on to the huge crystal punch bowl sitting in the middle of the dessert table.

Carla and Michelle also liked Tasha's new look, both immediately recognizing the "Tamron Hall" look.

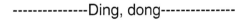
---------------Ding, dong---------------

"I'll get it," Michelle, who was closer to the door than Mrs. Green, announced over her shoulder as she headed for the door. Erica had arrived with her husband and three beautiful children in tow, all dressed for a family outing.

This was Tasha's first time seeing Erica's family in person so she, not wanting to intrude, stood quietly at the dessert table and watched admiringly as Michelle, Carla and Mrs. Green showered the girls with hugs and kisses.

"Excuse me," Carl smirked, his arms held open in a "where's my hugs and kisses" kind of way. "What am I, chopped liver?" He

Gary Norman

laughed as he and Erica stood over a very familiar scene, family and friends fussing over their girls.

"I'm sorry Carl...how have you been?" Mrs. Green was the first to stand up and hug Carl. Carla and Michelle were next, with Rhonda hugging him last. They never mean to ignore Carl and Erica when their girls are in the room, but how could they not ignore them when their girls look as adorable as they do. All three of the girls were sporting ponytails, their facial features resembling both Erica and Carl. Kim, Teri and Jessica (nine, seven, and two) wore the cutest little dresses; all three dressed in red and green, a celebration of the Christmas season. Jessica, the youngest, is the darkest of the three while Kim, the oldest, is the lightest and tallest (their complexion, and height, leveling off like stairs in a staircase).

"I've been fine, how about you? Or should I ask you if you've been staying out of trouble? I heard about how you wouldn't let go of some guy's candy cane," Carl and Erica grinned from ear to ear, though Erica's grin was more of an "I'm sorry, it slipped out" kind of grin.

"Big-mouth," Unable to conceal her embarrassment, Mrs. Green slipped an elbow to Erica's side before rejoining Carla and Michelle in cheek pinching and kissing, along with some dress adjusting. It was as if Erica's little girls were being prepped for a pageant set to begin in five minutes. The very sight of everyone fussing over Erica's little darlings took Tasha back to her own childhood, at her grandparent's home in Maywood, IL. Gram and Grandpa used to spoil her to death, spoiling her with ice cream whenever she hit them with that "sad puppy" face all the little kids learned to perfect.

"I'm sorry, Tasha, I didn't see you standing over there. Come on over and meet my family," Erica's voice jolted Tasha from her pleasant daydream. "Carl, this is Tasha, the newest addition to the group. And Tasha, this is my husband, and soul mate, Carl," Erica snuggled against his left arm. He shook Tasha's hand. "And these are my little angels, Kim, Teri, and Jessica," Erica tapped each of their heads as she said their names. "And what's all this?" Standing akimbo, Erica asked after noticing the dining room table and the dessert table.

"It's my surprise 'pre-Christmas' dinner," Mrs. Green said, smiling like a proud parent.

"I'm sorry, but we can't stay. We're taking the girls to see the Chocolate NutCracker. Actually, we only stopped by because they wanted you all to see them in their dresses...I'm so sorry."

"That's okay. You all go and have fun and I'll just put something away for you and the girls," Mrs. Green said.

"Thanks, Mrs. Green," The girls said in unison.

"Everything looks so good, I hate to leave. Where's Ronald? I want to thank him before we go," Erica asked.

"He's not here. In fact he's taking Tara to see the same play you're headed off to see, so you'll probably see him there," Tasha answered for Mrs. Green.

"Well, well, well…It sounds like somebody is getting pretty close to Mr. Ronald Marks. Is there anything you'd like to share with the group? Anything exciting? Or do I need to ask the kids to leave the room before you can answer that question?" Carla teased as everyone looked on as if they were actually expecting a reply.

"Whatever do you mean?" Tasha responded slyly.

"I'm not letting you off that easy. We'll talk later, miss 'hot-to-trot'," Carla winked.

"I'd like to hear about you and Ronald too, but we have to get going. I'll just have to get the details later," Erica winked.

"Okay girls, say good-bye to everybody if you want to make it to the play on time," Carl announced, glancing at his watch.

Good-byes took over ten minutes because Mrs. Green just had to take a few pictures of the girls in their dresses. That led to Mrs. Green suggesting a group picture, leaving Carl to play photographer. Rhonda, Erica, Tasha, Carla, Michelle, and Mrs. Green, is how they were arranged in the picture. Rhonda held up two fingers behind Erica's head. Carla's smile was an opened mouth smile; the camera's flash captured her in mid laughter. Michelle and Mrs. Green both smiled from ear to ear, while Tasha's 'ooo-oop' and Erica's 'skee wee' held the same enthusiastic clatter as it had when they both were neophytes at their first student center party.

After the pictures were taken, and the Danials' family had gone, Carla and Rhonda led Tasha to the living room where they'd drill her for information about her and Ronald before it was time to eat. Mrs. Green wanted to give Amanda an extra fifteen minutes to arrive. She could've sworn she'd seen Amanda's Camaro pass by when she opened the door to let Erica and her family out. Carla and Rhonda got to hear all of the juicy details, which really weren't juicy at all. Carla felt Friday's evening of shopping was kind of romantic, but inviting Ronald to her gym for a light workout could actually lead to something.

"Dinner is served," Mrs. Green interrupted. She gave Amanda more than enough time to find a parking space, if that was Amanda. "I guess that wasn't her car," Mrs. Green shrugged, mumbling to herself as she took her seat at the head of the table where she paused briefly before going into a pre-meal grace that seemed to last forever. Thank God she was hungry.

Scene 61

For the first time since she's been Mrs. Thompson, Amanda spent Christmas without her husband. Things were moving as fast as an Indy driver so Amanda did all she could to keep herself focused on maintaining what little control she had over her immediate well-being, which meant getting a J-O-B. That was the only way she could begin to put her life back together. She needed to start somewhere, anywhere, but finding a job this deep into the holiday season would be next to impossible, especially with no degree. "You can always wait tables down at Expose`," Keri suggested. "So you're saying I should be a barmaid?" Amanda sneered at Keri's suggestion, three days earlier. "Look Amanda, I'm not suggesting that you dance at the damn club. I'm just talking about being a waitress. They make more money than you think, some of the girls bringing home close to one hundred dollars in tips, a night. And you look just as good, if not better, than most of them. So I know you'll do well. Whatdaya say?" Keri's question weighed heavily on Amanda's mind for one full week before she finally agreed to give it a shot. Amanda looked at it as a temporary pit stop on the way to reaching her goal which is to finish school and get a better job.

During her first visit to Club Expose` Amanda quickly learned the ins and outs of waitressing in a gentleman's club. Since she was new to the club her section of tables sat closer to the club's entrance. The girls that have been at the club the longest had seniority. They got the best sections, which were the sections closest to the stage. They also got to work the V.I.P. room on the best nights, leaving the newer girls to choose from Sunday to Wednesday. All of the "non-dancing" girls wore identical outfits, usually a cream-colored form fitting mini dress they'd have to purchase themselves. On special 'theme' nights they'd wear whatever costume the night's theme called for. On those nights the club provided their costumes. The waitresses made most of their money from tips, since the club's hourly wage was somewhere around minimum wage. So a kind word and a smile would usually bring in a generous tip, especially after a patron has downed a few drinks. At that point anything's possible. Men would offer hundreds, sometime as much as one thousand dollars for a little extra attention. After working one full week at the club, Amanda found that most of the girls, waitresses included, did provide that extra attention the men, and sometimes women, were so eager to pay for. To those girls providing that extra attention, Keri and Wanda

Gary Norman

included, the men were nothing more than sugar daddies, with an occasional romance springing to life every so often. "When that happens the girl usually quits," Craig, a freckled faced, red head, offensive lineman size bouncer, explained some of what he's seen during his three years of working the crowd.

Craig and Amanda talked so much on her first day that a few of the dancers thought they were an item. "But not all the girls break the rules and get involved with the costumers. Some of the girls that have worked here, at one time or another, actually used this job to put themselves through school... and you know what? The determined ones do make it," He nodded, adding encouragement with his effortless head movement. "Now get over there and take those orders," He teased, nudging her towards her section. That table left a measly five-dollar tip. "Five grown ass men sat at that table, and that's all they could come up with," Amanda hissed in Craig's ear. "Welcome to *Club Expose'*," he laughed.

Pink October.doc

Scene 62

"So you're thinking about dancing, huh?" Keri asked, grinning as she poured maple syrup over her butter soaked French toast. This late Sunday afternoon Keri and Wanda treated Amanda to an IHOP breakfast to celebrate her second week of working at the club. To their surprise, moments before the waitress returned to their booth with their orders, Amanda revealed how she, after witnessing the club's devotion to professionalism and it's secure working environment, was seriously considering becoming a dancer. Dancing equaled money, money she needed now, is how Amanda began to look at things. It took her two weeks to earn six hundred dollars. Some dancers make that much in one night. With that kind of money coming in she could get her own place, a used car, pay court fees, and still be able to start school this coming summer semester. Those were the positives she used to weigh her decision towards going through with this dancing thing. But those positives didn't carry as much weight as she had hoped. She still couldn't make up her mind on what she should do, which is why she decided to share her dilemma with Keri and Wanda over breakfast. She figured they'd lay it on her straight. That, along with what she's already witnessed over the past two weeks, should be enough to sway her decision in favor of dancing, or not. She'd already witnessed the good and bad, though the bad usually ended abruptly with one of the bully security guards escorting a drunken patron from the club.

In the middle of her third week of waitressing, Amanda met Rene`, a dancer who would usually work second shift, but, on the that day, switched shifts with a friend in order to take care of some personal business later on that evening. Since Keri and Wanda were the only dancers at the club to officially welcome Rene` aboard, back when she was "brand new' to the dancing scene, she was happy to meet Amanda. "Any friend of theirs, is a friend of mine," Rene` smiled before walking over to the end of the bar and introducing herself to Amanda, who stood smiling with her eyes glued on the few full tables in her section. Keri and Wanda told Rene` how Amanda was considering dancing as a means to further her education, which was something Rene` could relate to since she was dancing to pay her med-school tuition. "The hours are great and the money is even better," Rene` proclaimed in one breath, then warned with the next. "You just gotta stay focused, and that means not getting caught up in this life-style. I mean the parties are there, the drinking and drug, but is it really worth it?" She said with the seriousness of a high school

Pink October.doc 185

guidance counselor. She's seen a lot in her two years of dancing at the club; girls came and went, some leaving in worse shape than when they came. But not Rene`. She arrived right after graduating from the University of Illinois (with a degree in Chemistry) on her way to the University of Chicago Medical School, on a full scholarship. But when the Internet company behind her scholarship went bankrupt, nearly bankrupting her dreams right along with its financial pitfalls, a friend of hers, who was dancing at the time, suggested dancing as a means for her to keep her dream alive. At first Rene` was reluctant, but, after realizing that without the proper finances her dream of becoming a doctor would die like a Texas death-row inmate, soon came to see dancing as a blessing in disguise. Since she worked only three, sometimes four days a week, she was able to put more time into studying. That's the main reason she'll be graduating in three years instead of four. "And, believe me.... If I can do it, anybody can," Rene asserted.

"How did you even attempt to prepare yourself emotionally to actually get up there and take your clothes off in front of total strangers?" Amanda asked, hoping for some sort of magic answer that would erase her own ill feelings about a job she once referred to as being degrading to women, but now looked at as a money earning option.

"I wanted to turn my dream into a reality and this was the only way I could do that without, having to work two or three jobs," Rene` shrugged before sharing with Amanda how, after stumbling across a book entitled Ivy League Stripper (written by a woman who paid her Ivy League tuition with money she earned by stripping), she found the strength to go through with her decision to strip.

"I'll make sure I pick that up", Amanda remarked, quickly penciling the book's title on the top page of her order pad, which she tore off and placed in her pocket. She bought the book the next day. Amanda read that book three times during that same week. She also watched The Player's Club twelve times during the same week. That movie scared her more than it did help, but then again she knew she wouldn't end up like the main character's cousin.

By the end of the week Keri and Wanda were giving Amanda dance lessons in the middle of Wanda's living room. Everything from the appropriate table dance and lap dance to a sure-to-please stage show, Keri and Wanda held nothing back, sharing secrets Amanda needed to know in order to be successful.

Gary Norman

Monday, five weeks after she took the waitress job, she was about to dance for the first time in front of strangers and not even Mike's refusal to sign the divorce papers was a strong enough distraction to subdue the millions of butterflies fluttering in her stomach. In fact, time had passed so fast that she didn't even realize she'd missed over five group meetings until she stood backstage waiting to be introduced to the crowd, desperately searching her mind for anything she could use as brakes for her runaway emotions. "It's probably best that I didn't attend any meetings. I'm sure that'll be the first place he looks, if he hasn't already," Thinking of how Mike had probably put Mrs. Green's house under surveillance, Amanda muttered to herself just as the baritone voice DJ introduced ' Pink-Lace", the name Keri and Wanda had christened her with. "Here goes nothing," Amanda, shaking like a leaf in a windy city breeze off the lake, ran her hands over her white lace lingerie, took a deep breath, and walked out onto the stage.

Scene 63

Amanda's first night as an exotic dancer didn't go as smoothly as she had hoped. Yet it wasn't a total disaster either. During her first stage appearance she was so nervous that when it came time for her to remove her bra she stalled so long one of the patrons yelled, "Am I supposed to pay you to take it off, or keep it on?" Then when a patron reached up to place a folded five-dollar bill beneath her garter, but then guided his hand up to her crotch where he tucked the bill into her panties, brushing his fingers over her pubic hair, she wanted to scream, cry, kick and spit. He had violated her "no-touch" zone, smiling up at her as if she was supposed to enjoy the brief violation. She was mortified. She stood frozen, fighting the urge to run and hide the tears that had begun to swell. Luckily Keri and Wanda were there. They came in early, sneaking backstage while Amanda prepared to work the crowd, planning to congratulate their friend after her first stage appearance. Once they saw Amanda freeze, first they laughed, then they set out to help her through her first time on stage. They joined Amanda on stage where they coaxed her into following their lead. That night Amanda made one hundred and seventy five dollars, and that was after the one hundred-dollar tip-out.

"I know you're not laughing at her. Not when you had that same 'I wanna go cry' face during your first night of dancing," Wanda interjected, defending Amanda's first night "near breakdown" before continuing with a tale she seemingly saved specifically for this Sunday night's slumber party in celebration of Amanda's first full week of dancing.

As they sat around Wanda's glass coffee table in their tank tops and pajama bottoms, stuffing their faces with Jay's Bar B.Q. potato chips and washing it down with Dr. Pepper, Wanda could hardly contain her laughter as she told of how Keri's first customer was a man-dressing, man-looking, woman. "She had everybody in the club fooled, except me," Wanda laughed to Keri's dismay. Back then Keri considered herself one hundred percent heterosexual. She was even a tad bit homophobic. That is until she became friends with Tasty Treat, one of the club's former dancers.

Tasty Treat, whose real name was Sarah Cardin, was a five foot five inch beauty with hazel eyes and shoulder length blonde hair. She had huge 38DD-implanted breasts that matched her curvy hips perfectly. She bared a striking resemblance to Sharon Stone, before the wrinkles. She was fine! Capital F-I-N-E, fine. She was also openly bi-sexual. She also had a crush on Keri. "It'll happen one day, trust me," She'd always say after yet another one of Keri's "No it won't. I don't go that way" speeches. But one night, after a very profitable night of stripping and more than their share of champagne, it did happen. That was six months after Keri's encounter with the man looking patron. The same patron Keri now dates (Sam).

"I know you're not laughing at me," Keri interrupted Wanda's high pitched laughter before going into her own tale about Wanda and how she had cried for a week after attending her first bachelor party.

"That's different...they wanted me to do things I had never done in private, let alone in front of a room full of drunken strangers," Wanda winced as she thought back to that evening. An evening ending with her climbing out of a first floor bathroom window moments before she was to engage in a four woman sex-show, complete with the kinds of toys she thought were illegal. "Girl, I'm not gay, but I will be for the kind of money they're paying," One of the three other girls had said in an attempt to persuade Wanda to think of it as method acting. "You know you're not gay and that's all that matters," The girl continued. She was right. There was no way Wanda would've been able to look in another mirror if she had chosen to compromise her sexual preference for financial gain.

Hearing about their past encounters made Amanda look at her first week in a totally different light. It wasn't as bad as it could've been, even though for two days, after she'd arrive home from an evening of stripping, she would go into the bathroom and throw-up. Just the thought of strangers touching her body made her stomach turn. It was during those times that she would reread Ivy League Stripper, but only the parts of the book she thought pertained to whatever her situation was at the time.

"So when was the last time you attended one of your cancer-group meetings?" Keri asked out of the blue, catching Amanda completely off guard because they were talking about the adventures associated with being a dancer, not group meetings.

"It's been a while," Amanda sighed, suddenly remembering the friends she hadn't seen in over a month. But how could she go back when it was highly likely Mike would probably look for her at Mrs. Green's house?

"Are you going back?" Keri asked. It was a simple question, but to Amanda it was the one thousand-dollar Jeopardy question.

"Sooner or later," She answered with a shrug.

Scene 64

With the holidays behind her, Tasha eagerly crossed into the New Year with a whole new outlook on life and love. Life's simple pleasures would no longer be taken for granted. "Life's a lot shorter than we think it is, so whenever possible make sure you take time out of your day to stop and smell the flowers, watch the birds fly and listen to them sing. Enjoy the simple things life has to offer, because one day you won't be able to enjoy those simple things," Tasha still remembered those words spoken by her girl scout leader, Mrs. Barbrie, but it was only recently that she began to take heed. Fortunately, Tasha is blessed with family and friends she can share those pleasures with. Simple pleasures like Sunday breakfast at her parent's house and watching movies with friends.

The last six weeks went by so fast Tasha had joked, "I must've had a lot of fun." And she really did. From attending a R. Kelly concert with Carla, Erica, Mrs. Green and Michelle to seeing the look on Kevin's face when she entered the gym with a new workout partner, she had a ball. "Who's he?" Kevin quizzed after watching Tasha's workout buddy enter the locker room. He was so worried about who she was with that he didn't even notice her new hairstyle. Tasha thought that was funny. The pitiful "I can't believe she disrespected me by bringing another brother to our gym" look on his face had Tasha biting her lip to keep from laughing out load. "He's none of your business," She responded dryly, continuing with her pre-workout five mile hike as if he wasn't standing right next to her treadmill. "But if you must know, he's what you didn't have the tools to be... he's my new man, the bigger and better version," Knowing how sensitive men are about being compared to their ex-lover's new partner, Tasha smiled broadly as she attacked his manhood with simple, yet ego shattering, words. "Now if you'll excuse me, please leave before he gets back," She added without as much as a glance in his direction. She still smiled when she thought about that day, making Kevin feel as uncomfortable as she felt during her first day back to the gym, after their breakup. And referring to Ronald's size as being larger than Kevin's, even though at that point she had not slept with Ronald, was like adding salt to an open wound. The dagger in Kevin's heart coming when he walked out to the parking lot to find that Tasha's new beau had parked right next to his used, 98, Explorer with its dented passenger side door and balding tires. Watching Tasha smile from the passenger's seat of Ronald's Range Rover made

Kevin feel even lower than he had already felt, as if a man's possessions determined his worth in life.

That night Tasha laughed so hard during her phone conversation with Carla that tears ran down her face, her side hurt, and her face turned a bit crimson. "You should've seen his face... looking like somebody stole his puppy," Tasha said. "You mean his kitty," Carla responded. They both laughed at that one.

During the holiday season Tasha was also able to become better acquainted with Tara, which was easy to do considering she spent most of her free time at Ronald's house. Even if she hadn't spent as much time as she did at Ronald's, Tasha still would've liked his daughter. She was just that adorable.

Scene 65

Dressed and ready for whatever Carla's night of dancing could throw her way, Tasha looked absolutely stunning in the outfit she picked out for the night. At least that's what her bedroom mirror told her as she modeled in front of it, conceitedly admiring how good she looked in her black Donna Karen dress with its thigh high split, low cut bust line and exposed back. She would definitely turn heads tonight, and she knew it. Since their last outing was to a jazz club on 21st and Halsted, tonight Tasha and Carla were headed to a place called Maria's, a Latin club on the northwest side. This is where Carla would go whenever she was in the mood for a little salsa. "I hope you're ready to experience some real dancing, not like that steppin' stuff," Carla joked during last night's phone conversation. Tasha was more than ready. She'd been talking about her up and coming introduction to salsa dancing since Carla made the suggestion during Tuesday night's phone conversation, a few days earlier. Their nightly conversations had become a daily occurrence since Christmas, which was a little more than six weeks ago. They talked like teenagers tying up their parent's phone to the point that even twenty minutes after their conversation ended you could still feel warmth being emitted from the phone like heat from a hot engine. And today was no exception. They had already spoken to one another three times today, twice while both were at their place of employment. Carla, a car saleswoman at a south suburban Toyota dealership, just had to share with Tasha how happy she was about having sold a Land Cruiser, only her fourth such sale in the two years she's been employed at one of the state's most productive car dealerships. And Tasha just had to call Carla after Dr. Rhay E. Street, the school's namesake and one of the city's most successful dentist for over twenty years, and his wife, Allison, left her school. Tasha couldn't believe that she'd met Dr. Street, who was also one of the most vocal participants of the Civil Rights movement, as well as one of today's strongest supporters of bringing Emmit Till's Killers to justice.

When Dr. Street, the morning's guest speaker, reached the end of his motivational speech he allowed the kids to ask him whatever they wanted to know about him, with some exceptions of course. With dozens of hands waving in the air, Dr. Street pointed at each child until he had graciously answered every single question from "How old are you?" to "Was microbiology hard?" He answered them all. "Sixty three," Tasha uttered in disbelief after Dr. Street shared his age with the entire auditorium. "They aged well," Was all she could say as she admired Dr. and his wife from where she stood on the auditorium floor, near the visitor 's locker room entrance. If it wasn't for the salt and pepper hair they both possessed they could easily pass for being in their forties. Dr. Street was five foot nine inches tall, with a medium build and a slightly protruding belly. His teeth were straight and sparkling white, which was of no surprise considering his profession. All in all, he resembled a much older "P. Diddy," while his wife, Allison, resembled the principal on the Steve Harvey Show, only older, shorter and prettier, for her age.

"I hope I age as well as they have," Tasha said as she and Carla watched the surprise ending of the Bulls-Blazers game. The Bulls, led by Brand and Mercer, won.

"The way you describe them, I hope I can do the same," Carla cheerfully added between applauding her Bulls. They played a near perfect game, Mercer scoring 39 points, Brand adding 29, so her already "great sales day" good mood was heightened. "I hope you're ready for some hot spicy dancing," Carla added with an overly accented tongue.

"Hot and spicy?" Tasha Laughed. "I don't think I'm ready for hot and spicy. Maybe I should start off with plain old hot."

"You'll be just fine, trust me...But if you don't think you're ready for the hot and the spicy I'm willing to give you a crash course before we go."

"No thank you," Tasha smirked at the thought of the two of them engaging in one of the most erotic dances around.

"Maybe you're right," Carla, embarrassment all over her face, shook her head as if she'd read Tasha's mind. "But I'm sure if my name was Ronald you wouldn't have turned me down."

"You're absolutely right about that, but with him I'd be after the closeness, not the dance lesson...I already know how to Salsa. Well, I sort of know how. I've seen a few videos that featured Salsa dancing and it looks easy enough."

"So you think you can learn how to Salsa from some video?"

"There's only one way to find out," Tasha stood from Carla's couch as if to say, 'I'm ready when you are.'

Smiling from ear to ear, Carla stood up, turned off the TV, and then retrieved their coats from the closet at the foot of the stairs in the foyer.

As Tasha slid her arms into the sleeves of her stylish leather coat her heart smiled when she noticed the pre-Christmas dinner 'group picture' sitting on Carla's mantel, next to her grandmother's ashes.

"I see you moved the picture from your bedroom," Tasha replied.

"No, I still have that one in the bedroom, I just had another copy made," Carla said proudly. "I needed one out here so that everybody that visits can see without me having to invite them into my room."

"You know you want people all up in your 'hot and spicy' bedroom," Tasha poked fun at Carla's earlier statement. Carla was caught completely off guard by Tasha's wisecrack. Her facial expression said it all.

"That's cold," was all she could say as they headed out the door.

Scene 66

Tasha's Friday night intro to salsa was a night funny enough to win the grand prize on America's Funniest Home Videos. Needless to say, watching an occasional video didn't turn Tasha into the salsa queen. She was terrible, so terrible that after only thirty minutes on the dance floor men began to avoid her like she had Ebola. She'd accidentally banged her right knee into the left knee of her first dance partner of the night, a five-foot-eight inch Latin man named Jose. While dancing with Hector, her second salsa coach of the night, she raised her left foot when she was supposed to put it down, causing her to knock knees with partner number two, lose her balance and fall backwards, taking Hector to the floor with her. After that nifty move other would-be dance partners went as far as avoiding her side of the club altogether. "They treated me like a red-headed stepchild," Tasha recanted the night's events to Tracey at a teacher's lounge table, both enjoying their morning coffee and Old Fashion Donuts, a popular South side donut establishment. "If it wasn't for Mark coming to my rescue, I would've left an hour after I got there," Tasha continued to fill Tracey in on the one guy brave enough to approach her after she had taken out her two previous partners like a Mafia hit man.

Mark, a twenty nine year old, light skinned brother from the Westside, was a little heavier than medium build with tree trunk thighs that held his six foot three inch frame firmly planted on the dance floor. His hazel eyes were cat-like the way they looked an entirely different color when hit by a sudden stream of light.

Mark approached right after Carla had offered to give Tasha a crash course in salsa dancing, which Tasha had decided against. "Excuse me, but if you really want to learn how to salsa then please, allow me," Was all the handsome man said, holding out his hand, waiting patiently for a sign of acceptance. Tasha still found herself smiling at the fact that she was hit on by fine, younger men.

They started off slow, finally pepping things up by the start of the second song. From then on they were inseparable. From steppin' to salsa, they jammed. That is until Mark's excitement became apparent. "Girl, it was like he had smuggled a flash light into the club, I mean one of those police flash lights," Amazement still covered Tasha's face as she shared her story with Tracey, holding her hands about a foot apart as to demonstrate his size. "I couldn't continue to dance after that, so we sat at a table close to the dance floor and watched Carla dance circles around some poor guy, who, to my surprise, turned out to be her ex-husband," Tasha said, emphasizing

Pink October.doc   195

the words 'to my surprise'. Carla hardly ever talked about her ex-husband. In fact Tasha could only remember one other time that Carla had even mentioned her ex. This was mainly because she was tired of everybody predicting a near-future reconciliation. That's not what she wanted, not when things were better now than when they were married. She loves him to death, 'but why fix it if it ain't broke,' is how she sees their relationship. Jesse sees things differently and she knows it, though she acts like she doesn't. His actions scream 'I WANT MY WIFE BACK!' which Carla did her best to ignore. Luckily for her, he hadn't found the nerve to turn his ignored actions into words. That would force Carla to hear him. He was just as scared of starting over and failing as she was, but that wouldn't stop him from eventually trying again. He didn't feel that kind of fear. That kind of fear was reserved for Carla.

At the end of her workday, Tasha stopped at Subway and bought herself a steak and cheese sub, and a Diet Mountain Dew to wash it down with. Once she made it home, she enjoyed her meal while watching a Jamie Foxx rerun. After finishing her meal and soft drink she turned off the TV in the middle of a Steve Harvey rerun, retrieved a cup of banana yogurt from the frig, then went upstairs to prepare her bath. Once in the tub she stayed submerged with only her hands, head and shoulders above water, relaxing in the hot sudsy water while enjoying her therapeutic treat. With Sade's Cherish The Day filtering into the bathroom through the seven inch speakers connected to the portable CD player sitting on the counter-top across from the tub, Tasha soaked herself until her extremities were prune-like.

On her way to Mrs. Green's house, Tasha stopped at the Blockbuster Video closest to her home to return The Best Man, The Blair Witch Project and Big Momma's House, all of which she had rented Sunday night to watch with Ronald, at her place. After watching The Best Man, Ronald was set to leave, but, since it was nearing 1am, Tasha protested by saying, "Now you know you can stay here, that's unless you're scared of me." "Now what makes you think I just go around sleeping with strange women?" Ronald jokingly responded. "Who said anything about sleeping together? You're sleeping on the couch, mister Marks," Tasha said as she slapped the middle seat cushion. That was the plan, Ronald sleeping on the couch, but, with the sexual tension being as thick as it was, especially after watching The Best Man thirty minutes earlier, they were drawn to one another like a moth to a flame. Their lovemaking began with

Ronald tracing the length of her body with an expert tongue, right there in the den. When his tongue reached its destination, Tasha had to bite her lip to keep herself from singing out like a Sunday school choir. It was as if he knew exactly where each and every one of her "spots" were, the way he touched, nibbled, licked and kissed his way to Tasha's river of passion. And when he entered her, pleasingly filling her with girth and width, Tasha's toes remained curled for as long as it took the waves of pleasure to subside. The next morning, before Tasha's trek to work, Tasha surprised Ronald, as well as herself, by waking him up with her mouth. Well, that part of his body was already woke. Thank God for the extra condoms Tasha had stashed away in the right-hand corner of her dresser drawer.

"What's going on in here?" Hearing high-pitched laughter coming from inside of Mrs. Green's house, even before the front door was opened, Tasha quizzed as she stepped into the foyer, leaving Chicago's harsh winter weather on the other side of the door.

"Jessica's birthday is Saturday so Erica is showing a tape of Jessica's second birthday party," Still smiling from watching the adorable images Carl had captured the previous year with his camcorder, Mrs. Green said as she hung Tasha's coat in the downstairs closet. "You have to see this," She said before leading Tasha to the den, where every eye in the room was glued to the fifty five-inch TV across from the sofa and chair.

"Awww, look at my poor baby," Erica cooed as her youngest child appeared on the screen, seated in her high chair, with a cone-shaped birthday hat secured to her head and a slice of birthday cake in front of her on an oversized Styrofoam plate. She was crying her little eyes out. She was terrified of the white-faced clown, the same clown trying desperately to get her to smile, laugh or talk, anything but cry, which she did in high-pitched squeals every time the clown got within five feet of her high chair. "Maybe you need to take off your wig," You could hear Erica's voice offering the clown some advice, but she wasn't on the screen. "Mommy, she's scared of the nose, not the wig," You could hear a child offering input to a puzzling, yet comical, situation. "Is that right?" Erica asked with a chuckle before the screen suddenly swung to the left, catching Erica's oldest child's response on film.

"Awww, look at them," the room cooed in unison when Kim and Teri, who were making funny faces at the camera, appeared on screen sitting side-by-side at the kitchen table, both wearing their Easter dresses in celebration of their younger sister's birthday.

Pink October.doc 197

"You heard Teri, Rhonda, off with the nose," Carl, dressed in his only tux for his little girl's birthday, came into view to sit ice cream and cake in front of Kim and Teri. "Hi honey," He waved at the camera before disappearing once again.

"Rhonda! That's you in the clown suit?" Tasha, standing unnoticed in the den's entranceway, asked before moving a few feet closer to the screen for a better look at the red nose, white face clown.

"Hey...I didn't know you were here. Yeah, that's me...the clown," Tilting her head towards the clown on the TV screen, Rhonda couldn't smile any wider if that was her family being showcased on Mrs. Green's floor model TV "Watch this," Rhonda instructed, pointing at the screen. "Here, see...it's only me...see, look," Standing to the left of Jessica's high chair, Rhonda cooed as she removed her red sponge nose. The crying came to an immediate halt. After recognizing Rhonda's face behind that scary red nose, Jessica couldn't stop smiling. This looks like an episode from the Cosby Show, Tasha thought as she watched the love filled home video, Erica's prize possession.

"Why don't I take the camera so you can give the birthday girl a kiss," Carla's voice was heard moments before the picture on the screen experienced minor turbulence. When steadiness resumed Erica appeared on screen for the first time. She was wearing her favorite long-sleeved black dress with her braids pulled back into a ponytail, same as her two little girls. Erica had those braids woven into her head after Carl told her how much he liked Angela's braids in How Stella Got Her Groove Back.

"Keep doing that. Go Rhonda. Go Rhonda. Get busy. Get busy," Erica sang encouragingly as Rhonda resorted to her ace-in-the-hole when it came to getting Jessica to laugh. She danced like Carlton from *The Fresh Prince of Bel-Air.* Everybody in the room, on screen and off, laughed. And when Kim and Teri got out of their chairs and joined Rhonda, dancing on either side of her, they left Erica with one option. Join them. "Look at mommy! Look at mommy!" Teri laughed as her mother danced, looking just as silly as the rest of the dancers in the room.

Gary Norman

Scene 67

Watching Erica's home video before the customary opening prayer had a heart-warming effect on the entire group. Just seeing Erica's little girls having so much fun was enough to cause the kind of lump in your throat you get when a movie's happy ending is just too powerful for a simple gracious nod. And when Jessica screamed, "That's auntie! That's auntie," while pointing from her high chair at the dancing clown, Rhonda and Erica weren't the only ones in the room to shed a few tears.

"Girl, you need to quit it. You're making everybody cry," Erica teased her good friend as they both sat teary eyed on the sofa, reveling in the beautiful moment just displayed on screen. Erica's children love their auntie Rhonda, and their auntie Rhonda loves them. The fact that Rhonda is white didn't matter. Rhonda always found time, during her visits with Erica, to interact with the girls whether she played board games or read a Harry Potter story. It was during those times that she would always feel better about her own situation, which, even though Harry swore to never father another child, she still deemed temporary. Even after being married for seven years, with no significant progress made on the matter, Rhonda still believed that one day he'd change his mind and father her child.

"And please Lord, look after Amanda. Guide her through these times of troubles and let her be safe and far from harm. And please Lord, lead her back to her friends, we miss her. We ask this in Jesus' name, Amen," After finally tearing themselves away from Erica's home video, Mrs. Green concluded the opening prayer the same way she's been ending it since finding out about Amanda's martial troubles, over two weeks ago. She called Amanda to make sure she was all right, since she had missed two meetings without as much as a phone call, and that's when Mike told her that his wife had moved out. "I don't know where she is, or has been. I haven't heard from her since she left," Mike said dryly. Mrs. Green wanted to unleash a barrage of questions starting with 'why? Where? And how long?' but instead settled on leaving her name and number with a brief plea. "Please, call me when you hear from her so I'll know she's okay," she calmly asked, knowing full well that the chances of Mike calling with any information were slim to none. But what else could she do? She didn't know Mike well enough to pry, which is probably how he would have viewed her had she asked any questions.

Mrs. Green has had a strange feeling about Mike ever since Amanda's first meeting, when he accompanied his wife to her house a

Pink October.doc 199

few months before Tasha joined the group. He seemed to be more interested in who the members were than he was in his wife's fight for her life. And when he saw that one of the members was a man, he suddenly became overly affectionate, like he had just recently been released from prison and just had to have her right then and there. Like he needed to show Thomas that his wife was off limits. "That guy has some serious issues," Were Mrs. Green's exact words after Amanda's first meeting. Once Mike saw that Thomas wasn't the least bit interested in his wife he no longer had to miss every other Monday from work to escort her to Mrs. Green's weekly gatherings. That much was obvious to Mrs. Green.

"Where's the meat?" Carla asked, reminiscent of the popular '80's commercial, as she inspected the sandwich she'd taken from the serving tray Mrs. Green had brought into the den.

"There is no meat. These are grilled vegetable sandwiches...and before you go turning your nose up, try it first," Mrs. Green instructed, sounding like a mother trying to get her child to eat liver for the first time.

"Grilled vegetable sandwiches!" Seated on the sofa between Tasha and Rhonda, Erica turned her nose up. Mrs. Green moved from Carla to in front of the sofa, between all four ladies seated (Tasha, Erica, Rhonda and Michelle) and the TV 'Take a sandwich, then I'll move,' is what the ladies figured Mrs. Green's body language was screaming. Each one of them took a sandwich. "Are you supposed to grill vegetables? I mean, I've eaten them raw, broiled, baked but never grilled and definitely never as the main ingredient in a sandwich. This is where the meat is supposed to be," Erica continued as she watched Tasha take a bite from the sandwich. If Tasha had given any indication that the sandwich was unpleasant, Erica was ready to set the sandwich right back on the tray.

"Aw...this is terrible. Absolutely terrible," Tasha uttered, her face twisted like she could spit out the small bite she'd just taken.

"I'll pass," Erica sat her sandwich back on the tray.

"I'm just playing with you...this is really good... really," Tasha laughed.

"Anyway, if you touch it, you eat it," Taking a seat on the ottoman next to the sofa, Carla carefully balanced her own sandwich on a paper towel spread across her lap.

"That only applies to my husband," Erica winked before retaking the sandwich she'd just put back down.

"You're a freak," Rhonda shook her head as she took a sandwich from the tray.

"Again, that only applies..."

"That only applies to my husband!" The entire room interrupted, mockingly finishing Erica's statement.

Erica took a bite out of her sandwich then laughed so hard that Tasha had to pat her on the back to help move the small bite down her throat. Once her breathing passage was free from obstruction, Erica blurted, "I'm thinking about asking Carl to get a vasectomy," Nobody said a word.

Scene 68

It was 11:55pm when Tasha finally drifted off into a peaceful nights sleep, her mind replaying the joy-filled scenes she'd seen earlier in the evening. When she woke the next morning she still found herself smiling about what she'd seen on Erica's home video, the smiles, hugs, love and affection. Tasha could hardly wait until Friday, the day of Jessica's birthday party, so that she could experience the joy up close. This year's birthday party will be different than last year's simply because the entire group was invited. Last year Carl only wanted family at his youngest daughter's second birthday celebration. Erica didn't tell anybody about her husband's wishes, so the entire group showed up. Luckily, the girls loved all the attention or Carl would've been upset a lot longer than just a few days. Back then Carl feared that he'd lose his wife to cancer, though he never said it to Erica. He has always maintained his composure when in his wife's presence, though, once alone, late at night after his wife and kid's were sound asleep, he'd lock himself in the bathroom and shed soundless tears while looking at his reflection in the mirror over the sink. But as time passed his fear subsided a bit, allowing him to once again look forward to the future he and his wife had all planned out. He had to learn to live life one day at a time all over again. He no longer needed to spend every single minute at Erica's side for fear of not being there when and/or if cancer came to take his wife, because she had beaten it. Erica was now a cancer survivor, the group had taught her that, and she taught Carl. Nobody could say for sure that the cancer would never return, but the odds were against it because Erica, like most of the group, was lucky enough to catch it early.

It was 6:35am when Tasha finally rolled out of bed. She showered, dressed and ate a microwave sausage, egg, and cheese sandwich, washing it down with a glass of orange juice, all in record time. An hour and ten minutes later she stood behind her desk handing out room assignments to the substitute teachers standing in front of her. The computer teacher was out with a severely sprained ankle and one of the gym teachers was out with the flu. "You're definitely in for a very interesting day," Tasha smirked, shaking her head as she watched the young and very attractive, light skinned, woman walk out of her office. The woman, Mrs. Simms, who was assigned to Mrs. Parker's computer class, had shoulder length, black hair atop a pie-shaped face, sort of like Sister Souljah, only with hazel eyes. She wore a dark colored skirt suit with a light colored blouse that strained against the sides of her ample breasts. Porn star-size breasts, only real and attached to a five foot three inch frame.

"What class is big tits taking?" Tracey asked, entering Tasha's office moments after the two subs exited.

"She's subbing for Mrs. Parker," Tasha answered. "But lets not refer to Mrs. Simms as big tits...how would you like it if she referred to you by the size of your ears?" Tasha responded with a playful retort. Tracey sat down in the chair in front of her desk.

"I'd kick her ass," Tracey responded with zest.

"Why would you do that when you started with the name calling?" Tasha said in a matter-of-fact kind of way.

"I can do that, she can't ...my brother is the only person I let get away with talking about these ears," Tracey smiled, tilting her head to the right as to expose her left ear.

"And how is Gary?"

"Fine, now that he knows he'll be home in April."

"Really! When did you find this out? And didn't you call and tell me?"

"I just found out yesterday. My cousin called the parole board in Texas and they said he'd been granted parole, but his release date is in April, 2002."

"Damn, why so far away?" Tasha quizzed, realizing Tracey's brother, a first time offender, had been locked up for more than nine years on a possession charge yet the parole board still decided to make him do another year before setting him free. Shit, child molesters in Texas don't do that much time.

"We all said the same thing when we got the news, but then we figured at least we finally know when he'll be coming home. And that means more to us than anything."

"I know that's right!" Tasha said, knowing how much Tracey missed her big brother. He used to take up most of their teacher's lounge chat time, especially when he had decided to focus his time and energy on writing a book, a little over a year ago.

---Ring--Ring--

"Excuse me," Tasha politely interrupted their early morning talk so that she could answer the phone.

"Principal Mills...Hey, you ...Yes I did...I did too know it was you," Tasha smiled into the receiver like a love-struck teenager, instantly oblivious to Tracey's presence. And Tracey took note,

Pink October.doc

203

waiting to tease her once her phone conversation ended. "Ok then... I'll be waiting ...Bye," Tasha said 'bye' in a low, sexy voice.

Tracey pounced before the phone could be placed back onto its cradle. "Somebody did the nasty," she teasingly sang, finally noticing that familiar glow on Tasha's face, the same glow emitted after Tasha's first night with Kevin over two years ago.

"Where did that come from?" Tasha asked, trying in vain to hide what her face so easily gave away.

"Don't play dumb with me. I saw how your face lit up while you were talking to Ronald... And don't try to tell me that wasn't Ronald, because we both know it was," Tracey held her hand out, palm towards Tasha, halting Tasha's protest before she could get it off the ground.

'How does she do that?' Thinking back to when Tracey said the exact same thing after she and Kevin slept together for the first time, Tasha shook her head before sharing the goods with Tracey. She knew that if anybody would notice her 'I've gotten laid' glow, it would be Tracey, not the members of the group. They haven't known her long enough to be able to detect that kind of thing. But Tracey knew. Tasha's body language during the morning's staff meeting gave her away, something Carla had not yet learned to read.

"It was that good, huh?"

"Yes, it was," Tasha grinned like the cat that ate the canary, elbows on top of her desk, fingers clasped underneath her chin. "I think it was as good as it was because of the sexual tension that had been building between us since our first date...God, I hope he's that good every time," Tasha finished her statement by slapping her hand against her desk for emphasis.

"I know what you mean. And for your sake, I hope he's good every time or at least a little more than half the time."

"Yes, Lord."

"You know what you gotta do if you really want to find out," Tracey smiled a mischievous smile, winking across the desk at her friend. Tasha smiled the same smile in response. She knew exactly what she needed to do. And she planned on doing it again real soon. Tonight soon.

"On a school night?" Tracey teased after hearing of Tasha's plan to spend the night with Ronald at his place. "So I guess tomorrow you'll be wearing a crocodile smile."

"God, I hope so," Tasha stood and leaned over her desk to give Tracey a high-five.

Scene 69

"When I got home I started getting ready for a long night of passion, you hear me. I had nothing but passion on my mind."

"I know that's right," Tracey settled into the leather and wood chair in front of Tasha's desk, listening as Tasha went over the details of last night's sleep-over at Ronald's.

"I picked out my sexiest lingerie, wore my sexiest black dress, you know, the strapless one with the thigh high slit. And oh yeah, no panties."

"Oh, you did the white girl thing, huh?" Tracey laughed.

"Let me finish, thank you," Tasha rolled her eyes playfully. "I also brought along some scented candles along with my favorite bath and massage oils, and a bad-ass mood tape. You know the kind you put on when you want to get your groove back."

"Is that the same as doin' the nasty?" Tracey interrupted.

"Will you please let me finish my story," Tasha rolled her eyes. "Anyway, before I was so rudely interrupted, it was going better than good. He cooked a fabulous dinner, which turned out to be the best pepper steak I've ever had. There was wine, candle light, soothing music and to top it off we ate in front of a small fire he had going in the fireplace."

"Small compared to the fire you had burning in your fireplace."

Tasha smiled, rolled her eyes once more, then continued. "After dinner we slow-danced next to the table. At that point I think M&M's would've melted in my hand, I was just that ready. And from the bulge in his pants, I could tell that he was too," Tasha paused for emphasis. "And that's when the unexpected happened."

"He went down on you right in front of the fireplace," Tracey, anticipation pushing her to the edge of her seat, interjected with a 'come on with the story' tone of voice.

"You really need to stop watching Sex in the City," Tasha gave a brief 'Girl you need to quit' look before continuing. "Tamara dropped Tara off so that she could go console her sister."

"You're lying!"

"I wish I was, but I'm not. Apparently her sister's husband has been dipping his spoon in some other woman's bowl, so Tamara had to ruin my party," Tasha shook her head in disbelief. "I couldn't believe it. That was the second time she's interrupted my groove. It's like she has some kind of hard dick signaling device hidden in Ronald's house that alerts her every time it looks like he's about to get

Pink October.doc   205

some. That way she can speed over and run interference, using their daughter to ensure a successful block."

"I thought you knew. Nobody's better at cockblocking than a baby's momma."

"How about an ex-wife slash baby's momma?" Tasha nodded as if to say top that.

"How did the evening turn out, or did you pack up and go home?"

"I wanted to, but Ronald really didn't want me to leave, so I stayed. And you know what? I'm glad I did," Tasha said, pausing a moment before going into detail about the pleasant night she spent with Ronald and Tara. How they had a rice crispy treat cook-off before Ronald declared it past Tara's bedtime. Ronald cooked the treats on his daughter's behalf and Tara was the judge. Ronald's treats were made according to the recipe, except for a dash of something he refused to share with either Tara or Tasha. It was of no surprise to Tasha when Tara named her father's treats the winner, but when she winked then whispered, "Yours taste better, but he is my daddy, so I had to make him feel good about himself," Tasha almost cried.

That night Tasha slept in the guest bedroom alone, that is until Ronald crept into her bed after he made sure that Tara was "sound" asleep. They talked until their eyelids were too heavy to hold up any longer. At 5:30am, Tasha woke to find that Ronald had made her breakfast in bed. With breakfast out of the way so early in the morning, they had enough time to have sex, lay in each other's arms and shower before Tara got up and they both had to leave for work. "And it was good," Tasha said emphatically before sharing most of this morning's surprise session, only to stop just when the story was getting good. If Tracey wanted to hear the extended version she'd have to come back to Tasha's office later, after the morning's scheduled fire drill. Like always, Tracey wanted to hear.

Scene 70

By twelve o'clock, two hours into her work day, Amanda had already made sixty dollars, forty dollars coming from her most faithful customer, Tom, who's one of the many C.P.A.'s with a downtown office near the club. He usually stops by on his lunch break hoping to catch Amanda before any of the other patrons could lasso her time, which is also his time since it wouldn't be long before he'd have to be back at his office. Tom was Amanda's first lap-dance recipient, and the only patron she'd ever considered dating out side of the club, but decided against it. But if she were to ever date someone she'd met at the club, Tom would be that somebody. Amanda found him appealing. He's six foot, three inches tall with blond hair. And his ass is the tightest she's ever seen. At least that's how it looks in slacks. He is the man she's been dreaming about since adolescence. The perfect man for her, physically. The only drawback being the gold wedding band he wore on his long, salon tanned finger. That, and it being against club rules for employees to date patrons, was more than enough reason to keep their relationship strictly business, even though he did remind her of her favorite Calvin Klein underwear model. The one she had taped to her dorm room wall throughout her brief collegiate career. She loved that poster, which was actually the back page of a Playboy magazine she'd taken from a friend's apartment while they were away taking a biology exam.

"He is hot, ain't he?" Cori, a dark haired, naturally large breasted dancer, nudged Amanda's arm, snapping her out of her gaze. "I think he likes you," Cori added. She and Amanda stood scantly dressed next to the table Tom had just vacated, watching him stroll out of the club on his way back to his office.

"What makes you say that?" Amanda asked purely as an attempt to disguise the fact that she's known how he felt for quite sometime. In fact, Tom has asked her out on several occasions to which she declined. Not because of the club's rules and his being married, but because she was married. Although her marriage was in the process of being terminated, she still viewed it as cheating.

"I've been working here long enough to spot that kind of thing in my sleep. I bet he told you he and his wife were having problems. They're probably headed for a divorce, and the only reason he hasn't left yet is because of the kids. After telling you all that, I bet he still finds a way to ask you out to dinner or a movie. They do that to make it look like they're interest in us isn't just sexual," Cori, who has been dancing at Expose` for three years, nodded for emphasis. "If I were you I'd milk that cash cow," She winked then abruptly walked off, heading towards the elderly gentleman that had just taken a seat two tables to their left. He was Cori's cash cow, and it was obvious.

Cori was right about everything she said about Tom and his personal situation, but her suggestion about using him as a cash cow went in one ear and out the other. Having a cash cow wasn't on, or anywhere near, Amanda's agenda. Her plan was to go back to college and complete her mortuary science studies, not become a prostitute. And that's what Cori was suggesting, indirectly. "Girl, it's not prostitution when you know the guy...You get money from your boyfriend or husband, don't you? It's the same thing. If I feel comfortable enough to have sex with a guy, he can feel comfortable enough to give me what I want," is how Cori felt about it. Amanda saw it differently, especially since most of the girls at the club with cash cows/sugar-daddies were having sex with them. That was a route Amanda refused to take.

At the end of her shift, Amanda caught a cab back to Wanda's Oak Park apartment, which subtracted twenty dollars from the two hundred thirty dollars she made for the day. Between going to and from work, Amanda spent forty dollars a day, over two hundred dollars a week on transportation. That money could've been used to purchase her own car or on getting her own place, is how Amanda started to feel. "Get the car first and worry about finding a place later," Wanda suggested before Amanda could respond to this morning's cab driver, who had gotten out of his car and repeatedly pressed his finger against the buzzer. "When you get home from work call this number and ask for Stan. Tell him you're the friend I told him about and he'll give you a great deal on a nice used car. But wait until you get home. That'll give me time to sweet talk him into giving you what you want," Wanda winked, then jotted down her friend's business number on a torn piece of paper towel. Amanda made sure to put the number in her purse before she headed down stairs to her cab.

Amanda called Stan as soon as she made it home. "Come on in tomorrow and I promise I'll have you in a car within an hour," His voice beamed with the kind of arrogance reserved for the city's top salesman.

By the end of their conversation, during which Stan collected all of the information he would need to secure Amanda's loan, Amanda felt as if a huge load had been lifted from her shoulders. She stood at the kitchen window sipping hot chocolate as she stared out into Chicago's cloudless winter sky, smiling at the thought of leaping her second hurdle since leaving Mike. And it felt good. Damn good, actually.

Scene 71

"Would you like anything else?" The freckle-faced teenager asked, his voice cracking because of the onset of puberty.

"No, that'll be all. Thank you," Amanda answered then watched the Subway cashier ring up her purchase.

After paying for her six-inch seafood sub, small bag of potato chips and diet Mountain Dew, Amanda took her order over to one of the empty window booths where she would be able to see Tasha and Carla pulling into the health club parking lot across the street. But that wasn't the only reason she took a window seat. She was now the proud owner of the black Honda Accord sedan, '95 model, parked right outside of the window. Stan followed through with his promise, though it took him more than an hour because of the extra doctoring he did to her loan application in order to secure the loan. With that done, Amanda chose something she could have paid off in no time, thanks to the sizable discount Stan gave on the 'like new' used car. She would definitely have to thank Wanda later.

After driving off the lot, Amanda's subconscious mind took over and guided her to where she needed to be, which explains how she ended up sitting in Subway waiting on Tasha and Carla to pull into the parking lot across the street. The only time she'd really think about her weekly meetings was on Mondays, the group's day to meet. That was until Wanda asked, "When was the last time you've been to a meeting?" From that day on she couldn't stop thinking about her friends, but, at the same time, she couldn't take a chance of going back to Mrs. Green's place where there was a possibility she'd run into a disgruntled, soon to be ex-husband. Especially with the group still in the dark about her marital woes, another reason her subconscious mind led her here on this Thursday evening.

Having finished off her meal, Amanda went out to her car where she placed her coat in the passenger seat before coming to rest in the driver's seat. She sat in her car, listening to the radio, until she spotted Tasha's BMW turning into the health club parking lot. It was a little pass 6pm. The time had finally arrived. She was about to be reunited with her friends, at least two of them. She'd figure out when it would be best for her to rejoin the group another time. For now, Tasha and Carla were in her sights.

"Tasha...Carla, wait!" After pulling into a parking space four spaces over from where Tasha and Carla had parked, then jumping out of her car and hastily walking after her friends, Amanda called out just as they stepped in front of the automatic sliding doors at the gym's entrance. Both Tasha and Carla turned to face whoever it was calling out their names. Huge grins spread across their faces when they saw their estranged friend. They raced into each other's arms like they were starring in an old black and white movie. They stood in the parking lot locked in a wordless, three-way embrace for what seemed like an eternity.

"I'm sorry it's been so long," Amanda uttered. "I know I should've called...but things started happening so fast..."

"Don't worry about that...as long as you're all right. You are all right, aren't you?" Carla asked teasingly, breaking from their embrace so that she could get a good look at Amanda's expression. The same Amanda she used to make fun of. The same Amanda she missed dearly.

"Oh yeah, I'm fine. My marriage, now that's a different story," Amanda added without a hint of sorrow in her voice.

"You want to talk about it?" Tasha hesitantly asked, unsure if she was reading Amanda's body language correctly.

"With all that she's put us through, of course she wants to talk about it," Carla interjected. "Now lets go inside and talk. It is cold as hell out here, ladies," She grinned, holding out her left hand as if re-introducing Tasha and Amanda to the bitter cold.

Once inside they gathered around one of the small tables in the gym's south lounging area and listened as Amanda told of a marriage that had actually failed before it began. The verbal abuse, the physical abuse, the insecurity and the forced sodomy, which turned out to be the last straw. She shared almost everything within an hour; her current occupation being the only subject she avoided. She figured they wouldn't understand and at this point she didn't know how to make them understand. Dancing wasn't something she was particularly proud of herself, but it was how she planned to pay for her education which will allow her to move on to a more respected career.

"I'm glad to hear that everything is okay," Tasha said consolingly, unable to believe what she'd just heard. She never understood why women would choose to stick around so long after the first signs of abuse. "Will you be able to make Jessica's birthday party, tomorrow? Everybody's going to be there."

"I wouldn't miss it for the world," Amanda said, fighting back the tears Tasha and Carla's show of support had stirred deep within her soul. "I wouldn't miss it for the world," She repeated, a single tear breaking loose and running down her left cheek. She couldn't hold back forever.

Scene 72

Tasha found herself thinking back to Amanda's horrifying tale of abuse the rest of the night. She was so shaken by Amanda's stories of being physically attacked that she passed on hoagies and fries with Ronald, which she's been craving ever since he'd taken her to The Home of The Hoagy (on 111th and Loomis) during Christmas break. She just didn't understand why Amanda put up with his shit for as long as she did, and she didn't ask her why. She couldn't ask something like that. Not without seeming like she placed some of the blame on her for allowing it to happen, which is exactly how she felt. In her eyes Amanda was as much at fault as he was. Tasha did feel for her for having been abused, but she also felt that Amanda could've left years ago, sparing herself the deep emotional and physical scars he undoubtedly left behind. Tanya felt the same way. They talked about it later that evening, before Tasha went to bed. Neither Tasha nor Tanya have ever been in an abusive relationship, yet they still considered themselves leading authorities on what Amanda could've/should've done, never-mind the years of being manipulated by Mike and his promises to change and seek help for his illness. Never-mind how Amanda had, at one time, felt somewhat responsible for his behavior. It was her own infidelity that lit the abuse fuse in the first place, at least that's how she felt. She didn't share that part of her story with Tasha and Carla. Even if she had shared that small bit of information it still wouldn't have changed Tasha's mind about women that allow such abuse to go on. There's no excuse and there never will be, as far as Tasha is concerned.

Friday afternoon Tasha still found herself drifting back to Thursday's surprise meeting with Amanda. Not even Tracey's news about her brother's parole date being moved up a few months could keep her from reliving each of Amanda's words as if they were spoken moments ago. It was as if Amanda's situation had brought an unwanted gloom into Tasha's life. Luckily she's the principal at Dr. Rhay E. Street Magnet Elementary and Greg Clark is still a real life version of Dennis the Menace. Today's dilemma involved someone posting unkind, and completely untrue statements about a sixth grader named Craig on an adult bulletin board, on the Internet. The bulletin board catered to those people who enjoyed S&M, particularly the spanking and hot wax part. Craig accused Greg because he'd heard that Greg had been accused of the same thing before. And since he's been teasing Greg about being teacher's pet for a

Gary Norman   212

substitute teacher, in his eyes, the evidence pointed directly at Greg. The teasing even went as far as someone, probably Craig, leaving a note on the sub's desk asking that she meet her admirer at locker sixty-five between forth and fifth period. Locker sixty-five is Greg's locker. Craig didn't know anything about any of that, at least that's what he told Tasha when he told her why he felt it was Greg Clark who posted his name, number, and home address on the adult web-page. Either way, after that embarrassing 'lunch time' meeting with Mrs. Simms, Greg declared war, which also led to Craig's accusations being aimed at Greg. But, same as before, with no real evidence Tasha was powerless. What could she do when all Craig had were his accusations? He didn't have any real proof. And since Greg didn't admit to it, there was nothing Tasha could do but laugh. Of course she had to wait until she was alone in her office to do that.

At the end of her workday, Tasha drove straight home. She showered, dressed and finished off the remainder of last night's spaghetti all before retrieving the gift wrapped Venus and Serena Williams dolls from the downstairs closet and driving over to Erica's house for Jessica's birthday party. The entire group had planned on joining the Danials' family in celebrating their youngest daughter's third birthday, but Michelle couldn't make it because of a bad chest cold and Amanda was a no show. That was apparent when Erica greeted Tasha at her front door by asking, "Is Amanda with you?" before greeting the person standing in front of her.

"Hello to you, too," Tasha said, playfully rolling her eyes at Erica, who had gone as far as scanning the area in front of her house in hopes of stopping Amanda. "She's not out there, but she is coming," Tasha entered the house with a reassuring smile, calming Erica with a simple flash of her pearly whites. Everybody wanted to see Amanda, and, moments after the first slice of birthday cake had been placed on a Styrofoam plate and sat in front of the birthday girl (who was decked out in the cutest pink and green dress), the doorbell rang. It was Amanda.

Without saying a word Carla, after answering the door, hugged Amanda like she'd just returned from war before ushering her into Erica's home towards the dining room. Everybody's face lit up when they saw Amanda standing next to Carla, in the dining room's entranceway. Carl, working the camcorder just like he'd done the year before, captured every smile, tear, and hug on film.

"Ladies...Ladies...You're making the birthday girl cry," Handing the camera to Kim, his oldest angel, so that taping could continue, Carl interrupted their tearful reunion/huddle before assuring

Pink October.doc   213

his little girl that everybody was crying because they were happy, not sad.

"I think now is a good time to give Jessica her presents," Erica whispered, using the back of her hand to wipe tears from her cheeks. "She'll feel better and we'll be able to talk in the kitchen while she and her sisters play," She winked at Amanda before tending to her youngest child. Kim, the film's new director, captured the exchange on film.

While Kim and Teri helped Jessica with her toys, that's what they called what they were doing since they figured they were getting too old to play with toys, Erica left Carl to his taping while she joined the group in the kitchen.

"Aren't you supposed to be out there with the kids, Bozo?" Looking back over her shoulder, Tasha's comment drew laughter from the group as four of them took seats around the kitchen table, two of them standing nearby.

"I stopped being a clown when Jessica looked up at me and said, 'I'm too old for the clown thing, auntie Rhonda,'" Rhonda, wearing the same clown make-up and costume from last year, smiled as she shared Jessica's announcement with everybody. "I think she just needs a new clown...What do you think, Erica?" She winked at her friend, who standing behind Tasha's chair, then leaned over Tasha's shoulder and pressed the side of her face against Tasha's, smearing clown make-up all over her left cheek.

After the laughter had subsided, Amanda tried to apologize for not calling during her hiatus but Mrs. Green wouldn't have it. "With all that you've been through, we're just glad you were able to get out in one piece," Mrs. Green reached across the table and took both of Amanda's hands, consoling her with the kind of tenderness a mother has for her daughter. Carla told everybody about Amanda's situation earlier so that when she arrived no one would bring up the painful past by asking uncomfortable questions. "You know what this calls for?" Mrs. Green asked the entire room, an 'up to no good' look covering her face. "A girls night," She smiled.

"When?" Amanda asked with the same enthusiasm as a child when he or she learns of an upcoming trip to Great America.

"Is next Friday all right with everybody?"

"Can we make it Saturday?" Tasha asked as if suddenly remembering an engagement already scheduled for next Friday.

"Oh yeah, your follow-up is on that day," Mrs. Green smiled, obviously surprising Tasha with how she had remembered.

Gary Norman

"So that'll make three things we'll need to celebrate," Carla added nonchalantly.

"What's the third thing?" Mrs. Green asked the question any of the other women would've asked, if she hadn't beat them to it.

Carla didn't answer immediately. First she scanned the faces of the women around her, heightening the anticipation a bit, then blurted, "I'm pregnant," Catching the entire room completely off guard. A few of the women wanted to say 'I told you so', but didn't. They knew Carla wouldn't like that, not when she used to deny the possibility of her ever getting back together with her ex-husband, even though their relationship was much stronger now that they were divorced.

"Thanks for stealing my spotlight," Amanda teased, whispering in Carla's ear as they hugged.

The group was whole again. Whole and safe...

Scene 73

Even though both women did nothing particularly different from their normal routines, the week still seemed to fly by for both Tasha and Amanda. While Amanda eagerly anticipated her first "girl's night out," Tasha dreaded her upcoming follow-up for fear of receiving bad news. And nothing she did was enough to put an end to that fear, though, between being pampered by her parents and Ronald, it was made more bearable. Her nightmares, which had returned a few days before her scheduled follow-up, didn't pack that 'I'm too scared to open my eyes' kind of punch, not like her pre-support group nightmares had done.

During Monday night's meeting everybody gave encouraging words and personal testimonies to help ease Tasha's fear. They had all lived through the same run-wild emotions she was undoubtedly experiencing, so their input was invaluable. When she thought about it later that night while watching the news from her bed, she saw that they were right. "Early detection equals high survival rate," Carla said in between sampling one of the honey-whipped peanut butter filled celery sticks Mrs. Green had prepared for the group function. "Don't let your imagination get the best of you...you'll be fine, trust me," Erica added convincingly.

With that said, Tasha was able to take hold of her out-of-control emotions and drift off into what turned out to be her only pleasant night's sleep of the week, which didn't last that long. Fear, anxiety, and anticipation put an end to her pleasant sleeping, which in turn added exhaustion to her already unstable emotional state.

"Why don't we both call in sick tomorrow, that way I'll have an entire day to take your mind off of Friday's follow-up," Ronald made this suggestion Wednesday night as they stood in line at The Home of the Hoagy, waiting on their number to be called.

"If that includes a deep tissue massage and breakfast in bed the next morning, you got a deal," Tasha responded with a seductive glint in her eye. Ronald agreed to her terms, without hesitation.

Friday morning, after a night of tension relieving sex, Ronald greeted Tasha with a pre-dawn breakfast in bed fit for a Queen. Grits. Eggs. Canadian bacon. Homemade buttermilk biscuits with grape jelly and orange juice. I can really get used to this, Tasha thought as Ronald, sitting next to her on the bed, fed her the last bit of a jelly-topped biscuit.

Gary Norman

After breakfast Ronald ran her bath water, then, while Tasha soaked in the hot sudsy water enjoying her banana yogurt as R. Kelly crooned in the background, picked out her wears for the day, which he laid over the arm of the plush chair next to Tasha's bed.

When Tasha emerged from the bathroom she jokingly rubbed the back of her hands over her eyes as if she was trying to make sure that what she was seeing wasn't a figment of her imagination. She could hardly believe how complete their relationship seemed in such a short period of time. Short compared to how long it took her to feel that close to Kevin. It was as if she and Ronald had been together for years, not months. The thought of how much better off she was with Ronald as opposed to Kevin made her smile. It also made her horny, which led to her having to take another shower before her noon appointment.

"Don't worry, baby...everything will be fine," Tanya assured her daughter. Tasha had called to let her know she was on her way to her appointment and, as brief as the call was, Tanya was still able to sense her daughter's fear and uneasiness. The same fear and uneasiness Tasha had so expertly hid from Ronald. Tasha couldn't hide her feelings from her mother. Tanya knew her only child like the back of her hand. "I'll be over right after I leave the doctor's office," Tasha added before ending her call. She had talked her parents into letting her go to this appointment alone. She told them that she wouldn't be able to keep herself from breaking down if she saw that her parents were just as scared as she was. The truth is, she wanted to be alone just in case she received bad news today. Tanya sensed as much, so she didn't argue. Today her daughter will face her fears alone and she will be triumphant. At least that's how Tanya's dream ended.

Scene 74

"Ladies, I'd like to propose a toast," Mrs. Green stood at her stage side table, raised her champagne glass and announced over the boisterous crowd at The Rodeo, a male strip club on Chicago's north side. "This is to pure joy. The pure joy Tasha felt the moment Dr. Jordan gave her the negative mammogram results. The pure joy Carla feels now that she and Jesse are expecting their first child. The pure joy we all feel now that we can, once again, look across a table at Amanda. We love and missed you," Mrs. Green tilted her glass towards Amanda, who was seated two seats to her left, before ending her toast with, "This is to pure joy. May we always experience it."

"Wait. Wait...before we toast I want to add something," Erica added just as everyone raised their glasses to complete Mrs. Green's toast, surprising them all with her last second appeal. "I just wanted to add this exact moment to our toast, because it is the first time the entire group has enjoyed a girl's night out, together. And, it's the first time we've ever had a non-member join us," Erica smiled at Tanya, who was seated two seats to her right, next to her daughter. "Maybe two firsts in one night means something...I don't know what, but hopefully it's something good. Anyway, here's to tonight. May we experience many more," Erica raised her glass. They all raised their glasses. Amanda, Michelle, Mrs. Green, Erica, Rhonda, Tasha, Tanya and Carla shared one of the large round tables close to the stage.

"That was corny," Seated at Erica's right, Rhonda teased after taking the customary 'end of toast' sip of champagne.

"That wasn't corny, Erica. It was a nice thing to say, and you're right, this is a special night. So lets be sure to enjoy every inch of it," Smiling like the Hamburglar, Mrs. Green added the last part of her statement just as the club's lights dimmed and the first stripper of the night was set to take the stage.

"Mrs. Green, I hope you know we're at The Rodeo and not a petting zoo," Carla yelled over the thunderous hoots, hollers, and catcalls the first dancer of the night received when he strutted out on stage dressed in a Chicago Police officer's uniform. He had his holster strategically positioned in a way that allowed his lone weapon to rest in it.

"I know where we are, smart-ass," Mrs. Green smiled as she hastily searched through her purse for the wad of singles she made sure to grab off of her dresser before leaving her bedroom earlier that evening. "Now watch momma reel him in," She kissed the money and wink at Carla before turning her attention back to the now half naked stripper dancing suggestively in front of Amanda, two seats to her left. "Come to momma!" Her words had already begun to slur as she yelled at the stripper in front of an obviously 'too timid' Amanda.

"I hope this doesn't turn out like your first outing," Recalling what Tasha had told her about the first 'girl's night out' she'd attended, Tanya whispered in Tasha's ear, nodding her head towards Mrs. Green. Their mouths fell open as they watched Mrs. Green tuck money into the dancer's holster with one hand, while helping him out of his shirt with the other hand.

"Ma, all I can say is be prepared for a long night or a very short one," Tasha shrugged. Just hope Mrs. Green doesn't get too drunk, is what she wanted to say. Tanya was hoping the same thing.

Tanya joined tonight's outing to help her daughter celebrate her great news. There weren't any suspicious masses to investigate, meaning the cancer had not returned. And if statistics were correct, probably never will. "I knew everything would be all right," Tanya embraced her daughter (yesterday) when Tasha showed up at her house with the good news. "Woman, please stop crying all over my baby and let her in the house before she freezes to death," William fussed from a few feet behind their embrace, Tanya's tears of joy smearing her daughter's make-up. Tanya purposely ignored his remark long enough to whisper, "I love you," over a dozen times in Tasha's ear. She was a nervous wreck, shaking like she'd been standing in the cold for hours in a pair of shorts and a tank top. Though the shaking didn't start until Tasha's car pulled in front of her house. At that point she was on the verge of an emotional breakdown, needing only a somber look on Tasha's face to push her over the edge. "Momma, I'm fine...I'm okay, really...there was no sign of cancer, so it looks like you and daddy are stuck with me for a little while longer," Tasha's voice was low and full of tenderness as she looked into her mother's teary eyes, through her own teary eyes. The mother-consoling-daughter role had reversed as Tasha took her mother by the hand and led her to the kitchen, with William silently leading the way, choking back his own tears. When they reached the kitchen, both women went from tears to smiles, though each smile held a different meaning. Tasha's smile said 'surprise!' Tanya's was the kind of smile that glows on your face after unwrapping a gift and finding something you had hoped to find underneath the wrappings and card board box. That turned out to be a pretty good Friday.

Pink October.doc 219

"Momma, I'll get him to come our way," Tasha's voice jolted Tanya back to a place where women went wild over half nude men. Tasha had moved closer to the stage where she frantically waved a ten-dollar bill over her head, trying to get the dancer's attention. "Hurry up before he gets over here," Tasha impatiently waved her mother over to the unoccupied space beside her, in front of the stage. Tanya complied, joining her daughter in waiting on 'Twelve Inch' (the strong-safety built stripper) to reach the area in front of their stage side seats. He was four patrons over, in front of Amanda, his pelvis thrusting forward, his crotch only inches from her face.

Amanda looked more than happy as she tucked that bill into his g-string. Mrs. Green looked just as happy as she eased her way closer to the stage. Once she reached the stage, 'girl's night out' was officially over. She took the snake out of the bag.

Scene 75

Monday's snow flurries added two inches to the three inches that fell on Saturday and the two inches that fell on Sunday. The snow, along with the minus fifteen degree wind chill factor, was more than enough reason for Mike to put his car in gear and drive straight home where he'd enjoy a cup of hot chocolate and a Friends rerun. But he couldn't leave yet. Not now, not when his insides were telling him that he had finally cornered the most elusive creature ever tracked by man; An estranged wife. Amanda was inside that house. He could feel it in his bones. He hasn't seen her since that incident back in December, two months ago, yet he still feels like once he's face to face with his wife he'll get her to see how silly a divorce would be. "We shouldn't even be thinking about a divorce. We should be doing all we can to make our marriage work," Just last night he stood in front of his bathroom mirror rehearsing what he'd say if he ever got the chance to talk to his wife face to face.

"Hopefully her nosy ass friends haven't poisoned her into thinking she's better off without me," He said to himself as he watched Mrs. Green's front door from half a block away.

He'd been sitting in his car for the last thirty minutes, engine running, heat blasting, waiting on the meeting to end in hopes of finally talking with his wife. She was still his wife, whether she wanted to be or not. That simple truth meant she was obligated to allow him one last chance to plead his case. At least that's what that fifth of Jim Bean told him last night. The same fifth he took swigs from on this cold Monday evening while sitting in his car watching Mrs. Green's house. And the more he said it, the more it became his truth. She had betrayed him in the most hurtful way imaginable, not the other way around. She was the reason he became the focus of snickering and pointing everywhere he went, on and off campus. He became the white guy that lost his woman to a black man, which led to his decision to leave school for a semester or two to find himself. That's what he told his parents, but it didn't take them long to find out the truth. The neighbor's son was a junior at the same school Mike and Amanda attended, and his big mouth ass told his parents what he'd heard. His parents told Mike's parents. Mike never told Amanda that his parents knew, nor did he tell her what they had to say about it. "Son, the girl's tainted goods," Mike's father confronted him with what the neighbors told him about Amanda and her black lover. "Now dump her sorry ass and get yourself a woman who hasn't been fucked by a nigger!" Mike remembered his father's exact words as if they were spoken yesterday. Up until that phone conversation, many years ago, Mike had never heard his father use the 'N' word. It was as if a black man had fucked his wife, that's how pissed Mike's father was. After that there was no way either of Mike's parents would have accepted Amanda into their family. No matter how long Mike waited, hoping things would die down. That just wasn't going to happen, not in this lifetime. As far as his parents were concerned, Amanda was the forbidden fruit and Mike would be forever cursed if he chose to take a bite. Mike took that bite when he and Amanda secretly wed down at City Hall. His parents have been estranged ever since.

Suddenly there was movement. Mrs. Green's front door opened and three seasonally dressed women stepped out onto the porch, lights from the inside of the house brightening the cold night air in the immediate area of the front porch. Mike's heart rate quickened, immediately reaching a pace consistent with that of a person who'd just completed a ten-mile run. He didn't recognize the black leather coat or the dark colored scarf wrapped around her head and neck, but he did recognize Amanda. He also recognized Carla from when he would attend the meetings with his wife. He didn't recognize the black woman, but he assumed she was Tasha, the new addition his wife had told him about back in October.

"Damn!" Mike cursed, pounding the steering wheel as he watched the three women head towards the line of parked cars in front of Mrs. Green's house. There was no way he could approach her now, not with them around. Not after what happened between them, which is probably group business by now.

"Nosy bitches!" Mike spat as the three women hugged, said a few words, laughed, said a few more words, then headed to three different cars. His mind raced and his blood boiled. "She's already fucking somebody else," was all he could think when he saw his wife standing next to a black Accord, looking through her purse as if she were trying to find her keys. "That's probably her boyfriend's car. Probably the same guy Jake told me about," His thoughts continued a downward spiral towards a harmful untruth. An untruth that will eventually get him in trouble.

"Lying Bitch!" He huffed as he put his Camaro in gear and slowly pulled away from the curb. His anger began to boil all over again, an active imagination fanning the flames of a fire that had all but died out. It was bad enough he found those birth control pills she'd obviously been taking for sometime, even though she knew how much he wanted to have a baby. But to see her getting into her new

Gary Norman

lover's car was the straw that broke the camel's back. She needed to pay for all the pain she's caused, the finger pointing and the name-calling. She needed to pay.

Amanda heard a car's engine approaching and figured it was Carla pulling away from the curb. She looked up from rummaging through her purse to give a final wave good-bye before she got in her own car. What she saw struck her with a 'disabled fawn being stalked by a tiger' kind of fear. Mike, who had double-parked alongside Amanda's car, had already exited his car and was rounding her trunk heading straight for her. His open hand slap across her face landed before she could get her scream airborne, knocking her backwards into seven inches of bitter cold snow.

"Whose car is this?" Mike hissed through clinched teeth, his eyes red from either anger or Jim Bean, as he stood over her. "Did you hear me? Whose car is this?" He demanded, his fist held out in front of him as if to say 'you better not take too long with that answer'. In an instant he went from wanting to reconcile to losing any chance he may have thought he had of winning his wife back. Whether it was a mistake or not, she was unfaithful once before, which, considering what he viewed as evidence (her new leather coat and access to somebody's car), left him no choice but to see the truth. She was at it again, is what his misinformed heart told him, the Jim Bean causing his feeling about his wife and their marriage to flip back and forth like a teenager in front of a satellite equipped television. Too bad Mike listened to the negative.

"Mike, please don't do this," The left side of her face stinging like an open wound splashed with alcohol, Amanda begged as she crawled backwards on her elbows, trying to keep at a safe distance. She couldn't get to her feet because he hovered over her, daring her to even try.

"Answer the fuckin' question," He spoke with a venomous tongue, widening his stance a bit as if he were prepared to kick the answer out of her. "Who's car are you drivin...UMPH!" He was so into extracting an answer from his wife that he didn't realize Tasha had inched close enough to deliver a menacingly effective kick to his groin until it was too late.

Tasha, who had been sitting in her car (which she parked two cars and an SUV in front of Amanda's car) listening to her Carl Thomas CD while her car warmed up, didn't realize Amanda was in trouble. She heard Amanda's voice (her words indecipherable), glanced in her side mirror and saw that she had fallen into the snow. Tasha laughed, that is until Mike appeared in her mirror seemingly out

Pink October.doc   223

of nowhere. The SUV parked behind Tasha's car blocked most of her view of anything behind it, so she wasn't able to see Mike until he stepped away from Amanda's car door. Then she saw the terrified look in Amanda's eyes. That's when she used her cellphone to call the police. She didn't have time to go over her personal information a million times with the dispatcher so she ended the call after giving her information only once. Then she slid her arms out of her winter coat, for extra mobility, before exiting her car with the least amount of noise possible. Since Mike was so into Amanda he had no idea Tasha had planted herself behind him, preparing to make her move. When she thought Mike was about to kick Amanda, she kicked him. Hard!

"Shit!" Mike groaned, pain gripping his entire body as he fell over into the snow whimpering in a fetal position. He spit out a few more undesirable words aimed at his assailant, but Tasha was undeterred as she helped Amanda to her feet.

"He hit you," Tasha noticed the redness and swelling on the left side of Amanda's face. She didn't see him hit her, but it was obvious that he had.

"I'm all right," Amanda spoke softly, her bottom lip still trembling with fear as she backed up a few feet further away from Mike's motionless body, keeping an eye on him the entire time. "Thanks for the help," She uttered, still unnerved by her husband's uncharacteristic attack. Their personal problems have always stayed behind closed doors, not outside for the whole world to see. Things have definitely gone from bad to worse, and Mike still wasn't finished.

As he laid motionless in the snow waiting on the perfect moment to unleash his vengeance on the nosy bitch that had kicked him, he listened to them with his eyes closed tight, whimpering softly all the while. He acted as if the pain was unbearable when in fact Tasha's kick slammed into the athletic support cup he wore to work, not his groin. When he heard them walking away, their voices growing distant, he knew it was time to strike. He looked up and saw that they were heading back towards the house. He also saw that Carla had joined his wife and the black woman. He knew they were talking because he could see their breath in the cold night air, but he couldn't make out their words. Now is the time, he told himself before leaping to his feet and rushing the three women from behind, focusing his rage on Tasha. Just as he was about to run straight through Tasha like a Bears linebacker and a Lions running back, she turned slightly, stuck out her leg, and sent him flying with a precisely timed

Gary Norman

hip toss. Snow crunching beneath his feet ruined his surprise attack. The same snow softened his fall to earth.

"Bitch!" He cursed, springing to his feet like he'd practiced this move over a thousand times, cutting them off before they could reach the house. "I know you're not leaving already? The party's just started," His squinted eyes and crazed stare burned holes in Tasha like a magnifying glass held over a fleeing ant. Tasha didn't flinch or blink. Her adrenaline wouldn't allow her to.

"I called the police, Mike…They should be here…"

"Don't say my name like you know me!" He barked, cutting Tasha off before she could finish. Then he rushed her, catching them off guard with his sudden lunge.

Tasha and Amanda were side by side, back peddling a few steps in front of Carla. Tasha tried to kick him, only this time he sidestepped her leg, grabbed it before she could recoil, then tried to slam her to the ground but instead lost his balance and fell on top of her. Carla ran to Mrs. Green's house for help. Amanda jumped on his back and choked him from behind, trying to stop him from hitting Tasha, who was lying underneath Mike's "two hundred-plus pound" frame trying to protect her face with her arms. He was only able to punch her in the face one good time before Amanda was able to pull him off of her. Tasha lay dazed in the snow, rocking from side to side, her hands pressed tightly against her face like it would fall to pieces if she moved them away.

"Tasha!" Ronald's voice rang out as he charged from Mrs. Green's house to Tasha's aide.

With Amanda's arm still wrapped around his neck, Mike froze as he watched the black man, first, check on the black woman he'd just attacked then jerk his head in his direction. Ronald's murderous gaze scared Mike to the bone, sobering him up even. Suddenly Mike was the one thinking about the police, and why was it taking them so long.

Scene 76

Ronald wasn't able to catch Mike like he had hoped. He would have if the police had arrived a few minutes later. By then he would've caught him. Mike couldn't have run around those cars forever. Ronald knew it and so did Mike. That's why when Mike saw the police turn onto Mrs. Green's street he took off running towards their car like he was the one who had been victimized. He might as well had handcuffed himself, he was that eager to get in the back seat and away from Ronald. "Ronald please, let the police take care of him," Mrs. Green, Erica, Michelle, and Carla had all pleaded with Ronald at some point during his pursuit of Mike, hoping that Mike could keep himself at a safe distance until the police arrived. It's not that they cared about Mike's well being, because they didn't. It was Ronald they cared about. The homicidal look in his eyes scared them just as it did Mike. Nobody wanted to see him get into any legal trouble behind beating Mike half to death, but they did want to see Mike get what he had coming, which he got the moment they arrived at the police station to press charges and sign witness statements. And this time the charges would stand. There was no chance that either Tasha or Amanda would decide against filing their complaints. Even if Amanda wanted to drop the charges, she couldn't. Things had gotten well out of control. Not that she wanted to drop the charges, especially with what he'd done, striking Tasha's face with his fist and smacking her in public, both of which were first time occurrences, like when he hit her with an open hand for the first time a few months ago. If she didn't go through with filing her complaint, what would be the next first? "A broken leg? A broken arm? A stabbing? A gunshot wound? Could he kill her like so many other abusive men wind up doing, purposely or accidentally?" Each of these scenarios played inside Amanda's mind like a motion picture based on her life, past, present, and future. A future that she, as of the moment she decided to leave her husband, now felt she had control of. That feeling was like a ray of sunshine breaking through darkened clouds, bringing a chance at life to a delicate flower. Amanda being that flower.

"You look like you're going to be just fine," Amanda's ruminations were jarred by the pretty faced, heavyset, policewoman with dark wrinkle-free skin and salt and pepper hair. The police officer was preparing to take Amanda's statement when she noticed Amanda's smile, a smile that had appeared out of nowhere.

Gary Norman

"Everything is finally all right," Amanda's smile widened even more as she sat in a metal folding chair on the other side of the officer's desk, visualizing a brand new life without Mike.

After the complaints had been filed, witness statements written and signed, the group disassembled, with most of them heading home to their warm beds hoping to sleep off the evening's exhausting events. Mrs. Green saved Michelle's son a trip by driving Michelle home. Erica and Rhonda left the station within twenty minutes of their arrival. Neither of them witnessed the attacks, Rhonda was on the phone with Harry and Erica was in the bathroom, so they excused themselves after making sure everybody involved was okay. Then it was off to a more pressing engagement.

Erica had volunteered to bake cookies for all thirty kids going on Kim's class field trip to the Shed Aquarium tomorrow. Her cookies were to be a part of the sack lunches prepared by two of the other parents. Erica needed to bake sixty cookies for the kids, two per child, plus an extra fifteen to twenty more for the parents, teachers and bus driver. All of that baking added up to two girlfriends, Erica and 'auntie' Rhonda, talking and laughing over a bottle of white wine, in Erica's kitchen, until each and every cookie had been baked, wrapped, and bagged.

Amanda returned to Wanda's apartment exhilarated, her spirits reaching cloud nine and beyond. She had finally completed her transformation from being weak and afraid to being standoffish and strong-willed. She'd taken the stand she should've taken years ago, only back then the fear of an uncertain future held her in place at Mike's side. Now she had a newly found sense of value, as if that single act of filing a complaint had opened her eyes to the obvious. She could do better, much better. And once she gets her life back together, after her divorce is final, she plans to.

"Looks like somebody's in a good mood," Wanda was on the living room sofa watching the Rams slaughter the Lions on Monday night football when Amanda entered the apartment bubbling over with laughter. Wanda just had to see that fine ass Kurt Warner before she left for the club. She was late, but so what!

"A great mood!" Amanda responded, winking at Wanda before going into the evening's excitement. Wanda's response was a simple, "Good for you, girl...Good for you."

Before heading to her Hyde Park duplex, Carla, now in her fourth week of pregnancy, stopped at Jewels for a half gallon of butter pecan. She needed to curb her sudden craving for something cold and sweet. When she made it back to her duplex she was lucky

**Pink October.doc** 227

enough to find a parking space a half a block down from her place. Finding that spot is considered luck when you live in Hyde Park, especially in the evening.

While walking back to her place Carla noticed Jesse sitting in his car, which he'd parked right across from her home. He had a nervous look on his face and a familiar glint in his eyes. Carla could see the glint in his eyes as he stepped out of his car and started his approach. His smile widening with each step he took. He also had a nervousness about him that made Carla feel a bit uneasy, but she didn't let it show.

Carla entered her house and headed straight for the kitchen, Jesse in tow rambling on and on about how happy he was about being so close to becoming a complete family. "There's only one piece missing," He added as Carla placed the ice cream in the freezer, her back facing him as he sat at the kitchen table. Carla stood frozen in front of the open freezer door, cool air assaulting her face and neck. His voice cracked, which meant he was about to say or do something that would effect both of them. Carla knew this because his voice cracked that same way the night he proposed and the night they decided to separate. Either one would be a surprise, though she did expect him to propose soon. The way he glowed with pride, after finding out she was pregnant, gave away all of his secrets. If he did propose tonight she'd say yes. She loved him more now than when they first fell in love with one another years ago, but she's been reluctant to admit it to herself or anyone else. That is until she found out she was pregnant. That's when everything changed. That's when she started to realize the group was right. They will eventually be together, for a second time, though this time things will be different, better. Jesse knows it, and so does Carla. Only if he proposed, Carla held her breath, anticipating his next words. She shut the freezer door and turned around to face Jesse. He was still sitting there at the table. Carla's wishful thinking started to get the best of her, wishful thinking that started materializing right before her eyes. There he was, in her kitchen, on one knee, holding up a black velvet box as if it were a sacrifice to the Gods. "Yes," Carla gave her teary-eyed answer before he could even ask his question.

Tasha arrived at her University Park home tired, battered, and bruised. Thirty minutes later Ronald arrived with his overnight bag hanging from his shoulder, a large supreme pizza from Pizza Hut and a six pack of Mountain Dew, which he balanced on top of the pizza box. There was no way he was going to let her spend this night alone, not after what she'd been through.

After a few slices of pizza and two Dews between the two of them, which Tasha ate tenderly, favoring the left side of her face, Ronald set his surprise night of TLC in motion. A platonic night of TLC, that's how he planned it when he packed her favorite bath salts, massage oils and scented candles into his overnight bag. But when he ran his tongue from her pretty little toes to the inside of her knees he knew he had to go further north, the sounds of arousal egging him on like he was a long distance runner on the last leg of a race.

By the end of the night she had returned the favor with a skilled mouth of her own. His oral talents curled her toes, fingers and any other part of her body that could be curled. That's never happened to her, not even on Kevin's best day, so it was befitting that she please him the same way he pleased her. Besides, she knew how men felt about oral sex. She'd have a better chance of experiencing the feel of his talented tongue again if she'd lend a talented mouth of her own. That was a trade she was willing to make. "Things are going well," her insides smiled before she drifted off to sleep, her left arm and left leg draped over his chest and right thigh, her head on his shoulder.

Surprisingly, as she lay next to Ronald, completely satisfied, Tasha had one of her usually terrifying nightmares, only this time she wasn't frightened at all. It started just as all the other nightmares had, with Tasha, her non-existent husband and children, along with her mother and father, all at her funeral. But this nightmare changed before the funeral services could begin. Out of nowhere Mrs. Green, Michelle, Rhonda, Amanda, and Carla arrived, all dressed in black, all mourning their friend, all seated to her left.

Pink October.doc

Gary Norman

Scene 77

Saturday morning, three and a half weeks after Monday night's melee, Mrs. Green received a call that sent her heart plummeting into the pit of her stomach. Easing herself into one of the chairs surrounding her kitchen table, she fought back tears as she listened to the prognosis. "A week at best is what the doctors are saying," She could feel the pain in Carl's voice as he gave her the prognosis verbatim. "It's a miracle she's still conscious, is what I've been told," He continued, his voice cracking as the reality of what he'd been told twisted his heart in knots. His wife was dying right before his eyes and besides staying at her side and showering her with enough love to last three life times, there wasn't a damn thing he could do about it. He couldn't undo what the cancer had done to her brain. He could only see to it that her last days, weeks, however long God allowed her to wake up to another day, were spent surrounded by the people who loved her most.

After he and his wife spent over an hour crying in each other's arms, Carl left her side so that he could make the phone calls they had agreed he'd make if/when her cancer ever progressed to this exact point. The girls and her parents would keep her company until he finished making the calls then the both of them would painstakingly explain the situation to their children, something neither of them looked forward to doing. They're so young, too young to handle something like this. Hell, Carl is a grown man and he could hardly handle it himself. How were they supposed to look their children in the eyes and tell them that soon they will be without a mommy? How does anyone even begin to prepare for something like that?

"I'll call everybody else. You just go back to your wife and kids...We'll see you all when we get there," After Carl told her about the inoperable tumor the doctors found on his wife's brain, Mrs. Green exhaled deeply then, with sadness saturating her every word, did what she was supposed to do. Sent Carl back to his family.

"Mrs. Green," Carl uttered, pausing to gather the strength he needed to keep his tears at bay. "Pray for my family," was all he could muster before hanging up the phone.

Scene 78

After talking with Carl, Mrs. Green held herself together long enough to call the rest of the group before she finally broke down, crying harder than she'd ever cried in all of her life. Having the strength to stand by and watch a friend, who had become as close as any family member, die is something she and Michelle never thought about when they discussed the good and bad points of starting a breast cancer support group. They had joked about the possibility of getting a member who was a kleptomaniac or maybe a member with gas so bad that they would have to conduct meetings in the backyard, even in the winter. Those were the worse points they could come up with. They didn't even consider the possibility of losing a member, or even themselves, to cancer. Now, years after their decision to form the group, a devastating reality slammed into her heart like a runaway EL train into a terminal. A reality she and Michelle should've had sense enough to consider. Not that they didn't know about the millions of lives cancer has claimed throughout history, up until the present date. They just never thought it would claim one of their members, especially in such a small group. The odds would be against it. Most of the members caught the cancer relatively early, which lessened the chances of it reoccurring. At least that's how it was supposed to be. Surely Erica wasn't supposed to be lying in some hospital bed waiting for her life's light to fade out like stage lights in between scenes, but she was. And the only thing the group could offer at this point was their prayers and love, same as her family.

After finally mustering up enough strength to stand up from the table, Mrs. Green grabbed three strawberry breakfast bars from the cabinet next to the refrigerator and a twenty ounce bottle of water from inside the frig then left her home headed for the hospital. Twenty minutes later she pulled into the hospital parking lot where she was lucky enough to find a space close to the entrance, three cars over from Rhonda's car.

Entering the hospital, blowing her warm breath on her cold hands, Mrs. Green went straight to the information desk where a young blonde woman pointed her towards the waiting room at the end of the hall, to the left, across from Erica's room.

When she turned the corner and stepped into the spacious waiting room, Mrs. Green scanned the immediate area for any sign of Rhonda, Carl, the kids, anybody. Nobody else had arrived. Not unless they were all waiting on her in Erica's room, which was likely the case. At least that's what she told herself when she turned and walked out of the waiting room heading for Erica's room.

"Come in," Mrs. Green heard Carl's voice after she'd knocked on Erica's door, room 136B.

"Hey, girl," Her arms wrapped around a sleepy Jessica, who was lying with her head just under her mother's breast, Erica greeted Mrs. Green without the slightest hint of sadness in her voice.

"Hey," Mrs. Green responded in the same manner, as best she could, before extending her greetings to everyone else in the room, Rhonda, Carl, Kim, Teri, Jessica, and Erica's parents, Joan and Ivan Carter.

Erica's parents were standing at the foot of Erica's bed. Joan had her hand underneath Erica's covers tickling her daughter's left foot when Mrs. Green entered the room. Tickling her daughter's foot was her way of attempting to make light of the situation, for the sake of the girls.

Joan and Ivan arrived moments after Carl and Erica had their talk with the girls, during which they cagily explained the severe changes their lives would soon undergo, and how they would have to be 'big girls' and help daddy when mommy's gone. The girls were beyond devastated, crying hysterically, holding onto their mother's arms and neck as if by doing so they could keep her forever. It took the combined efforts of Erica, Carl, Rhonda, Ivan and Joan to calm the girls. Their hysterical crying scared everyone in the moderate size hospital room, including the nurse who had looked in after hearing the commotion while sitting at her station, all the way down the hall. Luckily, for Mrs. Green's sake, by the time she arrived things had calmed down, though she could see evidence that the girls had been crying, actually everybody's eyes were red and puffy. If she had been present during the downpour of tears and heavy sobbing, Lord only knows what it would've taken to get her to stop crying.

"Where is everybody? Or are you the only one willing to come, besides Rhonda?" Erica managed to feign a show of strength by forcing a smile on her face.

"Girl, you know everybody's coming," Mrs. Green walked over to the left side of the bed and gave Erica's thigh a soft whack for even asking such a question.

"Don't pay her any mind, Mrs. Green. She's just a little tired," Standing over his wife and youngest child, holding his wife's hand, Carl responded, apologizing for his wife's comment.

Pink October.doc

"I'm not tired, honey! I'm just joking. God...when did everybody lose their sense of humor?" Erica snapped, obviously annoyed.

"It's not that we've lost our sense of humor...that just wasn't funny," Standing on the right side of Erica's bed, Rhonda responded in a low, sorrowful tone, tears threatening the banks of her eyelids.

A mournful silence filled the room as the reality of Rhonda's words touched each and every soul assembled. Carl squeezed Erica's hand. Erica repeatedly rubbed her hand over Jessica's curly mane. Jessica, lying with her head just below her mother's breasts, her arms wrapped around her mother's mid-section, tightened her embrace. Kim and Teri, sharing the plush sofa/sectional their father had pushed closer to the head of their mother's bed, looked at their parents with tears starting to swell, their trembling lips signaling a possible breakdown. Mrs. Green reached down and placed her hand on Erica's thigh, transferring her strength to her friend with that one simple touch, if that were at all possible. Ivan and Joan stood at the foot of Erica's bed, speechless, an anchor of heartache and distress weighing their hearts down like concrete shoes on a Mafia snitch. Solemnity descended upon the room like storm clouds over the Florida Keys. Tasha's arrival broke the deafening silence, diverting all teary-eyed stares to the door.

"Hey," Poking her head into the room, Tasha's tone was soft and suspicious. The demeanor of everyone in the room gave her the impression that she'd interrupted something. Maybe things had somehow gotten worse, if that were possible.

"Come on in here," Erica spoke up, struggling to keep steadiness to her voice. "Don't worry, nobody in here has rabies, so if you get bit you won't need any shots," Teri's laughter lightened the mood instantly. Thanks to her mother's wit.

Tasha took off her coat as she entered the room, greeting everybody as she hung her coat in the small, crowded, closet to her immediate left. Joan and Ivan introduced themselves. Rhonda excused herself from the room, "nature is calling" was the excuse she gave, but her glistening eyes said otherwise. Silence filled the room again. Carla and Michelle knocked then entered the room, followed by Amanda moments later. Fifteen minutes later, after everyone had a chance to introduce themselves, Rhonda returned with a box of half eaten chocolates that she picked up at the hospital gift shop.

"These are for you," She smiled nervously, holding the box in front of Erica's face, flaunting it teasingly before laying it on the bed next to Erica's free hand. "I hope you like 'em."

"Ah, Rhonda...how can you say you got them for me when you ate, it looks like, half the box?" Erica's smile was half cocked.

"Now what kind of friend would I be if I didn't make sure they were safe for you to eat?" Rhonda, trying as hard as she could to keep a smile on her face, reached down and took another one of the chocolate treats from the rectangular box.

Ostentatiously, Erica looked to her parents then to Mrs. Green in absolute shock, jokingly of course. "Girls, do you want some candy?" Erica asked. Of course they wanted some candy. "Then come get this box before auntie Rhonda starts making pig noises," Everyone laughed. Rhonda rolled her eyes and handed Kim the box after Erica removed a few pieces for herself and Jessica. "Thank God they've stopped crying," Erica breathed a sigh of relief as she watched her girls enjoy the last of the chocolate. "Momma's babies," A smile spread across her face and tears threatened to swell.

It wasn't long before the atmosphere in the room became more like that of a family reunion, the way family and friends were standing around laughing at past antics. Time slipped by unnoticed, that is until a knock at the door produced a nurse with a 'ten minute' warning. Carl, Ivan, and Joan took the girls down to the cafeteria, allowing Erica a few minutes alone with her friends. They still hadn't asked her about the specifics concerning her condition. Nobody wanted to upset the kids and or Erica, but now that the girls were gone Erica made it easy for them. She began without waiting for them to ask, whether they were going to or not.

"Tuesday morning I woke up with numbness up and down my left side. I figured I must've slept wrong so I didn't pay it no mind," Erica exhaled deeply before continuing slowly and methodically, her words full of pain. "When I woke up Friday morning, not only had the numbness persisted, it had gotten worse. I mean I could barely make a fist with my left hand," Her eyes were full of restrained tears as she attempted, once again, to make that same fist she couldn't make earlier. She still couldn't make that fist. "I knew then that something was wrong so I told Carl I needed to go to the hospital. A CAT scan and MRI later, I found out that the cancer had not only returned, but it returned and spread to my brain," Rhonda's grip on Erica's hand tightened, tears running down her cheek as she waited on her friend to continue. At this point there wasn't a dry eye in the room. "Well, you know the rest," Erica waved off a painful topic only to address an

Pink October.doc   235

even more painful one with her next breath. "I'll be checking out of the hospital in the morning. I don't want to spend my last days in this hospital bed, and since there's nothing they can do to..." Erica paused briefly in order to clear her throat and wipe tears from her eyes with the back of her hand. "Anyway, I'm checking out tomorrow," She squeezed Rhonda's hand for strength, hers and Rhonda's alike.

Erica didn't dare tell them what she had instructed her husband to do in regards to life support, not now. "If it comes to that, I don't want to be kept alive by some machine. Please don't let that happen," is what she'd told Carl during their 'what happens when' talk with the doctor. Reluctantly Carl nodded, his heart crying as he agreed. He would honor his wife's wishes, though he prayed things never reached that point.

"Ladies, visiting hours are over," A soft knock, followed by an even softer voice, broke the mournful silence in the room. The nurse had returned. She hated this part of her job, telling friends and family they had to be going.

"Okay, thank you...I guess we have to leave," Mrs. Green looked from the door to Erica.

"Okay, then...I'll see you all later..."

"Tomorrow!" Rhonda corrected, giving Erica's hand a loving squeeze. Everyone agreed.

"Okay, okay...tomorrow," Erica rolled her eyes playfully, trying unsuccessfully to hide her fear. "Since I don't have a choice in the matter," She shrugged. Rhonda leaned down, kissed her forehead, said her good-byes, then excused herself to the cafeteria. "I'll see you tomorrow, but right now I really need to get something into my stomach," She squeezed Erica's shoulder before leaving the room. Mrs. Green, Michelle, Tasha, Carla, and Amanda all followed suit. Down in the cafeteria they ate with Carl, the girls, Joan and Ivan. Rhonda was nowhere to be found.

Pulling out of the parking lot, Tasha noticed Rhonda sitting in her car crying with her forehead pressed against her steering wheel. "She wasn't there when I passed her car a minute ago," Tasha could've sworn as she pulled out into traffic. The driver behind her expressed his impatience, honking his horn when traffic had to slow down so that Tasha could look back over her shoulder towards the hospital parking lot, just to make sure that that was Rhonda. It was. Tasha decided to go back to the parking lot, circling the block as fast as she could. When she got back to the lot, Rhonda was gone.

Nobody wanted to intrude on Jessica, Kim, and Teri's fleeting time with their mother, but Erica insisted on having Monday night's meeting at her house, the first time a meeting had ever been held outside of Mrs. Green's house. This meeting, which was attended by Carl, the girls, Joan, Ivan and Ronald, was more for the girls than anything else. Ice cream, cake, and Liar, Liar on DVD and permission to stay up as long as they wanted to. Jessica, bless her little heart, was out like a light forty minutes into the movie, her sisters followed suit thirty minutes later. Carl captured every single minute on tape.

"I told you they couldn't hang," Carl whispered as he lifted Jessica from the couch, Erica waking Kim and Teri for their trek upstairs to their rooms.

Back downstairs they sat with the group for another forty minutes, the group's laughter masking their true feelings of sadness. A sadness they couldn't reveal in Erica's presence. "If you're walking around all sad looking, I won't be able to keep this fake smile on my face," Seated on Carl's lap, on the sofa between Rhonda and Tasha, Erica exaggerated her smile, jestingly showing as many of her teeth as she could. She made this little speech twenty minutes after the group had arrived. Rhonda looked like she was on the verge of tears. "And you know my girls need to see a smile on my face. They're already dealing with so much, bless their hearts. So please, don't take what little strength I have by crying. That wouldn't be fair to the girls," Erica instructed for the second time since leaving the hospital, her tears on the verge of swelling beyond containment. But Erica wouldn't allow that to happen, not with the girls in the same house. At this point they were so fragile that someone else's tears would send them into a teary hysteria for at least an hour. So everybody had to abide by Erica's 'no crying' rules, that's if they wanted to visit Erica and her family. Especially Rhonda, who loved Erica's children like they were her own. So of course she'll do what she has to do to protect their fragile emotions. But who would protect hers.

Later that night, after their company had gone home, after Ivan and Joan drifted off into a deep slumber down the hall in the guest room, Carl and Erica made love until sunrise, resting periodically, enjoying each other as if it were their first time. They experimented like newlyweds. Tuesday morning a teary eyed, sexually satisfied Erica laid in her husband's arms and made him promise her that he'd make love to her with the same passion until the day she died, whenever and wherever the mood struck her. He promised, kissing her from her lips to her lips, sealing the deal.

Wednesday morning Thomas flew in from Texas, joining the group's daily pilgrimage to Erica's house. "The same Erica I remembered seeing back in October," He thought when Erica opened her front door and cheerfully stepped aside so that he and Mrs. Green could enter. Once inside they were treated to a very special 'Surprise' dinner with all the trimmings. Ronald, with help from a few friends from work, helped to make Wednesday night's gathering look more like Thanksgiving dinner. Turkey, dressing, ham, macaroni and cheese, mash-potatoes, with and without cheese, dinner rolls, chittlins, two kinds of Greens, cabbage and cranberry sauce. And for dessert there was sweet-potato pie, a three-layered coconut cake, pound cake, and banana pudding.

Erica's girls loved dessert, especially on this day, a day their parents let them sample as many of the desserts as they wanted. Anything to keep them smiling. Good parents to the very end, Erica smiled as she watched Jessica steal a spoonful of her sister's (Kim) banana pudding when she wasn't looking.

Sunday evening Thomas caught a flight back to Texas. Monday morning Erica slipped into a coma. One week later, Carl, honoring his wife's wishes, took Erica off of life support. She was pronounced dead three minutes later at 10:55pm, Monday night, March 5th, 2001. Carl, who had been the picture of strength and courage throughout the entire ordeal, stood at his wife's bedside holding her lifeless hand, his sobs growing louder with each breath he took. They were supposed to grow old together with matching rocking chairs and all, Carl with his English bull dog, Erica with her cat, it didn't matter what kind. That's what they use to say, joking or not. It wasn't supposed to end like this. She wasn't supposed to leave him. Carl's cries grew louder as each memory of their happier times replayed in his mind. He collapsed onto his wife's torso as if his body weight could keep her soul from rising to heaven so soon, thus giving her more time with him and the girls. He stayed that way for over fifteen minutes, but the beeping didn't return. His sobs and the death-affirming buzz from the telemetry monitor were the only sounds in the room, his sobs spilling out into the waiting room across the hall. The girls heard their father's cries and, starting with the youngest then up to the oldest, their silent tears went from being soft sobs to half-hysterical screams. Mommy was gone, they knew because their daddy was crying. Rhonda consoled Kim as best she could, but there

Gary Norman

was no way she could silence their cries when her own cries saturated the room, blending with sobs and whimpers from everyone gathered in the waiting room.

Suddenly the air in the room was too thick to breathe, growing harder to breathe with each scream for a mother that wasn't coming back, ever. Rhonda barely made it to her car, tears dripping from her face to the freshly waxed floors, her screams bordering hysterical, same as the screams she ran away from. She couldn't escape those screams, no matter how fast she ran.

Scene 79

Three weeks after Erica's death, Michelle stood in the middle of Mrs. Green's living room, tearfully sharing her latest mother-in-law/daughter-in-law incident with the group. The animosity between the two most important women in her son's life had been put to rest. "Finally," Michelle whimpered, wiping her eyes with the back of her hand while Mrs. Green patted her back consolingly. Everybody in the room understood Michelle's joy and, at the same time, her pain. She'd made groundbreaking progress with a daughter-in-law she never thought she'd like, much less get along with. "Hell will freeze over before this hatchet gets buried," Were her exact words, almost two years ago, after Erica had joked about them one day becoming the best of friends. Erica said they'd be together, and she meant just that. It was as if she was the older and wiser of the two. Now the clouds of resentment and ill-feelings had finally lifted, allowing rays of understanding and acceptance to shine down and nurture a budding relationship and Erica wasn't around to say 'I told you so'. Michelle's joy and pain.

"I'm sorry about that," Michelle sighed nervously, stepping away from Mrs. Green's embrace, wiping the tears from her face like she'd been caught wearing makeup by a paddle wielding nun. Everybody agreed that there would be no crying at group meetings, but Michelle couldn't help it. Erica's death had forced her to step back and take a look at herself, and what she saw wasn't pretty. Here she was, refusing to accept the woman her son chose as his wife, the mother of her only grandbaby, simply because of the color of her skin. "Was I wrong for wanting my son to marry a strong black woman?"

"No you weren't wrong for wanting your son to marry a strong black woman, but when he chose to marry a strong white woman, you tripped out. That's when you were wrong," Carla's voice was caring and stern, her eyes misty. Everyone nodded their heads in silent agreement, their eyes also misty. "You're lucky he chose a white woman, because if he had married a Latino woman you wouldn't have been able to get away with the kind of stuff she let you get away with…we don't play that," she added jokingly, attempting to lighten the mood a bit. The smile stretching across Michelle's face was an acknowledging smile. She knew Carla was right, not the part about Latino women having less tolerance, about being lucky her son chose a woman like Robin, who was more understanding and forgiving than anyone she'd ever met. It was Robin who made their recent attempt

Gary Norman

at being more than just in-laws possible. That's something most women would have never considered if they had been in Robin's position, Michelle included. There's no way Michelle would've been able to get over someone choosing a dope fiend over her simply because she was black. "That was more insulting than anything else you've ever said or did," Robin joined Michelle at the kitchen table for a late night, woman to woman, talk one week after Erica's death, tears and ice cream included. Michelle's tears apologizing for her past misdeeds, Robin's tears accepting the apology. The following afternoon Michelle and Robin went shopping together, which marked the first time they've done something together, without Bryan being present. And they actually enjoyed each other's company.

Michelle started laughing as she pictured Erica shaking a finger at her while practically singing 'I told you so'. "Keep it up and before you know it you'll be marrying a white man," The mere thought of what she knew Erica would say, if she'd been here today, caused Michelle's laughter to reach sidesplitting heights. Everybody stared confusedly, as if Michelle was losing her mind right before their eyes. They all burst into the same sidesplitting laughter after Michelle's explanation.

Later that night an exhausted Amanda slid underneath her comforter and into a dreamed-filled sleep twenty minutes after WGN's news at nine ended. She started her apartment hunting in the middle of last week, finally ending her search this Monday afternoon after she, accompanied by her mother, came across a spacious one bedroom place in Country Club Hills, less than ten miles from Mrs. Green's home. "It has a patio and a fireplace," Amanda beamed while sharing the particulars of her find with the group, earlier in the evening. "And my mother absolutely loves the place," She continued, sharing with the group her personal choice as to what made the apartment so attractive. Her mother loved it. That meant more to her than anything else. They had been at odds for so long that if her mother said she loved a one-bedroom apartment in the Robert Taylor Homes Projects, Amanda would've found a way to feel just as pleased. That's how much she missed her mother.

The thought of something happening to her while she and her mother were still at odds scared her so bad that her fingers trembled as she pressed her mother's phone number into her phone's numeric key pad, almost four weeks ago. "I'm sorry," Both Amanda and Gretchen nervously blurted, breaking the awkward silence that followed their initial hellos. "Ma, you were right," Amanda began, her voice cracking with emotion. It took her nearly twenty minutes to

Pink October.doc 241

recap her marital woes to her mother, but when she finally reached the end of her horrid tale Gretchen responded just as any loving parent would have responded. Her words were as comforting as medicated lotion rubbed on irritated skin. "Believe me, I didn't want to be right," Gretchen began in a somber tone. "I wanted you to be happy. I wanted Mike to be good to you. Hell, no mother wants her daughter to end up with the same kind of asshole your stepfather was. My mother didn't want that for me and I damn sure didn't want it for you. You saw how bad things were with your stepdad and I. Lord knows I wouldn't wish that on my worse enemy," She said as a matter-of-factly. And she meant every word. "But you've learned from it...we've both learned from it. Just thank God it didn't take you as long as it took somebody we both know so well," Her voice was smiling and Amanda knew it. "Now it's time for you to heal, with my help of course," She added before proclaiming that night 'pizza night'. Amanda and Gretchen both smiled at the official title, which was first used the day Gretchen's late husband (that's how Amanda chose to refer to him) died, leaving Amanda and Gretchen behind with no choice but to be happy. Ironically, he was killed when his car was broadsided by a late model pickup truck driven by a man being chased by police after he fled the scene of a domestic disturbance. The man that killed him was also a wife beater.

By the time Amanda had gotten off the phone, she and Gretchen had made plans to get together the following day, the day after, and the day after that. Amanda couldn't wait to share this news with the group, which she did this Monday night, right before Michelle shared her tale. Erica's death was the catalyst that set their reconciliation in motion. Erica's death scared Amanda that much.

"Mike was actually good for something," Tasha had jokingly accredited Mike with getting Amanda and Gretchen to resume being a loving mother and daughter team. Amanda smiles in her sleep at that one.

Tuesday morning Rhonda woke to the sounds of water running in the adjoining master bathroom. Harry's voice could be heard over the hum of running water, butchering a familiar song as he undoubtedly rinsed remnants of last night's activities down the drain. He didn't come home last night, Rhonda was sure of that. She stayed up past 1am waiting on him to arrive home, but he never showed up. He'd spent the prior two days in Canada meeting with N.B.A. team owners in hopes of persuading them to name him the newest owner of the Grizzlies. "Didn't even call," Rhonda sighed as she smoothed out the sheets next to her. And to think she wore her most easily accessible outfit to bed, a T-shirt minus the panties. He'd usually wake her up after arriving home to find her nude from the waist down, but last night was different. Nothing happened. "He was cheating, he had to be," Rhonda was sure of it, but she didn't dare make her feelings known because she knew what his response would be. And the only thing she hated more than his response, which she knew would be an out right lie, was the way she allowed him to manipulate things, making himself seem free of all wrongdoing. He'd do that even though he knew she knew better. He also knew how badly she wanted to believe his lies, which made telling them so much easier. "Baby," He'd always begin so arrogantly, smiling as if he already knew his lie would be believed. "I'm sorry about last night. I really meant to call but I guess I was so exhausted after the all day meetings, one after another, I just fell asleep when I got back to my room. You know I'm not as young as I used to be. Those meetings take a lot out of me," He's said that a number of times after previous out-of-town business trips. Rhonda knew he was lying then, and she knew he'd lie again if she accused him now. She still remembered when she was his mistress, lying in bed next to him in the townhouse he was paying for, listening as he called his secretary to make sure all of his bases were covered in case Cathy checked on his whereabouts. "If you're so sure he's cheating why don't you have a private investigator follow him for a few days, hell, maybe even a few weeks. That way you'll have proof, one way or the other," Erica said during one of the many times she's consoled Rhonda after her suspicions had gotten the best of her.

Rhonda had actually given it some thought but decided against it, fearing knowing the truth would be a thousand times worse than not knowing. At least that's what she'd tell herself as she'd listen to one of Harry's well rehearsed lies, accepting the expensive gifts he'd shower her with in hopes of smoothing over her anger. He'd always accomplish exactly what he set out to do and that was to steer her thoughts as far away from divorce proceedings as he could. "You have him by the balls, and he knows it. Why do you think he always has some kind of gift when he comes through that door? It's not because he's sorry, because if he was he wouldn't do the same shit again and again," Erica had once ranted before trading in her more vocal stance against Harry's blatant infidelities for more of a support/shoulder to cry on stance. She knew that no matter what Harry did, Rhonda would still search for ways to make their marriage work.

Pink October.doc   243

Rhonda lay in bed, tears running from the corners of her eyes onto her pillowcase, replaying Erica's words in her mind over and over again. She was absolutely right. Rhonda had seen the undeniable evidence over the past few years. The late night business meetings he'd forget to mention until after the fact. The personal cell-phones he'd try to hide, even though he'd claim it was for business purposes. The time he spent at the club claiming his presence was needed to keep business in order, even though he sold his share of the club years ago. "The present owners are also close friends of mine," He'd say with a shrug as if to show Rhonda his patience was dwindling and he was getting fed up with her unfounded accusations. "If I can help them get the most out of their investment, of course I'll help," He'd sound so sincere she'd almost believe him. If Rhonda had never been the 'other woman' she would've believed him. Maybe that was the problem, having been the other woman she knew too much about him. Or she thought she did. He could've changed, now choosing to be with only one woman instead of many. He did choose her over Cathy. He could've continued their affair, but he didn't. He made his choice. Maybe, just maybe, she was overreacting. With that thought, Rhonda pressed her teary face into her pillow and cursed herself for being so weak when it came to her needing to confront her husband with the evidence she'd stockpiled against him. "Circumstantial evidence" She could almost hear the reply he'd give if confronted. In a way, he would be right. Rhonda's so called evidence was circumstantial, but that was only because she chose not to look too deep for fear of what she'd find.

Out of sheer force of habit, Rhonda, sniffling back her sobs, picked up the phone sitting atop the night stand next to the bed, and dialed the first three digits of Erica's home number. In that instant, the painful realization of her friend's death grabbed hold of her heart like a pitbull would a smaller dog.

"Damn," She uttered the single word before setting the phone back in its cradle then rolling over onto her back where she laid dazedly, staring at the ceiling. She needed to talk to Erica, her best friend. A friend she loved like a sister. A sister that had been so understanding when others would have tired and turned a deaf ear after they'd realize she had turned a deaf ear to any talk intended to prompt her to divorce the husband she loved so much. Erica knew how she and Harry met. She knew about their affair. She knew how Harry had chosen her over Cathy. Erica understood, the group wouldn't. Rhonda dismissed the thought of talking to the group just as fast as it popped into her head. "This is my problem and I'll deal with it as best I can, by myself," She suddenly declared as if gaining strength from dismissing such an absurd thought. Sharing her marital pitfalls with the group was something she just wasn't comfortable with, with or without Erica's presence.

"But if I do find out he's cheating I'll...I'll...," before she could turn her thought, a thought she really didn't mean, into a personal morale inspiring phrase, the shower cut off, leaving only Harry's brutal rendition of *Born in the U.S.A.* to spill out into the bedroom.

Rhonda sprang from her bed and dashed out of the room and down the hall to the guest bathroom where she splashed cold water on her face in hopes of concealing the fact that she'd been crying. Chances are he wouldn't have noticed or even cared about her tears, though she liked to believe he would have, thus proving, in a way only she could explain, her marriage was worth every one of her tears.

Rhonda stared somberly at her reflection in the mirror above the bathroom sink, water dripping from her face, her eyes red and on the verge of tearing once more, before suddenly remembering something even more painful than the thought of her husband being unfaithful. "I haven't visited Erica's girls in two weeks," She closed her eyes as if in silent prayer, the pain in her voice was evident. The pain of seeing the girls, knowing they missed their mother as much as she does, would magnify the pain she already felt by ten. That was one of her reasons for letting so much time go by without once seeing the girls. But that wasn't the only reason. As selfish as it may sound, Rhonda was mad at Erica for dying. Dying and leaving her to face the rest of her days alone, without a best friend to experience life's pleasures with, a best friend that would help her through the hard times. It wasn't that she didn't love the other members of the group, because she did. She just wasn't as close with any of the other members as she was with Erica. Erica knew things about her that she'd never share with the group. "And oh yeah, my life is no where near as perfect as it may look. I mean, things in my life go only two ways, bad or worse. The bad is I suspect that my husband is cheating on me, and I think he has been for years. The worse is, I allow it to happen by acting as if it's not...but then again, I don't have any proof...and that's only because I'm too scared to take the steps needed to find out the truth. Don't ask how I know he's cheating because I can't tell you how I started out as his mistress, probably one of many at that time," Rhonda stared at her reflection, shaking her head at how ridiculous she'd sound sharing such B.S. with the group. How could she seriously consider standing in front of the group with

Pink October.doc   245

such non-sense when Tasha stood up a few weeks ago to tell how Ronald's suggestion to go in for a "stress easing" mammogram helped to rid her of the nightmares that had returned after Erica's death.   A week later Amanda talked of how, because of the suddenness of Erica's death and her fear of losing her mother while they were at odds, she and her mother finally patched things up. Then, the same night Amanda shared her story, Michelle stood in the exact spot Tasha had occupied the previous week and told of how she and daughter-in-law had become closer since Erica's death. Michelle had even apologized for her past   "immature" behavior.

Rhonda's accusations weren't nearly as significant as either of their "shared tales of personal triumphs." Plus she really didn't have proof, is what she told herself, her seesawing feelings on the upswing for the fifth time this morning. The downward fall would come with the next beat of her heart, that's how often her feelings changed.

"Maybe I should focus all of my attention on my upcoming birthday," Rhonda flashed a teethy, emotionless, smile at her reflection. She nearly forgot about her upcoming fortieth birthday, which was understandable considering her best friend had recently died. A best friend who wouldn't be there to say 'Happy Birthday' as she's done in the past.

Scene 80

"I can't wait to see her face when she walks through that door," Tasha said as she joined Michelle, Amanda and Carla in putting up the decorations and setting the table.

"Tell me about it," Amanda said as she set the Styrofoam cups by the punch bowl. "She probably thinks we forgot."

"That's why this will be a total surprise, surprise party," Mrs. Green added as she entered the dining room, coming from the kitchen. It was Mrs. Green's idea to surprise Rhonda with a surprise birthday party two days before her birthday, during this Monday night's meeting. "If we wait until her birthday, or after her birthday, she'll suspect something," She unveiled her strategy during last week's meeting while Rhonda was in the kitchen talking to her husband via cellphone.

Everybody missed Erica, the pain of losing her still drew tears from each of them when they were alone, be it in the shower or under their covers. But Rhonda's pain went a lot deeper than that. Erica was her best friend, her confidant. Rhonda's pain went as deep as actually making her physically sick for the entire week following Erica's funeral. Rhonda told everyone that it was something she'd eaten, but they knew better. They understood. The way Rhonda broke down at the first meeting after Erica's funeral proved their theory of what actually made her sick to be true. On that night, Rhonda cried until she passed out, scaring everybody in the room until Mrs. Green and Michelle finally got her to open her eyes, which she did five minutes before the ambulance arrived. So Rhonda definitely needed this night. They all did.

"Do the Lakers play tonight?" Carla asked Michelle, both women standing at the punch bowl filling their cups.

"I think so...what time is it?"

"It's almost eight o'clock."

"I think the pre-game show started at seven," Amanda added, her interest in the Lakers had grown since they hired Phil Jackson as their coach. Plus she thinks Robert Horry is fine as hell.

"Did Rhonda call anyone to say that she'll be late? It's almost eight o'clock and I haven't heard from her," Mrs. Green asked no one in particular.

"I haven't heard from her," Tasha responded before running her pointing finger alongside the cake. The icing was calling her like Pookie from New Jack City. "I'll give her another ten minutes, then I'll give her a call...and I won't say anything about the surprise," Tasha

Pink October.doc
247

cut in before Mrs. Green could open her mouth. "Now lets go watch those fine ass Lakers," Tasha locked arms with Mrs. Green, leading her out of the dining room and into the den. It was two minutes to go before the end of the first quarter. That should take about ten minutes.

Scene 81

"Why today? God, why today?" Rhonda cried out, her slurred words echoing throughout the huge house like a single scream at the Grand Canyon. Her pain beginning to numb, thanks to the bottle of Remy Martin 'V.S.O.P.' she'd opened a little past seven. Almost an hour later, with more than a half of bottle consumed, all of her words echoed as her reality started to fuse with the unreal.

On this Monday, a few days before her fortieth birthday, a little more than a month after her friend's death, Rhonda's heart and spirit were crushed with one phone call. The same phone call she remembered being a part of so many years ago, when she was on the giving end and Cathy on the receiving end. It was funny then, but now it was too painful for words. Now she knew how Cathy must've felt after hearing her laughing in the background during one of Harry's "I have to attend a late meeting, so I'll be home kinda late" phone calls. Today she heard what she thought...no, what she knew was laughter in the background while Harry gave some excuse as to why he'd be home late. A woman was laughing in the background just like she'd done so many years before, only this time it was her heart crumbling like the Berlin Wall.

"How could he do this to me?" She asked as if Remy would answer. "Why," She flopped down in one of the chairs surrounding the kitchen table and tried to pour herself another glass of painkiller.

Deep down she knew why he'd sought the attention of another woman. She's always known about his attraction for younger women. The same attraction that fueled their affair years ago, when she was the young mistress and Cathy was the maturing housewife. Harry hasn't changed and she was a fool for thinking he would, is what she thought she heard Remy say. Or was it Cathy, who was seated next to her at the table, laughing and pointing. Pointing and laughing. Then she was gone. Then she was back again. Then Erica appeared. She was as consoling as ever, offering a solution to an easy to fix problem. "Divorce his no good ass," were her exact words. The same words Rhonda hated to hear, but needed to be heard. Then she was gone. Then she reappeared. Maybe it was the alcohol. Either way, seeing Erica right there in her kitchen scared Rhonda so bad that she couldn't move a muscle. It was like her entire body had locked, with breathing her only allowed function. Rhonda sat frozen in place, staring at Erica's image until it disappeared, came back, and disappeared again. She couldn't move. "Is Erica trying to tell me something, other than what she's told me before? Am I going

Pink October.doc   249

to die soon after I turn forty? Is Harry leaving me for a younger woman? Dying a lonely woman is not what I imagined would happen to me when I said 'I do," Rhonda cried, finally able to lift her glass of spirits to her mouth, doing her best to make sense of Erica's visit.

"How could I have been so stupid?" She cursed, slamming her left palm into the table as each word left her mouth. Thoughts of Harry with a younger, more attractive, woman flashed in her mind...or were those images happening right before her eyes? Was Harry actually having sex with another woman right there on the kitchen table? "No, that has to be the alcohol," Rhonda assured herself, another swig making the awful thoughts go away. Part of her still wanted to believe Harry loved her, and only her.

"We'll get through this," Rhonda uttered, her emotions going from love to fear to hate to love. "If you pass my test then we're meant to be together...If you fail, we're not," She got up from the table and staggered out of the kitchen, up the stairs and into the master bathroom.

Thoughts of dying of cancer, turning forty, losing her husband to a younger woman, the sound of a faceless woman's laughter all bombarded Rhonda as she opened the medicine cabinet over the sink. She couldn't think straight. She started to feel sleepy, really sleepy. An annoying ring coming from somewhere. Sleepy. Ring. Really sleepy...

Scene 82

Tasha's call to Rhonda's house proved to be a lifesaver. Incoherent babbling about joining Erica prompted her to dial 911 before gathering the troops and rushing over to Rhonda's house. They made it there just as Harry pulled into the driveway, an ambulance and squad car pulling in front of his house before he could turn off the car's ignition. Twenty minutes later the entire group, Harry included, all visibly shaken, sat in a hospital waiting room silently praying that Rhonda's attempt to reunite with Erica had been postponed. Thankfully it was. Rhonda made it, though the unborn child she carried did not. News of her pregnancy was a total surprise to her. She had stopped taking her pills over a month ago, Erica's death occupying the side of her brain that kept up with that sort of thing, so when the nurse informed her about the miscarriage she was hurt as well as relieved. Hurt because she wanted to have her husband's baby years ago, even though he was against it from day one. "I'm too old to be a new daddy," was his main 'baby argument' battle sword. Relieved because the pool guy could've gotten her pregnant. The pool guy with the tight body and the "too good to be true" ability to listen, which led to their three-day affair.

Rhonda stayed in the hospital for three days, with Harry at her side like a husband should be. Whether he actually cared or not was something only he knew the answer to, though Rhonda saw his being there as a sign that he did care. "He actually seems okay," Mrs. Green, Michelle, and Tasha all had the same feeling about Harry after meeting him at the hospital the night of the incident. Carla didn't like him, "He seems sneaky to me," was all she'd say about him.

Carl also visited Rhonda's bedside daily, though he didn't bring the girls. "I can hardly step into this hospital without thinking about my wife, I won't put my girls through this," He said as he stood at Rhonda's bedside. Rhonda understood.

One week after her release from the hospital, Rhonda sat on Mrs. Green's couch sharing her feelings as if she were a first time attendee. Feelings about her marriage, missing Erica and the fear Erica's death had re-ignited. They all experienced that same fear. What happened to Erica could easily happen to any of them. None of them had ever given much thought to the possibility of losing one of the group's members to cancer. Especially not Erica, someone the entire group secretly admired. From her loving husband to their beautiful girls to her career to their home, Erica's life had something every woman has, at one time or another, dreamed of one day having

Pink October.doc 251

in their lives. Now she was no more. Taken away by the same cancer each of them survived. And that scared them to death. "It was as if Erica's death made the threat of dying from cancer valid," Tasha stood, tears running down her face, attempting to help Rhonda make sense out of what she'd just gone through. What they'd all gone through.

Six months later Tasha, Mrs. Green, Carla, Michelle, Rhonda, and Amanda all stood in Grant park, yards away from the official starting point of this years Breast Cancer Awareness "Race For A Cure," taking pictures of the other participants, as well as snapping pictures of one another. Last month the entire country watched in total horror as two commercial airplanes were deliberately flown into the World Trade Center, so this year's Race For A Cure event had an added theme, REMEMBRANCE. Red, white, and blue ribbons were worn opposite the chest or arm bearing the pink ribbon. Race participants could be heard talking about where they were when the first plane struck. Most of them were at work, many of them were working in or near the downtown area, Tasha being one of them. She could still hear the crying, her own included, as she debated on whether or not she should evacuate her school for fear of an attack on one of Chicago's towering skyscrapers. News that all planes had been grounded helped Tasha's decision a lot easier to make.

"Shit! You couldn't have done this shit during the week!" An angry motorist's curse brought Tasha back to the present. She smiled. Just last year she sat in her car, cursing this same event. An event she was now a part of. An event that meant more to her now that she's a survivor, than when she was a pissed off morning commuter. Funny how things change...funny how they stay the same...THE END

Gary Norman

EPILOGUE

FROM THIS DAY FORTH...

TASHA AND RONALD MARRIED ONE YEAR LATER, on October 13th, 2002, making Tara possibly the happiest little girl in the world. Now she had two mommies, "more presents on my birthday and Christmas," is how she saw it. A year later she had a new little sister. Asia Tanya Marks was born on October 15th, 2003, two days after the annual Beast Cancer Awareness "Race For A Cure" event. Tasha was there, swollen belly and all. Needless to say, Tasha never experienced another nightmare, even though she did find a suspicious lump in her breast a year after Erica's death. It was benign.

RHONDA ACCEPTED HARRY'S APOLOGY, along with his gifts and meaningless promises to change. "He really means it this time. My near fatal suicide attempt scared him straight," is how Rhonda explained his welcomed change for the better. Carla felt that Rhonda should give it a little time before recommitting herself to a marriage she had doubts about. Especially after her "if he makes it home before I die, we're meant to be together" love test. Carla's suggestion went in one ear and out the other. Rhonda was determined to make it work and she did just that. She made it work, at least for a little more than a year. That's how long it took before Harry's wandering eye, once again, settled on a much younger prize. This time Rhonda was smart enough to hire a private investigator, who, after only three months of surveillance, was able to take pictures of Harry with his old, wrinkled dick down another woman's throat. Their divorce was final on October 25th, 2003.

After months of intense therapy, Rhonda was able to move on to a better life. The transition was made a lot easier since Rhonda kept their Olympia Field's home, the summer home in Miami, three of their seven cars, a sizable percentage of Harry's assets and the pool

**Pink October.doc**   253

guy. "Consider the pool guy your compensation," were the words spoken by Rhonda's two hundred dollar an hour shrink. "A well deserved compensation," is how Rhonda saw it.

CARLA AND JESSE WED ON DECEMBER 1ˢᵗ, 2002, two days before the birth of their first child, Jesse Jr. Six months into the following year Jesse's old ways resurfaced. He felt that the man was supposed to be the provider, not the woman. Her job was to stay home and raise Jesse Jr., not pay for daycare. That's what he, "the man of the house," was supposed to do.

When Carla refused to quit her job their snowball size dispute turned into an avalanche sized dilemma. They divorced in August 2003, strengthening their relationship just as it had done in the past. They couldn't get along as a couple, but they were the perfect parenting team as 'ex' husband and wife/lovers. They remained this way until the day Jesse Jr. died as a result of a vicious mauling by two stray pit bulls seven months after their divorce was final. Carla survived the attack, which happened a few blocks from her Hyde Park duplex (She had taken her son on an afternoon walk along the lake front, stopping his stroller every so often to tend to his every, wine, cough, cry or laugh. On that day Jesse Jr. didn't make it home, dying in the hospital five minutes after his arrival. Jesse blamed Carla, though he never said it aloud, but Carla knew. Though she never said anything about it).

After the death of their child Carla and Jesse went from seeing each other seven days a week to seeing each other every other seven days to going months without seeing each other. They eventually severed their ties altogether.

ON THANKSGIVING DAY, 2002, MICHELLE TOOK HER son's favorite sweet potato pie from her daughter-in-law's oven and placed it in the center of the dessert table, in the living room. Even though she only prepared one of the many desserts, she looked at it as a start. "Before you know it, I'll be helping with the turkey," She joked with Mrs. Green one week after being allowed near "Robin's" stove. The following year she did help to prepare that turkey, solidifying her relationship with her daughter-in-law.

AMANDA WENT BACK TO SCHOOL IN THE SUMMER OF 2002.
She completed her studies the following year, graduating at the top of her class, making her mother the proudest mother at the graduation ceremony. The entire group attended.

Mike underwent counseling for both his alcohol abuse and his spousal abuse. The counseling helped him deal with his trust issue, which was the cause of all their problems. Three months after seeking counseling, he and Amanda were back together. Two months after their reconciliation he broke her jaw because she was thirty-five minutes late getting home from one of her support group meetings. They split for good after that. She went on to work at a funeral home on the south side. He went to jail, where he served two and a half years of a five-year sentence.

Mrs. GREEN MOVED TO TEXAS TWO WEEKS AFTER AMANDA'S
graduation. The night before she was scheduled to leave, Michelle decided to surprise her, as well as the rest of the group, with a special 'girl's night in', complete with Mrs. Green's favorite male stripper, 'Twelve Inch'. The look on their faces when Mrs. Green took hold of his "snake," was priceless (the things she put that poor man through, on that night, I'm sure he'll never forget. He had no idea a woman of her age could have such a strong grip).

The next morning she woke up to the last empty bed she'd experience for quite some time. She couldn't wait to wake up in Thomas' arms, everyday, for the rest of their lives, whether they decided to marry or not. All she knew was that she didn't want to grow old by herself. And if that means she has to move across the country, leave the group that she had co-founded, to be with a man that she has to fuck from time to time...then that's what she has to do...

Pink October.doc

ABOUT THE AUTHOR

A Chicago native, Gary Norman Jr. attended the University of Northeastern IL. before going to Southern IL. University-Carbondale. He currently resides in Harvey, IL. where he's working on his second novel.